Becoming Human:
The Seven of Nine™ Saga

The STAR TREK® SCRIPTBOOKS

Book Two:
Becoming Human:
The Seven of Nine™ Saga

POCKET BOOKS
New York London Toronto Sydney Tokyo Singapore

An *Original* Publication of POCKET BOOKS

 POCKET BOOKS, a division of Simon & Schuster Inc. 1230 Avenue of the Americas, New York, NY 10020

 STAR TREK is a Registered Trademark of Paramount Pictures.

A VIACOM COMPANY

This book is published by Pocket Books, a division of Simon & Schuster Inc., under exclusive license from Paramount Pictures.

ISBN: 0-671-03447-2

First Pocket Books trade paperback printing January 1999

10 9 8 7 6 5 4 3 2 1

POCKET and colophon are registered trademarks of Simon & Schuster Inc.

Printed in the U.S.A.

CONTENTS

ABOUT THE SCRIPTS

The contents of this book consist of *Star Trek* shooting scripts presented in much the same form as the actors and production staff would have originally received them at the start of filming.

Due to changes made on the set and in postproduction, it is possible that these scripts are not absolutely word-for-word identical to the final broadcast version of each episode.

Becoming Human:
The Seven of Nine™ Saga

STAR TREK: VOYAGER

"Scorpion, Part One"

#40840-168

Written
by
Brannon Braga & Joe Menosky

Directed
by
David Livingston

STAR TREK: VOYAGER

''Scorpion, Part One''

CAST

JANEWAY

PARIS

CHAKOTAY

TUVOK

TORRES

DOCTOR

KES

NEELIX

KIM

BORG

DA VINCI

Non-Speaking

N.D. SUPERNUMERARIES

STAR TREK: VOYAGER

''Scorpion, Part One''

SETS

INTERIORS

VOYAGER
    BRIDGE
    BRIEFING ROOM
    CORRIDOR
    ENGINEERING
    HOLODECK/DA VINCI'S WORKSHOP
    JANEWAY'S QUARTERS
    READY ROOM
    SCIENCE LAB
    SICKBAY

BORG COLLECTIVE

BORG CUBE
    CORRIDOR #1
    CORRIDOR #2
    CORRIDOR #3

ALIEN BIO-SHIP

EXTERIORS

VOYAGER
BORG CUBE

STAR TREK: VOYAGER

"Scorpion, Part One"

PRONUNCIATION GUIDE

AMASOV	AH-muh-sahv
BENE	BEN-ay
BUONA	boo-OH-nuh
CATARINA	cah-tah-REE-nah
CATZO	CAHT-soh
CHE	KAY
CROCE	CROW-chay
ESSATTO	ay-SAHT-toh
FIESOLE	fee-AY-soh-lay
HEPHAESTOS	huh-FEH-stohs
MARAVIGLOSO	mah-rah-vil-YOH-soh
SCUDI	SKOO-dee
VERROCCHIO	vay-ROH-kee-oh

STAR TREK: VOYAGER

"Scorpion, Part One"

FADE IN:

1   EXT. SPACE—THE BORG (OPTICAL)   1
In the distance, <u>TWO BORG CUBES</u> are approaching camera. The massive
ships come closer . . . ominous. We HEAR the VOICE of the COLLEC-
TIVE:

> BORG
> We are the Borg. Existence as you know it is over. We
> will add your biological and technological
> distinctiveness to our own. Resistance is futile. You
> will be—

Without warning, TENDRILS of CRACKLING ENERGY whip out from just
offcamera, RIPPING and TEARING RIGHT THROUGH THE BORG
SHIPS, <u>OBLITERATING</u> THEM IN A MAELSTROM OF FIRE AND DE-
BRIS. Off the mass destruction—someone or something has just beaten the
Borg . . .

FADE OUT.

END OF TEASER

<u>ACT ONE</u>

FADE IN:

(NOTE: Episode credits fall over opening scenes)

2 CLOSE ON A GEOMETRIC FIGURE   2

as artist's sketch study of geometry and perspective.

> DA VINCI'S VOICE
> The Cardinal is a thief . . .

2A CAMERA PANS   2A

along a series of sketches, models, pigment jars, half-prepared canvases . . .

> DA VINCI'S VOICE
> (continuing)
> I delivered <u>two</u> portraits of his mindless nephew more
> than three months ago . . .

We continue to REVEAL the materials of a magical, fifteenth-century artist's workshop . . .

> DA VINCI'S VOICE
> (continuing)
> ''To be depicted in the heroic mode of a Hercules or
> an Achilles''—so specified our contract . . .

The camera stops at a mechanical arm.

An ELBOW JOINT built out of bronze and iron, the joint creaking with movement. CAMERA SLOWLY PULLS BACK to REVEAL a mechanical FOREARM and HAND, a complex, almost whimsical design replete with gears, pulleys, counterweights—a kind of medieval ''contraption.''

> DA VINCI'S VOICE
> And so I complied. Making that young fool of a
> nephew look far more heroic than nature ever
> intended. An act on my part, greater than <u>anything</u>
> accomplished by Hercules <u>or</u> Achilles . . .

We can now see that the mechanical arm is attached to a life-sized artist's manikin—a half-torso made of wood. LEONARDO DA VINCI leans into view, making an adjustment to the arm.

This is da Vinci in his prime—a vital 50 years old, with the distinctive beard, bushy eyebrows and Renaissance artist's clothes. He turns to someone offcamera, speaks English with a light Italian accent.

> DA VINCI
> (continuing)
> And what have I—the "Divine Leonardo da Vinci"—
> received in payment?

3   NEW ANGLE—THE ROOM (OPTICAL)   3

We can now see that JANEWAY is there, wearing her Starfleet uniform. She and da Vinci are surrounded by a magical confusion of sketches, models, inventions and contraptions. This is DA VINCI'S WORKSHOP—a late 15th century wonderland of imagination and creativity. The room is lit by soft light from an open window.

> JANEWAY
> (a smile)
> The Cardinal's eternal gratitude?

> DA VINCI
> Essatto! In other words, Signorina . . . less than
> nothing.

Janeway sees an opportunity to pursue something she was after before we joined this scene . . .

> JANEWAY
> All the more reason to accept my proposal . . .

> DA VINCI
> Money is beside the point . . .
> (recalling her name)
> Catarina, is it?

> JANEWAY
> Yes.
> (indicates workshop)
> I'm only asking for a corner . . . one bench . . . a
> place to work on my own projects—paintings . . .
> sculptures . . . Just being here . . . in your company, is
> inspiring to me.

> DA VINCI

Flattery, Catarina, is <u>also</u> beside the point. I prefer my solitude.

He releases a small pin on the contraption in front of him—and the arm begins to slowly move up and down on its own, driven by the counter-weights and creaking gears. Da Vinci smiles at the result.

> DA VINCI
> (proudly)

<u>Maraviglioso</u> . . .

Janeway smiles—forgetting her proposal in the charm of the moment . . . getting a sense of da Vinci and how his mind worked is the primary reason for her being here in the first place.

> JANEWAY

What will you call it?

> DA VINCI

"The Arm of Hephaestos."

> JANEWAY

The god of the forge . . .

> DA VINCI
> (nods)

Every blacksmith who has ever swung a hammer will thank me for this creation.

> JANEWAY

Someone once said . . . all invention is but an extension of the body of man . . .

Leonardo glances at her—he can't help but respect the quickness of her mind. He wags a finger at her—but there is a growing affection in his voice.

> DA VINCI

Do not think because I have enjoyed your visit today, that I am prepared to turn my workshop into a traveller's inn—

A mechanical SCREECH. The mechanical arm freezes up—one of the gears has broken. Da Vinci moves to it, annoyed.

DA VINCI
(cursing)

Che catzo . . .

He tinkers with the arm, trying to remove the broken gear. Janeway moves to lend him a hand.

JANEWAY
Here, let me help you . . .

Da Vinci eyes her, holding up his blackened hands.

DA VINCI
And get your hands covered with goose grease . . . ?

JANEWAY
It's good for the skin . . .

Leonardo motions "come here" with his hand.

DA VINCI
(re: gear)
Let's find his big brother—hopefully he will be stronger . . .

Da Vinci and Janeway move to a tabletop with a wooden box of mechanical parts and start sorting through the gears . . .

Janeway picks up a couple of sketches of Da Vinci's famous "FLYING MACHINE" to get at a box of gears—she's almost reverent about the way she handles them.

JANEWAY
(eyes sketches)
These look like designs for a flying machine . . .

Da Vinci shakes his head—the invention is one of his great failures, and a source of sadness and irritation.

DA VINCI
Because my imagination takes flight so easily . . . I thought my body might do so as well. I was wrong.

He goes back to a box of gears, as Janeway considers the drawings.

And she sees an opportunity to press her proposal in a different way. She moves to join him, eyeing the model of his flying machine hanging nearby, gives it a tap of her hand as she passes . . .

> JANEWAY
> It's this "flapping approach." You designed your machine to mimic the way a bat or a sparrow flies—

> DA VINCI
> —Yes, yes. So?

He distractedly puts the gear in place, still giving Janeway his attention.

> JANEWAY
> So what if you based it on the hawk, instead?

Da Vinci suddenly stops what he's doing, the gear in place.

> DA VINCI
> A creature who glides through the air . . .

> JANEWAY
> (smiles)
> Essatto.

Da Vinci considers, impressed. Then he too, smiles.

> DA VINCI
> We'll design a new machine . . . and you, Catarina, will help me fly it.

Janeway indicates the workshop.

> JANEWAY
> I'll need someplace to work . . .

> DA VINCI
> (quoting her)
> A corner . . . one workbench.

> JANEWAY
> That will be fine.

Da Vinci turns back to the mechanical arm—but he's definitely sold on the proposal.

                              DA VINCI
Ten scudi per week . . . and you provide your own
materials . . .

                              JANEWAY
Seven . . .
                    (glancing at the magical confusion)
And I might need to borrow a few things—on
occasion.

Da Vinci releases the pin on the mechanical arm as before—and it starts
working perfectly. He turns to Janeway.

                              DA VINCI
Then we have an agreement.

                    CHAKOTAY'S COM VOICE
Chakotay to Janeway.

                              JANEWAY
                    (taps combadge)
Go ahead.

                    CHAKOTAY'S COM VOICE
Captain—we need you in Engineering. There's
something here you should see.

                              JANEWAY
I'm on my way.
                              (to com)
Computer, end program.

As she walks offcamera (we do not see the program end) . . .

Janeway heads for the door, removing her leather apron . . .

                                                            CUT TO:

4   INT. ENGINEERING   4

CHAKOTAY and TORRES are working at a console. N.D.s in the b.g.
Janeway ENTERS and Chakotay turns to her.

                              JANEWAY
What have you got?

CHAKOTAY

Some bad news.

(beat)

One of the long range probes we sent out two months
ago has stopped transmitting.

TORRES

At first I thought it was a problem with the
communications grid . . . then I cleared up the last
few seconds of telemetry. Take a look at <u>this</u> . . .

Torres taps a control on the console and they all watch a monitor . . .

5   CLOSE ON THE MONITOR (OPTICAL)   5

It shows a variety of TELEMETRY and a VISUAL IMAGE—the "POV" of
the PROBE. We see a starfield . . . and then a <u>BORG CUBE</u> flies into
view . . .

The image suddenly FRITZES . . . and is replaced by the vast INTERIOR of
a BORG COLLECTIVE . . . the telemetry readings are now scrambled. The
image FRITZES again . . . and we see a row of BORG ALCOVES . . .

And then—the face of a BORG DRONE! It reaches into camera and the
image FRITZES OUT completely. The monitor goes dark.

6   RESUME   6

Janeway reacts.

CHAKOTAY

This could be it, Captain . . . <u>Borg space</u>.

CUT TO:

7   INT. BRIEFING ROOM (VPB)   7

At impulse. Janeway is on her feet, facing the troops. Chakotay, Torres,
TUVOK, PARIS, KIM, NEELIX, and the DOCTOR (who's wearing his
mobile emitter) are sitting around the table. Everyone looks tense—this is
the day they've all been dreading. Mid-conversation.

JANEWAY

We don't know exactly how many vessels are out
there . . . but their space appears to be vast . . . it

includes thousands of solar systems . . . all Borg.
(beat)
We are no doubt entering the heart of their
territory . . . there's no going around it . . . but there
may be a way <u>through</u> it.

She looks to Chakotay, who picks up the ball. He moves to the wall monitor
and taps a control. A STAR MAP comes up—a narrow ribbon of space is
HIGHLIGHTED.

CHAKOTAY
(off graphic)
Before the probe was disabled, it picked up a narrow
corridor of space devoid of Borg activity. We've
nicknamed it the "Northwest Passage."

TORRES
(chiming in)
Unfortunately, the passage is filled with intense
gravimetric distortions . . . probably caused by a
string of quantum singularities.

PARIS
Better to ride the rapids than face the hive.

CHAKOTAY
Exactly. We're going to set a course for that
corridor . . . and go into full Tactical Alert.
(to Tuvok)
Where do we stand with weapons?

TUVOK
I have reprogrammed the phaser banks to a rotating
modulation. But I suspect a Borg vessel will adapt
quickly.

CHAKOTAY
We can use every edge.
(to Kim)
Ensign?

KIM
I've already configured the long-range sensors to scan
for transwarp signatures. An early warning system.

                    CHAKOTAY
Good work. Doctor, how are you coming on the
medical front?

                     DOCTOR
I've analyzed every square millimeter of the Borg
corpse we recovered three months ago. I'm closer to
understanding how their assimilation technology
works . . . and I may be able to create some sort of
medical defense.

                    CHAKOTAY
Redouble your efforts. This is your top priority.
                     (beat)
Neelix, I doubt we can resupply the ship any time
soon . . .

                     NEELIX
No problem, sir. I'm working on a plan to extend our
food and replicator rations.

Chakotay nods.

                    JANEWAY
                     (to all)
We have to act fast. The Borg have captured one of
our probes . . . they know we're out here.

Janeway looks at her people, tries to bolster their spirits and prime them for
the challenge ahead.

                    JANEWAY
                   (continuing)
We'll do everything in our power to avoid a direct
confrontation . . . but if and when we do engage the
Borg, I'm confident that we'll be ready. I have faith in
each and every one of you.
                     (beat)
Let's do it.

As the crew moves into action . . .

                                                            CUT TO:

A MONTAGE OF IMAGES:

The crew working, urgent, focused:

8   INT. ENGINEERING   8

Torres and N.D.s working. Every panel that can be opened has been opened—we get the sense that major work is being done.

9   INT. CORRIDOR   9

Several N.D.s carrying equipment . . . a few others racing down the hall . . . urgent.

10   INT. SCIENCE LAB   10

(SEE ADDENDUM FOR DIALOGUE)

Tuvok and Paris, working on a PHOTON TORPEDO. They have a panel open, and are making adjustments inside the weapon . . .

11   INT. ENGINEERING—SECOND LEVEL   11

Three N.D.s pulling phaser rifles out of the weapons locker, making adjustments. Janeway looks on . . .

12   INT. BRIDGE   12

(SEE ADDENDUM FOR DIALOGUE)

At warp. Chakotay and Kim on the Bridge at the aft station, studying the Voyager schematic there. A couple of N.D.s can be seen in the b.g., hurriedly carrying equipment cases across the scene, urgent . . .

                                                      END MONTAGE.

13   INT. SICKBAY   13

The Doctor and Kes working at a bio-bed, where several BORG BODY PARTS are laid out—an arm, eyepiece, inner workings, etc. This is the Borg corpse last seen in "Unity," which has been dissected. The Doctor is studying a Borg HAND, which has dagger-like "assimilation tubules" sticking out of the fingertips (as seen in "First Contact," when the N.D. was stabbed in the neck).

                              DOCTOR
                         (to Kes, re: tubes)
              These injection tubules are the first step in the Borg

assimilation process. Once inside the skin, they
release a series of nanoprobes into the bloodstream.

> KES
> Maybe we can develop some kind of protective
> shielding against them . . .

> DOCTOR
> Unlikely. The tubules are capable of penetrating any
> known alloy or energy field. Which means our battle
> must be waged inside the body itself.

The Doctor moves to a monitor, taps a few controls . . .

14   INCLUDE MONITOR (OPTICAL)   14

It shows a MICROSCOPIC VIEW of healthy human BLOOD CELLS.

> DOCTOR
> The first tissue to be attacked by the nanoprobes is
> the victim's blood . . .

On the graphic, we see a cell-sized BORG NANOPROBE race into view . . .
it attaches to a blood cell . . . and in a frightening chain reaction all of the
blood cells are BORGIFIED . . . turning dark and more elongated.

> DOCTOR
> Assimilation is almost instantaneous.

> KES
> (studies console)
> They take over the blood-cell functions . . . like a
> virus . . .

> DOCTOR
> Which suggests to me that we should try to enhance
> the immune system . . . create an "assimilation
> antibody," as it were.

They move back to the bed with the Borg body parts.

> DOCTOR
> I doubt we can actually destroy the nanoprobes, but
> we might be able to slow them down . . .

15   CLOSE ON KES   15

as she listens . . . staring down at the Borg body parts, suddenly transfixed by them . . .

> DOCTOR
> Let's perform a submicron dissection on the probes we've collected so far . . . see if we can find the DNA recoding mechanism.

16   KES'S POV—THE BORG BODY PARTS   16

CAMERA PUSHING IN on the arm and circuits . . .

17   CLOSE ON KES   17

CAMERA PUSHING IN on her face as her eyes widen . . . and she is hit by a:

18   MENTAL FLASH (OPTICAL)   18

A nightmarish image: TWENTY BORG BODIES PILED HIGH and FUSED TOGETHER. Limbs mangled and askew, faces twisted, eyes open—a surreal sculpture of death.

18A   RESUME KES   18A

as she reacts to the vision . . . hit by another:

18B   MENTAL FLASH (OPTICAL)   18B

CLOSER ANGLE on some DEAD BORG in the pile, their faces blank with shock . . .

19   RESUME KES   19

as she braces herself on the table, recovering from the vision.

> DOCTOR'S VOICE
> Kes, what's wrong?
> (beat)
> Kes.

He takes hold of her arm, and she turns to him. She looks startled and breathless.

> KES
> I saw Borg . . .

DOCTOR
You've had a . . . telepathic experience?

KES
(nods)
There were bodies . . . dozens of them . . . all
dead . . .

Off the mystery . . .

CUT TO:

20   EXT. SPACE—VOYAGER (OPTICAL)   20

at warp.

21   INT. BRIDGE   21

Janeway and Chakotay in command, Kim, Paris and N.D.s all at their
stations, working. The mood is focused and tense. Tuvok ENTERS from a
Turbolift and crosses to Janeway and Chakotay.

JANEWAY
How's Kes?

TUVOK
Unsettled . . . and uncertain . . . Over the past two
hours, she has experienced several telepathic
"visions" about the death of Borg . . . and the
destruction of Voyager.

CHAKOTAY
Some sort of . . . premonitions?

TUVOK
Possibly.

Janeway considers.

JANEWAY
We can't just ignore her "intuition" . . . but I see no
reason to alter our plan.
(beat)
Tuvok, I want you to keep an eye on—

Just then Kim's console sends out an ALARM.

                              KIM
                          (off console)
          Captain . . . long range sensors are picking up
          transwarp signatures . . . five point eight light years
          distant . . . closing from behind . . .

                           CHAKOTAY
          Red Alert.

The ship goes to RED ALERT.

                           JANEWAY
          Evasive maneuvers.

Paris works and the ship immediately SHUDDERS.

                           CHAKOTAY
          What's happening?

                            PARIS
                          (off console)
          We've dropped out of warp . . .

                           JANEWAY
                        (quickly, to com)
          Bridge to Engineering—what's going on down there?

22   INT. ENGINEERING   22

Torres and N.D.s frantically working.

                            TORRES
                           (to com)
          I'm not sure, Captain. Some kind of subspace
          turbulence is preventing us from creating a stable
          warp field.

The ship starts TREMBLING slightly . . .

23   INT. BRIDGE   23

Tension rising. TREMBLING . . . we hear a low, ominous RUMBLING
noise.

                            TUVOK
                          (off console)

Turbulence is increasing . . .

                        KIM
I'm reading two Borg vessels . . . three . . . four . . .
five . . .
                        (works)
Fifteen Borg vessels. Distance: two point one light
years and closing!

The trembling gets worse . . . the rumbling louder . . .

                        JANEWAY
Shields to maximum! Stand by all weapons!

                        TUVOK
They're in visual range . . .

Tuvok works . . .

24   INCLUDE VIEWSCREEN (OPTICAL)   24

We see an ARMADA of FIFTEEN BORG CUBES rapidly approaching—an
awesome sight.

                        CHAKOTAY
        My God.

The LIGHTS start to FLICKER.

25   EXT. SPACE—VOYAGER (OPTICAL)   25

dead in space, the onslaught of FIFTEEN BORG CUBES coming at us from
the rear. Suspense as the Cubes approach at high speed . . . closer . . .
closer . . .

26   NEW ANGLE (OPTICAL)   26

As the BORG CUBES ROAR DIRECTLY PAST on either side of Voyager,
tossing the tiny ship in their wake. It's like being caught in a stampede.

27   INT. BRIDGE   27

SHAKING hard! Lights and consoles flickering! Everyone hanging on for
dear life!

28   OMITTED   28

29   INT. BRIDGE (OPTICAL)   29

On the Viewscreen, the last few Borg Cubes are RACING away from us.
The shaking dies down . . . the rumbling subsides . . . and the lights and
console come back to life. Everyone recovering. Chakotay looks up at the
Viewscreen.

                        CHAKOTAY
          Captain . . .

The Viewscreen shows one last BORG CUBE looming, not moving. Kim
scrambles to his station as a greenish BORG SCANNING BEAM begins to
SWEEP across the Bridge.

                          KIM
          We're being scanned . . .

                        JANEWAY
                         (wry)
          Think good thoughts . . .

A long, tense beat . . . and then on the Viewscreen, the Cube RACES OFF,
flying away from us.

                         TUVOK
                      (off console)
          The last Cube has rejoined the others . . .

Off our stunned reactions . . .

30   OMITTED   30

                                                    FADE OUT.

                    END OF ACT ONE

ACT TWO

FADE IN:

31   INT. BRIDGE   31

Continuous from Act One. Everyone a little shaken—checking readings, etc. Janeway looks tense—that was too close for comfort.

> JANEWAY
> Did we sustain any damage?

> KIM
> No. Shields held . . . warp engines are coming back on-line . . . all primary systems are stable.

> JANEWAY
> Stand down Red Alert.

The ship goes out of Red Alert. Janeway tries to make sense of what just happened.

> JANEWAY
> Harry . . . maintain a long-range sensor lock on that Borg "armada." They seemed to be in quite a hurry . . . I'd like to know what they're up to.

> KIM
> Yes, Ma'am.

> JANEWAY
> (somber)
> I'll take this near-miss as a good omen. Resume our course.

Paris works. Chakotay turns to her.

> CHAKOTAY
> If we needed any more evidence that we've entered Borg space . . . I think we just got it.

Janeway doesn't answer, lost in her own thoughts . . .

> JANEWAY
> (taut)
> I'll be in my Ready Room.

And she leaves, looking intent. As Chakotay watches her go . . .

CUT TO:

32   EXT. SPACE—VOYAGER (OPTICAL)   32

at warp.

33   INT. READY ROOM—CLOSE ON A MONITOR   33

The screen reads "STARFLEET DATABASE. CLASSIFIED. THE BORG."
Blocks of text are visible.

34   INCLUDE JANEWAY (OPTICAL)   34

studying her desktop monitor. Warp stars out the window. She's focused,
intense. The door CHIMES, and she jumps a little, startled out of her
concentration.

> JANEWAY
> Yes . . . come in.

Chakotay ENTERS, holding a PADD.

> CHAKOTAY
> (re: PADD)
> We've just completed the latest sensor sweep. So far,
> so good. The "Northwest Passage" is still clear of
> Borg activity.

> JANEWAY
> (terse)
> I'd like to see a tactical update.

He nods. Janeway returns to her monitor. Chakotay can see that she's
troubled . . . tries to lighten the mood a little.

> CHAKOTAY
> According to my calculations, neither of us has eaten
> since last night. Join me for dinner?

JANEWAY

No, thanks. I'm not hungry. And I've got a lot of work
to do.

CHAKOTAY

I see.

A beat. She leans back in her chair, a little fatigued, indicates the desktop
monitor.

JANEWAY

I've been looking through the personal log entries of
all the Starfleet Captains who encountered the Borg.
I've gone over every engagement, from the moment Q
flung the Enterprise into the path of that first
Cube . . . to the massacre at Wolf Three-Five-Nine.
Every battle, every skirmish . . . anything that might
give me an insight into the mind of the Collective.

CHAKOTAY

And?

JANEWAY

In the words of Jean-Luc Picard . . .

As Janeway reads, we can hear a hint of formality in her tone and phrasing
(but not an accent).

JANEWAY
(continuing, reads, off monitor)
"In their Collective state, the Borg are utterly without
mercy . . . driven by one will alone: the will to
conquer. They are beyond redemption . . . beyond
reason."
(beat)
And then there's Captain Amasov of the Endeavor . . .

Again, Janeway reads with a subtle change in her inflection (but no accent).
Chakotay begins to smile slightly.

JANEWAY
(off monitor)
"It is my opinion that the Borg are as close to pure
evil as any race we've ever encountered.
All attempts to negotiate with them have failed. They
are ruthless in their pursuit of . . ."

She trails off when she sees that Chakotay is smiling slightly.

                    JANEWAY
     What's so funny?

                    CHAKOTAY
     Nothing.

                    JANEWAY
     You're smiling. Obviously, I've said something
     amusing . . .

                    CHAKOTAY
     You sounded just like Amasov.

                    JANEWAY
     What?

                    CHAKOTAY
     Just now, while you were reading his log. You were
     using his inflections.

                    JANEWAY
     I was not.

                    CHAKOTAY
     Yes, you were. And before that, you were doing a
     pretty good Picard.

Janeway hesitates.

                    JANEWAY
     Was I . . . ?

                    CHAKOTAY
     It's nothing to be ashamed about . . . echoing the
     Greats. Ensign Hickman in Astrophysics does a
     passable Janeway.

A beat, then Janeway can't help but break a smile. Chakotay has disarmed her with humor, and for a moment, some of her tension melts away.

                    JANEWAY
                    (lightly)
     If we manage to survive the next few days, I'm going

to have a little chat with Ensign Hickman. Imitating
the Captain . . . surely that violates some kind of
Starfleet protocol.

She stands, starts moving about the room . . . serious again, but opening up
a little . . . taking this opportunity to share her concerns with a trusted
colleague and friend.

                    JANEWAY
     This day was inevitable . . . we all knew it . . . and
     we've all tried to prepare ourselves for the challenge
     ahead . . .

She looks at him, probing, asking the hard questions.

                    JANEWAY
                    (continuing)
     But at what point is the risk too great . . . at what
     point do we come about and retreat to friendly
     territory? Could the crew accept living out the rest of
     their lives in the Delta Quadrant?
                    (glances at monitor)
     I keep looking to all these Captains . . . my "comrades
     in arms." But the truth is . . . I'm alone.

A quiet beat.

                    CHAKOTAY
     If that moment comes . . . we'll face it together. And
     we'll make the right decision.
                    (beat)
     You're not alone, Kathryn.

She looks at him, appreciative. His quiet solidarity is reassuring.

                    JANEWAY
     Three years ago . . . I didn't even know your name.
     Today . . . I can't imagine a day without you.

A warm beat between them.

                    TUVOK'S COM VOICE
     Captain Janeway to the Bridge.

As they head out the door . . .

35   INT. BRIDGE—CONTINUOUS   35

Janeway and Chakotay ENTER. Tuvok is standing at the aft science station
with Kim, studying the console. Kim and Tuvok look up.

                              KIM
        Something strange is going on . . .

                             TUVOK
        The power signatures of those Borg vessels have
        terminated.

                            CHAKOTAY
        All of them?

                              KIM
                            (nods)
        They're dead in the water . . . about five point two
        light years from here.

                            JANEWAY
        Cause?

                             TUVOK
        Unknown.

A mystifying beat. Janeway makes a decision.

                            JANEWAY
                           (to Paris)
        Mister Paris, set a course for their position . . . warp
        two.

                             PARIS
        Aye.

As Paris works . . .

36   EXT. SPACE—VOYAGER (OPTICAL)   36

at warp.

                                                            CUT TO:

37   INT. BRIDGE   37

Red Alert. A short time later. Everyone at their stations.

KIM

We're approaching the ships.

JANEWAY

Slow to impulse. On screen.

38   INCLUDE VIEWSCREEN (OPTICAL)   38

The crew reacts with amazement as they see the WRECKAGE of the BORG ARMADA.

CHAKOTAY

Lifesigns?

KIM

A few . . . but they're erratic.

TUVOK

Captain, I'm detecting two residual weapons signatures in the debris. One is Borg . . . the other is of unknown origin.

An ominous beat.

PARIS

Who could do this to the Borg?

39   EXT. SPACE—VOYAGER (OPTICAL)   39

Slowly cruising through the cemetery of decimated ships. Fifteen Borg Cubes blown to pieces . . . a graveyard of debris, chunks of hull, flotsam . . . some of the larger pieces still crackling with energy. Incredible devastation.

FADE OUT.

END OF ACT TWO

ACT THREE

FADE IN:

40   INT. BRIDGE   40

As before. Red Alert. Everyone looking at the (offcamera) Viewscreen.

> JANEWAY
> Someone more powerful than the Borg . . . it's hard to imagine . . .

> KIM
> But they did it—fifteen Cubes! We might've just found our ticket through Borg space . . . an ally.

> PARIS
> I'd like to shake their hands . . . if they have hands.

> CHAKOTAY
> Let's not jump to conclusions. Scan the vicinity for other vessels.

> TUVOK
> There are none . . .

> KIM
> (reacts to console)
> Hold on . . . I'm picking up some sort of <u>bio-readings</u> . . . they're coming from the outer hull of one of the Borg ships.

> JANEWAY
> Let's see it.

Kim works . . .

40A   INCLUDE VIEWSCREEN (OPTICAL)   40A

It shows a CLOSER VIEW of a large, broken-off CORNER of a Cube. There is a small, organic-looking BIO-MASS on the hull. It's bulbous and ashen. Strange.

> JANEWAY
> Magnify.

Tuvok hits a control, and the Viewscreen changes to a CLOSER VIEW of the bio-mass. We can now see what looks like the body of a "squid" attached to the hull . . . no tentacles . . . but it definitely looks like an organism of some kind.

                    KIM
          It's definitely organic . . . but our sensors can't
          penetrate its surface.

                    JANEWAY
          Send a standard greeting.

                    TUVOK
                    (beat)
          No response.

                    CHAKOTAY
                    (eyeing it)
          This could be a space-dwelling organism . . . or a
          biological weapon . . .

                    JANEWAY
          I'd like to know what kind of weapon could destroy
          the Borg . . .
                    (to Tuvok)
          Can we beam it away from the ship?

Kim works a beat.

                    KIM
          I can't get a lock on it . . .

                    CHAKOTAY
          Tractor beam?

                    TUVOK
                    (works console)
          No effect.

                    KIM
          Whatever that thing is . . . it seems impervious to our
          technology.

                    JANEWAY
          Tuvok—are you reading an atmosphere in the Cube?

>   TUVOK
>   (works)
> Affirmative.

Janeway turns to Chakotay.

>   JANEWAY
> Commander, I want you to take an Away Team
> inside . . . try to get a short-range scan of the bio-
> mass.

>   TUVOK
>   (off console)
> There are still Borg lifesigns . . . but they're unstable.

>   JANEWAY
>   (to Chakotay)
> We'll keep an open comlink and an active Transporter
> lock . . . we'll pull you out of there at the first sign of
> trouble.

Chakotay nods.

>   CHAKOTAY
>   (quickly)
> Tuvok, Harry—you're with me.

Chakotay, Tuvok and Kim head for the Turbolift. Janeway glances at the Viewscreen. Off the image of the "bio-mass" gripping the side of the Cube . . .

                                                              CUT TO:

41   INT. BORG CUBE—CORRIDOR #1 (OPTICAL)   41

The familiar maze of Borg alcoves. The Cube has taken heavy damage—walls are scorched, lights are flickering and a haze fills the air. Two dead Borg can be seen on the floor, one other is slumped lifelessly in its cubicle. Chakotay, Tuvok and Kim MATERIALIZE inside the ship, carrying phaser rifles. They immediately shine their phaser beacons in the darkness. No active Borg in sight. Chakotay pulls out his tricorder.

>   CHAKOTAY
>   (off tricorder)
> This way . . .

They cautiously start down the corridor . . .

42   INT. BORG CORRIDOR #2   42

The Away Team ENTERS and stops at what they see . . .

43   NEW ANGLE   43

Three BORG DRONES are methodically making repairs—they look injured
and one of the Borg is missing an arm. But despite their injuries, they are
single-minded in their objective. They pay no attention to our team.

                              KIM
          Looks like they're a little preoccupied . . .

                              TUVOK
          Lower your phasers. If we don't appear threatening,
          they should ignore us.

A tense beat . . . then the CAMERA FOLLOWS as Chakotay leads the way
down the narrow passageway. They carefully make their way past the Borg,
who completely ignore them . . .

Finally, they reach an intersection. Chakotay stops for a moment . . .
indicates one of the adjoining corridors.

                              CHAKOTAY
                           (off tricorder)
          The alien bio-readings are getting stronger . . . we're
          close.

Just then Kim sees something down one of the opposite corridors. He reacts,
startled—

                              KIM
          Commander!

They turn to see—

44   THEIR POV (OPTICAL)   44

The corridor is piled high with DEAD BORG—their bodies mangled and
mashed together in a bizarre "sculpture of death." <u>This is the exact same
image that Kes saw in her mental flash</u> in Act One—but now this is the real
thing.

45   CHAKOTAY, TUVOK, KIM   45

take in the shocking sight.

TUVOK

Curious.

CHAKOTAY

That's not the word I had in mind . . .

TUVOK

Those bodies are reminiscent of one of the
premonitions Kes described.

KIM

Didn't she say we were all going to die?

A creepy moment.

CHAKOTAY

Let's keep moving.

As they walk . . .

46   INT. BORG CORRIDOR #3   46

Chakotay, Tuvok and Kim ENTER.

47   THEIR POV   47

At the far end of the corridor there is a BORG working on a section of the
wall. But we can't see what he's doing . . .

48   THE AWAY TEAM   48

moves toward the Borg . . .

49   THEIR POV—MOVING   49

As we approach the Borg, we can see that he is standing next to a large,
irregular OPENING in the wall. The perimeter of the opening is covered
with glistening alien FLESH. It's as though something dissolved through the
Borg wall from the other side and latched onto the perimeter with its
"skin." We cannot see clearly inside the opening, but it is dark and we get
the sense there might be a large chamber beyond.

50   THE AWAY TEAM   50

reacts to the sight.

                              CHAKOTAY
                      (off tricorder, re: skin)
              It looks like it dissolved right through the Borg
              hull . . .

51   CLOSE ON THE BORG (OPTICAL)   51

He raises his hand toward the "fleshy" perimeter . . . and assimilation
"tubules" extrude from the Borg's fingers and penetrate the alien flesh.
(These are the same kind of tubules seen in Sickbay in Act One.) Instantly,
the "flesh" CRACKLES with energy that jolts the Borg backward slightly.

52   THE AWAY TEAM   52

observes with interest.

                                TUVOK
              The Borg is attempting to assimilate it.

A beat . . . then the Borg tries again (offcamera), single-minded. He's
JOLTED backward again.

                                 KIM
              Doesn't look like he's having much luck . . .

Chakotay takes a step closer . . . scans through the opening (the Borg
ignores him).

                              CHAKOTAY
                           (off tricorder)
              There's a chamber beyond this opening . . . forty
              meters wide . . . . . . high concentrations of antimatter
              particles . . .
                             (reacts)
              It looks like some kind of propulsion system.

                                 KIM
              It's a ship?

                                TUVOK
              Starfleet has encountered species that use organic-
              based vessels. The Breen, for example.

CHAKOTAY
(off tricorder)

There doesn't seem to be anybody on board . . .

(taps combadge)

Chakotay to Voyager.

JANEWAY'S COMM VOICE

Go ahead.

CHAKOTAY

Captain, we've found an entrance to the bio-mass . . .
we think it may be a ship of some kind. Permission to
go inside.

JANEWAY'S COM VOICE

Granted.

Chakotay indicates a nearby CIRCUIT BOX—a "distribution node."

CHAKOTAY

Harry . . . that's a Borg distribution node. See if you
can download their tactical database—it might contain
a record of what happened here.

KIM

Aye, sir . . .

Kim moves to the circuit box and starts working his tricorder.

CHAKOTAY

Tuvok.

Phaser rifles in-hand, Chakotay and Tuvok EXIT through the weird opening
in the wall, careful to avoid the "fleshy" perimeter. Off Kim as he
works . . . glancing nervously at the Borg working just a few feet away . . .

53   INT. ALIEN BIO-SHIP—CONTINUOUS   53

The walls are ROUNDED, organic-looking, with pulsing VEINS of ENER-
GY running along the walls and fleshy MEMBRANES hanging from the
ceiling. In the center of the room there is a raised STRUCTURE that looks
like a chair that's grown out of the floor of the vessel. The only source of
light is a weird GLOW from certain sections of the walls . . . and there is a
low, rumbling SOUND. It's like being inside a BODY CAVITY—dark and
glistening and utterly alien.

Chakotay and Tuvok ENTER . . . take in the mysterious setting. They stop first at the large "chair-like" structure. The form-fitting shape of it suggests that a very large humanoid might sit there—someone over ten feet tall. A prolonged and creepy silence as they get a good look at its various features . . .

Chakotay notices a nearby wall with several pulsing "veins" running through it. He moves to the wall and scans it.

> CHAKOTAY
> (re: veins)
> They seem to be organic conduits . . . they're carrying electrodynamic fluid.

> TUVOK
> Maybe an energy source . . .

> CHAKOTAY
> Maybe.

They take a few steps . . . stop at a section of the wall that is BLINKING colorfully with what can only be described as "neurochemical pulses."

> CHAKOTAY
> (off tricorder)
> This looks like a binary matrix . . . but it's laced with neuropeptides . . .
> (eyes it)
> Could be their version of a computer core . . .

54   INT. BORG CUBE—CORRIDOR #3   54

Kim scanning the circuit box with his tricorder, downloading information. A quiet moment . . . then we hear a distant SCRAPING sound from somewhere in the corridors. He glances around . . . another SCRAPE echoes through the ship. Unnerving. Kim glances at the Borg, who continues working, ignoring the sounds.

55   INT. ALIEN BIO-SHIP   55

Chakotay and Tuvok are on different sides of the chamber, studying its various features.

Tuvok is eyeing a large section of the wall that is SCORCHED and TORN. He scans it.

> TUVOK
> (off tricorder)
> This damage was caused by a Borg disruptor beam.
> (beat)
> The wall appears to be regenerating itself.

Just then something in an adjoining chamber catches his eye . . . he moves to it, looks down to see . . .

56   A DEAD BORG   56

on its back, eyes wide with shock. There is a thin alien TENDRIL sticking out of its mouth, wrapped around its head, leading into its nostrils. A startling sight.

> CHAKOTAY
> (calls out)
> Tuvok . . .

57   INT. BORG CORRIDOR #3   57

As before. Kim at the node; the Borg next to him. There's another SCRAPING sound followed by a distant, booming sound, almost like a weapon being fired.

Closer now. Kim completes the download . . . and then starts scanning the corridor with his tricorder. Another SCRAPE . . .

Suddenly, the Borg next to Kim stops what he's doing . . . looks past Kim from where the sound is coming, reacts to it . . . turns and walks in the opposite direction, as though in hasty retreat. Kim watches him go . . . curious . . .

CRASH! A loud and jolting noise comes from somewhere nearby, like metal being twisted apart. Kim whirls, startled at the noise—

                                                        SMASH CUT TO:

58   INT. SICKBAY   58

Kes working at a console. She reacts to a sudden—

59   MENTAL FLASH (OPTICAL)   59

Kim's face, screaming in agony!

60   RESUME KES   60

As she falters slightly, overwhelmed by the vision. The Doctor rushes to her.

                         DOCTOR
            Kes . . .

She looks at him, panic rising.

                          KES
            Harry's in danger . . .

                         DOCTOR
            What are you—

                          KES
      Get them out of there.

                         DOCTOR
                        (to com)
            Sickbay to Janeway . . .

61   INT. ALIEN BIO-SHIP   61

Chakotay and Tuvok looking around.

                      KIM'S VOICE
                        (urgent)
            Commander!

They react, head for the opening in the wall where they entered . . .

62   INT. BORG CUBE—CORRIDOR #3—CONTINUOUS   62

Chakotay and Tuvok ENTER quickly. Kim is standing in the corridor, tricorder open.

                          KIM
            There's someone in here with us . . . and it's not a
      Borg.
                        (works)
            I can't localize it . . . but it's within twenty meters . . .

                         TUVOK
            Perhaps the ''pilot'' has returned.

JANEWAY'S COM VOICE
Voyager to Away Team.

CHAKOTAY
(taps combadge)
Go ahead.

63   INT. BRIDGE   63

Janeway in command. Paris at Conn, Torres filling in at Ops. Kes is there, standing next to the Captain, worried.

JANEWAY
Stand by for transport. We're getting you out of there.

CHAKOTAY'S COM VOICE
Good idea.

JANEWAY
(to Torres)
Energize.

Torres works the Ops console . . . it BEEPS.

TORRES
I can't get a lock on them . . .

JANEWAY
What's the problem?

TORRES
It looks like bio-electric interference . . . from whatever's coming toward them . . .

64   INT. BORG CUBE—CORRIDOR #3   64

Chakotay, Tuvok, Kim. Tension rising. There's another SCRAPE and an alien SHRIEK of some sort.

CHAKOTAY
(off tricorder)
It's within seven meters . . . let's get out of here . . .

CAMERA FOLLOWS as the Team starts moving quickly down the hall . . .

65   INT. BRIDGE   65

Torres working Ops; Janeway at her side.

                    JANEWAY
          Narrow the confinement beam . . .

                    TORRES
          No effect. I'm going to try a skeletal lock . . .

                    JANEWAY
          A what?

                    TORRES
          I think I can get a clean lock on the minerals in their
          bone tissue . . .
                         (off her look)
          I just came up with it, but I think it'll work!

66   INT. BORG CUBE—CORRIDOR #2   66

The Team ENTERS, moving. TWO BORG are a few feet ahead of them, also
in retreat along the darkened hall. Chakotay checking his tricorder as he
goes . . .

                    CHAKOTAY
          The lifeform's five meters away . . . closing . . .

                    KIM
          From where?

67   NEW ANGLE—THE TWO BORG (OPTICAL)   67

As an ALCOVE beside them EXPLODES OUTWARD IN A SHOWER OF
SPARKS AND DEBRIS! IN A VIOLENT BLUR OF MOTION WE GLIMPSE
A LARGE ALIEN—VAGUELY HUMANOID, BUT OF INHUMAN
PROPORTIONS—IT ATTACKS THE BORG SO FAST THAT WE GET
ONLY A GLIMPSE OF IT!

68   CHAKOTAY AND TUVOK   68

are knocked to the ground by debris. We HEAR the RIPPING of METAL off
camera.

69   KIM   69

on the floor nearby. He looks up to see—

70   THE ALIEN (OPTICAL)   70

standing over the dead Borg, barely visible in the darkness down the hall. It
TOWERS—at least ten feet tall—its limbs cramped in the narrow corridor.
It wears an alien breathing apparatus. Without warning, it LUNGES at Kim
with blinding speed, and SLASHES at him, sending Kim FLYING BACK-
WARD!

71   OMITTED   71

72   NEW ANGLE (OPTICAL)   72

As Kim HITS the floor and DEMATERIALIZES. In the b.g., Chakotay and
Tuvok DEMATERIALIZE as well.

73   INT. VOYAGER BRIDGE   73

Torres and Janeway at Ops.

                              TORRES
                            (off console)
            I got them.

                              JANEWAY
            A ''skeletal lock'' . . . we'll have to add that one to the
            Transporter manual.

                              PARIS
            Captain!

She looks up to see:

74   THE VIEWSCREEN (OPTICAL)   74

which shows the view seen earlier of the BIO-SHIP attached to the Borg
Cube. The alien vessel starts to SHIMMER with incandescent COLORS.
Angry-looking, turbulent.

75   ON KES   75

staring at the Viewscreen . . . and she's hit by a:

76   MENTAL FLASH (OPTICAL)   76

Inside the alien bio-ship. The <u>ALIEN FACE MOVES INTO VIEW, STAR-ING RIGHT AT US!</u>

77   RESUME KES   77

as she falters backward from the telepathic blast, slumps against Chakotay's chair.

                          JANEWAY
              Get us out of here—maximum warp!

Paris works . . .

78   EXT. SPACE—VOYAGER (OPTICAL)   78

as it turns away from the Borg graveyard . . . the alien BIO-SHIP SENDS OUT a CRACKLING TENDRIL of ENERGY, whip-like, powerful, the same effect seen in the Teaser.

The tendril narrowly MISSES Voyager, but even so SENDS our ship SPINNING WILDLY!

79   INT. BRIDGE   79

Red Alert. SHAKING! Everyone hanging on! Paris working frantically . . .

80   EXT. SPACE—VOYAGER (OPTICAL)   80

as it STOPS its tailspin and JUMPS into WARP!

81   INT. BRIDGE   81

Moments later. Everyone recovering. Paris checks his console.

                          PARIS
              The alien ship is not pursuing.

Janeway moves to Kes, who is slumped in Chakotay's chair, a little dazed.

                          JANEWAY
              Kes . . . ?

                                    KES
        I could hear its thoughts . . . the pilot of the bio-
        ship . . . it tried to communicate with me . . .

Kes concentrates, trying to make sense of the impressions.

                                    KES
        They're a telepathic species . . . I think I've been
        aware of them for some time now . . . the
        premonitions . . .
                                  (beat)
        Captain, it's not the Borg we should be worried
        about . . . it's them.

                                 JANEWAY
        What did it say to you?

Kes looks at her.

                                    KES
        It said . . . "The weak . . . will perish."

Off the moment . . .

                                                        FADE OUT.

                        END OF ACT THREE

ACT FOUR

FADE IN:

82   EXT. SPACE—VOYAGER (OPTICAL)   82

hanging in space.

> JANEWAY (V.O)
> Captain's Log, Stardate 50984.3. It's been twelve
> hours since our confrontation with the alien lifeform.
> There's no sign that we're being pursued . . . and
> we've had no further encounters with the Borg . . .

83   INT. CORRIDOR   83

Janeway walking along . . . passing a few crewmembers . . . she nods to
them with an encouraging look.

> JANEWAY (V.O.)
> (continuing)
> I've decided to hold our course. The "Northwest
> Passage" is only one day away . . . and I won't allow
> fear to undermine this crew's sense of purpose . . .

She EXITS into Sickbay . . .

84   INT. SICKBAY—CLOSE ON KIM   84

eyes wide open and staring, lying on the surgical bed. Awake. The WOUND
on his chest is covered with ALIEN TISSUE—strange, thin tendrils are
wrapped around his torso and neck and face like a python . . . and they
have also entered his nose and throat.

> JANEWAY (V.O.)
> (continuing)
> . . . even if that fear is justified.

85   WIDER (OPTICAL)   85

The Doctor is standing next to the surgical bed. He turns and walks
THROUGH the forcefield, which FLASHES on and off. A Security N.D.
stands guard. The Doctor joins Janeway and they move a discreet distance
away from Kim.

> DOCTOR
> (low, to Janeway)
> The infection is spreading. What began with a few
> stray cells contaminating the chest wound . . . is now
> infusing every system in his body.

> JANEWAY
> It looks like he's being transformed in some way . . .

> DOCTOR
> Not exactly. The alien cells are consuming his body
> from the inside out . . . in essence, Mister Kim is
> being eaten alive.

Janeway eyes Kim, disturbed.

> JANEWAY
> He's still conscious . . .

> DOCTOR
> I tried giving him a sedative, but it was rejected
> immediately. In fact, every treatment I've tried has
> been neutralized within seconds.

He moves to a console MONITOR (the same monitor where he was looking
at human blood cells in Act One), and he taps a control.

86   INCLUDE MONITOR (OPTICAL)   86

It shows a MICROSCOPIC VIEW of ALIEN CELLS and various technical
data. The cells are similar to human blood cells, but they are in constant,
violent motion, agitated, the cell membrane itself luminescent.

> DOCTOR
> These are alien cells. Each one contains more than a
> <u>hundred</u> times the DNA of a human cell. It's the most
> densely coded lifeform I've ever seen . . . even I
> would need years to decipher it.

Janeway eyes the technical data.

> JANEWAY
> They have an extraordinary immune response.
> Anything that penetrates the cell membrane . . .
> chemical . . . biological . . . <u>technological</u> . . . it's all
> instantly destroyed.

(beat)
That's why the Borg can't assimilate them . . .

DOCTOR
(nods)
Resistance in this case is far from futile. Nevertheless,
I believe Borg technology holds the key to saving
Mister Kim.

JANEWAY
How so?

DOCTOR
I hope to unleash an army of modified Borg
nanoprobes into his bloodstream . . . designed to
target and eradicate the infection.
(explains)
As you know, I've been analyzing the nanoprobes . . .
they're efficient little assimilators . . . one can't help
but admire the workmanship. But they're no match
for the alien cells . . .
(beat)
So I successfully dissected a nanoprobe . . . and
managed to access its re-coding mechanism. I was
able to <u>reprogram</u> the probe to emit the same
electrochemical signatures as the alien cells. That
way, the probe can do its work without being
detected.
(beat)
Observe.

He hits another control . . . and on the MONITOR we see a BORG
NANOPROBE enter frame and begin to ASSIMILATE a few alien cells,
turning them dark and oblong.

DOCTOR
(continuing)
Unfortunately, I've only created a few prototypes. I'll
need several days to modify enough nanoprobes to
cure Ensign Kim.

JANEWAY
Does Harry have several days?

DOCTOR
I wish I knew.

She nods. The Doctor keeps working. Janeway walks past the surgical bay . . . glances at Kim, who is lying awake. Kim's eyes look into hers. He's obviously conscious and aware . . . but can't speak.

> JANEWAY
>
> Fight it, Harry.
>
>   (softly)
>
> That's an order.

But Kim can only stare back at her . . . no response at all . . . an affecting sight. Off the moment . . .

                                                                CUT TO:

87   INT. ENGINEERING (VPB)   87

Tuvok and Torres are reporting to Chakotay. A nearby MONITOR shows various BORG DATA scrolling across the screen—starmaps, Borg vessel diagrams, telemetry, etc.

> TORRES
>
> We've analyzed the Borg's tactical database. They refer to these new aliens as "Species Eight Four Seven Two."

> TUVOK
>
> Over the past five months, the Borg have been attacked by them on at least a dozen occasions. Each time, they were defeated . . . swiftly.

> TORRES
>
> The Collective has very little information about the species . . .

> CHAKOTAY
>
> Is anything known about where they come from?

Tuvok and Torres exchange a look.

> TORRES
>
> I'm afraid so.

She turns to the console and taps a few commands. Chakotay watches the monitor (which is now offcamera). As he reacts to what he sees, his expression turning grim . . .

                         CHAKOTAY
Get the Captain.

                                                              CUT TO:

87A INT. BRIDGE—ANGLE ON VIEWSCREEN (OPTICAL)   87A

It shows a murky region of space that is FILLED with ALIEN BIO-SHIPS.
From this distance, we can see at least twenty or thirty ships of various
shapes and sizes. All of them glowing and moving.

87B NEW ANGLE—THE CREW   87B

Red Alert. Tuvok, Paris, Torres at Ops. Janeway and Chakotay on their feet.
Kes standing nearby, also on her feet. Everyone is staring at the viewscreen
in shock.

                         JANEWAY
                 (bleak, re: Viewscreen)
The "Northwest Passage" . . .

                         CHAKOTAY
It's clear of Borg activity for a very good reason . . .

Beat.

                         TUVOK
                    (off console)
I'm picking up one hundred and thirty-three bio-
ships . . .
                         (reacts)
More are appearing . . .

                         JANEWAY
From where?

                         TUVOK
They seem to be coming from a quantum
singularity—

                         TORRES
I'm localizing the gravimetric distortions . . .

                         CHAKOTAY
On screen.

The Viewscreen changes to show a large, undulating FISSURE in space. A
BIO-SHIP flies out of the fissure . . . and then another BIO-SHIP. Everyone
reacts with growing concern. Janeway turns to Kes.

                        JANEWAY
            Kes . . . anything?

87C   ON KES   87C

slowly PUSHING IN on her face as she stares at the Viewscreen, "sensing"
the aliens.

                        KES
            Yes . . . I can hear them . . .

87D   MENTAL FLASH (OPTICAL)   87D

A BIO-SHIP flying past camera . . .

87E   KES   87E

reacting . . .

87F   MENTAL FLASH (OPTICAL)   87F

CLOSE ON an ALIEN HAND moving over one of the control modules in a
bio-ship (as seen earlier) . . .

87G   KES   87G

takes in the impressions . . . trying to put them into words . . .

                        KES
            They come from a place where they're alone . . .
            nothing else lives there . . .

                    CHAKOTAY
            Some kind of parallel universe . . .

                        KES
            I don't know . . .

Kes shivers a little, struck by a sudden malevolence . . .

> KES
>
> I feel . . . malevolence . . . a cold hatred . . .
> (thinks)
> The weak . . . will perish . . . it's an <u>invasion</u> . . . they
> intend to destroy everything . . .

> JANEWAY
>
> Tom . . . reverse course, maximum warp. Take us five
> light years out and hold position.

> PARIS
>
> Aye, Captain.

> JANEWAY
> (to Tuvok)
>
> Maintain Red Alert.

Janeway considers the shocking discovery, then heads for her Ready
Room . . .

> JANEWAY
> (to Chakotay)
>
> Commander.

Chakotay follows her and they EXIT to . . .

87H   INT. READY ROOM—CONTINUOUS (OPTICAL)   87H

Janeway and Chakotay ENTER. She looks at him:

> JANEWAY
>
> That moment we spoke about . . . it's here.
> (beat)
> Any thoughts?

> CHAKOTAY
>
> Just one. Flying into that corridor would mean certain
> death.

> JANEWAY
>
> Agreed. The "Northwest Passage" is no longer an
> option. So now the choice is between facing the Borg
> in their space . . . or finding ourselves a nice planet
> here in the Delta Quadrant . . . and giving up on ever
> getting home.

> CHAKOTAY
> We'd be turning around, but we wouldn't be giving
> up. We might find another way home . . .

But the words sound hollow. They both know that's unlikely. Janeway
starts pacing, not willing to give in.

> JANEWAY
> I'm not ready to walk onto the Bridge and tell the
> crew we're quitting. I can't do that. Not yet.
> (beat)
> There must be an alternative . . .

A somber beat.

> CHAKOTAY
> Kathryn . . . you haven't slept in two days. Try to get
> some rest, clear your head. We're safe, for the
> moment . . .
> (beat)
> We can tell the crew tomorrow, if we have to.

She looks pensive . . . but she nods.

> JANEWAY
> See you in the morning.

Chakotay heads for the door. Off Janeway's troubled face . . .

DISSOLVE TO:

88
thru   OMITTED   88
92   thru
                                                             92

93   OMITTED   93

94   INT. JANEWAY'S QUARTERS   94

Janeway lying on her bed in the darkness, still in uniform . . . eyes wide
open. She sits up . . . takes a deep breath . . . there's no way she's going to
get any sleep tonight. As she stands . . .

CUT TO:

95   INT. CORRIDOR   95

Janeway walks up to the set of Holodeck doors.

                    JANEWAY
          Computer—activate Da Vinci workshop program,
          Janeway seven.

As the Computer works . . .

96   INT. DA VINCI'S WORKSHOP—NIGHT   96

Janeway steps inside . . . the workshop is lit by candle and oil lamp
light . . . the flickering shadows lend an almost dream-like mood to the
scene. Janeway moves further inside . . .

                    JANEWAY
          Maestro?

She moves slowly through the light and shadows . . . not finding him . . .

                    JANEWAY
                    (continuing)
          Leonardo . . . ?

Janeway rounds a shelf of manuscripts . . .

97   INCLUDE DA VINCI   97

seated at a bench. He seems almost fixated by something off-screen.

Janeway steps closer, cautiously. Leonardo takes notice, comes out of his
reverie, but only a little . . .

                    DA VINCI
          Catarina . . . buona sera . . .

Her eyes attempt to follow his gaze—but he appears to have been staring at
the blank wall nearby.

                    JANEWAY
                    (puzzled)
          Am I disturbing you?

Leonardo doesn't answer the question. Instead, he indicates the wall.

DA VINCI

What do you see?

Janeway considers—she's used to his unexpected questions and musings.

JANEWAY

A wall . . . with the light from a lamp reflecting on it.
(beat)
Why? What do you see?

DA VINCI

A flock of starlings . . . the leaves of an oak . . . a
horse's tail . . . a thief hanging from a noose . . .

He smiles, coming further out of his reverie.

DA VINCI
(continuing)
And a wall. With the light from a lamp reflecting on
it.
(musing)
There are times, Catarina, when I find myself
transfixed by a shadow on the wall, or the splashing
of water against a stone . . . I stare at it, and hours
pass . . . the world around me drops away, replaced
by worlds being created and destroyed by my
imagination . . .
(beat)
A way to focus the mind.

Janeway stares at him for a very long moment, thinking of her own
dilemma. She turns back to the shadows on the wall.

JANEWAY
(re: wall)
There's a path before me . . . the only way home. And
on either side, mortal enemies bent on destroying
each other. If I attempt to pass between them . . . I'll
be destroyed, as well. But to turn around . . . that
would end all hope of ever getting home.

She turns to Da Vinci.

JANEWAY
(continuing)
No matter how much I focus my mind . . . I can't see
an alternative.

Leonardo considers her for a beat, as if sensing that she is speaking of a
dilemma in her actual life. He offers his guidance . . .

DA VINCI
May I suggest . . . that you turn to the Divine.

She looks at him.

DA VINCI
When one's imagination fails to provide an
answer . . . one must seek a greater imagination.
There are times, when even I find myself kneeling in
prayer.

Da Vinci stands . . . moves to a table and picks up a foot-tall object wrapped
in muslin.

DA VINCI
(encouraging)
I must deliver this bronzetto to the Monks at Santa
Croce. Come with me . . . we will wake the Abbot . . .
visit the chapel . . . and appeal to God.

JANEWAY
Somehow, I don't think that's going to work for
me . . .

Janeway turns one last time to the light dancing against the wall . . . but this
time, Da Vinci's words and the shifting patterns give her an idea.

JANEWAY
But . . . there is an alternative I hadn't considered . . .

She turns to him.

JANEWAY
What if I made an appeal . . . to the Devil?

Da Vinci reacts, a little startled by the remark, unsure what she means.
Janeway stands, mind working.

JANEWAY

Thank you, Maestro.

She heads for the door. OFF the mystery of the flickering light . . .

FADE OUT:

END OF ACT FOUR

ACT FIVE

FADE IN:

98   EXT. SPACE—VOYAGER (OPTICAL)   98

hanging in space.

99   INT. BRIEFING ROOM   99

Janeway standing at the head of the table, addressing Chakotay, Tuvok, Paris, Torres, the Doctor, Kes and Neelix. Everyone looks surprised by something she has just said. Mid-conversation.

> PARIS
> An alliance . . . with the Borg?

> JANEWAY
> More like . . . an exchange. We offer them a way to defeat their new enemy . . . and in return, we get safe passage through their space.

She turns to the Doctor.

> JANEWAY
> In developing a treatment for Harry, the Doctor has found a way to attack the aliens at a microscopic level.

> DOCTOR
> It's still in the experimental stages, Captain . . . I've only made a few prototypes.

> JANEWAY
> Nevertheless, if we teach the Borg how to modify their own nanoprobes . . . They'd have a blueprint to create a weapon to fight the aliens.

> DOCTOR
> In theory . . . yes.

> JANEWAY
> (to Torres)
> B'Elanna, it's clear from the Borg database that they

know practically nothing about "Species Eight Four
Seven Two."

Torres sees where she's going, intrigued.

> TORRES
> That's right. The Borg gain knowledge through
> assimilation. What they can't assimilate, they can't
> understand.

> JANEWAY
> But we don't assimilate . . . we investigate. And in
> this case, that's given us an edge. We've discovered
> something they need.

> NEELIX
> The Borg aren't exactly known for their diplomacy.
> Can we really expect them to cooperate with us?

> KES
> Normally, the answer would be no. But if what I've
> learned from the aliens is true . . . the Borg are <u>losing</u>
> this conflict.

> JANEWAY
> In one regard, the Borg are no different than we
> are . . . they're trying to survive. I don't believe
> they're going to refuse an offer that will help them do
> that.

> TUVOK
> (doubtful)
> What makes you think the Borg won't attempt to <u>take</u>
> the information . . . by assimilating Voyager and its
> crew.

> JANEWAY
> That won't get them anywhere.
> (beat)
> Doctor, you're the only one on board with full
> knowledge of the nanoprobe modifications. I want you
> to transfer all of that research into your holo-matrix.

> DOCTOR
> Certainly.

> JANEWAY

You're my guarantee. If the Borg threaten us in any
way, we'll simply erase your program.

The Doctor looks a little startled at the notion.

> JANEWAY
> (reassuring)

But it won't come to that . . . it's in the Collective's
own interest to cooperate.
> (beat)

Voyager's only one ship . . . our safe passage is a
small price to pay for what we're offering in
exchange.

Silence as they all consider. Janeway is determined, confident.

> JANEWAY

B'Elanna, assist the Doctor with his transfer. Mister
Paris . . . locate the nearest Borg vessel, and lay in a
course. They shouldn't be difficult to find.

> PARIS

Yes, Ma'am.

> JANEWAY

Dismissed.

The crew rises and starts to EXIT. But Chakotay hangs back, troubled by
what he's heard. Janeway can sense his discomfort . . . and waits until
everyone else is out of the room.

> JANEWAY

You were awfully quiet.

> CHAKOTAY

I didn't want to say this in front of the others . . .
> (beat)

But I think what you're proposing is too great a risk.

> JANEWAY

How so?

He chooses his words carefully, taking a tactful approach . . .

> CHAKOTAY

There's a story I heard as a child . . . a parable . . . I never forgot it . . .

> (recalls)

A scorpion was walking along the bank of a river, wondering how to get to the other side . . . when suddenly he saw a fox. He asked the fox to take him on his back across the river. The fox said no . . . I'll get halfway there, and you'll sting me, and I'll drown. But the scorpion assured him . . . if I did that, we'd both drown. The fox thought about it and finally agreed. So the scorpion climbed up on his back, and the fox began to swim . . .

> (beat)

But halfway across the river, the scorpion stung the fox. As the poison filled his veins, the fox turned to the scorpion and said why did you do that? Now you'll drown, too.

> (beat)

I couldn't help it, said the scorpion. It's my nature.

A long moment as Janeway takes this in, thoughtful.

> JANEWAY

I understand the risk . . . and I'm not proposing that we try to change the nature of the beast. But this is a unique situation. To our knowledge, the Borg have never been so threatened . . . they're vulnerable . . . I think we can take advantage of that.

> CHAKOTAY

Even if we do somehow negotiate an exchange . . . how long will they keep up their end of the bargain? It could take months to cross Borg territory . . . we'd be facing thousands of systems . . . millions of vessels . . .

> JANEWAY

But only one Collective. And we've got them over a barrel. We don't have to give them a single bit of information . . . not until we're safe. We just need the courage to see this through to the end . . .

> CHAKOTAY

There are other kinds of courage . . . like the courage to accept that there are some situations beyond your

control. Not every problem has an immediate
solution.

JANEWAY

You're suggesting we turn around . . .

CHAKOTAY

Yes. We should get out of harm's way . . . let them
fight it out. In the meantime, there's still a lot of the
Delta Quadrant we haven't explored . . . we may find
another way home.

JANEWAY

Or we may find something else. Six months, a year
down the road . . . after Species Eight Four Seven Two
gets through with the Borg . . . we could find
ourselves back in the line of fire. And we'll have
missed the window of opportunity that exists right
here . . . right now.

A beat. Chakotay takes another tack.

CHAKOTAY

How much is our safety worth?

JANEWAY

What do you mean?

CHAKOTAY

We'd be giving an advantage to a race guilty of
murdering <u>billions</u>. We'd be helping the Borg
assimilate another species . . . just to get ourselves
back to Earth. It's wrong.

JANEWAY

Tell that to Harry Kim.
                    (beat)
He's barely alive thanks to that species. Maybe
helping to assimilate them isn't such a bad idea . . .
we could be doing the Delta Quadrant a favor.

CHAKOTAY

I don't think you really believe that. I think you're
struggling to justify your plan . . . because your desire
to get this crew home is blinding you to other options.
                    (beat)

I know you, Kathryn . . . sometimes you don't know
when to step back.

The tension rises a notch. They're at an impasse and it's getting more
emotional.

> JANEWAY
> Do you trust me, Chakotay?

> CHAKOTAY
> That's not the issue . . .

> JANEWAY
> But it is.
>> (beat)
> Only yesterday, you were saying that we'd face this
> together . . . that you'd be at my side.

> CHAKOTAY
> I still have to tell you what I believe. I wouldn't be
> any good to you if I didn't.

> JANEWAY
> I appreciate your insights . . . but the time for debate
> is over. I've made my decision.
>> (beat)
> Do I have your support?

> CHAKOTAY
> You're the Captain . . . I'm the First Officer. I'll
> follow your orders.
>> (beat)
> But that doesn't change my belief that we're making a
> fatal mistake.

> JANEWAY
> Then I guess I'm alone, after all.
>> (formal)
> Dismissed.

Chakotay turns and EXITS. Off Janeway's face . . .

                                                    CUT TO:

100   EXT. SPACE—VOYAGER (OPTICAL)   100

at impulse. It flies past . . . and the CAMERA PANS to reveal Voyager is entering a <u>BORG SOLAR SYSTEM</u>. In the distance we see a SUN . . . and a BORGIFIED PLANET. There are five BORG VESSELS flying about.

101   INT. BRIDGE   101

Red Alert. Janeway, Chakotay, Paris, Tuvok, Torres at the Engineering Station, N.D.s at their stations. Everyone staring at the (off camera) Viewscreen.

                          TUVOK
                       (off console)
            There are three planets in this system . . .
            inhabitants . . . all Borg. A vessel is approaching.

                         JANEWAY
            All stop. Shields up.

102   EXT. SPACE—VOYAGER (OPTICAL)   102

holding position as a BORG CUBE flies into view . . . and then STOPS right in front of Voyager.

103   INT. BRIDGE (OPTICAL)   103

As before. The Borg Cube on the Viewscreen.

                          TUVOK
            They're hailing us.

                         JANEWAY
            Open a channel.

The COLLECTIVE is heard over the com:

                           BORG
            We are the Borg. You will be assimilated. Resistance
            is futile.

The ship JOLTS slightly.

                          TUVOK
            They've locked onto us with a tractor beam . . .

> JANEWAY
> (to com)
> Borg vessel, this is Captain Janeway of the Starship
> Voyager—I have tactical information about "Species
> Eight Four Seven Two." I want to negotiate.

> BORG
> Negotiation is irrelevant. You will be assimilated.

Janeway turns to Torres, nods.

104   CLOSE ON OPS CONSOLE (OPTICAL)   104

Torres working. A MONITOR shows what we saw in Sickbay in Act Four—
alien cells being assimilated by a Borg nanoprobe. After a beat, the image is
replaced by the words "DATA TRANSMITTING . . ."

105   RESUME SCENE (OPTICAL)   105

As everyone waits, tension rising.

> JANEWAY
> (to com)
> Borg vessel . . . what you're receiving is a sample of
> the knowledge we possess. If you don't disengage
> your tractor beam immediately . . . I will have that
> data destroyed.
> (beat)
> You have ten seconds to comply.

A tense beat. Janeway glances to Tuvok.

> TUVOK
> Their tractor beam is still active . . .

> JANEWAY
> (to com, pressing on)
> We know you're in danger of being defeated . . . you
> can't afford to risk losing this information. Disengage
> your tractor beam.

Janeway suddenly DEMATERIALIZES in a BORG EFFECT . . .

106   INT. BORG COLLECTIVE—WIDE (OPTICAL)   106

Janeway MATERIALIZES on a narrow bridge in the middle of the vast interior, a tiny figure among the thousands of Borg drones that line the walls.

> BORG
>
> State your demands.

106A NEW ANGLE—JANEWAY (OPTICAL)   106A

facing the hive. She's a little awed, but stands her ground—her opening gambit appears to be working.

> JANEWAY
>
> I want safe passage through your space . . . once my ship is beyond Borg territory, I'll give you our research.

> BORG
>
> Unacceptable. Our space is vast. Your passage would require too much time. We need the technology now.

> JANEWAY
>
> If I give it to you now, you'll assimilate us.

> BORG
>
> Species Eight Four Seven Two must be stopped. Our survival is your survival. Give us the technology.

> JANEWAY
>
> No. Safe passage first. Or no deal.

A pause as the Collective "thinks."

> BORG
>
> Your demand is unacceptable.

Janeway hesitates.

> JANEWAY
>
> All right . . . then I'll take the first step . . . but you're going to have to meet me halfway.

A pause—the Borg are not used to the "give and take" of negotiations.

> BORG
>
> State your proposal.

> JANEWAY

Let's work together . . . combine our resources.
Even if we give you the technology now, you're still
going to need time to develop it.
>   (beat)
By working together, we can create a weapon more
quickly. If you escort us through your space . . . we
can perfect the weapon as we—

BOOM! The ship SHAKES. Janeway reacts. BOOM—another SHAKE.

> JANEWAY

What's going on?

But the Collective doesn't answer. Another JOLT! Janeway grabs hold of the
railing . . .

106B EXT. SPACE—THE BORG CUBE (OPTICAL)   106B

which has Voyager in its tractor beam. We see an alien BIO-SHIP as it FLIES
PAST the Cube, sending out an ENERGY TENDRIL as it goes. The Cube is
ROCKED by the blast, shaking Voyager with it.

107   INT. BRIDGE   107

SHAKING. Chakotay, Tuvok, Paris, Torres, N.D.s. The shaking subsides.

> CHAKOTAY

Where did that ship come from?

Tuvok checks his console.

> TUVOK

A quantum singularity has appeared twenty thousand
kilometers away.
>   (beat)
The bio-ship is heading directly toward the planet.

> TORRES
>   (off console)

The Borg shields are weakening . . . we might be able
to break free of the tractor beam . . .

> CHAKOTAY

Can you lock onto the Captain?

> TUVOK
> (works)

Not yet . . .

> PARIS
> (off console)
> Commander—nine more bio-ships have just come out
> of the singularity!

Reactions . . .

107A INT. BORG CUBE (OPTICAL) 107A

As before, Janeway facing the Hive.

> BORG
> We have made our decision.

Before Janeway can respond, the ship TREMBLES with power . . .

108 EXT. SPACE—ALIEN BIO-SHIPS (OPTICAL) 108

An entire fleet of them—nine in all. They are RUSHING toward camera . . .

Suddenly, all of the ships GLOW with power and send out CRACKLING TENDRILS from their bows . . . the tendrils CONVERGING to form one MASSIVE intertwining BEAM of ENERGY . . .

108A NEW ANGLE—THE BORG PLANET (OPTICAL) 108A

as it is HIT with the massive TENDRIL of ENERGY. After a moment of being continuously struck, a SHOCKWAVE ripples across the surface of the sphere . . . and the planet EXPLODES IN A TITANIC BLAST!

108B NEW ANGLE (OPTICAL) 108B

FIRE and DEBRIS BLOWING PAST US. And out of the maelstrom two ships come ROARING THROUGH: THE BORG CUBE with VOYAGER locked in its tractor beam! They RACE past the screen, narrowly avoiding destruction . . .

109 REVERSE ANGLE—THE CUBE AND VOYAGER (OPTICAL) 109

as the ships race off at high impulse. HOLD ON the image as the two vessels recede in the distance, smaller and smaller . . . locked together . . . until finally they are tiny dots lost among the stars . . .

SUPER: TO BE CONTINUED

END OF ACT FIVE

THE END

ADDENDUM

SCENE 10 (AS NEEDED)

            PARIS
         (re: torpedo)
Getting one of these things to penetrate the Borg
shields isn't going to be easy.

            TUVOK
Perhaps that is the wrong approach.

            PARIS
What do you mean?

            TUVOK
         (re: torpedo controls)
By altering the detonation parameters, I believe we
can target the shields themselves.

            PARIS
         (getting it)
Use the torpedoes to blow through the outer
defenses . . .

            TUVOK
And then follow with concentrated phaser fire.

            PARIS
It just might work . . .

SCENE 12 (AS NEEDED)

            CHAKOTAY
I want to cut down on the time it takes to seal off the
decks.

            KIM
In case we take on some uninvited guests . . .

            CHAKOTAY
Exactly. And I want to increase the magnitude of the
forcefields.

KIM

We can do both. If I dedicate the emitters on decks
seven and eight, that should give us a few more
seconds activation time . . . and an increase in
magnitude of at least ten percent . . .

STAR TREK: VOYAGER

"Scorpion, Part Two"

#40840-169

Written
by
Brannon Braga & Joe Menosky

Directed
by
Winrich Kolbe

STAR TREK: VOYAGER
"Scorpion, Part Two"

CAST

JANEWAY

PARIS

CHAKOTAY

TUVOK

TORRES

DOCTOR

KES

NEELIX

KIM

BORG

SEVEN OF NINE

Non-Speaking

N.D. SUPERNUMERARIES

STAR TREK: VOYAGER

''Scorpion, Part Two''

SETS

INTERIORS

VOYAGER
    BRIDGE
    BRIEFING ROOM
    CARGO BAY TWO
      JEFFERIES TUBE
    HOLODECK/DA VINCI'S WORKSHOP
    READY ROOM
    SICKBAY
      MED LAB

BORG CUBE
    CHAMBER
    CORRIDOR

EXTERIORS

VOYAGER
BORG CUBE
BIO-SHIPS
ALIEN REALM

STAR TREK: VOYAGER

''Scorpion, Part Two''

PRONUNCIATION GUIDE

DENATURATE	dee-NATCH-your-rate
DISPURSIVE	diss-PURSE-iv
FLUIDIC	flue-ID-ick
ISOTON	EYE-so-ton
LOCUTUS	low-CUTE-us
MULTIKINETIC	mull-tie-ken-ET-ick
NANOPROBES	NAN-oh-probes
NEUTRONIC	new-TRON-ick
PHOTON	FOE-tawn
TERTIARY	TERSH-ee-air-ee

STAR TREK: VOYAGER

"Scorpion, Part Two"

<u>TEASER</u>

FADE IN:

A1   RECAP FROM PART ONE   A1

1   EXT. SPACE—BORG CUBE (OPTICAL)   1

as it ROARS past camera at warp, Voyager locked in its tractor beam (as
seen in Part One).

2   INT. VOYAGER BRIDGE   2

Red Alert. Just moments have passed since we escaped the destruction of
the Borg planet. CHAKOTAY, TUVOK, PARIS, N.D.s at their stations,
TORRES at Ops. Fast action, tense:

> CHAKOTAY
> Report.

> TORRES
> (working)
> The Borg shields are off-line. I've got a lock on
> Captain Janeway . . .

> CHAKOTAY
> Get her out of there . . . and break us free of the
> Cube. Stand by all weapons.

Torres starts to work . . .

> TORRES
> I'm trying to energize . . . the Borg are scattering the
> beam . . .

> CHAKOTAY
> Compensate.

A minor SHAKE.

                         TORRES
No effect . . .

Suddenly Tuvok's console BEEPS.

                          TUVOK
We're being hailed.

                        CHAKOTAY
On screen.

3   INCLUDE VIEWSCREEN (OPTICAL)   3

JANEWAY is standing in the vast Borg Collective (as seen in Part One).

                        JANEWAY
     Commander—cut the transporter beam.

                        CHAKOTAY
     Captain . . . ?

                        JANEWAY
Do it.

Chakotay nods to Torres, who works. He turns back to Janeway with a
questioning look.

                        JANEWAY
     I've reached an agreement with the Collective. We're
     going to help them design a weapon against Species
     Eight Four Seven Two. In exchange, they've granted
     us safe passage through their space.

                         PARIS
                   (reacts to console)
     The Cube is altering course . . . they're heading
     toward the Alpha Quadrant.

                        JANEWAY
     That's part of the plan. We'll work on the weapon en
     route. Once we're across their territory . . . we'll give
     them the nanoprobes.
                         (beat)
     They appear to be holding up their end of the
     bargain . . . I suggest we do the same.

Chakotay hesitates . . . all of his instincts tell him this alliance is wrong . . . and for a moment, it looks as if he might protest . . . then:

> CHAKOTAY
> How do you propose we begin this "collaboration"?

> JANEWAY
> I'm going to work here . . . on the Cube. They have technology that'll make the job go faster. I want to take advantage of it.

> CHAKOTAY
> (concerned)
> It's not necessary for you to stay there. We can set up a comlink with the Borg and—

> JANEWAY
> It's part of the deal. I work here.

An awkward beat—we can sense the tension between them.

> CHAKOTAY
> All right.
> (beat)
> As long as we're cooperating . . . maybe the Borg would be willing to disengage their tractor beam. We can match their course without a leash.

> JANEWAY
> I'll propose it.
> (to Tuvok)
> Mister Tuvok . . . transport to my coordinates.

> TUVOK
> Understood.

> JANEWAY
> (to Chakotay, pointed)
> We're going to make this work, Commander. Janeway out.

She blinks off. A long moment as the crew waits for Chakotay to take the next step. Everyone is on edge. Finally, he turns to Tuvok.

CHAKOTAY
(even)
You heard the Captain.

Tuvok moves into action. OFF Chakotay's face—he's not happy about this . . .

FADE OUT.

END OF TEASER

ACT ONE

FADE IN:

(NOTE: Episode credits fall over opening scenes.)

4   MICROSCOPIC VIEW—BORG NANOPROBES (OPTICAL)   4

as seen in Part One, but now there are MANY of them, agitated, knocking
into each other, as if looking for something to attack.

> DOCTOR (V.O.)
> I've replicated nearly ten million Borg nanoprobes . . .
> each of them reprogrammed to my specifications . . .

REVEAL we are in—

5   INT. SICKBAY—MED LAB—CONTINUOUS   5

Chakotay is looking through a microscope at the nanoprobes. The DOCTOR
stands nearby.

> DOCTOR
> (continuing)
> . . . each capable of targeting the alien tissue.

> CHAKOTAY
> Assimilating it?

The Doctor pulls a vial out of the microscope.

> DOCTOR
> Just momentarily. The Borg technology will
> denaturate within seconds . . . taking the alien tissue
> along with it.

6   NEW ANGLE—HARRY KIM   6

lying on the surgical bed, his face and upper torso now nearly covered with
ALIEN TISSUE and TENDRILS—the infection has spread. Even though
Kim is still conscious, his eyes are covered with the alien tissue. The Doctor
and Chakotay move over to the bed. KES is there, working a console.

87

DOCTOR
(to Kim)
Mister Kim . . . I'm about to inject your carotid artery.
You'll feel a tingling sensation . . . don't be alarmed.

Kim doesn't respond. The Doctor applies the hypospray to Kim's neck and
INJECTS.

7   ON KIM (OPTICAL)   7

A section of his face begins to TRANSFORM. The alien tissue around his
right eye and cheekbone DARKENS . . . and then SPROUTS BORG
TECHNOLOGY . . . metallic nodes and tubes start to form . . . a terrifying
effect . . . but then a moment later, the entire section of Borgified tissue
DISSOLVES AWAY . . . leaving Kim's normal flesh and his now uncovered
eye and cheekbone beneath. The eye blinks.

8   RESUME SCENE   8

DOCTOR
(pleased)
Nice to see you again, Ensign.

Kes glances at a nearby read-out.

KES
It's working . . .

DOCTOR
(to Kes)
Prepare another dose of nanoprobes.

KES
Yes, Doctor.

Kes heads for the Med-Lab.

CHAKOTAY
(to Doctor)
Good work. Let me know when he's back on his feet.

Chakotay turns to go.

DOCTOR
Commander.

He stops.

> DOCTOR
> I must tell you, I have my doubts about this . . .
> "alliance." You may have convinced the Borg the
> nanoprobes can defeat their enemy. But a medical
> treatment is a long way from a weapon of war.

A beat. Chakotay obviously has his own doubts . . . but at the moment, he doesn't voice them.

> CHAKOTAY
> Leave that to the Captain.
> (beat)
> This situation is . . . unpredictable. So we're going to
> stay at full Red Alert. Keep all information about the
> nanoprobes stored in your holo-matrix.

> DOCTOR
> Don't worry. I'll delete myself at the first sign of
> trouble.
> (dry)
> Well . . . maybe not the <u>first</u> sign.

Chakotay doesn't respond to the humor . . . heads for the door . . .

CUT TO:

9   INT. BRIDGE   9

Still at Red Alert. Chakotay ENTERS and resumes command. Torres at Ops, Paris and N.D.s at their stations. Chakotay is more on edge than we've ever seen him—uneasy about this situation but trying to carry out orders despite his doubts.

> TORRES
> (to Chakotay)
> Tuvok beamed to the Cube . . . he's joined the
> Captain.

> CHAKOTAY
> Keep a Transporter lock on both of them.

> TORRES
> I'll try. But the Borg are already regenerating their
> shields . . .

                              CHAKOTAY
Try matching their shield frequencies . . .

                               TORRES
It won't work. They'll be able to adapt too quickly.

                              CHAKOTAY
                               (sharply)
I don't want to hear what we can't do, Lieutenant.
Just find a way to get our people out of there if we
have to.

Beat.

                               TORRES
     Aye, sir.

Torres keeps working. The ship TREMBLES briefly.

                               PARIS
                     (off console, surprised)
They've released their tractor beam.

                              CHAKOTAY
Match their course and speed.

Paris works.

                               PARIS
     I never thought I'd hear myself say this . . . but it
     looks like the Borg are cooperating.

Chakotay doesn't respond. OFF his somber expression . . .

                                                              CUT TO:

10   INT. SICKBAY—MED-LAB   10

Kes is busily working at a console. The Doctor is in the main Sickbay, out of
view.

11   ANGLE ON CONSOLE (OPTICAL)   11

which shows a variety of DATA. We can see Kes' REFLECTION on the
surface. A moment goes by, and then in the reflection we see a <u>BIO-ALIEN</u>

RISING INTO VIEW BEHIND KES—its huge and terrifying shape just inches away!

12   KES   12

whirls around, startled! <u>There is nothing there</u>. A beat as she catches her breath. Then a low, alien VOCALIZATION is heard . . .

Slowly, Kes turns around to see—

13   A BIO-ALIEN (OPTICAL)   13

standing a few feet away, in the doorway leading to Sickbay! It LUNGES right at her!

14   CLOSE ON KES   14

screaming!

> DOCTOR'S VOICE
> Kes . . . <u>Kes</u>!

WE PULL BACK to see the <u>Doctor</u> gripping Kes by the shoulders . . . trying to snap her out of her trance. She reacts . . . coming out of it . . . stunned and shaken . . .

> KES
> They're watching us.

Off the creepy moment . . .

CUT TO:

15   INT. BORG CUBE—CORRIDOR   15

The dark and eerie interior of a Borg ship (NOTE: This section of the Cube has no visible damage). Janeway and Tuvok are being led down the corridor by TWO BORG DRONES—one in front of them and one behind. Tuvok carries an Engineering kit and PADD. CAMERA FOLLOWS as they talk:

> TUVOK
> (to Janeway)
> May I ask where we're being taken?

> JANEWAY
> "Grid nine-two of subjunction twelve."

(off his look)
Our very own workspace. It's near the center of the
Cube.

Tuvok hands her a PADD.

TUVOK

These are my tricorder readings of the bio-ship we
examined. I believe you will find them most
revealing.

She glances at the PADD, reacts with interest.

JANEWAY

Have you compared this to the Doctor's analysis of
the alien tissue?

TUVOK

Yes. Many of the cellular structures are identical.

JANEWAY

The aliens and their ships . . . are made of the same
organic material.

TUVOK

Apparently so.

As this sinks in, the Borg Drone ahead of them abruptly turns a corner. As
they follow . . .

16   INT. BORG CHAMBER   16

A room filled with Borg equipment, alcoves and a few Borg Drones.

Janeway and Tuvok ENTER, flanked by the two Borg Drones. The
Collective Voice booms through the room:

BORG

You have entered grid nine-two of subjunction twelve.
Proceed.

Janeway stays calm and determined.

JANEWAY
(to Collective)
All right. We've analyzed one of the alien vessels . . .

and it appears to be constructed of organic material
vulnerable to the modified nanoprobes.
(beat)
I suggest we begin thinking about a large-scale
delivery system . . . a way to infect their ships and
destroy them at the microscopic—

BORG

We will begin.

Suddenly, the two Borg grasp Janeway and Tuvok by the arms. The Borg
Surgeon moves to them, holding a small, distinctive-looking Borg device—a
NEURO-TRANSCEIVER—and ATTACHES it to the back of Janeway's
neck. (NOTE: This is the same device seen in "Unity.")

TUVOK
(quickly)
What are you doing?

The Borg Surgeon keeps working the device. The disembodied Collective
speaks:

BORG
A neuro-transceiver is required for maximum
communication. We will work as one mind.

JANEWAY
No . . . that wasn't the agreement.

A beat, as if the Borg are processing the response—the give and take of
dealing with individuals is not familiar to them.

BORG
The neural link is temporary. You will not be
damaged.

JANEWAY
I don't care . . . I prefer to communicate verbally,
thank you.

Pause.

BORG
Your primitive communication is inefficient.

TUVOK

On the contrary . . . we work better with our
individuality intact. Surely, we've proven that to you
by now . . .

BORG

Irrelevant. You must comply.

JANEWAY

We "must" do nothing. Tell your drone to remove the
transceiver.

The Surgeon keeps working. A scary moment. Janeway thinks fast—this
situation is spinning out of control.

JANEWAY

What about choosing a representative? A single Borg
we can work with . . . and talk to directly.

BORG

Elaborate.

JANEWAY

You've done it before . . . when you transformed
Jean-Luc Picard into Locutus.
(firm)
We will not be assimilated. Choose a
representative . . . or the deal's off.

A long moment . . . then the Borg Surgeon removes the device from
Janeway's neck. There is a HISSING sound from somewhere in the room.
They turn to see—

17   NEW ANGLE—BORG ALCOVE (OPTICAL)   17

A single BORG FEMALE is standing in the alcove, like a vampire in her
coffin. Several CABLES BREAK AWAY from her body . . . a brief PLAY OF
CRACKLING ENERGY around her body . . .

. . . and then she is DISCONNECTED from the alcove with a BLAST of
VAPOR—

The Borg female steps out of the alcove and through the vapor . . . and for
the first time we get a clear look at her. She's young, striking, covered with
Borg technology but clearly once human.

Her demeanor is cold and passionless—even though she speaks in an individual voice, she's still connected to the Hive Mind. (NOTE: This is a character we will come to know as <u>SEVEN OF NINE</u>.)

She eyes Janeway and Tuvok with an impassive stare.

> SEVEN OF NINE
> I speak for the Borg.

Off the moment . . .

                                                    FADE OUT.

<u>END OF ACT ONE</u>

ACT TWO

FADE IN:

18   INT. BORG CHAMBER (VPB)   18

As before. Janeway and Tuvok facing Seven of Nine, the Borg representative. Janeway is cautious, gauging this Borg, taking this all one step at a time. Seven of Nine is incisive, almost arrogant . . . and she speaks in a precise Borg-like manner.

> JANEWAY
> I'm Captain Janeway . . . this is Lieutenant Tuvok.

> SEVEN OF NINE
> We are aware of your designations.

> JANEWAY
> What's your . . . designation?

> SEVEN OF NINE
> Seven of Nine, Tertiary Adjunct of Unimatrix Zero
> One. But you may call me . . . Seven of Nine.
> (to business)
> You are proposing a large-scale weapon. We concur.

> JANEWAY
> I thought you might.

> TUVOK
> (an idea)
> We could encase the nanoprobes in some of our
> photon torpedoes . . . in essence, turn them into bio-
> molecular warheads.

> SEVEN OF NINE
> Your torpedoes are inadequate. They lack the
> necessary range and dispursive force.

> JANEWAY
> Do you have a better idea?

> SEVEN OF NINE
> (obviously)
> We are Borg.

Seven of Nine moves to a nearby console.

> TUVOK
> (to Janeway)
> I take that as a ''yes.''

Janeway and Tuvok join Seven of Nine at the console, which is crammed with exotic controls and a large MONITOR. Seven of Nine quickly works the controls . . . and the monitor shows a GRAPHIC of a BORG WEAPON with a variety of complex technical data.

> SEVEN OF NINE
> (re: graphic)
> A multikinetic neutronic mine. Five million isoton yield.

> TUVOK
> (reacts)
> An explosion that size could affect an entire star system.

> SEVEN OF NINE
> Correct. The shock wave will dispurse the nanoprobes over a radius of five light years.

> JANEWAY
> That's somewhat larger than I had in mind. You're proposing a weapon of mass destruction . . .

> SEVEN OF NINE
> We are.

> JANEWAY
> Well, I'm not. You'd be endangering innocent worlds.

> SEVEN OF NINE
> It would be . . . efficient.

Janeway sees a difference in philosophy here . . . realizes she has to convince them on their own terms. Tuvok, who has been studying the graphic of the Borg weapon, turns to Seven of Nine with an argument of his own.

> TUVOK
> (re: graphic)
> We'd need approximately fifty trillion nanoprobes to

arm this mine. It would take several weeks for the
Doctor to replicate that amount.
                    (pointed)
You are losing this conflict . . . are you willing to risk
further delay?

                    JANEWAY
                    (urging)
Right now, your enemy believes it is invulnerable. If
we create smaller weapons using our torpedoes . . .
and destroy a few of their bio-ships, it may be enough
to deter them . . . convince them to give up this war.

Seven of Nine considers . . . takes a couple of steps around the room . . .
then turns to them, having made a decision with the Hive Mind.

                    SEVEN OF NINE
You are individuals. You are small, and you think in
small terms.
                    ("listening" to the hive)
But the present situation requires that we consider
your plan.

Janeway and Tuvok exchange a look—a small triumph. Seven of Nine
moves to the console, taps a few controls. The monitor changes to show a
VOYAGER WEAPONS INVENTORY—schematics and detailed technical
data.

                    SEVEN OF NINE
                    (off monitor)
Voyager's weapons inventory. Photon torpedo
compliment: thirty-two. Class Six warhead. Explosive
yield: two hundred isotons.

                    TUVOK
                    (surprised)
How did you obtain this information?

                    SEVEN OF NINE
                    (simply)
We are Borg.

                    TUVOK
Naturally.

As they work . . .

CUT TO:

19   EXT. SPACE—BORG CUBE & VOYAGER (OPTICAL)   19

at WARP, flying side by side. The tractor beam seen earlier is now gone.

20   INT. SICKBAY   20

The Doctor is examining Kes, who is sitting on a bio-bed. Kes looks agitated—she's been receiving a constant barrage of telepathic "flashes" and it's starting to unnerve her. Chakotay ENTERS and moves to them.

> DOCTOR
> Commander . . . we have some disturbing news.

> CHAKOTAY
> At this point, I'm getting used to it.

> DOCTOR
> (re: Kes)
> Her telepathic visions are increasing . . . both in frequency and intensity.

As she speaks, CAMERA PUSHES IN on Kes . . .

> KES
> It feels different this time . . . like they're right here . . . in the room . . .

21   MENTAL FLASH (OPTICAL)   21

CLOSE ON an ALIEN EYE—dark and striated, strange—its pupil DILATES.

22   RESUME KES   22

reacts to the shocking image, tries to stay in control.

> KES
> I'm trying to block them out . . . I can't . . .

23   MENTAL FLASH (OPTICAL)   23

CLOSER on an ALIEN EYE. We can see KES' FACE REFLECTED in the pupil.

24   KES   24

reacts, breathless. Chakotay takes her arm to steady her. The Doctor scans with his tricorder.

>   DOCTOR
>   (off tricorder)
>   There it is again . . .
>   (explains)
>   Every time she has a vision . . . specific regions of her
>   cerebral cortex go into a state of hyper-stimulation.
>   Memory engrams . . . perceptual centers.
>   (beat)
>   I can't be sure . . . but I think there's more going on
>   here than just a simple "hello."

                                                          CUT TO:

25   INT. BORG CHAMBER (OPTICAL)   25

Janeway and Tuvok are standing at the monitor seen earlier—the screen shows a BORGIFIED Voyager photon torpedo. Seven of Nine is working at a console in the b.g.

>   JANEWAY
>   (points to graphic)
>   Enhance this grid . . . I want to take a closer look at
>   the detonator.

Seven of Nine walks up to them.

>   SEVEN OF NINE
>   (to Janeway)
>   We must analyze the bio-ship.
>   (beat)
>   Your data.

Janeway hands Seven of Nine a PADD. Seven of Nine turns to a console at the table and works. Janeway eyes the Borg woman's face . . . curious.

>   JANEWAY
>   You're human . . . aren't you?

SEVEN OF NINE
(matter of fact)
This body was assimilated eighteen years ago. It
ceased to be human at that time.

Her indifference is unsettling.

JANEWAY
I'm curious . . . what was your name . . . before you
were—

SEVEN OF NINE
Do not engage us in further irrelevant discourse.

Clearly, Seven of Nine is unresponsive to this "personal" approach. A tiny
ALARM is heard. Seven of Nine reacts.

SEVEN OF NINE
We are being hailed by your vessel.

Seven of Nine moves to a MONITOR—this one is smaller, twelve inches in
diameter, like a lens on the end of a snake-like tube. Seven of Nine hits a
control and the screen ACTIVATES to show Chakotay standing in Sickbay.

JANEWAY
Commander, what is it?

CHAKOTAY
It's Kes. The Doctor believes that the aliens are
accessing her memory.

The implications are chilling.

JANEWAY
If that's true, they may already know what we're
planning . . .

CHAKOTAY
(nods)
I've ordered long range scans for bio-ships . . . nothing
so far.

JANEWAY
(to Seven of Nine)
We should alter course . . . try to throw them off.

                    SEVEN OF NINE
        Agreed.

Seven of Nine thinks for a moment . . . at one with the Hive Mind . . .

                    SEVEN OF NINE
        Our course and heading have been changed.

                    JANEWAY
                    (to Chakotay)
        Match them. Keep me apprised of any changes in Kes.

                    CHAKOTAY
                    (nods)
        Chakotay out.

He BLINKS OFF the monitor. Seven of Nine crosses the room to join
Tuvok . . . Janeway following . . .

26   NEW ANGLE—TUVOK (VPB)   26

who is working at the monitor seen earlier. It now shows a Voyager photon
torpedo that is bristling with Borg technology—various projections and
tubes. Seven of Nine indicates the monitor.

                    SEVEN OF NINE
        We now require one of your photon torpedoes . . .
        and the nanoprobes.

                    JANEWAY
        One step at a time. We're not safely across your
        territory yet.

Seven of Nine stares at her—a new urgency in her voice.

                    SEVEN OF NINE
        We must construct and test a prototype—now. The
        risk of attack has increased.

                    JANEWAY
        Irrelevant. We have an agreement. You're asking me
        to give up my only guarantee that you won't
        assimilate us. I won't risk it.

Seven of Nine studies her.

SEVEN OF NINE
Are you willing to risk a direct confrontation with us?
(beat)
If we transport five hundred drones onto your
vessel . . . do you believe you could offer sufficient
resistance?

A charged moment. Seven of Nine is forcing the issue . . . but Janeway
won't back down.

JANEWAY
(even)
We'd die trying.

Stand-off. They gauge one another . . . Borg and human . . . this alliance a
precarious one . . . finally, Seven of Nine stands down.

SEVEN OF NINE
That won't be necessary.

She turns back to the console.

SEVEN OF NINE
We must construct a launching system to
accommodate this design.

As Tuvok and Janeway exchange an uneasy look . . .

                                                            CUT TO:

27   INT. BRIDGE—ON TURBOLIFT   27

as the doors slide open to reveal <u>Harry Kim</u>. He's back in uniform and ready
for duty.

28   INCLUDE—THE BRIDGE   28

Red Alert. Chakotay, Paris, Torres at Ops, N.D.s at their stations. Everyone
turns to Harry, pleased to see him—a welcome sight in an otherwise
somber day.

PARIS
Harry . . . welcome back.

KIM
Thanks.

(to Chakotay)
Reporting for duty, sir. The Doctor gave me a clean
bill of health.

(ironic)
Did I . . . miss anything?

CHAKOTAY
(smiles)
Not too much. Take your station, Ensign.

Kim takes over Ops. Torres stands aside.

TORRES
(casually)
You've still got a tendril up your nose.

Kim checks . . . realizes she's joking . . . shoots her a look. Torres moves to
the Engineering station. Just then an ALARM sounds on Paris' console.

PARIS
Commander . . . I'm picking up gravimetric
distortions . . . twelve thousand kilometers aft . . .
(reacts)
It's a singularity!

29   INT. BORG CHAMBER   29

As before. Seven of Nine turns to Janeway with concern.

SEVEN OF NINE
We are under attack.

30   EXT. SPACE—BORG CUBE & VOYAGER (OPTICAL)   30

at warp. An ALIEN BIO-SHIP swoops into view, also at warp, and in
pursuit. The bio-ship begins to GLOW, charging its weapons (the same
effect seen in Part One).

31   INT. VOYAGER BRIDGE   31

As before.

PARIS
They're charging weapons . . .

CHAKOTAY
Shields! Keep a lock on the Away Team!

The ship rocks!

TORRES
Direct hit to our secondary hull!

KIM
Transporters are off-line! Shields and weapons are
down!

32		32
thru	OMITTED	thru
33		33

34   EXT. SPACE—BORG CUBE & VOYAGER (OPTICAL)   34

at warp. The Borg Cube FIRES a blinding onslaught of torpedoes out of
various portals . . .

35   NEW ANGLE—THE ALIEN BIO-SHIP (OPTICAL)   35

is repeatedly STRUCK by the torpedoes . . . each and every strike AB-
SORBED by its hull in a remarkable effect, impervious to the bombard-
ment.

36   INT. BORG CHAMBER   36

Janeway, Seven of Nine, Tuvok. Urgent:

TUVOK
(checks console)
Voyager has taken heavy damage.

SEVEN OF NINE
We cannot let the nanoprobes be destroyed.

Off Seven of Nine's concern . . .

37   EXT. SPACE—ALIEN BIO-SHIP (OPTICAL)   37

GLOWING again, weapons charging!

38   INT. VOYAGER BRIDGE   38

As before.

PARIS

We're being targeted!

CHAKOTAY

Brace for impact!

39   EXT. SPACE—THE BORG CUBE (OPTICAL)   39

suddenly DROPS BACK toward the bio-ship to protect Voyager!

40   THE BIO-SHIP (OPTICAL)   40

FIRES the ENERGY TENDRIL meant for Voyager—but it BLASTS into the
Cube instead! The tendril takes a HUGE CHUNK out of the Borg ship!

41   INT. BORG CHAMBER (OPTICAL)   41

A thin ALIEN ENERGY TENDRIL WHIPS THROUGH THE CHAMBER!
Everyone ducks for cover as the TENDRIL CRACKLES around them!

42   JANEWAY (OPTICAL)   42

The ENERGY TENDRIL HITS a WALL next to her—BLOWING OUT a
piece of the WALL and sending her FALLING violently to the deck.

43   EXT. SPACE—THE BORG CUBE (OPTICAL)   43

COLLIDES with the bio-ship and the two EXPLODE in a devastating effect!

44   INT. VOYAGER BRIDGE   44

SHAKING HARD! A hair-raising moment . . . and then the shaking subsides. Chakotay gets to his feet . . .

CHAKOTAY

The Cube?

PARIS

Destroyed . . . and they took the bio-ship with them.

TUVOK'S COM VOICE

Tuvok to Chakotay.

Reactions.

                              CHAKOTAY
                              (to com)
                    Go ahead, Tuvok—where are you?

45   INT. CARGO BAY TWO   45

CLOSE ON TUVOK, lying on the floor, propping himself on one elbow,
injured. His face and uniform are scorched, and we can't see who or what is
around him in the dim light.

                              TUVOK
                             (ragged)
                 I'm in Cargo Bay Two . . . along with the Captain . . .
                 and a number of Borg. We were beamed over just
                 before impact.
                         (losing consciousness)
                 We require . . . assistance . . .

46   INT. BRIDGE   46

As before.

                              CHAKOTAY
                 Tuvok . . . <u>Tuvok</u>?
                         (quickly, to Torres)
                 Seal off that deck.
                         (to com)
                 Security Team to Cargo Bay Two.
                         (to Paris, on the move)
                 Tom, you have the Bridge.

As he races for the door . . .

47   OMITTED   47

48   INT. CARGO BAY TWO   48

Chakotay ENTERS, flanked by two Security Guards and a MEDICAL N.D.
armed with phaser rifles. They stop at what they see . . .

49   THEIR POV—THE BAY   49

BORG TECHNOLOGY is visible in the room—consoles, hardware, tubes,
etc.—and SEVERAL BORG are quickly moving about. But the room is dark,
and from this angle, we can only see a small section of the Bay (We will see
the Borgified Cargo Bay in its entirety later, in scene 57).

50   ON JANEWAY AND TUVOK   50

Both of them lying on the floor, injured. Janeway's face and uniform are
badly scorched and bloodied—it looks bad.

51   CHAKOTAY AND THE SECURITY GUARDS   51

eye the setting, tense. The medic moves to Janeway and Tuvok . . .

> SEVEN OF NINE'S VOICE
> Lower your weapons.

52   NEW ANGLE—SEVEN OF NINE   52

as she steps into view, eyes the team.

> SEVEN OF NINE
> We are here with your Captain's consent. It was
> necessary to sacrifice our vessel to protect yours.

Chakotay keeps his rifle aimed straight at her.

> SEVEN OF NINE
> We have an alliance . . . do we not?

Off the moment—Chakotay and Seven of Nine face-to-face . . .

                                                      FADE OUT.

END OF ACT TWO

ACT THREE

FADE IN:

53   EXT. SPACE—VOYAGER (STOCK-OPTICAL)   53

at warp.

54   INT. SICKBAY   54

A short time later. Chakotay is briefing Tuvok, who is sitting on a bio-bed, being treated by Kes. He's alive and well, his injuries gone. The Doctor can be seen in the b.g., working on Janeway who is lying on the surgical bed. Mid-conversation.

> CHAKOTAY
> They've assimilated Cargo Bay Two . . . and they're
> drawing energy from the secondary power couplings.

> TUVOK
> But they've gone no further . . .

> CHAKOTAY
> Not yet. I've sealed off Decks Nine through
> Thirteen . . . and posted security details at every
> access point.

> TUVOK
> I suggest we increase security around Sickbay, as
> well . . .

> CHAKOTAY
> Already done.
> (beat)
> How far did you get on the weapon?

> TUVOK
> We're ready to construct a prototype.

Kes completes her scan of Tuvok.

> KES
> You're fit to return to duty, Lieutenant.

                    TUVOK
And <u>you</u>, Kes?

She's unsettled, but hanging in there.

                     KES
I'm . . . all right. The visions have stopped . . . for
now.

Tuvok nods. Kes moves off. Chakotay takes a moment . . . unsettled by
these turn of events. The Doctor walks up to them.

                   DOCTOR
               (re: Janeway, somber)
The plasma burns to her thoracic region I can
treat . . . and I've already stopped the internal
bleeding. But her neural injuries are going to require
some creative thinking.

                    TUVOK
                (to Chakotay)
Before we beamed out, an alien energy discharge
struck very near the Captain.

                   DOCTOR
Well, it appears to have disrupted all her
neuroelectrical pathways. I'll have to induce a coma
to protect her higher brain functions. But I must tell
you . . . unless I can repair the damage, she may
never regain consciousness.

This is devastating news. Chakotay turns to Tuvok.

                  CHAKOTAY
Make sure those Borg stay put . . . I want tactical
updates every twenty minutes.

                    TUVOK
Aye, sir.
                    (beat)
Shall I resume working with them?

Chakotay glances toward the injured Janeway.

                  CHAKOTAY
Stand by for now.

Tuvok heads for the door.

> DOCTOR
> (to Chakotay)
> The Captain wishes to speak with you. Please keep it
> brief.

Chakotay nods . . . heads to the surgical bay . . .

55   NEW ANGLE—JANEWAY   55

lying on the bed, eyes open, barely conscious. Chakotay walks up to her . . .
and for a moment their eyes meet. They haven't spoken privately since
their argument at the end of Part One, when their very friendship seemed at
stake. Janeway gathers her strength . . . it's difficult to speak . . .

> JANEWAY
> The Doctor . . . explained . . . my condition.
> You're . . . in command.

> CHAKOTAY
> I understand.

> JANEWAY
> They'll push you . . . threaten you . . . anything they
> can . . . to get their way . . .
> (beat)
> But they <u>need</u> you . . . they need this . . . alliance.

She looks straight into his eyes . . . tries to underscore her own position.

> JANEWAY
> You have to make this work . . . I want you . . . to
> make this work.
> (beat)
> Get the crew . . . home.

Chakotay doesn't answer . . . conflicted . . . he's loyal to this woman but
still has grave doubts about this alliance with the Borg. The Doctor walks up
to him.

> DOCTOR
> I must begin.

A beat, then Chakotay moves away. OFF Janeway . . . as her eyes begin to
close . . .

CUT TO:

56   OMITTED   56

57   INT. CARGO BAY TWO—WIDE ANGLE   57

An incredible sight. It looks like we've stepped onto a Borg Cube—the
entire Cargo Bay has been TRANSFORMED into a Borg Collective. Alcoves
line the walls, filled with Borg Drones. Other Borg move to and fro as
though they belong here. The lighting and sounds are those of Borg, as well.

58   ANGLE—CHAKOTAY   58

as he steps further inside flanked by two security guards armed with phaser
rifles. He's here to get a better sense of what he's dealing with . . . because
at this moment he's undecided about what to do. Seven of Nine turns from a
console and moves to him.

> SEVEN OF NINE
> Where is your Captain?

> CHAKOTAY
> In our medical bay . . . recovering. You'll be dealing
> with me, now.

Seven of Nine considers him . . . then gets down to business.

> SEVEN OF NINE
> Circumstances have changed.

> CHAKOTAY
> I'd say so.

> SEVEN OF NINE
> The loss of our vessel requires that we modify our
> agreement.

> CHAKOTAY
> I've been giving that some thought . . .
> (beat)
> I'm willing to let you stay on board . . . and we'll
> continue to work with you on the weapon. Once
> we're safely out of your territory, we'll give you the
> nanoprobes, shake hands and part company.

> SEVEN OF NINE
> Insufficient. Our latest tactical projections indicate
> that the war will be lost by then.
> (beat)
> The nearest Borg vessel is forty light years away. You
> will reverse course and take us to it.

Chakotay is taken aback.

> CHAKOTAY
> Even at maximum warp, that's a five day journey . . .
> in the wrong direction. We're supposed to be heading
> out of Borg space . . . not deeper into it.

> SEVEN OF NINE
> There is no alternative.

> CHAKOTAY
> (firm)
> Look . . . I'll honor the original agreement, but I'm
> not turning this ship around. It's too dangerous.

She takes a step toward him, menace in her voice.

> SEVEN OF NINE
> Denying our request . . . is also dangerous.

A tense beat as Chakotay stares at her . . . then:

> CHAKOTAY
> I'll think about it.

> SEVEN OF NINE
> Think quickly.

Seven of Nine turns away to work. Chakotay stares at her for a moment, then heads for the door with the two Guards . . .

CUT TO:

59   INT. BRIEFING ROOM (OPTICAL)   59

At warp. Chakotay is on his feet, facing the team—Tuvok, Paris, Kim, Torres, Kes and NEELIX. The tension is high—the past few days have taken their toll on everyone. Mid-scene.

                    CHAKOTAY

A five day trip back into the heart of Borg territory.
It's too risky. With those drones and the nanoprobes
on board, we might as well have a bull's-eye painted
on our hull. We're a prime target for Species Eight
Four Seven Two. We'd never survive another attack.

                    NEELIX

What's the alternative?

Chakotay stares at each of them in turn . . . about to make a major
decision . . . one he knows is controversial . . .

                    CHAKOTAY

I'm going to end this alliance . . . here and now.

Surprised reactions.

                    CHAKOTAY

Mister Paris . . . in your estimation, how long before
we clear Borg space?

                    PARIS

According to long-range sensors, the concentration of
Borg star systems is decreasing. I'd say another
week . . . ten days.

                    KIM
                  (onto idea)
If we avoid the regions of heavy Borg activity, there's
a chance we could slip through . . .

                    CHAKOTAY

Exactly. We're going to drop the Borg off on the next
uninhabited planet . . . give them the nanoprobes, and
take our chances alone. They can wait for a Borg Ship
to pick them up, and finish the weapon.

Everyone takes this in . . .

                    NEELIX

But . . . the Captain made an agreement. Isn't it worth
a detour to keep the Borg on our side?

                    CHAKOTAY

I've asked myself that question a hundred times . . .

and if I thought the Borg could be trusted to uphold
their end of the bargain, I'd say yes.

                    KES
They did sacrifice their ship to protect Voyager . . .
isn't that an indication that they're committed to this
alliance?

                    TORRES
These are Borg . . . whether they "sacrifice" a
thousand drones, or a million . . . it's no loss to them.
They don't value individual life.

                    PARIS
That may be true . . . but the bottom line is they died
to save us. We can't just ignore that . . .

                    TORRES
              (emotions rising)
They were protecting the nanoprobes . . . they don't
care what happens to us.

                    KIM
I'm with B'Elanna. The Borg are just stringing us
along until they can take what they want . . .

                    TUVOK
I'm not certain the Captain would agree with you. As
long as we posses the nanoprobes, we still maintain
the advantage.

An uncomfortable pause at the mention of the Captain. Chakotay knows
this is a sensitive issue . . . and his voice is diplomatic.

                    CHAKOTAY
You're right, Tuvok . . . if she were here, she'd
probably say our best chance was to do what they're
asking.
              (beat)
I just don't see it that way. I'm in command, now . . .
and I have to do what I think is best for this crew.

A moment as he glances around the room. Everyone seems to respect his
position.

                              CHAKOTAY
                    Tom, scan for the nearest uninhabited planet . . . and
                    set a course.

                              PARIS
                    Aye, sir.

                              TUVOK
                    I must caution you, Commander . . . the Borg may not
                    go quietly.

                              CHAKOTAY
                    We'll see.
                                    (beat)
                    Bring that female drone to the Ready Room.

Tuvok nods.

                              CHAKOTAY
                    Dismissed.

As the crew rises to go . . .

                                                                    CUT TO:

60   INT. READY ROOM (OPTICAL)   60

At warp. A short time later. Seven of Nine is facing Chakotay, who has just
explained his position. Two Security Guards stand nearby.

                              CHAKOTAY
                    Once we've beamed you to the surface . . . we'll send
                    down the nanoprobes and all our research.

                              SEVEN OF NINE
                    Unacceptable. We don't have time for—

                              CHAKOTAY
                    This isn't open for discussion. I'm not turning this
                    ship around. You're getting what you wanted. I
                    suggest we part ways amicably.

Seven of Nine is displeased.

> SEVEN OF NINE
> There is another option. We could assimilate your
> vessel.

> CHAKOTAY
> If a single drone steps one millimeter out of that
> Cargo Bay . . . I'll decompress the entire deck. You
> won't pose much of a threat floating in space.

Seven of Nine sees that at the moment, she's not going to win this argument.

> SEVEN OF NINE
> When your Captain first approached us, we suspected
> that an agreement with humans would prove
> impossible to maintain.
> (cutting)
> You are erratic . . . conflicted . . . disorganized. Every
> decision is debated . . . every action questioned . . .
> every individual entitled to their own small opinion.
> You lack harmony . . . cohesion . . . greatness.
> (beat)
> It will be your undoing.

Chakotay eyes her calmly.

> CHAKOTAY
> That's . . . a matter of opinion.
> (to Guards)
> Escort our guest back to the Cargo Bay.

The Guards move into position . . . a beat, then Seven of Nine EXITS with them. Chakotay leans back in his chair and let's out a breath . . . this situation is far from over . . .

61   OMITTED   61

62   INT. SICKBAY—CLOSE ON JANEWAY   62

lying on the surgical bed, unconscious. Her face looks almost peaceful. The room is dimly lit. Silent. MOVE TO REVEAL—

63   CHAKOTAY   63

moving to Janeway's bedside. He's come here to contemplate everything that's happened. Finally, he speaks in a quiet voice . . .

CHAKOTAY

Well . . . I made my decision.

(beat)

If it were only a matter of going against the orders of my superior officer, I wouldn't have that much of a problem with it. But you're more than just my Captain . . .

(beat)

You're my friend. And I hope you'll understand.

He is silent, watching her. OFF the moment . . .

FADE OUT.

<u>END OF ACT THREE</u>

ACT FOUR

FADE IN:

64   EXT. SPACE (OPTICAL)   64

A vast starfield. Space itself begins to RIPPLE and DISTORT . . . and then a
QUANTUM SINGULARITY OPENS with a flash of light and energy.
THREE ALIEN BIO-SHIPS come roaring out of the rift and into our space!

CAMERA PANS to find several BORG CUBES in the distance, already
under attack by a small fleet of bio-ships. As the three new bio-ships swoop
in to join the fight . . .

65   OMITTED   65

66   INT. CARGO BAY TWO—CLOSE ON SEVEN OF NINE   66

CAMERA PUSHING in on her troubled face . . . she is "linked" to the
Collective . . . so she knows everything that is happening . . . she can
"see" and "feel" these images. We HEAR the VOICES of the COLLECTIVE
in her head (NOTE: There should be a unique audio effect here to clarify that
these voices are in her mind):

> BORG (V.O.)
> Species Eight Four Seven Two has penetrated Matrix
> Zero-One-Zero, Grid Nineteen. Eight planets
> destroyed . . . three hundred twelve vessels
> disabled . . . four million, six hundred twenty-one
> Borg eliminated.
>   (an order)
> We must seize control of the Alpha Quadrant vessel,
> and take it into the alien realm.

> SEVEN OF NINE
>   (aloud)
> We understand.

Suddenly we see two Borg Drones open a WALL PANEL, revealing a
narrow JEFFERIES TUBE. As Seven of Nine moves to the Tube with
intent . . .

                                                              CUT TO:

67   67
thru   OMITTED   thru
68   68

69   INT. BRIDGE   69

Red Alert. Tuvok, Torres, Kim, N.D.s at their stations. Chakotay is standing
next to Paris at the helm.

                          PARIS
                       (off console)
          Class H moon . . . oxygen-argon atmosphere.

                        CHAKOTAY
          It'll do. Take us out of warp and enter orbit.

                          PARIS
          Aye, sir.

Paris works.

                        CHAKOTAY
          Tuvok . . . stand by to transport the Borg directly
          from the Cargo Bay. After they're on the surface, have
          Security run a sweep of—

Kim's console sends out an ALARM.

                           KIM
                       (off console)
          I'm reading power fluctuations in the deflector
          array . . .

                        CHAKOTAY
          Cause?

                           KIM
          It looks like the Borg have accessed deflector control.
          They're trying to realign the emitters . . .

                        CHAKOTAY
          Shut them out.

70   INT. CARGO BAY TWO—JEFFERIES TUBE   70

Seven of Nine is now inside the Tube seen earlier, rapidly making
adjustments to the circuitry . . .

71   INT. BRIDGE   71

As before.

KIM
They've bypassed security protocols . . .

72   EXT. SPACE—VOYAGER—ANGLE ON DEFLECTOR DISH (OPTICAL)   72

The dish sends out a THIN BEAM OF ENERGY . . .

73   NEW ANGLE (OPTICAL)   73

As the thin ENERGY BEAM strikes a region of space ahead of Voyager . . .
causing space itself to RIPPLE and DISTORT in a strange effect . . .

74   INT. BRIDGE   74

As before.

TORRES
(off console)
They're emitting a resonant gravitation beam . . . it's
creating another singularity!

CHAKOTAY
(to Paris)
Reverse course.

Paris works, but the ship TREMBLES.

PARIS
We're fighting intense gravimetric distortions . . . I
can't break free!

CHAKOTAY
(to com)
Bridge to Cargo Bay Two. Stop what you're doing, or
I'll depressurize that deck and blow you out into
space.
(no response)
This is your final warning.

Chakotay turns to Tuvok, nods. Tuvok works . . .

75   INT. CARGO BAY TWO—JEFFERIES TUBE   75

Seven of Nine working. We hear a violent HISSING NOISE—the SOUND of the Bay decompressing. She reacts with concern . . .

76   OMITTED   76

77   EXT. SPACE—VOYAGER—ANGLE ON THE HULL (OPTICAL)   77

The Cargo Bay DOOR OPENS. There's a rush of VAPOR and DEBRIS as the contents of the Bay are SUCKED OUT into the vacuum of space. FIFTEEN BORG DRONES come FLYING OUT!

78   INT. CARGO BAY TWO—JEFFERIES TUBE   78

WIND ROARING around Seven of Nine, who is holding onto an outcropping, barely hanging on . . .

79   OMITTED   79

80   INT. BRIDGE   80

As before.

                        TUVOK
            Decompression cycle complete.

Relief. Kim reacts to his console.

                        KIM
            I still don't have deflector control . . .

                        TUVOK
                      (works)
            A single Borg has survived . . .

The ship trembles.

                        PARIS
            We're being pulled in!

81   EXT. SPACE—VOYAGER (OPTICAL)   81

The energy beam still emitting . . . and its OPENING opening creating a <u>QUANTUM SINGULARITY</u> in front of the ship! <u>It is the same type of rift we saw alien bio-ships fly out of at the top of the Act.</u>

82   INT. BRIDGE   82

The ship TREMBLING continuously now. Everyone hanging on.

83   EXT. SPACE—VOYAGER (OPTICAL)   83

as its PULLED INTO the QUANTUM SINGULARITY—VANISHING in a flash of light. The singularity instantly COLLAPSES behind it.

84   INT. BRIDGE   84

The trembling subsides.

                          CHAKOTAY
        Report.

                          TUVOK
        We appear to have crossed an interdimensional
        rift . . .

                          PARIS
        We've definitely left our galaxy . . .
                    (checks readings)
        No stars . . . no planets . . .

                          CHAKOTAY
        Let's see.

85   INCLUDE VIEWSCREEN (OPTICAL)   85

It shows the ALIEN REALM. There are no stars. But space itself has a strange TEXTURE—shimmering with color and pulsating with a translucent, viscous FLUID. It's like being inside a WOMB.

85A   OMITTED   85A

85B   INT. BRIDGE   85B

As before.

                          TORRES
        I'm recalibrating sensors . . .
                    (works)
        The entire region is filled with some kind of organic
        fluid . . . this isn't space . . . it's matter.

Suddenly, we HEAR Seven of Nine's voice over the com:

SEVEN OF NINE'S COM VOICE
Commander Chakotay. We have entered the domain
of Species Eight Four Seven Two.
(beat)
Report to the Cargo Bay.

A grim moment. He turns to Torres.

CHAKOTAY
(to Torres)
Repressurize Cargo Bay Two.
(on the move)
Tuvok.

As Chakotay and Tuvok head for the Turbolift . . .

CUT TO:

85C   EXT. SPACE—ALIEN REALM (OPTICAL) FORMERLY 85A   85C

VOYAGER holding position in the strange, "fluidic" space.

86   INT. CARGO BAY TWO   86

Moments later. Chakotay and Tuvok are facing Seven of Nine in the "mini-
Collective," which has remained intact but is empty of Borg and in a state of
disarray—spewing gas, sparks, etc. Seven of Nine is confident, demanding.
Two Starfleet Security Guards stand nearby, armed.

SEVEN OF NINE
Our entry into fluidic space has created a compression
wave. They know we're here. A fleet of bio-ships is
already converging on our position. Time to intercept:
three hours, seventeen minutes.

Chakotay reacts to this information, suddenly realizing . . .

CHAKOTAY
You've been here before.

Seven of Nine doesn't answer.

CHAKOTAY
How else could you know about "fluidic space"?

> SEVEN OF NINE
> (ignoring him)
> We must prepare this ship for the altercation. We will
> construct—

> CHAKOTAY
> (pressing)
> Why? Why were you here?

Again, Seven of Nine hesitates. Chakotay is starting to put two and two together . . .

> CHAKOTAY
> (continuing)
> You started this war, didn't you?
> (beat)
> What's the matter . . . our galaxy wasn't big enough
> for you? You had to conquer new territory . . . but
> this race fought back . . . a species as malevolent as
> your own.

Seven of Nine glares at him.

> SEVEN OF NINE
> Species Eight Four Seven Two was . . . more resistant
> than we anticipated. Their technology is biogenically
> engineered . . . it is superior to that of all species we
> have previously encountered.

> TUVOK
> Which is precisely what you wanted.

> SEVEN OF NINE
> They are the apex of biological evolution. Their
> assimilation would have greatly added to our own
> perfection.

Seven of Nine takes a step toward him.

> SEVEN OF NINE
> My subspace link to the Collective has been weakened
> by the interdimensional rift. We cannot signal for
> help. We are alone.
> (beat)
> We must construct a compliment of bio-molecular

warheads . . . and modify your weapons to launch
them.

                        CHAKOTAY
                        (forceful)
I've got a better idea. Why don't you open that
singularity again and take us back.

                    SEVEN OF NINE
If I did that, you would no longer cooperate.

Suddenly:

                DOCTOR'S COM VOICE
Doctor to Chakotay.

                        CHAKOTAY
                    (taps combadge)
Go ahead.

                DOCTOR'S COM VOICE
Report to Sickbay at once.

                        CHAKOTAY
On my way.

Chakotay looks to Tuvok and they head for the door. OFF Seven of Nine's
inscrutable face . . .

                                                CUT TO:

87   INT. SICKBAY   87

Chakotay ENTERS, stops at what he sees—

88   CAPTAIN JANEWAY (OPTICAL)   88

is on her feet, reading over a PADD. Her wounds are gone—she's cured.
The Doctor is nearby, running some last minute scans. Chakotay reacts in
surprise.

                        CHAKOTAY
Captain . . .

DOCTOR
(to Chakotay)
As you can see, I've repaired her neural damage.
(pleased)
Ensign Kim . . . the Captain . . . I'm two for two.

JANEWAY
Doctor . . . if you'll excuse us a moment.

The Doctor glances at her grim expression . . . then at Chakotay . . .
realizes sparks are about to fly.

DOCTOR
Gladly.
(to com)
Computer—deactivate EMH Program.

The Doctor VANISHES. Janeway eyes Chakotay.

JANEWAY
The Doctor brought me up to speed . . . but he
couldn't tell me what I really wanted to know.
(an edge)
Why?

This is it . . . their conflict is about to ignite.

CHAKOTAY
The Collective ordered me to reverse course . . . travel
forty light years back the way we came . . . what
would you have done?

JANEWAY
I probably would've reversed course . . . maintained
the alliance as long as possible . . .

CHAKOTAY
In my mind, the alliance was already over.

JANEWAY
You never trusted me. You never believed this would
work . . . you were just waiting for an opportunity to
circumvent my orders.

CHAKOTAY
Trust had nothing to with it. I made a tactical
decision.

                              JANEWAY
And so did I.

                              CHAKOTAY
They were taking advantage of us from Day One . . .

                              JANEWAY
We made concessions . . . so did they.

                              CHAKOTAY
They lied to us. The Borg <u>started</u> the war with Species
Eight Four Seven Two.

A charged moment. Janeway is surprised at this revelation.

                              CHAKOTAY
                              (pressing)
We've only got one Borg left to worry about. We
should try to disable her . . . and get back to the Delta
Quadrant.
                              (beat)
We might be able to duplicate the deflector protocols
they used to open a singularity.

                              JANEWAY
<u>No</u>. I won't be caught tinkering with the deflector
when those aliens attack.
                              (resolved)
There's no other way out of this, Chakotay. It's too
late for opinions . . . too late for discussion. It's time
to make the call, and I'm making it.
                              (beat)
We fight the aliens . . . in full cooperation with the
Borg.

Chakotay moves to her, passionate.

                              CHAKOTAY
I was linked to a Collective once . . . <u>remember</u>? I had
a neuro-transceiver embedded in my spine . . . I know
who we're dealing with.
                              (urging)
We've got to get rid of that last Borg . . . take our
chances alone.

> JANEWAY
> (firm)

It won't work.

Again an impasse. They look at each other in frustration and exhaustion.

The past few days have taken their toll on them . . . both physically and emotionally.

> JANEWAY

This isn't working, either . . .
> (off his look)

There are <u>two wars</u> going on. The one out there, and the one in here.
> (beat)

We're losing both of them.

She's made an impact. Chakotay's voice softens . . . as he remembers Seven of Nine's words . . .

> CHAKOTAY

"It will be your undoing."

> JANEWAY

What?

> CHAKOTAY

Our "conflicted" nature . . . our individuality. Seven of Nine said that we lack the cohesion of a Collective mind . . . that one day, it would divide us . . . and destroy us.
> (beat)

And here we are, proving her point.

They consider—this is a wake-up call for both of them.

> JANEWAY

I'll tell you when we lost control of this situation . . . when we made our mistake. It was the moment we turned away from each other.

She moves to him.

> JANEWAY
> (continuing)

We don't have to stop being individuals to get through this.

                              (beat)
              We just have to stop fighting each other.

Off Chakotay . . . he knows she's right . . . and he wants to make this
work . . . but how? Off the razor tension between them . . .

                                                              CUT TO:

89   EXT. SPACE—ALIEN REALM (OPTICAL)   89

Voyager is slowly moving through FLUIDIC SPACE—we see ripples of
movement in space itself around the ship—the effect is like a creature
moving through the ocean.

90   INT. BRIDGE—ANGLE ON TURBOLIFT   90

Red Alert. Tuvok ENTERS with Seven of Nine. They stop at what they see.
INCLUDE—

91   JANEWAY   91

in the Captain's chair. She stands and turns to them. Paris, Kim, N.D.s at
their stations. Seven of Nine reacts in surprise.

                      SEVEN OF NINE
              Captain Janeway.

                        JANEWAY
              I've relieved Mister Chakotay of his duties, and
              confined him to the Brig.
                              (beat)
              I'm back in command.

Seven of Nine eyes her.

                      SEVEN OF NINE
              And you understand the situation?

                        JANEWAY
              Completely.

She stares at her a beat, then:

                        JANEWAY
              Tuvok . . . give her the nanoprobes . . . work with

her . . . build as many warheads as you can . . . and
start modifying our weapons systems.

Seven of Nine looks mildly surprised—she wasn't expecting this.

> JANEWAY
> (to Seven of Nine)
> I suggest we think about enhancing our <u>defenses</u>, as
> well. If we're going to fight this battle . . . I intend to
> win it.

> SEVEN OF NINE
> We are in agreement.

> JANEWAY
> Good. This is the plan: we engage the aliens here, in
> their space. We show them what they're up
> against . . . if they have any sense of self-preservation,
> they'll back off . . . pull their ships out of the Delta
> Quadrant.
> (beat)
> That's provided the weapons are effective. If they
> aren't . . .
> (to Seven of Nine, dry)
> It's been nice working with you.

The crew reacts to this sudden turn of events. Janeway turns to them.

> JANEWAY
> (to all)
> We've got to get this ship armed and ready in under
> two hours.
> (beat)
> We're going to war.

Off the moment . . .

FADE OUT.

END OF ACT FOUR

FADE IN:

| 92 thru 94 | OMITTED | 92 thru 94 |

| 95 | INT. BRIDGE | 95 |

Red Alert. Janeway in command. Kim at Ops, Paris, N.D.s at stations. Seven of Nine is working with Tuvok at Tactical. Kes is there, too, standing by Janeway.

> KIM
> The Borg modifications are complete.

> JANEWAY
> Bring them on-line.

Kim works . . .

| 96 | EXT. SPACE—ALIEN REALM—VOYAGER (OPTICAL) | 96 |

Moving slowly. A large section of Voyager's hull has been fortified with BORG TECHNOLOGY—it resembles the hull of a Borg Cube.

The Borg technology suddenly ACTIVATES, lighting up with power. Voyager is now part-Borg, part-Starfleet—muscular, aggressive, war-bound.

| 97 | INT. BRIDGE | 97 |

As before.

> KIM
> Torpedo launch tubes active . . . hull armor
> engaged . . . shield enhancements stable . . .

> TUVOK
> Bio-molecular weapons are ready . . . thirteen
> standard photon torpedoes . . . and one class ten,
> armed with a high-yield warhead.

Janeway takes a beat, then takes a moment to address her crew.

> JANEWAY
> (to com)
> All hands, this is the Captain. Ready your stations . . .
> seal all emergency bulkheads . . . and prepare to
> engage the enemy.
> (beat)
> Stand by for my orders.

Off the moment . . . as everyone prepares for battle . . .

TIME CUT TO:

98 EXT. SPACE—ALIEN REALM (OPTICAL)   98

TWO ALIEN BIO-SHIPS FLY INTO VIEW. CAMERA FOLLOWS BEHIND
THEM as they SLICE effortlessly through the fluidic space—they are
completely in their element, and they move as though they were born here,
like sharks through water. The two ships JOIN TWO MORE BIO-SHIPS and
the four now glide together, darting and moving in and around each other,
heading forward with intent.

CUT TO:

99 INT. BRIDGE   99

Janeway, Tuvok, Paris, Torres, Kim, Seven of Nine, N.D.s.

> PARIS
> Four bio-ships just entered sensor range.

> JANEWAY
> Battle stations.

We hear a special KLAXON sound. Everyone working, on their toes—this
is it.

> KIM
> I've got a visual.

> JANEWAY
> On screen.

100 INCLUDE VIEWSCREEN (OPTICAL)   100

FOUR BIO-SHIPS in the distance, quickly heading right for us. A fearsome sight.

101   ON KES   101

as she reacts to a—

102   MENTAL FLASH (OPTICAL)   102

An ALIEN FACE staring right at us!

103   KES   103

takes it in.

                              KES
          I can hear them . . . they want to talk . . . through
          me . . .

Kes concentrates . . . then turns to Janeway . . .

                              KES
          They say . . . we've contaminated their realm.

Janeway hesitates—this is a strange way to make First Contact.

                            JANEWAY
                            (to Kes)
          Tell them . . . we had no choice . . . we were only
          trying to defend ourselves . . .

                                                         INTERCUT:

104   MENTAL FLASH (OPTICAL)   104

An ALIEN FACE, aggressive, terrifying!

104A   RESUME KES   104A

as she "listens" to the aliens . . .

                              KES
          They say our galaxy . . . is impure. Its proximity is a
          threat to their . . . genetic integrity.

                              JANEWAY
Tell them we have a weapon . . . a devastating
weapon that can destroy them at the cellular level.
                              (beat)
If they don't stop their attacks on the Delta
Quadrant . . . we'll be forced to use it.

Kes thinks . . .

                               KES
They said: Your galaxy . . . will be purged.

105   EXT. SPACE—THE BIO-SHIPS (OPTICAL)   105

The four bio-ships are GLOWING . . . charging . . . and then two of the
ships FIRE ENERGY TENDRILS. The tendrils FLASH wildly through
"fluidic space"—"conducting" like electrical charges through water.

106   NEW ANGLE—BORGIFIED VOYAGER (OPTICAL)   106

As the tendrils CRACKLE around it, ROCKING the ship!

107   INT. BRIDGE   107

WHAM! The ship is ROCKED HARD! Everyone is THROWN about! Two
consoles BLOW OUT!

                               KIM
Shields and weapons are off-line!

                              TUVOK
                             (working)
I'm re-routing emergency power to the launchers . . .

                              PARIS
They're coming around for another assault . . .
                              (works)
I've lost thrusters.

                              TUVOK
Bio-molecular warheads are charged and ready.

This is it—the moment of truth.

                             JANEWAY
     Fire.

108   108
thru   OMITTED   thru
109   109

110   EXT. SPACE—BORGIFIED VOYAGER (OPTICAL)   110

As it FIRES a STACCATO BLAST of PHOTON TORPEDOES out of Borgified portals—a high-octane "gatling gun" effect. The weapons STREAK through fluidic space . . .

111   NEW ANGLE—A BIO-SHIP (OPTICAL)   111

One of the torpedoes STRIKES the ship, and is instantly ABSORBED into the hull . . . the same effect seen earlier. The ship is not damaged!

112   TWO BIO-SHIPS (OPTICAL)   112

are HIT by torpedoes. They ABSORB the weapons.

113   INT. BRIDGE   113

TUVOK
(off console)
Direct hit on all four vessels. No effect.

KIM
They're charging weapons!

Off the tension . . .

114   EXT. SPACE—THE FOUR BIO-SHIPS (OPTICAL)   114

Moving in for the kill . . . GLOWING with power . . . Voyager sitting helplessly in their sights . . .

115   NEW ANGLE—CLOSE ON A BIO-SHIP (OPTICAL)   115

Its trajectory becomes suddenly erratic . . . listing and rolling . . . and then BORG TECHNOLOGY BURSTS OUT FROM ITS HULL! Tubes and nodes and projections breaking out at an astonishing rate . . . until finally the Borg technology begins to dissolve away and the bio-ship EXPLODES in a blast of fire and organic debris! The blast sends SHOCKWAVES rippling through fluidic space!

116   TWO MORE BIO-SHIPS (OPTICAL)   116

Already BORGIFYING from within—they <u>EXPLODE</u>!

117   INT. BRIDGE   117

Voyager ROCKING from the shockwaves. Consoles flickering. Smoke.
Damage. Everyone recovering. The shaking settles.

> TUVOK
> (checks console)
> The nanoprobes were successful . . .if not prompt.
> (beat)
> All four bio-ships were destroyed.

Reactions all around—yes!

> JANEWAY
> (turns to Seven of Nine)
> I think we've made our point. Now, open a
> singularity, and get us out of here.

Seven of Nine works a console . . .

118   EXT. SPACE (OPTICAL)   118

A vast starfield—our normal space. Space distorts . . . a QUANTUM
SINGULARITY OPENS . . . and Borgified Voyager flies out and into normal space. The rift closes behind it.

Just then CAMERA PANS to reveal a <u>LARGE FLEET OF BIO-SHIPS</u>—
DOZENS of them heading right for Voyager. AMBUSH!

119   INT. BRIDGE (OPTICAL)   119

Everyone staring at the Viewscreen, which shows the BIO-SHIPS. Janeway
braces herself for the fight of her life . . . turns to Kes.

> JANEWAY
> Kes . . . are you still in contact?

> KES
> Yes . . .

> JANEWAY
> Tell them if they continue their attack . . . we'll use
> the weapon again.

Kes thinks.

                              KES
          They're not responding . . .

On the Viewscreen, the bio-ships are coming closer . . . <u>closer</u> . . .

                         JANEWAY
          Evasive maneuvers.

Paris works.

                              PARIS
          They're in pursuit.

                         JANEWAY
                         (to Tuvok)
          Prepare to fire the high-yield warhead. Aft Torpedo
          Bay.

Tuvok works . . .

120   EXT. SPACE—BORGIFIED VOYAGER (OPTICAL)   120

BANKS HARD to STARBOARD, just as DOZENS of BIO-SHIPS come
screeching at them! Several of them FIRE ENERGY TENDRILS. One CLIPS
Voyager, which goes SPINNING!

121   INT. BRIDGE   121

SHAKING hard.

                              TUVOK
          Ready, Captain!

                         JANEWAY
          <u>Do it</u>.

Tuvok hits a control.

122   EXT. SPACE—BORGIFIED VOYAGER (OPTICAL)   122

BIO-SHIPS flying all around. Voyager FIRES a HIGH-YIELD TORPEDO
out of the aft torpedo tube . . .

123 NEW ANGLE—THE TORPEDO (OPTICAL) 123

STREAKS into the thick of the BIO-SHIPS and <u>EXPLODES</u> in a series of concentric SHOCKWAVES—a MASSIVE BLAST that RIPS through dozens of the bio-ships, as it EXPANDS through SPACE . . .

124 INT. BRIDGE (OPTICAL) 124

SHAKING from the shockwaves . . . then it subsides. Tuvok checks his console.

> TUVOK
> Thirteen bio-ships have been destroyed . . . the others
> are in retreat.

Seven of Nine thinks a moment . . . communicating with the Hive Mind.

> SEVEN OF NINE
> I have regained full contact with the Collective . . .

> JANEWAY
> What are they saying?

She reacts as she begins to receive "messages" from the Collective . . . and a look of triumph crosses her face.

> SEVEN OF NINE
> All remaining bio-ships in the Delta Quadrant are
> returning to their realm.

Seven of Nine looks at her, satisfied.

> SEVEN OF NINE
> The Borg have prevailed.

Janeway eyes her, tense—she knows this is the moment of truth.

> JANEWAY
> With a little help from us.
> (beat)
> Now, it's time you fulfilled your end of the
> agreement.
> (beat)
> Tell the Collective we expect safe passage from here
> on out. We'll give you a Shuttlecraft . . . you can head
> for the nearest Borg ship.

Seven of Nine stares at her, considering her request. And for an instant, it looks like she may go along with it . . . but then:

> SEVEN OF NINE
> Unacceptable. This alliance is terminated. Your ship
> and its crew will adapt to service . . . us.

Reactions. Seven of Nine turns to the console and reaches out her arm—a BORG EXTENSION SLIDES out from her wrist and PENETRATES the console's Plexiglas surface.

> KIM
> (off console, urgent)
> Captain, she's tapping into helm control . . . she's
> trying to access our coordinates!

> JANEWAY
> Shut her out.

> KIM
> (works)
> I can't . . .

At that moment, Paris pulls a phaser from his console, takes aim . . .FIRES point-blank. The phaser hits Seven of Nine in the chest, but a BORG SHIELD deflects it.

> SEVEN OF NINE
> Resistance is futile.

Janeway eyes her . . . she's been waiting for this moment, and she's prepared for it. She speaks to the com with intent:

> JANEWAY
> Bridge to Chakotay.
> (with meaning)
> "Scorpion."

125   CLOSE ON SEVEN OF NINE   125

Working the console with her free hand. Suddenly, we hear CHAKOTAY'S VOICE in Seven of Nine's mind (with the same audio effect heard in Scene 66).

> CHAKOTAY (V.O.)
> Seven of Nine . . . stop what you're doing.

Seven of Nine reacts to the voice, taken aback by the intrusion.

126   INT. CARGO BAY TWO   126

CAMERA PUSHING IN ON CHAKOTAY, who is standing in a Borg alcove! He is wearing a BORG NEURO-TRANSCEIVER DEVICE (as seen in "Unity" and Act One). It has been placed on the back of his neck. The device is blinking, active. His eyes are open—he's aware, and he is "linked" directly to Seven of Nine's mind.

> CHAKOTAY (V.O.)
> You're human . . . a human individual . . .

127   NEW ANGLE   127

We now see that the Doctor is there, scanning Chakotay with a tricorder.

> DOCTOR
> (quickly, to Torres)
> His link is stable, but it won't be for long. You must
> hurry!

REVEAL that Torres is there, too, feverishly working at an opened panel.

> TORRES
> Just a few more seconds . . .

128   INT. BRIDGE   128

Seven of Nine still hooked to the console.

> CHAKOTAY (V.O.)
> I can see your memories . . . you remember being
> human . . .

Seven of Nine speaks aloud—

> SEVEN OF NINE
> (aloud)
> We are Borg.

Everybody on the Bridge watches Seven of Nine with anticipation . . . they know exactly what's going on.

> CHAKOTAY (V.O.)
> I see a young girl . . . a family . . .

Seven of Nine's expression is cold—Chakotay's tactic is not working.

                         SEVEN OF NINE
                            (aloud)
              Irrelevant. Your appeal to my "humanity" is
              pointless.

129   INT. CARGO BAY TWO   129

As before. Chakotay is sweating, tense, barely hanging on inside the alcove.
The Doctor looks worried.

                           DOCTOR
                    (to Torres, off tricorder)
              He's losing the link!

                           TORRES
              Initiating power surge—<u>now</u>!

Torres works a final control. The Doctor grabs hold of Chakotay by both
arms to support him. We HEAR the CRACKLE and HUM of energy
building. Chakotay stiffens suddenly.

130   INT. BRIDGE   130

As before. Seven of Nine is now feverishly working the console with her
free hand.

Suddenly, she goes <u>rigid</u>, reacting to an unseen surge of energy through her
body . . .

131   INT. CARGO BAY TWO (OPTICAL)   131

As before. The WHINE of building power hits a fever pitch and we see the
conduits where Torres was working CRACKLE with a SURGE of ENERGY.
The ENERGY SURGES along the wall until it hits Chakotay's alcove. The
neuro-transceiver on his neck CRACKLES and then BLOWS OUT in a
shower of SPARKS.

132   INT. BRIDGE (OPTICAL)   132

Seven of Nine cries out in pain as the back of <u>her</u> neck EXPLODES in a
SPRAY of SPARKS. She slumps to the deck, unconscious. Tuvok and the
Guard quickly move to her.

                    TUVOK
                (off tricorder)
    Her connection to the Collective has been severed.

                    JANEWAY
    Get her to Sickbay.
                    (to com)
    Bridge to Doctor. Report.

133   INT. CARGO BAY TWO   133

    Chakotay is lying on the floor, unconscious. The Doctor is scanning him.

                    DOCTOR
                (taps combadge)
    Commander Chakotay's going to be all right. Although
    he may wake up with a bit of a headache.

134   INT. BRIDGE   134

    As before.

                    JANEWAY
    Tom, plot a course out of Borg space. Maximum warp.

                    PARIS
    Yes, Ma'am.

    As he works . . .

                                                        CUT TO:

135   EXT. SPACE—VOYAGER (OPTICAL)   135

    Still Borgified, as before. At WARP.

                    JANEWAY (V.O.)
    Captain's Log, Stardate 51003.7. Three days, and no
    sign of Borg or bio-ships. We appear to be out of
    danger . . .

136   CLOSE ON A PIECE OF PAPER   136

    A feathered QUILL TIP dipped in ink is writing out Janeway's log on the
    paper. We can see the first part of the log (see above) written out on the page

in a cursive hand. The rest of the log is being written out as we hear it
spoken by Janeway:

> JANEWAY (V.O.)
> (continuing)
> . . . but the entire crew is still on edge . . . and so am I.

REVEAL we are in:

137   INT. DA VINCI'S WORKSHOP—NIGHT   137

Janeway is sitting at Da Vinci's upstairs worktable. She's been writing her
log entry as seen in Part One. The room is lit by candlelight, moody. As she
dips the quill into an inkpot . . .

> CHAKOTAY'S VOICE
> Am I interrupting?

Janeway looks up to see Chakotay. He's holding a PADD. There is a slight
awkwardness between them . . . they've worked through their differences
enough to get out of danger . . . but their personal relationship is still a little
strained.

> JANEWAY
> Not at all. Just finishing up my Log.

He eyes the paper and quill.

> CHAKOTAY
> The old-fashioned way . . .

> JANEWAY
> I wanted to get as far away from bio-implants and
> fluidic space and . . .
> (re: quill)
> This feels more . . . human somehow.

Chakotay hands her the PADD.

> CHAKOTAY
> I hate to spoil the mood, but you might want to look
> at this Engineering report.

She takes the PADD, looks it over.

> CHAKOTAY
> (continuing)
> It'll take at least two weeks to remove the Borg
> technology from our systems.
> (beat)
> B'Elanna did note that the power couplings on Deck
> Eight work better with the Borg improvements.

Janeway considers.

> JANEWAY
> Leave them.
> (beat)
> How's our passenger?

> CHAKOTAY
> The Doctor says she's stabilizing . . . her human cells
> are starting to regenerate.

Janeway looks thoughtful.

> JANEWAY
> I wonder what's left under all that Borg
> technology . . . if she can ever become human
> again . . .

> CHAKOTAY
> You plan to keep her on board . . .

> JANEWAY
> We pulled the plug . . . we're responsible for what
> happens to her now.

> CHAKOTAY
> She was assimilated very young . . . the Collective's
> all she knows.
> (beat)
> She may not want to stay.

> JANEWAY
> I think she might. We have one thing the Borg could
> never offer . . .
> (looks at him)
> Friendship.

This word hangs in the air. Their relationship has been strained by this adventure, and it's not clear exactly where they stand. An awkward silence, then:

> CHAKOTAY
>
> I want you to know . . . going against your orders was one of the most difficult things I've ever had to do.

> JANEWAY
>
> I understand. And I respect the decision you made . . . even though I disagree with it.
> (beat)
> What's important is that in the end, we got through this . . . together.
> (beat)
> I don't ever want that to change.

Chakotay nods.

> CHAKOTAY
>
> Agreed.

> JANEWAY
>
> Good.

Janeway stands.

> JANEWAY
>
> I think it's time we get back to our Bridge.

> CHAKOTAY
>
> No argument there.

And they head for the door, side-by-side, together. As they leave, CAMERA FALLS ON the quill and paper, which in the flickering candlelight looks warm and human . . .

DISSOLVE TO:

138   INT. SICKBAY   138

In stark contrast to the warm glow of the previous scene, we see <u>Seven of Nine</u> lying on the surgical bed. CAMERA IS SLOWLY MOVING IN on her face . . . she's unconscious, eyes closed . . . and her features would look almost peaceful, if they weren't covered with Borg technology.

As we linger on the image of this sleeping woman, we are left wondering what might happen . . . when she eventually wakes up.

FADE OUT.

<u>END OF ACT FIVE</u>

<u>THE END</u>

STAR TREK: VOYAGER

''The Raven''
(fka ''Resurrection'')

#40840-174

Teleplay
by
Bryan Fuller

Story
by
Bryan Fuller and Harry Doc Kloor

Directed
by
LeVar Burton

STAR TREK: VOYAGER

''The Raven''

JANEWAY	ANNIKA
PARIS	DUMAH
CHAKOTAY	FATHER
TUVOK	MOTHER
TORRES	GAUMEN
DOCTOR	
NEELIX	
KIM	
SEVEN OF NINE	

COMPUTER VOICE

Non-Speaking

N.D. SUPERNUMERARIES

STAR TREK: VOYAGER

''The Raven''

SETS

INTERIORS
VOYAGER
    BRIDGE
    BRIEFING ROOM
    CARGO BAY
    CORRIDOR
    MESS HALL
    SICKBAY
    TURBOLIFT
    HOLODECK (DA VINCI'S WORKSHOP)

PARIS' SHUTTLECRAFT
SEVEN OF NINE'S SHUTTLECRAFT

B'OMAR VESSEL
    COCKPIT

BORG SHIPWRECK
    CORRIDOR

EXTERIORS
SPACE
VOYAGER
B'OMAR SHIPS
SHUTTLECRAFTS
LUNARSCAPE
LUNAR ATMOSPHERE

STAR TREK: VOYAGER

"The Raven"

<u>PRONUNCIATION GUIDE</u>

AGRAT-MOT   ah-graht MOTE

ANNIKA   AH-nih-kah

B'OMAR   BO-mar

CHADRE KAB   chadreh KAHB

DUMAH   DOO-mah

GAUMEN   GAW-men

NASSORDIN   nass-or-DEEN

CORVIDAE   KORE-vih-die

HYPNAGOGIC   hip-nah-GOG-ik

STAR TREK: VOYAGER

"The Raven"

<u>TEASER</u>

FADE IN:

1   INT. DA VINCI'S WORKSHOP—DAY   1

JANEWAY and SEVEN OF NINE as Janeway shows her the workshop. This is a part of Janeway's "mentoring" of Seven, introducing her to aspects of humanity of which she remains unaware.

They are facing an incomplete clay sculpture that Janeway has been working on. Janeway grabs a small piece of raw clay.

> JANEWAY
> The first rule is: don't be afraid of the clay.

> SEVEN OF NINE
> I fear nothing.

Janeway adds the clay onto the sculpture.

> JANEWAY
> I mean you can't concern yourself with making a mistake . . . or whether the image you had in your mind is what's taking form in front of you. You just have to let your hands . . . and the clay . . . do the work.

Janeway takes a small piece of clay, hands it to Seven.

> JANEWAY
> Here.

Seven hesitates—it's an unnatural idea for her. Then she takes the clay.

> JANEWAY
> (indicates sculpture)
> Go ahead. I think the nose could be a little stronger.

Seven of Nine adds her small piece of clay onto the bridge of the "nose" of the sculpture—then stops. The effect is comical.

> JANEWAY
> Well, that's a start. Keep going.

Seven works it down for a couple of beats, thinking as she does so.

> SEVEN OF NINE
> This activity is truly . . . unproductive. The end result has no use, no necessary task has been accomplished . . . time has been expended—nothing more.

She steps back from the sculpture—no longer interested in working the clay.

> JANEWAY
> That depends on how you look at it. I find sculpting helps me unwind . . . relax.

Seven considers.

> SEVEN OF NINE
> The concept of "relaxation" is difficult for me to understand. As a Borg, my time was spent working at a specific task . . . when it was completed, I was assigned another. It was . . . efficient.

Janeway indicates the sculpting she's doing.

> JANEWAY
> So is this.
> (beat)
> It helps my own "efficiency" to forget about Voyager for a while . . .

Janeway steps back from the clay sculpture.

> JANEWAY
> I'd be embarrassed to show Maestro Leonardo something like this . . . but I get a great deal of pleasure in working the clay . . . creating something . . .

Janeway tosses a wet linen cloth over the clay, done for now . . . as Seven glances around the workshop, with its profusion of objects and images.

> SEVEN OF NINE
> But why here? In this simulation? Among these . . . archaic objects . . . in this disorganized environment.

> JANEWAY
> Frankly, it's refreshing to take myself out of the twenty-fourth century every now and then. And a little . . . disorganization can encourage the imagination.
> (beat)
> You might want to try it sometime.

> SEVEN OF NINE
> Are you suggesting that I create one of these— ''Holodeck programs''?

> JANEWAY
> You might find it interesting. It's a way of exploring aspects of yourself that probably didn't fit into your life as a Borg . . . imagination, creativity, fantasy . . .

> SEVEN OF NINE
> I'm uncertain why those things are necessary.

> JANEWAY
> Human progress . . . the human mind itself . . . couldn't exist without them.

She glances fondly at one of the da Vinci sketches.

> JANEWAY
> (continuing)
> When I was a child, I studied these drawings . . . I even built some of the models. Da Vinci has always been an inspiration to me.

Seven of Nine again takes in the vast profusion.

> SEVEN OF NINE
> He was . . . a busy man.

                                    JANEWAY
            Yes. A prolific artist . . . and a scientist as well . . . far
            ahead of his time.

Seven of Nine has spotted the "flying machine" hanging from the ceiling.
She stares at it, rapt.

                                    JANEWAY
            That design, for example. He conceived of an airplane
            centuries before one was actually built.

Seven doesn't respond, seems transfixed as she stares at the plane.

                                    JANEWAY
            Seven?

2   CLOSE ON SEVEN OF NINE   2

as she seems to be transported elsewhere: a montage of SURREAL IM-
AGES, intense, otherworldly.

3   INT. BORG SHIPWRECK—CORRIDOR (OPTICAL)   3

Heavily damaged, covered with dirt and rust, as though it were laid to waste
years ago. A haze of dust and silt permeates the stagnant air. Shafts of
sunlight stream down.

This is clearly a ship that has crash-landed.

A din of BORGIFIED VOICES—males, females, children all overlapping in
jumbled discord. An EERIE HYDRAULIC THUMPING AND HISSING
emulates the beating of a heart . . .

4   SURREAL FLASH   4

TWO BORG DRONES, aged and rusty, move menacingly toward camera.

The Borgified voices are slowly coming together in unity. What they are
saying is still indiscernible.

5   SURREAL FLASH   5

SEVEN OF NINE is running through a Borg Corridor. She appears as she
does now, two facial prosthetics and derma-plastic body wear. She looks
frightened, as though she is being chased.

6   SURREAL FLASH   6

The EYE of a RAVEN staring at us . . . a startling sight inside the Borg
Corridor . . .

7   SURREAL FLASH   7

The two Borg Drones move in on Seven of Nine. She pushes past them,
running down a narrow corridor . . .

The Borgified voices begin to harmonize.

                    BORGIFIED VOICES (V.O.)
                       (disjointed, repetitious)
              You will be assimilated . . . you will be
              assimilated . . .

Seven of Nine reaches a dead end. She turns to see—

8
         SURREAL FLASH   8

A long Borg Corridor . . . wrecked . . . shafts of SUNLIGHT streaming in
from jagged fractures in the walls . . .

A large, dark <u>RAVEN</u> is flying right toward camera . . . immense wings
flapping with a menacing WHOOSH . . . closer . . . closer . . . dust swirling in its wake . . .

9   SURREAL FLASH   9

Seven of Nine reacts to the sight . . . terrified . . . we hear the raven
SHRIEK . . .

10   SURREAL FLASH (OPTICAL)   10

The raven flying closer! CLOSER!

                    JANEWAY'S VOICE
              Seven . . . Seven . . .

                                                            CUT TO:

11   INT. DA VINCI'S WORKSHOP—DAY   11

Janeway has her hand on Seven of Nine's arm, trying to rouse her. She is
staring into middle distance, watching the images in her mind.

JANEWAY

<u>Seven?</u>

She blinks and recognizes the Captain, disoriented. Seven of Nine glances around the room, getting her bearings. She looks like she's pulling it together.

JANEWAY

What is it?

SEVEN OF NINE

I . . . don't know.

Off Seven of Nine's concern, we . . .

FADE OUT.

<u>END OF TEASER</u>

ACT ONE

FADE IN:

(NOTE: Episode credits fall over opening scenes.)

12   INT. SICKBAY   12

Seven of Nine stands next to an examination table. The DOCTOR scans her
with a medical tricorder. Janeway is there as well.

>   SEVEN OF NINE
>   It's happened three times now . . . in different
>   locations, at different times of day.
>   (beat)
>   I experience a series of . . . disjointed images in my
>   mind.

>   DOCTOR
>   Can you be more specific? Were these hallucinations?

>   SEVEN OF NINE
>   I don't know. I've never hallucinated.
>   (beat)
>   It's as if I were aboard a Borg vessel. But . . . I was
>   frightened . . . I felt fear.
>   (recounting)
>   Each experience has been similar. I'm being pursued
>   by the Borg . . . they want to assimilate me. I'm
>   running from them . . .
>   (frowns)
>   And then, each time, I see . . . a <u>bird</u>.

>   JANEWAY
>   A bird?

>   SEVEN OF NINE
>   Yes . . . a large, black one . . . flying toward me . . .
>   shrieking . . . attacking me . . .

She trails off, lost in the image, disturbed. The Doctor completes his scan.

>   DOCTOR
>   Hmmmm. Your hippocampus is in a state of agitation.

                              SEVEN OF NINE
What does that mean?

                                 DOCTOR
As your human physiology continues to reassert itself,
psychological symptoms are bound to manifest
themselves in a variety of ways . . . Through dreams,
hallucinations, hypnagogic regression . . .

                              SEVEN OF NINE
Hypnagogic regression?

                                 DOCTOR
"Flashbacks."
                                  (beat)
You could be experiencing some sort of post-traumatic
stress disorder.

                                JANEWAY
That makes sense . . . you were assimilated by the
Borg . . . you've gone through an intense, prolonged
trauma.

                              SEVEN OF NINE
I was not . . . traumatized. I was raised by the Borg. I
don't see them as threatening. Why would I
experience fear?

                                 DOCTOR
I don't know.

Seven of Nine frowns.

                              SEVEN OF NINE
Will I keep having these . . . "flashbacks"?

                                 DOCTOR
I'll need to study your neural scans further.
                                  (beat)
In the meantime . . . your digestive system is fully
functional. Now is as good a time as any to begin
taking solid and liquid nutrients.

                              SEVEN OF NINE
Oral consumption is inefficient.

DOCTOR
And unnecessary if you're lucky enough to be a
Hologram. But your human physiology makes it a
necessity.

Seven of Nine looks decidedly uncertain.

DOCTOR
I'll draw up a list of your nutritional requirements.
Take it to Mister Neelix, in the Mess Hall.
(lightly)
I hesitate to inflict his cooking on you . . . but it'll
have to do.

The Doctor moves off to work on a PADD.

SEVEN OF NINE
I do not enjoy this sensation—something is happening
to me, and I don't know what it is . . .
(beat)
It's as though I'm being driven somehow . . .

Before Janeway can reply:

CHAKOTAY'S COM VOICE
Chakotay to the Captain.

JANEWAY
Go ahead.

CHAKOTAY'S COM VOICE
Our guests have arrived. They're being escorted to the
Briefing Room.

JANEWAY
On my way.

She turns to Seven to explain.

JANEWAY
Representatives of the B'omar. I've been trying to
negotiate passage through their space . . . and so far
they've been difficult to deal with. I hope they've had
a change of heart.

                        SEVEN OF NINE
I'll wait here for the Doctor's instructions.

Janeway puts a hand on her shoulder.

                          JANEWAY
We'll help you through this, Seven. You'll be all right.

Janeway turns and EXITS, but Seven still looks troubled.

13   EXT. SPACE VOYAGER (OPTICAL)   13

facing three B'OMAR SHIPS.

14   INT. BRIEFING ROOM   14

Janeway, CHAKOTAY, and PARIS sit around the conference table with
TWO B'OMAR REPRESENTATIVES, GAUMEN and DUMAH. The B'omar
are suspicious, fastidious, and quirky, and more "sarcastic" than any aliens
we've met.

                          GAUMEN
Congratulations, Captain. Against our better
judgement, the B'omar Sovereignty has agreed to
grant your vessel passage through our territory.

Janeway exchanges a relieved look with her officers.

                          JANEWAY
On behalf of my crew . . . thank you. That will cut
three months off our journey.

                          GAUMEN
However . . . there are a few . . . stipulations.
Guidelines that you must adhere to.

                          JANEWAY
You'll have our complete cooperation.

                          GAUMEN
We expect nothing less.
                            (beat)
While in our space, your vessel will not exceed warp
three, and your weapons systems will remain off-line.
You will avoid unnecessary scans and you will not
conduct surveys of any kind. You will make no

attempt to explore our space. And you will avoid all
communications with non-military craft.

Janeway is a bit surprised at these restrictions.

> DUMAH
> We've also plotted the course your vessel is to follow.

Dumah goes to the monitor and pushes several controls. A DETAILED
STARCHART appears on the wall Viewscreen. A COMPLEX, BYZANTINE,
ZIGZAGGING LINE represents Voyager's intended course. Paris gives
Janeway a slow, sidelong glance.

> PARIS
> It'd take us weeks to follow that course.

> CHAKOTAY
> If not months.

Janeway takes it in. Gaumen stands and approaches the wall panel. Paris
takes a step back to give him room.

> DUMAH
> We've designed this course so your ship would avoid
> our populated systems and industrial areas. Deviation
> is not recommended.

> GAUMEN
> (re: dots)
> There are a total of seventeen checkpoints where you
> will submit your vessel for inspection.

Janeway exchanges glances with her officers.

> JANEWAY
> (to Gaumen)
> Chancellor Gaumen . . . If I may interrupt . . .

Gaumen stops as though Janeway's interruption is inexplicably rude.

> JANEWAY
> I appreciate your efforts in plotting this flight plan.
> But if we could, I'd like to negotiate a course that's a
> little more . . . direct.

The B'omar are taken aback by Janeway's suggestion. Off their surprise . . .

15   INT. MESS HALL   15

NEELIX is in his kitchen, slicing vegetables and quietly humming to himself. N.D.s at various tables as needed.

Seven of Nine ENTERS and stands just inside the door, surveying the room. Neelix sees her and moves to welcome her.

> NEELIX
>
> Well! An unexpected pleasure . . . would you like me to show you around the Mess Hall?

> SEVEN OF NINE
> (all business)
>
> My physiology has reasserted the need to process solid nutrients. The Doctor has prepared a list of dietary requirements. You will provide them for me.

Seven of Nine hands Neelix a PADD.

> NEELIX
>
> Let's see what we have here . . .
> (off PADD)
> Two hundred fifty grams glycoproteins consisting of fifty-three percent polypeptides, twenty-six percent fibrous glycogen . . . Doesn't sound very appetizing.

Neelix thinks a moment.

> NEELIX
>
> However . . . a plate of my Chadre-Kab should satisfy most of these . . . essentials . . . and provide a pleasurable culinary experience at the same time.

> SEVEN OF NINE
>
> Pleasure is irrelevant.

> NEELIX
> (cheerful)
>
> I beg to differ. A good meal involves much more than simply providing the proper nutrients.

> SEVEN OF NINE
>
> Why is that?

Neelix is a bit unprepared for the question.

> NEELIX
> Well . . . there's a certain—satisfaction—that comes
> from eating food which has been carefully prepared.
> I'm sure once you try it, you'll understand.
> (beat)
> How would you like your Chadre-Kab? Broiled?
> Baked? Stir-fried?

> SEVEN OF NINE
> Preparation is—
> NEELIX
> (overlapping)
> —is irrelevant. Maybe . . . maybe not.
> (thoughtful)
> This is your first time ingesting food in quite a
> while . . . let's go a little easy on your stomach . . .
> (decides)
> Steamed.

Neelix slaps a dollop of slop into a steamer and works. Seven of Nine is
puzzled, she hovers over him.

> NEELIX
> This recipe has been in my family for generations. It's
> a delicacy among my people.

Seven of Nine studies him.

> SEVEN OF NINE
> You are . . . Talaxian.

> NEELIX
> (good-natured)
> Guilty as charged.

> SEVEN OF NINE
> Species Two One Eight.

> NEELIX
> (uneasy beat)
> I suppose so.

> SEVEN OF NINE
> Your biological and technological distinctiveness was
> added to our own.

There is a surprised moment as Neelix looks up at her.

> NEELIX
> I hadn't realized that.

> SEVEN OF NINE
> A small freighter . . . containing a crew of thirty-nine.
> Taken in the Dalmine Sector.
> (beat, recollecting)
> They were easily assimilated. Their dense
> musculature made them excellent Drones.

Neelix casts her a glance, but realizes that Seven of Nine is not trying to be hurtful. She is simply honest.

> NEELIX
> Lucky for you, I guess.

Neelix quickly finishes the "Chadre-Kab" and slides in onto a plate.

> NEELIX
> Your . . . "nutrients."

He leads the way out of the kitchen carrying the plate. One the way, he grabs a small vase of flowers from the counter, a napkin, a knife and fork, and carries everything to a table. He puts the flowers in the center, places the plate and flatware, and pulls out the chair for Seven of Nine.

> NEELIX
> Please . . .

> SEVEN OF NINE
> Please what?

> NEELIX
> It's customary to sit while eating.

She regards him curiously for a moment, then sits as he slides the chair in.

It's a completely foreign feeling to her. She holds on to the sides of the chair.

NEELIX

Is something wrong?

SEVEN OF NINE

I am unaccustomed to this. Borg do not sit.

NEELIX

Well, this is a day of firsts, then, isn't it?

He fluffs open the napkin and puts it in her lap with a flourish. Then he sits opposite her.

NEELIX

Now. Take a bite.

She stares at the utensils, which look very strange to her. Neelix realizes the problem. He gestures toward the fork.

NEELIX

Try that one.

She picks it up, inspects it, hovers it over the food.

NEELIX

Just kind of . . . scoop some up.

Awkwardly, she does so. Neelix, without realizing it, is mimicking her, trying with body language to show her the idea. He brings his hand to his mouth.

NEELIX

That's the way . . . right into your mouth. Just like a little scout ship flying into a Shuttlebay.

Seven of Nine clumsily puts the fork in her mouth.

NEELIX

Now take it out . . . but keep your mouth closed.

She does so. The food remains in her mouth and she works it peculiarly.

NEELIX

That's it . . . chew, chew, chew—and then swallow.

She chews, but can't seem to swallow.

                    NEELIX
        Swallow.

He mimes a big swallow. She stares at him, and then gulps it down in an
ungainly fashion.

                  SEVEN OF NINE
        A curious sensation . . .

                    NEELIX
        You'll get used to it. Try some more.

Seven of Nine does so, more capably this time, though still not with
practiced ease. Then she stops suddenly, staring off into middle distance.
She seems to have gone into a trance, staring off at what seems to be
nothing—just as she did in the workshop with Janeway. But Neelix turns to
look where she's staring, in case.

                    NEELIX
        Is there something else I could bring you?

Camera PUSHES IN on Seven of Nine's face . . .

16   SURREAL FLASH (OPTICAL)   16

The Borg shipwreck corridor, as seen earlier. A Borg Drone walking toward
us . . . it throws back its head, opens its mouth and lets out the SHRIEK of a
bird! A bizarre sight.

17   RESUME SEVEN   17

reacting to the image in her mind. She turns to Neelix, stares at him . . . we
sense a change in her demeanor . . . as though she's driven by some inner
force.

                  SEVEN OF NINE
        You will be assimilated. Resistance is futile.

18   INSERT—SEVEN OF NINE'S ARM (OPTICAL)   18

Something is MOVING beneath the flesh of her arm.

19   BACK TO SCENE (OPTICAL)   19

Neelix stares at it in astonishment.

NEELIX
A soothing cup of tea, maybe . . .

Seven of Nine REELS from a SUDDEN PAIN. She gasps and clutches at her wrist.

A SMALL STAR-SHAPED BORG NODULE ERUPTS VIOLENTLY from beneath the skin of Seven of Nine's arm. Neelix recoils, hitting his combadge. Seven of Nine quickly recovers and rises, going to him.

NEELIX
Security to the Mess Hall—

WHAM! Seven of Nine knocks him off the chair and onto the floor, dazing him. Then she steps over him and moves intently toward the door. As N.D.s scramble to help Neelix . . .

FADE OUT.

<u>END OF ACT ONE</u>

<u>ACT TWO</u>

FADE IN:

20   INT. BRIEFING ROOM   20

As before. Janeway stands with Gaumen at the wall panel. We get the feeling that there is a battle of wills, and they've been negotiating for some time.

Chakotay indicates several points on the star chart, suggesting an alternate course. He is being as diplomatic as possible.

> CHAKOTAY
> What about this course? It's a marginal adjustment.
> The nearest populated system is more than three light
> years away.

> GAUMEN
> Definitely not. You would pass directly through the
> Agrat-mot Nebula. A key resource in our trade
> negotiations with the Nassordin.

> PARIS
> I could chart the nebula . . . try to avoid any—

> DUMAH
> No, no, no! Are your translators malfunctioning?

Suddenly, A KLAXON SOUNDS. <u>Red Alert</u>! Everyone reacts.

> TUVOK'S COM VOICE
> Captain Janeway to the Bridge.

> JANEWAY
> (to the B'omar)
> If you'll excuse me . . .

Off Janeway's movement . . .

21   INT. BRIDGE   21

KIM, TUVOK, and various N.D.s at stations. Janeway, Chakotay, and Paris ENTER from the Briefing Room.

Gaumen and Dumah follow on their heels. Paris and Chakotay take their stations.

                              JANEWAY
          Report.

                              TUVOK
          I've received an alert from Security. Seven of Nine
          attacked Neelix in the Mess Hall . . . and three other
          crewmen on Deck Two.

Shocked reactions.

                              JANEWAY
                           (to com)
          Janeway to Seven of Nine . . .
                           (beat)
          Seven . . . If you can hear me . . . respond.

No response . . .

                              CHAKOTAY
          What's her location?

                              TUVOK
          Deck Six, Section Twenty-Eight Alpha.

Janeway considers her options and gives Tuvok a nod.

Tuvok nods his understanding and quickly EXITS. Chakotay takes Tuvok's place at Tactical. Gaumen steps forward.

                              GAUMEN
          Captain . . . What's happening here?

                              JANEWAY
                           (to Gaumen)
          I wish I knew, Chancellor.
                           (to Chakotay)
          Chakotay . . . Seal off Deck Six.

Chakotay works Tactical.

                                                              INTERCUT:

22   INT. CORRIDOR   22

Seven of Nine on the move . . . She begins to HEAR a low-level cacophony
of BORGIFIED VOICES overlapping unintelligibly (like the surreal voices
in the Teaser).

                            BORG VOICE
          Seven of Nine.

She rounds the bend and runs head-on into . . .

23   SEVEN OF NINE'S POV   23

The TWO HAGGARD BORG DRONES from the surreal flashes. They are
menacing, they move in on her.

24   SEVEN OF NINE   24

takes a step back. She's frightened, her first instinct is to run . . . She looks
again, the two Borg Drones are . . .

25   HER POV   25

TWO SECURITY N.D.s, standing with hand-phasers drawn. There were
never really any Borg there . . .

26   SEVEN OF NINE (OPTICAL)   26

reacts, closes in on them. A guard takes aim and FIRES at her, grazing her
shoulder with the beam. Seven of Nine spins around reacting in pain.

She whirls on them. One of the Security N.D.s takes a step back and fires
again. This time the beam ACTIVATES SEVEN OF NINE'S BORG SHIELD-
ING. She keeps on moving down the hall.

27   INT. BRIDGE   27

As before.

                    SECURITY GUARD'S COM VOICE
                              (ragged)
          Security to the Bridge.
                              (beat)
          We just ran into Seven of Nine. Her Borg shields are
          fully operational. And they've adapted to our
          phasers . . .

Janeway reacts with surprise.

                        JANEWAY
                         (to com)
         Acknowledged.
                         (beat)
         Bridge to all security personnel. Configure your
         weapons to a rotating modulation, but keep them on
         stun.

Gaumen moves toward Janeway. He's incredulous, challenging.

                        GAUMEN
         Borg . . . ? You have <u>Borg</u> on your ship?

                        JANEWAY
                         (beat)
         It's not what you think. She's a member of my crew.
         We liberated her from the Collective. She's no longer
         a Borg.

                        GAUMEN
         Then why is she equipped with Borg shields?

                        JANEWAY
         I don't know . . .

28   INT. CORRIDOR (OPTICAL)   28

Seven of Nine on the move. She STEPS <u>THROUGH A CRACKLING
FORCEFIELD</u>.

29   INT. BRIDGE   29

As before.

30   ANGLE ON CHAKOTAY AT TACTICAL   30

                        CHAKOTAY
         She's able to cross through the security fields. She's
         entering the armory on Deck Six.

31   INT. CORRIDOR—CLOSE ON A SET OF DOORS   31

as they slide open, revealing Seven of Nine with a PHASER RIFLE. She
steps into the corridor, on the move . . .

32   INT. TURBOLIFT   32

Seven of Nine ENTERS.

                    SEVEN OF NINE
                       (to com)
        Deck Ten.

She works a touch pad.

33   INT. BRIDGE   33

Janeway stands at the ready, fielding reports.

                          KIM
                      (off console)
        She's in a Turbolift . . .

Janeway comes around to Kim's station.

                       JANEWAY
        Cut power to the Turboshafts.

                          KIM
                      (off console)
        She's blocking my commands with a Borg encryption
        code . . .

Janeway eyes Kim's console.

                       JANEWAY
        Janeway to Tuvok . . . Seven's apparently headed for
        Deck Ten. Can you get there before she does?

                   TUVOK'S COM VOICE
        I'm moving into position now, Captain.

34   INT. CORRIDOR—OUTSIDE TURBOLIFT   34

Tuvok and three SECURITY N.D.s march down the corridor with phaser
rifles in hand.

                        TUVOK
                (to Guards, on the move)
        We'll take position here.

They take up a flanking formation outside the TURBOLIFT. Their weapons CLICK AND CHARGE as they target the Turbolift doors. We HEAR the whine of the lift descending . . .

CLOSE ON Tuvok looking down the barrel of his phaser rifle at the Turbolift doors, he's focused and ready. Tension building . . .

35   ANGLE ON TURBOLIFT (OPTICAL)   35

As before. The Turbolift WHINES TO A HALT . . .

Tense beat . . . The doors UNDERLINE OPEN UNDERLINE.

Seven of Nine stands defiantly at the center of the Turbolift, a phaser rifle in her hand. She regards Tuvok with a vacant stare.

> TUVOK
> (to Seven)
> Lower your weapons and stand down.

She steps out of the Turbolift . . . and into the corridor. She's leaving Tuvok no choice.

> TUVOK
> (to N.D.s)

Fire.

Tuvok and the Security N.D.s OPEN FIRE. Their phaser bolts are AB-SORBED by Seven of Nine's CRACKLING BORG SHIELDS.

36   CLOSE ON SEVEN OF NINE'S FACE   36

as she lifts the rifle, takes aim, and begins firing. INTERACTIVE LIGHT plays on her face from the phaser fire.

Seven of Nine rounds the bend and disappears down the corridor.

37   ANGLE ON TUVOK   37

pulling himself to his feet. He moves over to a Security N.D. and checks for a pulse.

> TUVOK
> (taps com)
> Tuvok to Bridge. We were unsuccessful. I have
> wounded . . .

(beat)
She's moving toward junction thirty-two alpha . . .

38   INT. BRIDGE   38

As before.

                          JANEWAY
                         (realizing)
The Shuttle Bay.

                          CHAKOTAY
                         (quickly)
I'm erecting a forcefield . . .
                         (to Kim)
Harry, reroute all available power to Deck Ten!

                            KIM
                          (works)
Done.

39   INT. CORRIDOR (OPTICAL)   39

Seven of Nine HITS up against a FORCEFIELD around the Shuttle Bay
doors. She hesitates . . . realizes she can't get through . . . gets an idea . . .
then works a WALL PANEL next to the doors.

40   INT. BRIDGE   40

As before.

                            KIM
                       (off console)
She's accessing Transporter control!

41   INT. SHUTTLECRAFT (OPTICAL)   41

Seven of Nine MATERIALIZES at the rear of the shuttle! She works it . . .

42   INT. BRIDGE   42

As before.

CHAKOTAY
(off console)
She used a site to site transport . . . she's in a
Shuttlecraft . . . powering engines . . .

JANEWAY
Seal the launch doors!

43   EXT. SPACE VOYAGER (OPTICAL)   43

The main Shuttle Bay door EXPLODES OUTWARD, DECOMPRESSING
IN A GASEOUS FIREBALL.

Seven of Nine's SHUTTLE emerges from the VENTING EXHAUST, its
shields FLASHING AND CRACKLING IN BORG EFFECT.

44   INT. BRIDGE   44

The ship trembles from the explosion.

JANEWAY
Tractor beam!

CHAKOTAY
(off console)
No effect. She's neutralized the emitter array.

KIM
Captain . . . Seven's headed directly into B'omar
space . . . she's gone to warp.

45   ANGLE ON THE B'OMAR   45

as they exchange an incredulous glance.

PARIS
She's masked the shuttle's ion trail. I've lost her
signal.
(beat)
She's gone.

Off Janeway's frustration, we . . .

FADE OUT.

END OF ACT TWO

ACT THREE

FADE IN:

46   INT. READY ROOM   46

Red Alert. Chakotay and Janeway facing Gaumen and Dumah. The scene is tense, urgent:

> JANEWAY
> (To Gaumen)
> We'll do everything in our power to find her . . . but we'll need permission to enter B'omar space to track her shuttle effectively.

> GAUMEN
> (an edge)
> Very amusing.

Janeway gives him a look. The B'omar are angry, belligerent—but they still maintain their sardonic edge.

> GAUMEN
> Let's tally the events, shall we? First, you arrive uninvited and unwelcome . . . requesting a ''shortcut'' through our space.
> (anger rising)
> Then you proceed to unleash some sort of ''rogue Borg'' . . . and now you want us to help you get it back?

> JANEWAY
> I apologize for what's happened here . . . but we certainly didn't ''unleash'' anyone.
> (beat)
> We can resolve this situation quickly . . . if we work together.

> GAUMEN
> Captain Janeway . . . after what I've seen here, I question your competence.

Janeway's patience is wearing thin:

JANEWAY
(carefully)
May I remind you that you're still on my ship.

DUMAH
And you . . . are one vessel . . . among many of ours.

GAUMEN
(firm)
Your "Borg" will be dealt with, quickly and
efficiently. It's being tracked as we speak.

CHAKOTAY
Tracked . . . how?

DUMAH
Every vessel . . . every object . . . every particle of
dust that crosses our borders is immediately identified
and traced by our perimeter grid.

GAUMEN
The Borg will be found . . . and destroyed.

JANEWAY
Councilor . . .

GAUMEN
There will be no sharing of information. From this
point on, your vessel will maintain a distance of at
least five light years from our borders. Any
deviation . . . will be considered an act of aggression.
(wry)
It was a pleasure meeting you.

Janeway can see she's lost this argument . . . for now.

JANEWAY
(tight, to Chakotay)
Commander . . . escort our guests to the Transporter
Room.

Chakotay leads the B'omar to the Turbolift. Off Janeway's determination,
we . . .

CUT TO:

47   EXT. SPACE VOYAGER (OPTICAL)   47

at impulse.

                    JANEWAY (V.O.)
Captain's Log, Supplemental. I've assembled a team to
analyze every square millimeter of the Cargo Bay. I'm
determined to find something that might shed light on
Seven of Nine's actions.

48   INT. CARGO BAY   48

The room is bustling with activity—a detailed investigation is under way.
TORRES, Kim and FIVE N.D.s are scanning the room with tricorders,
checking in and around the Borg technology and alcoves, etc. Everyone is
looking for clues.

Torres and Kim are working together. Kim is a bit glum. Torres notices his
mood as she continues to scan, moving her tricorder up the length of the
alcove.

                    TORRES
Taking this kind of hard, aren't you?

                    KIM
What's that supposed to mean?

Torres shrugs and gives Kim a look that suggests she knows more then she
should. Kim catches on.

                    KIM
                (defensive)
We had a working relationship.

                    TORRES
                (inquisitive)
And . . . what's that supposed to mean?

                    KIM
It's not what you're thinking.

                    TORRES
                (innocently)
What am I thinking, Harry?

>   KIM
>   (flustered)
> Never mind.

Torres gives Kim a wry sidelong glance. She turns her attention back to the alcove.

She notices a small Borg implant attached to the headrest. She removes it and examines it in her hand.

>   TORRES
>   (re: Borg implant)
>   Take a look at this.

Janeway ENTERS, glances around. Torres and Kim walk up to her.

>   JANEWAY
> Anything?

>   TORRES
>   (re: implant)
>   A Borg data-link. It contains a succession of log
>   entries . . . written in Borg alphanumeric code.

>   KIM
>   I'm getting pretty good with the Borg language. I think
>   I can translate them . . .

>   JANEWAY
> Get on it.

Torres and Kim nod and step away as Chakotay ENTERS.

>   CHAKOTAY
>   (to Janeway)
>   It seems we've made quite an impression on the
>   B'omar.
>   (beat)
>   In the last hour, they've doubled the number of ships
>   patrolling their borders . . . and they've increased the
>   sensitivity of the perimeter grid by thirty-six percent.

>   JANEWAY
> So much for diplomacy . . .

> CHAKOTAY
>
> The Doctor analyzed the data from Seven of Nine's
> last transport.
>
> (beat)
>
> He's found something he wants us to see.

Janeway nods, and they head for the door.

49   INT. CORRIDOR—CONTINUOUS   49

Janeway and Chakotay EXIT the Cargo Bay and head for Sickbay.

> CHAKOTAY
>
> Maybe this was inevitable. Even if Seven did want to
> stay on Voyager . . . her Borg nature may have won
> out.
>
> (beat)
>
> We can remove implant after implant . . . but maybe
> at her core, she'll always be part of the Collective.

> JANEWAY
>
> No. I won't accept that.

They stop at the Turbolift doors. Janeway taps a control, the doors open,
and they EXIT to . . .

50   INT. TURBOLIFT—CONTINUOUS   50

Janeway and Chakotay ENTER.

> JANEWAY
> (to Lift)
>
> Deck Eight.
>
> (to Chakotay)
>
> She was responding to us . . . interacting with people
> outside the Collective for the first time.
>
> (beat)
>
> She was . . . adapting . . . to this environment . . . to
> this crew. But where is she going? We've scanned
> space for a distance of forty light years. There is no
> evidence of Borg ships. So she can't be trying to rejoin
> the Collective.

> CHAKOTAY
>
> She may plan to take the shuttle back to Borg space.

                         JANEWAY
Ten thousand light years from here? I don't think
so . . .
                         (beat)
There's something else going on. We're missing a
piece of the puzzle . . .

                         CHAKOTAY
In the meantime, the B'omar intend to find her. And
if they do, she'll probably resist them.

The Lift doors slide open . . .

                         JANEWAY
                         (determined)
One more reason for us to find her first.

As they EXIT . . .

                                                      TIMECUT:

51   INT. SICKBAY (VPB)   51

The Doctor is studying a GRAPHICS OF SEVEN OF NINE from the
Transporter information. It is covered with HIGHLIGHTED "HOT
SPOTS" of Borg activity. Janeway and Chakotay ENTER.

                         JANEWAY
What have you found, Doctor?

                         DOCTOR
Something most peculiar.
                         (re: "hot spot" graphic)
This graphic represents the matter conversion data
from Seven of Nine's last transport.

The Doctor refers to several of the "hot spots" on the Transporter-log
graphic.

                         DOCTOR
If you'll notice, there's a concentration of Borg
organelles in the bone marrow and lymphatic tissue.
                         (beat)
The dormant nanoprobes in Seven of Nine's cells are
reasserting themselves. They've taken over blood-cell
production and they're growing new Borg implants.

He eyes the graphic.

                    DOCTOR
Thirteen percent of the Borg technology I removed
three weeks ago has regenerated in a matter of
hours . . .

                    CHAKOTAY
You said the nanoprobes in her cells were dormant.
What reactivated them?

                    DOCTOR
I don't know. But I've developed a way to stop the
process.

The Doctor removes a cartridge from a storage container and loads it into a
hypospray.

                    DOCTOR
This hypospray contains a genetic resequencing
vector. It should neutralize the nanoprobes.

                    JANEWAY
That means someone needs to get close enough to do
it . . .

                                                    CUT TO:

52   INT. BRIDGE   52

Tuvok and Paris at an aft station. Various N.D.s at stations. Janeway and
Chakotay ENTER and approach . . .

                    JANEWAY
          Report.

                    TUVOK
We've analyzed the B'omar perimeter grid. It's
sophisticated . . . but not without vulnerabilities.
                    (explains)
It might be possible to penetrate the grid by re-
calibrating our shields to match its frequency.

                    PARIS
The trick is going to be our energy signature . . .
                    (beat)

Voyager's too big to hide. But a Shuttlecraft . . . with
the proper shield modulation and its engines powered
down . . . could "drift" right through without so
much as a peep.

                    JANEWAY
Nice work, gentlemen. Proceed.
                    (hands hypospray to Tuvok)
The Doctor's genetic resequencer should keep her
sedated until you get back to the ship.
                    (pointed)
Once you've penetrated the perimeter, there'll be no
<u>further</u> communication with Voyager. You'll be on
your own.

Tuvok and Paris nod their understanding.

                    TUVOK
Captain . . . it is possible that Seven will adapt to the
resequencer.

                    JANEWAY
I know. If it fails . . . and you're unable to reason
with her . . .
                    (grim)
You have my authorization to stop her . . . with any
force necessary.

                    TUVOK
Understood.

Off the sobering moment . . .

                                                    CUT TO:

53   SURREAL FLASH (OPTICAL)   53

The inside of the Borg shipwreck seen earlier. The din of BORGIFIED
VOICES haunts the air, once again overlapping in an unintelligible low-
level cacophony.

Seven of Nine is curled beneath a console. She hugs her knees to her chest,
like a terrified child hiding beneath her bed.

There is the eerie sound of the raven <u>shrieking</u> in the distance . . .

54   SEVEN OF NINE'S POV (OPTICAL)   54

as the two haggard Borg Drones peer beneath the console.

                         BORG VOICE (V.O.)
          Seven of Nine . . . Grid nine-two of subjunction
          twelve . . .

                                                           CUT TO:

55   INT. SHUTTLECRAFT   55

Seven of Nine staring into middle distance. She snaps out of her trance with
a start. The console is sending out an ALARM. She checks the console then
looks out the shuttle window . . . reacts with concern . . . Something outside of the shuttle's observation windows has attracted her attention.

56   EXT. SPACE—SHUTTLECRAFT (OPTICAL)   56

The shuttle is approaching a LINE OF FIVE B'OMAR VESSELS sprawled
out like a roadblock. A conflict is about to ignite . . .

                                                         FADE OUT.

                        <u>END OF ACT THREE</u>

FADE IN:

57   EXT. SPACE—SEVEN OF NINE'S SHUTTLECRAFT (OPTICAL)   57

approaching the LINE OF FIVE B'OMAR VESSELS sprawled out like a roadblock, as seen before.

58   INT. SEVEN OF NINE'S SHUTTLECRAFT   58

Seven of Nine works the helm controls . . . we HEAR Dumah's Com Voice:

> DUMAH'S COM VOICE
> Borg Drone . . . you have committed an infraction against the B'omar Sovereignty.

INTERCUT:

59   INT. B'OMAR VESSEL—COCKPIT—CONTINUOUS (OPTICAL)   59

OVER THE SHOULDER ANGLE THROUGH OBSERVATION WINDOWS

Dumah watches as Seven of Nine's shuttle approaches through the windows . . .

> DUMAH
> (to com)
> Cut power to your engines and lower your shields.
> Prepare to be boarded.

Seven of Nine's shuttle looms closer . . . almost filling the window now!

> DUMAH
> You will proceed no further. We will—

Seven's shuttle FILLS the WINDOWFRAME—and RAMS RIGHT INTO DUMAH'S SHIP!

60   EXT. SPACE (OPTICAL)   60

as Seven's SHUTTLE CRASHES through the B'omar barricade—SMASHING SHIPS out of her way.

CUT TO:

61   EXT. ANOTHER PART OF SPACE—SHUTTLECRAFT (OPTICAL)   61

at impulse. This shuttle is the <u>smaller</u> Voyager shuttle.

62   INT. SHUTTLECRAFT   62

Tuvok and Paris at the helm.

> TUVOK
> (off console)
> I'm detecting weapons signatures . . . Federation <u>and</u>
> B'omar.
> (beat)
> Five B'omar vessels are adrift . . . heavily
> damaged . . . lifesigns are stable.

Paris works the controls.

> PARIS
> I've located Seven's shuttle. She's two point five
> million kilometers from here . . .

> TUVOK
> Adjust course to intercept.

Paris works the helm.

63   EXT. SPACE—SEVEN OF NINE'S SHUTTLECRAFT (OPTICAL)   63

at impulse. Tuvok and Paris' shuttle comes roaring into view from behind,
in pursuit.

64   INT. TUVOK AND PARIS' SHUTTLECRAFT   64

Urgent:

> PARIS
> The implants in Seven's body are disrupting the
> Transporter signal. I can't get a lock.

Tuvok thinks, makes a decision, stands.

> TUVOK
> See if you can remodulate our transporters to match
> her shields . . .

PARIS
(surprised)
You want to beam over there?

TUVOK
Yes.

Tuvok pulls a phaser from his waist . . . grabs the <u>hypospray</u> seen earlier and adjusts it.

PARIS
(concerned)
I'm not sure that's a good idea, Tuvok . . . close quarters . . . Borg against Vulcan. You won't stand a chance if she decides to put up a fight . . .

TUVOK
It's my hope that the element of surprise will work in my favor.

Paris looks doubtful . . .

TUVOK
Do you have a better idea?

PARIS
Come to think of it . . . no.
(console beeps)
She's charging weapons . . .

TUVOK
Set my coordinates for the aft compartment.

Paris works.

PARIS
Ready . . .

TUVOK
<u>Energize</u>.

Paris works . . .

65   INT. SEVEN OF NINE'S SHUTTLECRAFT (OPTICAL)   65

Tuvok MATERIALIZES in the rear compartment and Seven of Nine is standing directly behind him. HE WHIPS AROUND WITH THE HYPO-SPRAY, BUT SHE KNOCKS IT FROM HIS HAND.

Seven of Nine SLAMS TUVOK AGAINST A CONSOLE PANEL AND THEN UP AGAINST THE OPPOSITE WALL.

Then she administers a VULCAN NECK PINCH. Tuvok collapses in her arms.

66   INT. PARIS' SHUTTLECRAFT   66

Paris at the helm.

                              PARIS
              Come on, Tuvok . . . Give me a sign.

WHAM! The shuttle is ROCKED!

67   EXT. SPACE—SEVEN OF NINE'S SHUTTLECRAFT (OPTICAL)   67

is firing at Paris' shuttle.

68   INT. PARIS' SHUTTLECRAFT   68

The cockpit is smoky.

                         COMPUTER VOICE
              Warning—propulsion systems are off-line.

                              PARIS
              Damn!

                                                            TIME CUT:

69   EXT. SPACE—SEVEN OF NINE'S SHUTTLECRAFT (OPTICAL)   69

at impulse.

70   INT. SEVEN OF NINE'S SHUTTLECRAFT   70

Tuvok is slumped in a corner at the rear of the ship. He's slowly regaining consciousness.

71   TUVOK'S POV   71

Seven of Nine is at the helm with her back to him.

Tuvok gets to his feet, he takes a step forward . . . runs into a greenish, Borg FORCEFIELD.

Seven of Nine does not even glance back.

SEVEN OF NINE

That's a level-five forcefield, Lieutenant. I suggest you be more careful.

Tuvok eyes her.

TUVOK

Why have you left Voyager?

SEVEN OF NINE

I am Borg.

TUVOK

You were Borg . . . but you're human, now . . . you're part of our crew.

She turns to him . . . Seven's expression is intense—not the usual remoteness we've come to expect. She's disoriented, hesitant, conflicted—driven by forces she doesn't understand.

SEVEN OF NINE

For a brief time . . . I was human . . .
(beat)
But I've come to realize . . . that I am Borg. I will always . . . be Borg.

Tuvok eyes her—sees that she going through some sort of internal struggle.

TUVOK

What prompted this . . . realization?

SEVEN OF NINE

Every Borg ship is coded to emit a distinct resonance frequency . . . to guide Drones who become separated from the Collective.

TUVOK

A homing beacon . . .

> SEVEN OF NINE
> Yes. I am following a signal. A Borg vessel is waiting
> for me.

> TUVOK
> We've scanned this entire region for Borg. There are
> none.

> SEVEN OF NINE
> You're wrong. They're here . . .

She stands . . . moves to him with sudden intent . . .

> SEVEN OF NINE
> Vulcan. Species Three Two Five Nine. Your enlarged
> neocortex produces superior analytical abilities. Your
> distinctiveness will be added to our . . .

She trails off . . . standing there, staring, caught in her own thoughts . . .
weird.

> TUVOK
> Seven?

She looks at him.

> SEVEN OF NINE
> No . . . I will not . . . assimilate you.
> (makes a decision)
> Once I return to the Collective, you will go back to
> Voyager . . . and tell Captain Janeway what's
> happened to me.
> (soft)
> Thank her . . . for her patience . . . for her kindness.

There is a hint of sadness and regret in her words . . . in her eyes.

> TUVOK
> Curious.
> (beat)
> Your behavior demonstrates affection and
> sentiment . . . traits of humanity . . . hardly Borg.

Tuvok ponders this seeming conundrum for a beat.

                         TUVOK
You've been experiencing hallucinations . . .
flashbacks . . .

                     SEVEN OF NINE
Yes . . .

                         TUVOK
Does that usually occur when a resonance signal is
activated?

                     SEVEN OF NINE
No . . .

73   SURREAL FLASH (OPTICAL)   73

Inside the BORG SHIPWRECKED CORRIDOR—dusty, shafts of
sunlight . . . a cacophony of BORG VOICES . . .

                     BORG VOICE (V.O.)
Seven of Nine . . . Grid nine-two of subjunction
twelve.

74   SURREAL FLASH (OPTICAL)   74

the RAVEN flying toward us down the corridor in SLOW MOTION (a re-use
of the shot seen earlier).

75   RESUME SEVEN OF NINE   75

she reacts . . . fear rising within her . . .

                     SEVEN OF NINE
But . . . I hear them . . . calling me . . . I'm
frightened . . .

                         TUVOK
That's understandable. Lower the forcefield . . . we
can return to Voyager . . . and find out what's
happening to you . . .

She looks at him, afraid . . . helpless . . . and for a moment, it looks as
though she might agree . . .

                              TUVOK
                            (pressing)
            I am your shipmate . . . We can return to Voyager
            together.

She takes a stop toward the forcefield . . . then <u>stops</u> . . . her expression
hardens . . .

                         SEVEN OF NINE
            I must rejoin the Collective.

She turns and moves back to the helm. Off Tuvok's face—what's going on
here . . . ?

76   OMITTED   76

77   EXT. SPACE—VOYAGER (OPTICAL)   77

at impulse.

78   INT. CARGO BAY   78

Janeway is alone in the room, sitting on a storage container. She contemplates Seven of Nine's Borg alcove. She is deep in thought, reflective.

Kim ENTERS.

                              KIM
                           (cautiously)
            Captain . . . Am I disturbing you?

                            JANEWAY
            Not at all, Harry.

Kim approaches, holding a PADD.

                              KIM
            I've managed to decipher Seven's log entries.

Janeway perks up with curiosity.

                            JANEWAY
            And?

> KIM

There's nothing that indicates she was planning to leave the ship. The entries are pretty unremarkable. She describes her daily routines . . . number of hours spent regenerating . . . that sort of thing. There were some personal log entries . . . mostly observations about the crew's behavior . . .
> (a little embarrassed)
> I'm mentioned in quite a few of them. Apparently, she finds my behavior "easy to predict." Whatever that means . . .

> JANEWAY
> (lightly)

Don't take it personally . . . coming from Seven, that's probably a compliment.

Kim hands her the PADD.

> KIM

The most recent entries are kind of strange . . . descriptions of bizarre images . . . almost like a record of her dreams.

> JANEWAY
> (taking the PADD)

The hallucinations . . .

> KIM

Maybe so. Sometimes she's in a Borg vessel . . . running . . . or hiding behind a bulkhead . . . falling down a shaft . . . Borg everywhere, chasing her . . .
> (beat)
> Nightmarish stuff.

> JANEWAY
> (studying PADD)

What about this . . . bird?

> KIM

She mentions it several times. It flies at her . . . shrieking . . .
> (shrugs)
> I don't know what it means.

                              JANEWAY
                           (reads off PADD)
"The feathers are black . . . wingspan approximately
one-half meter . . . the eyes are yellow . . . and it has
a powerful, triangular beak. When it looks at me, I am
paralyzed . . . I cannot move . . . it seems to know
me, but I don't understand how that's possible. It's
merely a bird . . . an inferior form of life . . . but the
sight of it fills me with fear . . ."

Janeway takes this in . . . trying to figure it out . . .

                              JANEWAY
It sounds like she's describing a member of the
corvidae family . . . like a crow . . .

She stops . . . struck by a sudden realization . . .

                              JANEWAY
        . . . or a <u>raven</u>.
                           (with meaning)
        <u>She's describing a raven</u>.

                               KIM
Why is that important?

Janeway stands . . .

                              JANEWAY
Because now I know what to look for . . .

Janeway EXITS to the Bridge, determined. Kim follows . . .

79   INT. BRIDGE—CONTINUOUS   79

Janeway ENTERS with Kim. Chakotay, N.D.s at their stations.

                              JANEWAY
Chakotay, calibrate our long range sensors to scan for
any Federation signature other than our two
Shuttlecraft.

                             CHAKOTAY
Captain . . . ?

JANEWAY

Do it.

She moves to the helm.

JANEWAY
(to helm N.D.)
Bring the ship about, Ensign . . . and lay in a course
for B'omar space.

The N.D. works. Off Janeway's intent face—what is she thinking . . . ?

FADE OUT.

<u>END OF ACT FOUR</u>

ACT FIVE

FADE IN:

80   EXT. SPACE—SEVEN OF NINE'S SHUTTLECRAFT (OPTICAL)   80

in orbit around an ALIEN moon.

81   INT. SEVEN OF NINE'S SHUTTLECRAFT   81

Seven of Nine is at the helm, Tuvok still behind the forcefield. She is studying the controls.

> SEVEN OF NINE
> The resonance signal is coming from the lunar surface.
> > (beat)
> The Borg are waiting for me there.

A hesitation, then she rises and goes to the wall console, prepares for transport.

> SEVEN OF NINE
> I don't know why I'm frightened. They are my people.

> TUVOK
> If you're afraid, then leave this place.

> SEVEN OF NINE
> Once I've been reintegrated into the Collective, my fears will disappear.

She is clearly disconcerted, uneasy about taking this step.

> TUVOK
> Seven . . . release the forcefield. I will accompany you to the surface.

She is surprised.

> SEVEN OF NINE
> You would be assimilated . . .

TUVOK
I don't believe so. I think this situation is not what it
appears.

This intrigues Seven, seems to give her hope.

SEVEN OF NINE
What do you mean . . . ? What else could it be?

TUVOK
I don't know. But I'm willing to go to the surface with
you and find out.

The slightest of hesitations, and she works controls. We HEAR the
forcefield fritz OFF.

82   EXT. SPACE—PARIS' SHUTTLECRAFT AND VOYAGER (OPTICAL)   82

at impulse.

83   INT. PARIS' SHUTTLECRAFT   83

Paris at the helm.

JANEWAY'S COM VOICE
Voyager to Paris.

PARIS
(to com)
Paris here, Captain. I'm glad to hear your voice.
(beat)
Tuvok is with Seven of Nine. I haven't been able to
establish communication with him since he
transported to her shuttle.

Paris works the console.

PARIS
(off console)
I've tracked them to a Class-M moon orbiting the fifth
planet of a yellow dwarf star.

INTERCUT:

84   INT. BRIDGE   84

Janeway in command. Chakotay, Kim and various N.D.s at stations.

                    PARIS
I'm picking up an unusual resonance signal from the
surface. It's erratic . . . I haven't been able to identify
it.

                    JANEWAY
Acknowledged.
                    (beat)
We've detected several B'omar ships closing in on
your position. What's your condition?

                    PARIS' COM VOICE
Warp engines are off-line and shields are at fifty
percent.

                    JANEWAY'S COM VOICE
Stand by . . . We're going to extend Voyager's shields
around your shuttle.

Janeway gives Kim the signal.

85   EXT. LUNARSCAPE—DAY (OPTICAL)   85

A murky yellow sky hangs over a black crater-marked lunarscape.

86   ANGLE ON PRECIPICE   86

Tuvok and Seven of Nine make their way along a rocky path. Tuvok is
scanning as they go.

                    TUVOK
The signal is getting stronger . . .

                    SEVEN OF NINE
                    (apprenhensive)
They're here . . . I'm sure of it.

                    TUVOK
                    (scans)
This way.

Seven of Nine stops, uncertain.

> TUVOK
> If you like, we can return to the shuttle.

She considers this briefly, then summons her courage.

> SEVEN OF NINE
> No. I have to find out.

He nods and they round a bend in the path.

87 ANOTHER ANGLE 87

as, surprised, they look down at something.

> SEVEN OF NINE
> (awed)
> What is it?

Tuvok scans.

88 CRASHED VESSEL—THEIR POV (OPTICAL) 88

A PARTIALLY BORGIFIED FEDERATION SHIP lies ruptured and broken in the alien sands, jagged hull rising from the dunes.

> TUVOK (V.O.)
> It is a Federation vessel . . . partially assimilated by
> the Borg.

89 TUVOK AND SEVEN OF NINE 89

> TUVOK
> There are no lifesigns. Tritanium decay suggests it has
> been here for nearly twenty years.

Seven of Nine, rapt, stares at the hulk. They start toward the ship.

90 INT. BORGIFIED SHIPWRECK 90

As seen in the surreal flashes. Shafts of murky sunlight intersect the ship's cracked frame. It appears to have been in the process of assimilation when it crashed.

As in Seven of Nine's surreal flashes, the vessel is heavily damaged, covered with rust. A haze of dust permeates the air.

The ship's impact has torn a jagged doorway in the hull. Tuvok and Seven of Nine ENTER, silhouetted by daylight, and carefully begin to explore the wreckage. Seven is a bundle of confusion, apprehension, and fascination.

                    SEVEN OF NINE
        This vessel is familiar . . .

She moves carefully toward a HALF-BORGIFIED CONSOLE. A flashing, beeping signal emanates from it.
0

                    SEVEN OF NINE
        This is the signal that's drawn me here . . .

Gingerly, she touches a control . . . and the signal goes off. This seems to provide a release of tension for Seven.

She gasps suddenly, caught in sense memory. A din of BORGIFIED VOICES begins their song . . .

                    BORG VOICES
        You will be assimilated . . . resistance is futile . . .
        your distinctness will be added to our own.

                    FATHER'S VOICE (V.O.)
                        (screaming)
        Annika . . . ! Annika . . . !

Seven of Nine whirls around . . .

91   SURREAL FLASH (OPTICAL)   91

A RUGGED MAN (Seven of Nine's father) is being pulled backward by a Borg Drone. He calls out, desperate—

                    FATHER
        Annika!

                    MOTHER'S VOICE (V.O.)
        Run . . . hide!

92   SURREAL FLASH (OPTICAL)   92

A WOMAN (Seven of Nine's mother) is lying on the floor, a Borg drone approaching.

                    MOTHER
        Run, Annika!

> BORG VOICES
> Resistance is futile . . .

93   RESUME SEVEN OF NINE   93

clutching her head, full of the cacophonous voices.

> SEVEN OF NINE
> Papa . . . help me . . .

> FATHER'S VOICE (V.O.)
> Annika . . . !

Seven of Nine turns suddenly and goes to a console, crawls UNDER it and
sits hunched up, reliving the past. Camera moves into her face.

94   SURREAL FLASH (OPTICAL)   94

A SIX-YEAR-OLD GIRL (young Annika) huddles under the console, just as
Seven of Nine did. She hugs her legs to her chest, terrified.

> MOTHER'S VOICE (V.O.)
> Hide, Annika . . .

> BORG VOICES
> Annika . . . Annika . . .

The little girl squirms in terror, helpless. DRONE LEGS appear before her,
and she shrinks back further.

95   ANNIKA'S POV   95

as a Borg Drone peers down at her, then extends a Borgified arm right at
her.

96   ON ANNIKA (OPTICAL)   96

in horror . . .

> ANNIKA
> (screaming)
> No! No!

97   RESUME SEVEN OF NINE   97

huddled under the console, eyes closed, head turning back and forth in anguish. Tuvok is there, kneeling, holding her wrists.

> SEVEN OF NINE
> (softly)
> No . . . no . . .

> TUVOK
> I'm here, Seven. Listen to me . . .

Slowly, she stops turning her head, and then her eyes open, still haunted by what she's gone through. She takes several deep breaths.

> TUVOK
> Come . . .

He helps her come out and stand up. She looks around, still shattered.

> SEVEN OF NINE
> It happened here . . . this is where it began.
> (beat)
> This is where I was assimilated.

She moves to a wall, brushes aside a Borg conduit to reveal . . .

98   CLOSE ON PLAQUE   98

words obscured by a layer of sediment. Seven's hand brushes the dust from the plaque, revealing the words: THE RAVEN.

99   BACK TO SCENE   99

> SEVEN OF NINE
> This was our ship.

She looks at Tuvok, calmer now, able to relate the story.

> SEVEN OF NINE
> We lived here for a long time . . . my father did
> experiments . . . they were very important, so we had
> to travel a long way . . .

She is recounting with the understanding of a six-year-old, imperfect and halting.

> SEVEN OF NINE
> I had my birthday here . . . my cake had six
> candles . . . and one more to grow on . . .

A look of ineffable sadness comes over her.

> SEVEN OF NINE
> And then the men came . . . Papa tried to fight them,
> but they were too strong . . . I tried to hide . . . maybe
> they wouldn't find me . . . because I was little . . . but
> they did . . .

Tuvok listens, fascinated.

> SEVEN OF NINE
> Then Papa said we were going to crash . . . and the
> big man picked me up . . . suddenly we weren't on
> this ship anymore. We were somewhere else . . .

She looks up at Tuvok, purged now, more like herself.

> SEVEN OF NINE
> (coolly)
> And then I became Borg.

> TUVOK
> Fascinating.

He gestures to the now-stilled signal.

> TUVOK
> This resonance signal must have been active since the
> ship was assimilated . . . and Voyager passed within
> its range.

WHAM! The ship is jolted hard.

Seven of Nine and Tuvok are shaken, they try to hold their footing.

We can HEAR the ship's structural integrity weakening.

> SEVEN OF NINE
> The ship is under attack.

> TUVOK
> (realizing)

The B'omar.

Several smaller explosions rock the ship, then BOOM! The ship is jolted again.

DEBRIS begins to fall from the ceiling as the ship is JOLTED.

TUVOK
We must get out of here. The ship will collapse.

100   EXT. SPACE—B'OMAR SHIPS (OPTICAL)   100

Three B'omar ships are in orbit around the moon, one firing at the lunar surface.

101   EXT. SPACE—ANOTHER ANGLE—VOYAGER (OPTICAL)   101

as it SWOOPS into view.

102   INT. BRIDGE   102

Janeway in command, Chakotay at Tactical, Kim and various N.D.s at stations.

KIM
The B'omar still aren't responding to our hails.

JANEWAY
(to Chakotay)
Target their weapons systems . . .

Chakotay works the Tactical station.

JANEWAY
(to com)
Tom . . . What's your status?

103   EXT. LUNAR ATMOSPHERE—PARIS' SHUTTLECRAFT (OPTICAL)   103

moving through the cloud layers.

104   INT. PARIS' SHUTTLECRAFT   104

Paris works the helm.

> PARIS
> (to com)
> I'm attempting to lock onto them now . . .

105   INT. BORG SHIPWRECK   105

Explosions continue to rock the scuttled mass. Debris falls from the ceiling.

106   ANGLE ON TUVOK AND SEVEN OF NINE   106

trying to make their way to the opening in the hull. It's difficult as the ship is jolting and shifting, and debris continues to pelt them.

Just as they come within reach of the portal, a particularly VIOLENT JOLT unlooses a BEAM, which falls across the opening—their only way of getting out of the collapsing ship.

Tuvok goes to the beam, tries to move it. It won't budge. He and Seven of Nine exchange a look as the ship SHUDDERS and JOLTS, almost throwing them off their feet. The ship is in real danger of disintegrating beneath them.

> SEVEN OF NINE
> My strength . . . added to your own . . .

Together, they apply Vulcan and Borg strength to the beam. It moves slightly.

107   INT. BRIDGE   107

As before.

> CHAKOTAY
> We've disabled two of their ships. The third is still
> firing.

> KIM
> We're being hailed. Audio only.

Janeway nods at him.

> GAUMEN'S VOICE
> You're committing an act of war, Captain.

> JANEWAY
> You've left me no choice, Councilor—

GAUMEN'S VOICE
Reinforcement are arriving. You will be destroyed.

Janeway makes the "cut" sign.

JANEWAY
(to Chakotay)
I don't have time for this. Target their weapons array.

108   INT. BORGIFIED VESSEL   108

The ship is SHAKING VIOLENTLY, near collapse. Tuvok and Seven of
Nine give it one last burst of strength . . . and pull the beam loose enough to
crawl through—

109   EXT. LUNARSCAPE (OPTICAL)   109

as Tuvok and Seven leap desperately from the ship, it COLLAPSES behind
them!

110   ROCKY PATH (OPTICAL)   110

Tuvok and Seven, covered with the dust from the vessel, turn back to stare
at the destruction of the ship—so nearly their own destruction.

Then they DEMATERIALIZE.

111   INT. BRIDGE   111

As before.

PARIS' COM VOICE
I've got them, Captain, and we're on our way to the
Shuttle Bay.

JANEWAY
Acknowledged. Good work.

An ALARM sounds from Kim's station.

KIM
(to Janeway)
I'm detecting a fleet of B'omar vessels
approaching . . .
(beat)
Sixty-eight ships.

JANEWAY
(to Conn.)
Lieutenant . . . As soon as Mister Paris's shuttle has
docked, take us out of B'omar space. Warp eight.
(to Chakotay)
It looks like there won't be any shortcuts this time.

TIME CUT:

112   EXT. SPACE—VOYAGER (OPTICAL)   112

at warp.

113   INT. DA VINCI'S WORKSHOP—NIGHT   113

Seven of Nine sits alone, staring at the "flying machine." Janeway ENTERS
and approaches.

JANEWAY
There you are . . .
(beat)
I wanted to tell you that the Doctor said he could
adjust one of your implants so you won't receive any
more "homing signals."

SEVEN OF NINE
Thank you.

She looks around the room.

SEVEN OF NINE
I hope you don't mind that I activated this
program . . .

JANEWAY
Not at all.

SEVEN OF NINE
I've been thinking about what you said . . . that this is
a place to . . . encourage your imagination.

JANEWAY
Is that appealing to you?

SEVEN OF NINE
I'm not certain.

There is a slight hesitation, as Seven begins to venture into territory that's new to her.

> SEVEN OF NINE
> I find myself . . . constructing scenarios . . .
> considering alternative possibilities . . .
> (beat)
> If my parents and I had not encountered the Borg . . .
> what would our lives have been?

She's struggling with her thoughts.

> SEVEN OF NINE
> (continuing)
> I would have been raised by them . . . learned from
> them . . . they would have influenced what I
> became . . . who and what I am.

Janeway is moved by this.

> JANEWAY
> And you would have done the same for them.

She continues to struggle with the idea. Janeway considers her for a moment, then:

> JANEWAY
> If you'd like to know more about your parents, there's
> information in the Federation database.

> SEVEN OF NINE
> Information?

> JANEWAY
> It seems they were fairly well known . . . for being
> unconventional . . . and for some rather unique
> scientific theories.
> (beat)
> You might like to read what's there. It might . . .
> encourage your imagination.

Seven of Nine seems to consider this proposal, but it's too much, too soon.

> SEVEN OF NINE
> Perhaps I will.

She rises.

SEVEN OF NINE

Some day.

(beat)

Good night, Captain.

She EXITS and Janeway looks after her. There are no miracles in a journey like this, only small steps.

FADE OUT.

<u>END OF ACT FIVE</u>
<u>THE END</u>

In a holodeck simulation of Renaissance Italy, Leonardo da Vinci builds one of his inventions in his workshop.
(Robbie Robinson)

In the alcoves of the Borg ship, the Borg drone known as Seven of Nine.
(C. T. Mathew)

The Borg assign Captain Janeway and Lieutenant Tuvok a representative of the Collective to aid in the completion of their shared weapon: the drone Seven of Nine, Tertiary Adjunct of Unimatrix Zero One. *(C. T. Mathew)*

Chakotay, who has spent a short time as part of the Borg Collective, is understandably suspicious when he encounters the drone Seven of Nine in *Voyager*'s cargo hold. *(C. T. Mathew)*

Seven of Nine. *(Robbie Robinson)*

Venturing out of her "quarters" in the *Voyager* cargo bay, Seven of Nine attempts to bond with the crewmembers in the galley. *(Robbie Robinson)*

Cut off from the support of Starfleet command, Captain Janeway can trust only her instincts and her crew. *(Peter Iovino)*

Captain Janeway decides to brief her senior staff on the Omega Directive. *(Robbie Robinson)*

Though her Borg implants were deactivated by the Doctor when she was rescued from the Collective, Seven of Nine finds that they have become active again. *(Robbie Robinson)*

Her suppressed memories becoming clearer, Seven of Nine remembers the attack on her father by the Borg aboard their ship the *Raven.* *(Robbie Robinson)*

A horrific vision of the past: Seven of Nine as young Annika Hansen, before her assimilation into the Borg Collective. *(Robbie Robinson)*

Seeking answers as to what her future may hold, Seven of Nine visits Captain Janeway's holodeck program of master visionary Leonardo da Vinci. *(Robbie Robinson)*

Plagued by disturbing dreams, Seven of Nine begins to wonder if her sanity is in danger. *(Robbie Robinson)*

Seven of Nine can work wonders with machinery but the crew of *Voyager* is a riddle wrapped in an enigma. *(Danny Feld)*

Seven of Nine, attempting to integrate herself into the *Voyager* crew, goes over Ensign Harry Kim's computations for the new Astrometrics lab. *(Robbie Robinson)*

Chakotay is relieved to discover his captain and Lieutenant Tuvok were transported to *Voyager* just in time following the Borg's suicidal run on the bio-ship. *(Robbie Robinson)*

Seven of Nine informs Chakotay and Tuvok that the development of the biological weapon will continue aboard *Voyager*. *(Robbie Robinson)*

The crew of *Voyager* sleeps in their shielded hibernation chambers, unaware of the danger all around them. *(Peter Iovino)*

The Doctor cautions Seven that what she is experiencing may be a form of cabin fever, brought on by isolation, and that she may not be able to trust her own perceptions. *(Peter Iovino)*

The only waking member of the *Voyager* crew, Seven patrols the decks in search of what she thinks is an intruder. *(Peter Iovino)*

Seven recovers in sickbay after successfully piloting *Voyager* through a highly irradiated section of space. *(Robbie Robinson)*

The mysterious Arturis assists Torres in fathoming the secrets of the prototype starship. *(Jerry Fitzgerald)*

Seven of Nine finds reason to be cautious on board the new Starfleet vessel, which may not be as innocent as it seems. *(Jerry Fitzgerald)*

Arturis is a man with a hidden agenda that will endanger the lives of everyone aboard *Voyager*. *(Ron Tom)*

Arturis confronts Captain Janeway and Seven.
(Jerry Fitzgerald)

Captain Janeway has no other choice but to trust Arturis when the mysterious Starfleet prototype ship begins its journey. *(Ron Tom)*

''The Omega Directive''
(fka ''The Omega Effect'')

Teleplay
by
Lisa Klink

#40840-189

Story
by
Jimmy Diggs & Steve J. Kay

Directed
by
Victor Lobl

STAR TREK: VOYAGER
''The Omega Directive''

JANEWAY

CHAKOTAY

KIM

PARIS

DOCTOR

TORRES

TUVOK

NEELIX

SEVEN OF NINE

COMPUTER VOICE

ALIEN CAPTAIN

ALLOS

Non-Speaking

N.D. SUPERNUMERARIES

STAR TREK: VOYAGER

''The Omega Directive''

SETS

INTERIORS

VOYAGER
BRIDGE
ASTROMETRICS LAB
BRIEFING ROOM
CARGO BAY
CORRIDOR
ENGINEERING
MESS HALL
READY ROOM
SCIENCE LAB
SICKBAY

ALIEN OUTPOST

EXTERIORS

VOYAGER
ALIEN MOON
ALIEN VESSELS

STAR TREK: VOYAGER

"The Omega Directive"

PRONUNCIATION GUIDE

ALLOS	AL-oss
ARITHRAZINE	ah-RITH-ra-zeen
DAKOTH	DA-koth
LANTARU	lan-TAR-oo
KETTERACT	ket-er-ACT

STAR TREK: VOYAGER

"The Omega Directive"

TEASER

FADE IN:

1   INT. CARGO BAY   1

The lights are dim in the Cargo Bay, and SEVEN OF NINE is regenerating in her alcove, eyes closed. It's somehow unsettling to see her here, surrounded by Borg hardware—we're reminded that she's still far from human.

There's a series of Borg beeps and mechanical sounds . . . and the lights come up . . . Seven of Nine's eyes open.

> COMPUTER VOICE
> Oh-six-hundred hours. Regeneration cycle complete.

Seven of Nine moves out of the alcove, instantly awake. She goes to the Borg console and briefly checks over some readings. She speaks to the com, recording a log entry—this is her daily routine.

> SEVEN OF NINE
> Daily Log, Seven of Nine, Stardate 51781.2. Today, Ensign Kim and I will conduct a comprehensive diagnostic of the aft sensor array. I'm allocating three hours twenty minutes for the task, and an additional seventeen minutes for Ensign Kim's usual conversational digressions.
> (beat)
> I'm scheduled to take a nutritional supplement at fifteen hundred hours, engage in one hour of cardiovascular activity, then I intend to review a text the Doctor recommended, entitled "A Christmas Carol." He believes it will have educational value.
> (beat)
> End log.

She heads out the door.

2   INT. MESS HALL (OPTICAL)   2

223

TUVOK and HARRY KIM sit at an isolated table, with a Kal-toh game between them. Kim holds one of the thin rods, trying to decide where to place it. He studies the chaotic haystack from one angle, then switches to another.

> KIM
>
> I'll get this . . . don't give me any hints.

> TUVOK
>
> I had no intention of doing so.

Seven of Nine ENTERS the Mess Hall and approaches Kim.

> SEVEN OF NINE
>
> Ensign.

> KIM
>
> Hi, Seven.

> SEVEN OF NINE
>
> Are you ready to begin our sensor diagnostic?

Kim looks up, surprised.

> KIM
>
> Is it oh-six-hundred already? We've been playing all night.

Seven of Nine glances at the game.

> SEVEN OF NINE
>
> Vulcan Kal-toh.

> KIM
>
> For a game of logic, you'd be surprised how addictive it is. Give me a few more minutes to figure this out . . .

He turns his concentration back to the game.

> TUVOK
>
> You should attend to your duties, Ensign. I'll accept your forfeit.

                        KIM

No way. This is the closest I've ever come to beating
you, and I'm not giving up now.

He continues to study the Kal-toh, from one angle, then another. Seven of
Nine waits for a few seconds, then loses patience. She takes the rod from his
hand, and places it, almost absently.

The Kal-toh SHIMMERS, and forms a perfectly symmetrical shape. Kim
stares at it, amazed. Tuvok nods.

                        TUVOK

Impressive.

                    SEVEN OF NINE

Elementary spatial harmonics.
                      (to Kim)
Are you ready now?

Kim acknowledges, still stunned.

                        KIM

Yeah . . . sure.

As they leave, he glances back at the game.

                        KIM
                      (to Tuvok)
I would've gotten that . . .

Off Tuvok, less than convinced . . .

3   INT. CORRIDOR   3

Kim and Seven of Nine head down the hallway.

                        KIM

Is there <u>anything</u> you don't know?

                    SEVEN OF NINE

I was Borg.

                        KIM
                    (overlapping)
"I was Borg." That's what you always say—but what

does it mean? You've got the knowledge of ten
thousand species in your head?

                    SEVEN OF NINE
Not exactly. Each Drone's experiences are processed
by the Collective. Only useful information is retained.

                    KIM
Still, that probably makes you the most intelligent
human being alive.

                    SEVEN OF NINE
Probably.

                    KIM
                    (lightly)
So what do you need the rest of us for?

Silence from Seven of Nine.

                    KIM
Forget I asked.

The ship TREMBLES mildly, and they both look around, curious.

                    KIM
What was that?

4   INT. BRIDGE (VPB)   4

CHAKOTAY's in command, PARIS and N.D.s are at stations. Tom's
checking a console.

                    PARIS
We just dropped out of warp.

                    CHAKOTAY
What's the problem?

                    PARIS
We were hit by some kind of shockwave.

                    CHAKOTAY
Source?

PARIS
(as he works)

Checking . . .

Suddenly, the monitor on his console goes blank, and an OMEGA symbol appears. Paris tries to work the console, but nothing happens.

PARIS

Hold on . . . I just lost all my sensor readings. The computer's bringing up some kind of message, but I can't access it. You'd better take a look at this.

On the monitor by his chair, Chakotay sees the same mysterious symbol. He looks around at other monitors on the Bridge—it's on all of them.

CHAKOTAY

I see it.

PARIS

What is it?

CHAKOTAY

I have no idea.

He works his console for a moment, then reacts with some surprise at the results.

CHAKOTAY

My command codes aren't working. The computer says I have insufficient clearance to access the message.

He looks around at the frozen Bridge monitors.

CHAKOTAY

We can't function like this. I'm going to get Harry up here to trace the source . . .

But before he can make the com call, the Turbolift doors OPEN and Janeway strides onto the Bridge, purposeful.

JANEWAY

Don't do anything. I'll take care of this.

She stops at an aft console, and enters a few commands. The Omega symbol disappears.

JANEWAY

Send all sensor data about the particle wave to my
Ready Room. Tom, disengage engines and hold
position here.

CHAKOTAY

Captain . . . what's going on?

JANEWAY

I can't explain right now. Don't discuss any of this
with the rest of the crew. I'll have further instructions
for you soon.

She EXITS into the Ready Room, leaving the Bridge crew to exchange
curious looks—what's going on?

FADE OUT.

END OF TEASER

ACT ONE

FADE IN:

(NOTE: Episode credits fall over opening scenes.)

5   INT. READY ROOM (OPTICAL)   5

Janeway ENTERS, and goes to her desk.

> **JANEWAY**
> (to com)
> Computer, seal the doors to this room. No entry
> without my authorization.

> **COMPUTER VOICE**
> Doors are sealed.

Janeway sits, and activates her desktop monitor. The Omega symbol
appears.

> **JANEWAY**
> (to com)
> Access secured datafile Omega One.

> **COMPUTER VOICE**
> Voiceprint confirmed. State clearance code.

> **JANEWAY**
> (to com)
> Janeway-one-one-five-three-red. Clearance level ten.

> **COMPUTER VOICE**
> Confirmed.

The image on the monitor changes to a graphic of a small starchart. There's
a DOT in the center, representing Voyager, and a line tracing a course from
it.

> **COMPUTER VOICE**
> Sensors have detected the Omega phenomenon within
> one-point-two light years of this vessel. Implement the
> Omega Directive immediately. All other priorities
> have been rescinded.

Janeway takes this in for a moment, grim.

> JANEWAY
> (to com)
> Display sensor data.

As she settles in to study the information . . .

6   EXT. SPACE—VOYAGER (OPTICAL)   6

holding position in space.

7   INT. ENGINEERING   7

Chakotay is giving out PADDS to Paris, Seven and TORRES.

> CHAKOTAY
> (to all)
> I've been informed that this is a highly classified
> mission. Information will be provided on a need-to-
> know basis. Captain's orders.

> TORRES
> Classified . . . by who? We're sixty thousand light
> years from Starfleet . . .

> CHAKOTAY
> Like I said—need-to-know.

They start looking over the PADDS.

> CHAKOTAY
> (to Torres)
> B'Elanna . . . she wants you to install multiphasic
> shielding around the warp core.

> TORRES
> (off PADD)
> I've never seen this shield configuration. I'd like to
> run a few computer simulations to make sure it's
> stable.

> CHAKOTAY
> No time. She needs this done by eleven hundred
> hours.

TORRES

Eleven hundred? I'm not sure that's possible . . .

CHAKOTAY

Make it possible. Seven of Nine will give you a hand.

SEVEN OF NINE

Are we attempting to protect the core from some form of subspace radiation?

CHAKOTAY

I don't know any more than you do.

SEVEN OF NINE

It will be difficult to complete the task without more data.

CHAKOTAY

The data you've got will have to do.
(to Paris)
Tom—start modifying a Shuttlecraft to withstand extreme thermal stress. Twelve thousand Kelvins, at least.

PARIS

Aye, sir.

Paris nods. Torres can't resist asking . . .

TORRES

Does all this have something to do with that secret message the Captain received?

Chakotay shoots her a glance.

CHAKOTAY

What have you heard?

TORRES

Rumors, mainly. Janeway's been locked in her Ready Room for the past sixteen hours . . . and something about an "Omega Directive" . . .

Seven of Nine reacts to this.

SEVEN OF NINE

Omega . . .

PARIS

Ring a bell?

CHAKOTAY

Look—the speculation ends right here. Now, I expect
you to carry out your assignments with a minimum of
gossip. Understood?

Everyone acknowledges.

CHAKOTAY
(lightly)
I know it's hard not to wonder . . . frankly, I'm
curious myself. But the Captain was very adamant
about this.
(beat)
Get going.

Everyone starts working. Chakotay pulls Seven of Nine aside, speaks
quietly.

CHAKOTAY
(to Seven)
The Captain wants to see you.

SEVEN OF NINE

I thought she might.

Chakotay gives her a puzzled look. But Seven EXITS without another
word . . .

CUT TO:

8   INT. READY ROOM   8

Janeway is at her desk, immersed in her work. She's surrounded by
PADDS, two desktop monitors, and a cup of coffee. The rumors are true—
she's been locked up in here for a while. The door CHIMES.

JANEWAY

Come in.

Seven of Nine ENTERS. Janeway eyes her.

> JANEWAY
> What do you know about the Omega Directive?

> SEVEN OF NINE
> Everything you do. Most likely.

A tense beat—even though we don't fully understand what's going on here, or what they're talking about, there's a sense of gravity to the situation.

> JANEWAY
> I thought as much. The Borg assimilated Starfleet Captains. You'd possess all of their knowledge.

> SEVEN OF NINE
> That's correct.
> > (beat)
> Do you intend to carry out the Directive?

> JANEWAY
> Yes.

> SEVEN OF NINE
> Then sensors have detected the molecule.

> JANEWAY
> So it appears. But we have to confirm it.

> SEVEN OF NINE
> We?

> JANEWAY
> You're going to help me carry out the Directive. Protocol forbids me from discussing this mission with any of my crew. But since you already know about it . . . my choice is to either work with you, or confine you to quarters.

> SEVEN OF NINE
> Perhaps you should do the latter.
> > (off her look)
> I will not help you destroy Omega. It should be harnessed.

JANEWAY

That's impossible.

SEVEN OF NINE

The Borg believe otherwise.

Janeway looks surprised.

JANEWAY

Explain.

SEVEN OF NINE

On one occasion, we were able to create a single
Omega molecule. We kept it stable for one trillionth
of a nanosecond before it destabilized.
(beat)
We didn't have enough boronite ore left to synthesize
more. But the knowledge we gained allowed us to
refine our theories.

JANEWAY

And the Borg have been waiting for the chance to test
them out . . .

SEVEN OF NINE

Yes. But we never found another source of the ore.
Until now.

JANEWAY

Sorry . . . if someone out there is experimenting with
Omega, I'm under orders to stop them. Otherwise,
this entire Quadrant would be at risk.

SEVEN OF NINE

Those orders were issued as a result of Starfleet's
ignorance and fear.
(pointed)
I can alleviate your ignorance. As for your fear . . .

JANEWAY

Sometimes fear should be respected.
(back at her)
Tell me . . . how many Borg were sacrificed during
this experiment?

> SEVEN OF NINE

Twenty-nine vessels . . . six hundred thousand
Drones. But that's irrelevant.

> JANEWAY

Not to me . . . not to my crew . . . and not to the
people who live in this quadrant. I'm going to
neutralize this threat . . . with or without your help.

A long, tense beat. Then:

> SEVEN OF NINE

I will assist you.

> JANEWAY
> (taken aback)

You will?

> SEVEN OF NINE

I've waited many years to observe this molecule
firsthand. I won't deny myself the experience.

> JANEWAY

All right. Go to your Cargo Bay . . . assemble all the
data you have about Omega. I'll expect a report
within the hour.

Seven acknowledges. But Janeway's still puzzled about something . . .

> JANEWAY

I didn't realize you had such a strong scientific
curiosity.

Seven hesitates . . . there is a deeper purpose in her words . . . almost a
sense of awe.

> SEVEN OF NINE

Not "curiosity" . . . desire. Omega is infinitely
complex . . . yet harmonious. To the Borg, it
represents . . . perfection.
> (beat)
I wish to understand that perfection.

Janeway looks at her.

                         JANEWAY
                         (lightly)
    The Borg's Holy Grail.

                     SEVEN OF NINE
    Captain?

                         JANEWAY
    Never mind.
                         (beat)
    I'll see you in an hour.

Seven turns and EXITS. Janeway sits at her desk, looks at one of the desktop
monitors . . .

8A   INCLUDE THE MONITOR (OPTICAL)   8A

It shows a graphic of an OMEGA MOLECULE—a crystalline, jewel-like
sphere, slowly spinning, glowing with energy, almost alive. As Janeway
studies it, troubled . . .

                                                        FADE OUT.

                    END OF ACT ONE

FADE IN:

9   INT. SICKBAY   9

The DOCTOR is facing Janeway, mid-conversation.

                    DOCTOR
                    (alarmed)
          Arithrazine? What for?

                    JANEWAY
          I'm going on an Away Mission.

                    DOCTOR
          What are you planning to do—stroll through a
          supernova?

                    JANEWAY
          Something like that.
                    (beat)
          Twenty milligrams. When can you have it ready?

                    DOCTOR
          Captain . . . arithrazine is used for the most extreme
          cases of theta-radiation poisoning. A physician must
          be present to monitor the treatment.

                    JANEWAY
          That won't be possible.

                    DOCTOR
          Then I'm afraid I can't accommodate you. I'd be in
          violation of Starfleet Medical Protocols.

                    JANEWAY
          Well, I'm overriding those protocols . . .

                    DOCTOR
          Don't tell me—''The Omega Directive.'' Whatever
          that might be . . .

                    JANEWAY
          The arithrazine, Doctor?

DOCTOR
It'll be ready in the morning.

JANEWAY
Have it sent to the Shuttle Bay.

Janeway turns to go.

DOCTOR
Captain . . . I don't know what's going on here . . .
but I'd hate this to be the last time I ever see you.
(beat)
Please be careful.

Janeway is touched by his sentiment, but she's resolved to see this mission through. She nods, then turns to go . . .

CUT TO:

10   INT. CARGO BAY (OPTICAL)   10

Seven of Nine is standing at the row of alcoves, working a control panel. A CONSOLE there displays a graphic of the OMEGA MOLECULE seen earlier, this time surrounded by Borg alphanumerics. Janeway is looking on.

SEVEN OF NINE
I've analyzed the sensor logs using Borg algorithms.
The shockwave we detected indicates not one . . . but
possibly hundreds of Omega molecules.

JANEWAY
(reacts)
Location?

SEVEN OF NINE
Within ten light years. I'm having difficulty isolating
the exact star system.

JANEWAY
Transfer your data to the Astrometrics Lab. I'll work
on it there.
(thinks)
Hundreds of molecules . . . that changes everything.
We're going to need more firepower . . . more
protection . . .

                    SEVEN OF NINE
        A shuttle mission may be insufficient. We require the
        resources of this entire crew.

Janeway considers . . . we get the sense this is something she's been
struggling with all along.

                    JANEWAY
        I've already considered that possibility . . . it's too
        dangerous. If something goes wrong, I want Voyager a
        safe distance away . . . so Chakotay can get this crew
        out of here.

Janeway looks at her.

                    JANEWAY
                    (continuing)
        Unless you think the risk is now too high . . . in
        which case, you can stay behind.

                    SEVEN OF NINE
        I have no intention of staying behind.

As they work . . .

                                                    CUT TO:

11   INT. SCIENCE LAB   11

Tuvok and Kim are working on a PHOTON TORPEDO, which has a panel
open on it. This is a delicate operation, and they're quiet and focused.

                    TUVOK
        Phase modulator.

Kim gives him an instrument, and Tuvok uses it on the internal circuitry of
the torpedo.

                    TUVOK
        Detonator circuits?

Kim checks a console reading.

                    KIM
        On standby.

>   TUVOK
> We're ready to load the gravimetric charge.

Kim very carefully hands Tuvok a narrow CYLINDER—the actual CHARGE.

>   KIM
> This looks like enough for a fifty isoton explosion.

Tuvok places the cylinder into the torpedo casing.

>   TUVOK
> Fifty-four, to be exact.

>   KIM
> What are we planning to do, blow up a small planet?

>   TUVOK
> I don't know.

>   KIM
> This warhead isn't standard issue . . . who designed it,
> the Captain?

>   JANEWAY'S VOICE
>   (lightly)
> Mister Kim . . . you ask too many questions.

REVEAL Janeway, who has just ENTERED the room. She moves to them.

>   JANEWAY
>   (continuing)
> Change of plans, Gentlemen. Increase the charge to
> eighty isotons.

A beat. Tuvok raises a brow.

>   TUVOK
> Aye, Captain.

>   JANEWAY
> Harry, when you're done here, give B'Elanna a hand
> with the shuttlecraft. She's reinforcing the hull.

>   KIM
> Right.

Janeway EXITS. A beat as they work. Kim is intrigued by the mystery of what's happening.

                    KIM
Ensign Hickman thinks it's Species Eight Four Seven
Two.

                    TUVOK
Pardon me?

                    KIM
That's his theory: there's an opening in fluidic space,
and Captain Janeway has to shut it down.

Tuvok doesn't respond.

                    KIM
Wanna hear what I think?

                    TUVOK
No.

                    KIM
I think there's a type-six protostar out there . . . and
the Captain's planning to detonate it and open a
wormhole to the Alpha Quadrant. In theory, it's
possible. And because she doesn't want to get our
hopes up, she's not telling anybody.

                    TUVOK
Don't get your hopes up.

                    KIM
Then what do you think it is?

                    TUVOK
I don't engage in idle speculation.

                    KIM
Come on, Tuvok, aren't you curious?

                    TUVOK
Yes . . . but we have a task at hand.
                    (an order)
The phase modulator.

Kim hands him an instrument. As they work . . .

CUT TO:

12   EXT. SPACE—VOYAGER (OPTICAL)   12

hanging in space.

13   INT. ASTROMETRICS LAB   13

Janeway is working at a console.

> JANEWAY
> Come in.

Chakotay ENTERS, having been called.

> JANEWAY
> Status report?

> CHAKOTAY
> Everything's going according to schedule.

> JANEWAY
> Good. The Omega Directive doesn't allow me to say
> much . . . but I want you to know what to expect.
> (beat)
> At oh-six-hundred hours, I'll be leaving in a shuttle
> with Seven of Nine.

> CHAKOTAY
> Would it be out of line to ask where you're going?

Janeway pauses—she'd like to tell him but she can't.

> JANEWAY
> I can tell you this: One of two things is going to
> happen . . . either Seven and I will succeed on our
> mission, and return within a few days . . . or your
> long-range sensors will detect a large explosion in
> subspace. If that occurs, you'll have less than ten
> seconds to jump to warp, and get the hell out of here.
> Head for the Alpha Quadrant and don't look back.
> (beat)
> Understood?

Chakotay doesn't like the sound of this . . . and this entire situation is starting to get under his skin.

                    CHAKOTAY
          I always thought Starfleet was run by duty-crazed
          bureaucrats . . . but I find it hard to believe that even
          they would order a Captain to go on a suicide mission.
                         (beat)
          This shuttle excursion is your idea, isn't it?

                    JANEWAY
          Let's just say I've had to . . . amend the Directive,
          given the circumstances.
                         (beat)
          You have your orders. . . . I expect you to follow
          them.

                    CHAKOTAY
          That's expecting a lot. You're asking me to abandon
          my Captain, and closest friend, without even telling
          me why.

                    JANEWAY
          If it were a simple matter of trust, I wouldn't hesitate
          to tell you. But we've encountered situations where
          information was taken from us by force. I can't allow
          knowledge of Omega to go beyond Voyager.

                    CHAKOTAY
          That's a reasonable argument . . . but you're not
          always a reasonable woman.
                         (off her look)
          You're determined to protect this crew . . . and this
          time you've taken it too far. A dangerous mission?
          Fine, I'll acknowledge that . . . but isn't it more likely
          to succeed with everyone behind you, working
          together?

His words have an impact—they strike to the heart of Janeway's dilemma.

                    JANEWAY
          Ordinarily, I'd agree. But this Directive was issued
          many years ago, and Starfleet didn't exactly have our
          predicament in mind . . . lost in the Delta Quadrant,
          with no backup. I can't ignore the orders . . . but I

won't ask the crew to risk their lives because of my
obligation.

CHAKOTAY

"<u>My</u> obligation." That's where you're wrong. Voyager
may be alone out here, but you're not.
(emphatic)
Let us help you. We'll keep classified information
limited to the Senior Staff . . . we'll take every
security precaution . . . just don't try to do this alone.

Janeway stares at him for a long beat . . . then:

JANEWAY

Assemble the troops.

Chakotay nods. There's a warm beat between them, then he turns to go . . .

CUT TO:

14   INT. BRIEFING ROOM (OPTICAL)   14

Janeway is on her feet, facing Chakotay, Tuvok, Torres, Kim, Paris, the
Doctor and Seven of Nine. The mood is tense, filled with anticipation.

JANEWAY

If we were in the Alpha Quadrant right now, we
wouldn't be having this conversation. I'd be in contact
with Starfleet Command, and they'd send in a
specialized team to deal with the crisis. In their
absence, we'll have to make do with the training I
received, and the knowledge Seven of Nine has
retained from the Borg.

Janeway moves to the wall MONITOR, taps a control. The OMEGA
SYMBOL seen earlier appears.

JANEWAY
(continuing)
You've all seen this symbol. <u>Omega</u>. The last letter of
the Greek alphabet . . . chosen by Starfleet to
represent a threat not only to the Federation, but to
the entire galaxy. Only Starship Captains and
Federation Flag Officers have been briefed on the
nature of this threat.
(beat)

What you're about to hear doesn't go beyond these
bulkheads . . . is that clear?

Nods all around. Janeway taps a few controls and the monitor CHANGES to
show a GRAPHIC of the OMEGA MOLECULE, spinning and pulsating.

> JANEWAY
> (re: graphic)
> This is Omega.

> PARIS
> A <u>molecule</u>?

> JANEWAY
> Not just any molecule . . . the most powerful
> substance known to exist. A single Omega molecule
> contains as much energy as a warp core. In theory, a
> small chain of them could sustain a civilization.

The crew takes this in.

> JANEWAY
> (continuing)
> The molecule was first synthesized over a hundred
> years ago, by a Starfleet physicist named Ketteract. He
> was hoping to develop an inexhaustible power source.

> SEVEN OF NINE
> Or a weapon.

Janeway throws her a look, but doesn't argue the point.

> JANEWAY
> Ketteract managed to synthesize a single molecule
> particle of Omega . . . but it only existed for a fraction
> of a second before it destabilized.

She works a control, and the monitor CHANGES to show a SPACE
STATION viewed from a distance which has EXPLODED from within. The
structure is barely holding together and is charred and smoking. TENDRILS
of CRACKLING ENERGY emanate from the station. As Janeway speaks,
the monitor shows three different views of the station . . .

> JANEWAY
> This was a classified research station in the Lantaru
> Sector. Ketteract and one hundred twenty-six of the

Federation's leading scientists were lost in the
accident.
                        (beat)
Rescue teams who tried to reach the site discovered
an unexpected, secondary effect. There were subspace
ruptures extending out several light years.

                        PARIS
                     (recalling)
The Lantaru Sector . . . it's impossible to form a stable
warp field there. You can only fly through it at
sublight speeds.
                        (beat)
But I was always told that was a natural phenomenon.
You're saying it was caused by a single molecule of
this stuff?

                      JANEWAY
                   (acknowledges)
Omega destroys subspace. A chain reaction involving
a handful of molecules could devastate subspace
throughout an entire Quadrant. If that were to
happen, warp travel would become impossible. Space-
faring civilization as we know it would cease to exist.
                        (beat)
Once Starfleet realized Omega's power, they
suppressed all knowledge of it.

                       DOCTOR
Have you detected Omega here . . . in the Delta
Quadrant?

                      JANEWAY
I'm afraid so.
                        (beat)
I'm authorized to use any means necessary to destroy
it.

A beat as everyone absorbs this.

                      JANEWAY
                     (to Paris)
Tom . . . I've calculated the location of the molecules.
I'll transfer the coordinates to the helm. Take us there
at full impulse.

PARIS

Aye, Captain.

She surveys her officers for a moment.

JANEWAY

I don't have to tell you what's at stake. If a large-scale
Omega explosion occurs . . . we'll lose the ability to
go to warp . . . forever.
(beat)
We've got our work cut out for us.

Everyone EXITS. Off Janeway's face . . .

FADE OUT.

<u>END OF ACT TWO</u>

ACT THREE

FADE IN:

15   EXT. SPACE—VOYAGER (OPTICAL)   15

at impulse.

> JANEWAY (V.O.)
>
> Computer—encrypt log entry.
>> (a beep)
>
> Captain's Log, Supplemental. We're approaching the
> star system where we believe we'll find Omega. I
> have to admit, I've never been this apprehensive
> about a mission . . .

15A   INT. CORRIDOR   15A

Janeway is walking along, carrying a PADD, lost in thought. FOUR
STARFLEET N.D.s are moving about, carrying equipment, etc.

> JANEWAY (V.O.)
>> (continuing)
>
> I know how Einstein must've felt about the atom
> bomb . . . or Marcus when she developed the genesis
> device. They watched helplessly as science took a
> destructive course . . .

                                               CUT TO:

16   INT. CARGO BAY (VPB)   16

Janeway ENTERS, carrying the PADD, glances around, looking for
someone.

> JANEWAY (V.O.)
>> (continuing)
>
> But I have the chance to prevent that from happening.
> I just hope it's not too late.

As the log ends, Janeway walks up to Seven of Nine, who is working at a
portable console.

> JANEWAY
>
> Status report?

Seven indicates a monitor . . .

16A   INCLUDE THE MONITOR (VPB)   16A

which shows a GRAPHIC of a large STEEL CHAMBER—cylindrical, high-tech, with two Plexiglass WINDOWS.

                        SEVEN OF NINE
            This is a <u>harmonic resonance chamber</u>. The Borg
            designed it to contain and stabilize Omega.

                        JANEWAY
            I thought I asked you to work on the photon
            torpedo . . .

                        SEVEN OF NINE
            The torpedo may be insufficient . . .
                        (re: graphic)
            I can modify this chamber to emit an inverse
            frequency. It will be enough to dissolve Omega's
            interatomic bonds.

                        JANEWAY
            Here's to Borg ingenuity.
                        (beat)
            Excellent work, Seven. We may need this.

                        SEVEN OF NINE
            The modification requires several complex
            calculations. Assist me.

                        JANEWAY
                        (lightly)
            I guess I will.

They start working the console. Janeway glances at her . . .

                        JANEWAY
            I'm curious . . . when did the Borg discover Omega?

                        SEVEN OF NINE
            Two hundred, twenty-nine years ago.

                        JANEWAY
            Assimilation?

                         SEVEN OF NINE
Yes . . . of thirteen different species.

                          JANEWAY
Thirteen?

                         SEVEN OF NINE
It began with Species Two-Six-Two. They were
primitive, but their oral history referred to a powerful
substance which could "burn the sky."
                         (beat)
The Borg were intrigued . . . which led them to
Species Two-Six-Three. They, too, were primitive . . .
and believed it was a drop of blood from their
Creator.

                          JANEWAY
Fascinating . . .

                         SEVEN OF NINE
Irrelevant. We followed this trail of myth for many
years . . . until finally assimilating a species with
useful scientific data. We then created the molecule
ourselves.

Janeway takes this in, working . . .

                          JANEWAY
Omega caused quite a stir among our own "species."
Federation cosmologists had a theory . . . that the
molecule once existed in nature . . . for an
infinitesimal amount of time . . . at the moment of the
Big Bang. Some claimed Omega was the primal source
of energy for the explosion that began our universe.

Seven isn't impressed.

                         SEVEN OF NINE
A creation myth, like any other. Your culture attempts
to explain what it doesn't understand in the context of
its own belief system . . . as all limited species do.

Janeway raises a brow.

                          JANEWAY
Perhaps.

(pointed)
What is it the Borg say . . . that Omega is "perfect"?

SEVEN OF NINE
Yes.

JANEWAY
Is that a theory . . . or a belief?

Seven pauses for a moment—she never thought of it that way. Before she can respond . . .

CHAKOTAY'S COM VOICE
Bridge to Captain.

JANEWAY
(to com)
Go ahead.

CHAKOTAY'S COM VOICE
We're approaching the coordinates.

Janeway and Seven exchange a look.

JANEWAY
(to com)
On my way.

She turns to Seven, indicates the monitor.

JANEWAY
I'm leaving this project in your hands. Use whatever resources and personnel you need.

SEVEN OF NINE
Understood.

Janeway heads for the door. As Seven turns back to the monitor, thoughtful . . .

CUT TO:

17   INT. BRIDGE   17

Janeway ENTERS from the Turbolift. Chakotay, Tuvok, Paris and Kim, N.D.s at their stations.

> CHAKOTAY
> (to Janeway)
> We've entered a planetary system.

> JANEWAY

Inhabited?

> CHAKOTAY

There's a pre-warp civilization on the outermost
planet. The source of Omega seems to be further in.

> PARIS

The damage to subspace in this region is extreme. We
won't be able to go to warp.

The ship TREMBLES.

> TUVOK
> (off console)
> We're encountering distortions . . .

> JANEWAY

Track their origin.

Tuvok works.

> TUVOK

An M-class moon . . . we're in visual range.

> JANEWAY

On screen.

18   INCLUDE THE VIEWSCREEN (OPTICAL)   18

It shows a craggy MOON. Immense TENDRILS of CRACKLING ENERGY
obscure part of the lunar surface—the same energy seen in the Lantaru
disaster on the Briefing Room monitor.

> TUVOK
> (off console)
> There's a subnucleonic reaction occurring in the upper
> atmosphere. It looks like it's emanating from a
> structure on the moon's surface.

JANEWAY
(to Kim)
Can your sensors penetrate the atmosphere?

KIM

Stand by . . .

Kim works for a moment. The image on the Viewscreen CHANGES to show
the burned-out WRECKAGE of an ALIEN OUTPOST on the lunar surface.
It's reminiscent of the charred space station we saw before, but this disaster
is clearly on a much larger scale.

JANEWAY

My God.

KIM
(off console)
Over three hundred thousand square kilometers . . .
destroyed.

JANEWAY

Scan the structure. Are there any Omega molecules
remaining?

TUVOK
(works)
I can't tell. Several sections of the outpost are still
shielded.

Kim reacts to a console reading, surprised.

KIM

I'm detecting lifesigns.

CHAKOTAY

How many?

KIM

A few dozen maybe . . . it's hard to get a clear
reading.

JANEWAY

Can we transport to the surface?

KIM

I can get you there . . . but conditions in the structure
aren't good. There are high levels of radiation.

Janeway turns to Tuvok.

> JANEWAY
> Assemble a rescue team and have them report to
> Sickbay for arithrazine inoculations. Tell the Doctor to
> prepare for casualties.

Tuvok nods and EXITS. Janeway turns to Paris.

> JANEWAY
> Move Voyager into a high orbit, then join the Away
> Team. We'll need a field medic.

> PARIS
> Yes, Ma'am.

He works the helm. Chakotay turns to Janeway, concerned.

> CHAKOTAY
> You're going with them?

> JANEWAY
> If Omega's still down there, I have to find it. I'll keep
> an open comlink with the ship.
> > (beat)
> You have the Bridge.

As Janeway EXITS to the Turbolift . . .

CUT TO:

19   INT. ALIEN OUTPOST (OPTICAL)   19

Janeway, Tuvok and TWO STARFLEET N.D.s MATERIALIZE in the ruins
of an alien research facility.

The WALLS and remains of the lab equipment are BLACKENED and
TWISTED from extreme heat. There are three ALIEN BODIES visible
among the wreckage. The N.D.s scan quickly, and find an ALIEN (ALLOS)
who is still alive. A second ALIEN SURVIVOR lies next to him.

The N.D.s move to the wounded man, and begin treating him. Tuvok and
Janeway use their own tricorders to scan the room.

JANEWAY
(off tricorder)
I'm picking up Omega's resonance frequency. It's
here . . . but I can't pinpoint a location.

Janeway moves to Allos, who is being treated by the N.D.s.

JANEWAY
I need to ask you about the experiments you've been
conducting here.

Allos looks up at her, groggy, badly burned.

ALLOS
There was . . . an accident. We lost containment . . .

JANEWAY
(nods)
The substance you were trying to create . . . did any
of it survive the explosion?

ALLOS
Yes . . .

JANEWAY
Where?

He turns his head, painfully, indicating a direction. Janeway looks up to
see—

20   A BLAST DOOR   20

Heavy steel, with alien markings resembling bio-hazard symbols. She nods
to Tuvok, who moves to examine the door.

ALLOS
(re: blast door)
Inside the primary test chamber.
(beat)
Who are you . . . ?

JANEWAY
Captain Janeway of the Starship Voyager. We're here
to help.

She stands.

> JANEWAY
> (taps combadge)
> Away Team to Voyager . . . two to beam directly to
> Sickbay.

Janeway moves to join Tuvok at the blast door . . . as we HEAR the two wounded aliens DEMATERIALIZE.

> TUVOK
> This door is solid duritanium, thirty centimeters thick.

> JANEWAY
> Can we get it open?

> TUVOK
> The duritanium has melted into the door frame. We'll need to cut through the metal with phasers.

> JANEWAY
> Do it.

Tuvok nods, but he's curious about something.

> TUVOK
> Captain . . . I would be negligent if I didn't point out that we are about to violate the Prime Directive.

> JANEWAY
> For the duration of this mission, the Prime Directive has been rescinded.
> (grim)
> Let's get this over with.

Tuvok moves off. Janeway contemplates the steel door, still unsettled about what she might find behind it . . .

CUT TO:

21   INT. CARGO BAY   21

The room is bustling with activity, but it's very organized, each person performing a single task. Seven of Nine supervises Kim, NEELIX and SIX N.D.s as they work around the nearly completed HARMONIC CHAMBER, a tall, cylindrical tank with transparent sides, sitting in the middle of the room.

Kim is methodically plugging isolinear chips into a series of small slots, part of the chamber. He gets them all arranged properly, and sets the processor aside.

Just as he does, Neelix approaches, with another load of isolinear chips, and sets them down beside Kim.

Seven of Nine stops a passing N.D.

> SEVEN OF NINE
> (to N.D.)
> Crewman Dell.

The N.D. stops.

> SEVEN OF NINE
> I'm assigning you a task more suited to your abilities.
> Calibrate the ionic-pressure seals on the observation
> ports.
> (beat)
> Your new designation is Three of Ten.

The N.D. nods and walks off.

21A   ON KIM   21A

who is methodically plugging isolinear chips into a small series of slots, part of the chamber. After a beat, Neelix walks up holding another tray of isolinear chips.

> NEELIX
> I've got more isolinear processors for you to install.

> KIM
> Thanks, but I need to get the power relays on-line
> first.

Kim stands.

> NEELIX
> Um . . . are you sure that's a good idea? Ensign
> Wildman was assigned to that.

> KIM
> This is ridiculous. I'm not going to waste time just
> because Seven wants to turn this team into her own,
> private Collective.

                        NEELIX
She says it's more efficient . . .

                        KIM
Maybe for a bunch of Drones.

Kim moves to a nearby console, starts working it. Seven of Nine walks up to
him.

                   SEVEN OF NINE
                       (to Kim)
Six of Ten . . . that's not your assignment.

                        KIM
Please stop calling me that.

                   SEVEN OF NINE
You're compromising our productivity.

Kim ignores her, keeps working. Seven takes a firm hand.

                   SEVEN OF NINE
I'm reassigning you to chamber maintenance. Your
new designation is Two of Ten.

                        KIM
Wait a minute . . . you're demoting me? Since when
do the Borg pull rank?

                   SEVEN OF NINE
A Starfleet protocol I adapted. It's most useful.

Kim looks at her . . . can't help but smile at this.

                        KIM
                       (lightly)
I'm glad you're not the Captain.

Chakotay is just ENTERING the Cargo Bay, looking around at the work in
progress. He approaches Seven.

                     CHAKOTAY
How's it coming?

                   SEVEN OF NINE
The crew can be efficient when properly organized.

The harmonic chamber will be completed within the
hour.

> CHAKOTAY
> Good. I'll let the Captain know.

> SEVEN OF NINE
> Has she retrieved any data from the surface?

> CHAKOTAY
> Not yet. They're still trying to access the primary test
> chamber.

> SEVEN OF NINE
> Are there survivors?

> CHAKOTAY
> (acknowledges)
> A few. The Doctor's treating them in Sickbay.

Seven of Nine reacts to this piece of news. Chakotay heads toward the door.
Kim catches up to him.

> KIM
> Commander . . .
> (off his look)
> Seven's taking this "hive mentality" just a little too
> far. Designated functions, numbered Drones . . . I
> wouldn't be surprised if she started plugging us into
> alcoves.

But Chakotay looks more amused than anything.

> CHAKOTAY
> When in the Collective, Harry . . . adapt.

He EXITS, leaving Harry far from reassured . . .

CUT TO:

22   INT. SICKBAY   22

Seven of Nine ENTERS, glances around the room—all four bio-beds are
occupied by wounded aliens. The Doctor glances over from where he is
preparing a hypospray.

SEVEN OF NINE
(re: aliens)
Which of them is the senior researcher?

The Doctor indicates Allos, who is groggy but recovering.

DOCTOR
This gentleman. Why do you ask?

SEVEN OF NINE
He has knowledge I require.

DOCTOR
He also happens to be barely conscious. Come back in
an hour.

SEVEN OF NINE
Unacceptable.

DOCTOR
Unavoidable. This is my Sickbay. The man needs to
recover.

SEVEN OF NINE
The Captain left me in charge of our efforts on
Voyager. I would be negligent to ignore a source of
new information.

She moves for the bio-bed, but the Doctor steps in her way. A brief face-off
between them . . . then the Doctor frowns, sees she won't take no for an
answer. He turns to Allos.

DOCTOR
How are you feeling, Sir?

ALLOS
(halting)
Better . . . thank you . . .

DOCTOR
Are you comfortable enough to speak to this . . .
individual?

Allos glances at Seven . . . nods.

DOCTOR
(to Seven)

Keep it brief.

He heads back to where he was working. Seven of Nine considers the alien
scientist.

SEVEN OF NINE
How many of the molecules were you able to
synthesize?

ALLOS
Two hundred million . . . ? I'm not certain . . .

SEVEN OF NINE
What is the iso-frequency of your containment field?

ALLOS
One point six eight terrahertz. We used the molecules'
own resonance to calculate the field.

Seven reacts, intrigued.

SEVEN OF NINE
That should've been enough to stabilize them.

ALLOS
Obviously, it wasn't.

SEVEN OF NINE
Obviously. But your approach is innovative . . .
perhaps I can adapt your technique, and improve
upon it.
(beat)
You will assist me.

Allos nods, struggles to sit up.

ALLOS
Our equipment was destroyed. If you can transfer the
molecules to your ship . . . maybe they can be saved.

SEVEN OF NINE
I have no intention of "saving" them.

Allos reacts.

ALLOS

What?

SEVEN OF NINE

My orders are to destroy the Omega molecules.

Allos is aghast.

ALLOS

This . . . this is my life's work . . . the salvation of my
people!

SEVEN OF NINE

Will you assist me, or not?

Allos' voice rises with desperation and anger.

ALLOS

Our resources are nearly gone . . . the future of my
people depends on this discovery!

SEVEN OF NINE

Then your answer is no.

ALLOS

Small-minded creatures! You destroy whatever you
don't understand!

Seven reacts to this—the scientist has echoed the Borg's own philosophy
about this situation.

ALLOS
(continuing, pointed)

Rescue ships are on the way. They won't let you do it!

The Doctor arrives—having heard the shouting.

DOCTOR

Please . . . try to be calm. Seven, you'll have to leave.

Seven turns to go—but Allos grabs her arm, staring into her eyes.

ALLOS
You don't realize what you're doing . . . you don't
know what this is . . . what this means . . .

The Doctor eases the man's hand away from Seven.

SEVEN OF NINE
On the contrary. I understand, perfectly.

She turns and leaves. FOLLOW and stay on her face—clearly disturbed by
this confrontation . . .

FADE OUT.

END OF ACT THREE

ACT FOUR

FADE IN:

<table>
<tr><td>23
thru
24</td><td>OMITTED</td><td>23
thru
24</td></tr>
</table>

24A   EXT. LUNAR SURFACE—ALIEN OUTPOST (OPTICAL)   24A

The wreckage of the outpost, as seen earlier. Tendrils of energy crackle around—a scene of destruction. (NOTE: This shot is a recycle of the Viewscreen shot used in Scene 18.)

25   INT. ALIEN OUTPOST (OPTICAL)   25

Tuvok and a Starfleet N.D. are standing at the steel blast doors, carefully CUTTING through the metal with THIN PHASER BEAMS—intricate work. After a beat, we hear a series of electro-mechanical CLACKS. Tuvok nods to the N.D. and they stop firing.

> TUVOK
> (to Janeway)
> We've disabled the locking mechanism.

Janeway moves to him. We can now see that the damaged room has been cleared of wounded and dead aliens.

> JANEWAY
> Narrow your phaser beams to cut through the inner seal . . .

> TUVOK
> Inadvisable. We'd risk penetrating the containment field.

> JANEWAY
> Then we'll have to use some elbow grease. Give me a hand.

Janeway moves to the blast doors and grabs hold of an outcropping. Tuvok and the N.D. holster their phasers and grab onto the doors. A beat, then Janeway nods and they all PULL. The doors resist . . . scraping . . . metal groaning . . . then finally they OPEN all the way. A deep blue, FLUORES-CENT GLOW spills out from beyond. Otherworldly.

25A   NEW ANGLE—THE CONTAINMENT CHAMBER (OPTICAL)   25A

Beyond a thick pane of GLASS, we get our first look at <u>OMEGA</u>.

Deep blue ENERGY with tiny particles streaming about, small pockets of light that burst and then vanish. And there's a SOUND—a deep, electromagnetic HUMMING that is weirdly reminiscent of human voices. Omega seems almost alive.

They stare at it for a moment, then Janeway scans it with her tricorder.

> JANEWAY
> (re: Omega)
> There's enough here to wipe out subspace across half the Quadrant.

> TUVOK
> I'll order the Away Teams back to Voyager . . . and target this facility with the gravimetric charge.

> JANEWAY
> It won't be enough. We'll have to go with our Borg option.
> (turns to N.D.)
> Return to the ship . . . tell Chakotay to help Seven complete the harmonic chamber.

The N.D. moves off.

> JANEWAY
> (thinks)
> We'll have to transport Omega directly to the ship. That means finding a way to shut down this containment field.

She nods toward a control panel by the doors. The two of them move to the panel and start working at it. As the blue glow plays on their faces . . .

> TUVOK
> It's unfortunate we can't study this phenomenon in more detail. We may not have the opportunity again.

> JANEWAY
> Let's hope we never do.

> TUVOK
> A curious statement . . . from a woman of science.

> JANEWAY
> I'm also a woman who occasionally knows when to
> quit.

She glances into the glowing portal . . .

> JANEWAY
> Take another look at your tricorder . . . Omega's too
> dangerous. I won't risk half the Quadrant to satisfy
> our curiosity. It's arrogant, and it's irresponsible.

As she stares into Omega . . .

> JANEWAY
> (continuing)
> The "Final Frontier" has some boundaries that
> shouldn't be crossed . . . and we're looking at one.

CUT TO:

25B   ANGLE—SEVEN OF NINE   25B

> SEVEN OF NINE
> We don't need to destroy the molecules. I believe I've
> found a way to stabilize them.

REVEAL we are in—

25C   INT. CARGO BAY   25C

Seven is talking to Chakotay. They're standing by the large harmonic
chamber seen earlier.

> SEVEN OF NINE
> (explains)
> The alien in Sickbay calibrated his containment field
> using Omega's own resonance . . . an approach
> unknown to the Borg. I've modified the chamber to—

Chakotay cuts her off, disturbed.

                        CHAKOTAY
Those weren't your orders. The Captain wants Omega
<u>eliminated</u>.

                        SEVEN OF NINE
That's still an option—if she insists on yielding to her
fear.

Chakotay eyes her for a beat . . .

                        CHAKOTAY
Show me what you've done.

Seven moves to a console, keys in a command . . .

25D   INCLUDE THE MONITOR (OPTICAL)   25D

which displays several OMEGA MOLECULES in graphic form, moving
chaotically.

                        SEVEN OF NINE
This simulation shows the molecules in their free
state—highly unstable.
                    (re: harmonic chamber)
I've modified the chamber to emit a harmonic
waveform that will dampen the molecules.

She keys in a command—the OMEGA MOLECULES gradually start to
SLOW DOWN . . . finally reaching a point where they are all VIBRATING
in SYNCH.

                        CHAKOTAY
Looks great in theory . . . but this is only a
simulation . . . how are you going to test it?

                        SEVEN OF NINE
On Omega.

                        CHAKOTAY
Bad idea. One mistake, and none of us will be around
for a second try.

                        SEVEN OF NINE
It will work.

He looks at her, sees how adamant she is.

CHAKOTAY
Someday, maybe. Hang on to your research . . .
                    (beat)
For now, we stick to the plan. Stand by to transport
the molecules into this chamber . . . and neutralize
them, as ordered.

But Seven won't let this go—her quest for Omega borders on obsession.

SEVEN OF NINE
I've been a member of this crew for nine months . . .
in all of that time, I've never made a personal request.
I'm making one now. Allow me to proceed.
                    (beat)
Please.

Chakotay is taken aback by the emotional appeal.

CHAKOTAY
Why is this so important to you?

Seven struggles with this . . . not quite sure how to convey her thoughts.

SEVEN OF NINE
Particle zero-one-zero. The Borg designation for what
you call Omega. Every Drone is aware of its
existence . . . we were instructed to assimilate it at all
costs.

Seven stares at the display of Omega molecules.

SEVEN OF NINE
(continuing)
It is . . . perfection. The molecules exist in a flawless
state . . . infinite parts functioning as one.

CHAKOTAY
Like the Borg . . .

SEVEN OF NINE
Precisely.
                    (beat)
I am no longer Borg . . . but I still need to understand
that perfection. Without it, my existence will never be
complete.

Chakotay looks doubtful. She moves to him, tries to make him understand.

                    SEVEN OF NINE
                      (pointed)
        Commander . . . you are a spiritual man.

                    CHAKOTAY
        That's right.

                    SEVEN OF NINE
        If you had the chance to see your God . . . your
        "Great Spirit" . . . what would you do?

Chakotay is surprised by her analogy—and moved by it.

                    CHAKOTAY
        I'd pursue it . . . with all my heart . . .

                    SEVEN OF NINE
        Then you understand.

                    CHAKOTAY
        I think I do.
                      (beat)
        I'll inform the Captain of your . . . discovery. For
        now, her orders stand.

                    SEVEN OF NINE
                      (beat)
        Thank you.

Chakotay nods . . . heads for the door. OFF Seven's face . . .

                                                    CUT TO:

25E   EXT. LUNAR SURFACE—ALIEN OUTPOST (OPTICAL)   25E

As seen before (same shot).

25F   INT. ALIEN OUTPOST   25F

A short time later. Janeway and Tuvok are setting TRANSPORT PATTERN
ENHANCER RODS in place around the steel blast doors. Two N.D.s work
in the b.g. Omega is offcamera, but GLOWS into the room from beyond the
blast doors.

                    JANEWAY
                 (re: enhancers)
Set the confinement beam to its narrowest dispersion.

                    TUVOK

Understood.

                    JANEWAY
We'll target this facility with the gravimetric
torpedo . . . if anything goes wrong during transport,
that'll be our only hope.

Suddenly:

             CHAKOTAY'S COM VOICE
Bridge to Janeway. We've detected two ships on an
intercept course.

                              INTERCUT WITH:

26   INT. BRIDGE   26

Chakotay in command. Paris, Kim and N.D.s at stations.

                  CHAKOTAY
                 (continuing)
They're not responding to hails.

                    JANEWAY
How long until they get here?

Chakotay looks to Paris.

                    PARIS
Less than four minutes, Captain.

                    JANEWAY
Standby to transport the molecules directly to the
harmonic chamber.

                  CHAKOTAY
Understood.

Everything starts to happen fast as the different teams move into action.

CHAKOTAY
(to com)
Bridge to Cargo Bay.

INTERCUT WITH:

27   INT. CARGO BAY   27

Seven is checking the harmonic chamber.

SEVEN OF NINE
(to com)
Yes, Commander.

CHAKOTAY
Get ready, Seven. We'll have to do this quickly.

SEVEN OF NINE
That's not advisable.

CHAKOTAY
We don't have a choice. The alien ships are on their
way.

She moves to the console and starts working quickly.

SEVEN OF NINE
Then I recommend moving the ship within five
thousand kilometers of the surface.

28   ON THE BRIDGE   28

PARIS
That'll take us right into the atmosphere. With our
shields down, we won't withstand the thermal
reaction for more than a few seconds.

CHAKOTAY
Then we'll only get one shot at this. Take us in.

Paris acknowledges, and works the helm.

PARIS
Aye, sir.

                             CHAKOTAY
                              (to Kim)
Transporter status.

                               KIM
                            (off console)
Targeting scanners are locked.

                             CHAKOTAY
                              (to com)
Captain? Are you ready?

29   IN THE ALIEN OUTPOST   29

We see that Tuvok and the N.D. have set up pattern enhancers near the
containment vessel. Janeway looks to Tuvok.

                              TUVOK
Pattern enhancers are active.

                             JANEWAY
                              (to com)
Do it.

30   ON THE BRIDGE (OPTICAL)   30

The Viewscreen is now filled with the crackling energy tendrils in the
atmosphere.

                              PARIS
We're eleven thousand kilometers from the
surface . . . if we get much closer, we'll incinerate.

31   IN THE ALIEN OUTPOST   31

Janeway is listening to this, concerned.

                         KIM'S COM VOICE
We're losing structural integrity.

                         PARIS' COM VOICE
Nine thousand kilometers . . .

                    JANEWAY
                    (to com)
We're close enough. <u>Energize</u>.

32   IN THE CARGO BAY (OPTICAL)   32

As Seven of Nine reacts.

                CHAKOTAY'S COM VOICE
Initiating transport.

The harmonic chamber LIGHTS UP with power—the windows GLOW
from within the DEEP BLUE color. Omega is inside the chamber! Seven of
Nine moves to the chamber, checks a readout.

                    SEVEN OF NINE
                (off console, to com)
The Omega molecules are stable.

She looks into one of the portals . . . a blue glow on her face.

                    SEVEN OF NINE
                    (to com)
Transport was successful.

33   ON THE BRIDGE   33

                        KIM
                    (as he works)
I've got the Away Team in Transporter Room Two.

                    CHAKOTAY
                    (to Paris)
Get us out of here, maximum impulse.

                        PARIS
                    (as he works)
Already on it.

                    CHAKOTAY
How far away are those ships?

                        PARIS
                    (off console)
Right on our tail.

34   EXT. SPACE—VOYAGER AND ALIEN VESSELS (OPTICAL)   34

Voyager speeds away from the alien moon at high impulse, with two ALIEN
VESSELS in pursuit.

                                                            FADE OUT.

            <u>END OF ACT FOUR</u>

ACT FIVE

FADE IN:

35   EXT. SPACE—VOYAGER AND TWO ALIEN VESSELS (OPTICAL)   35

Voyager flies through open space at maximum impulse, the two alien ships speeding after it.

36   INT. BRIDGE (VPB)   36

Tuvok and Kim are at stations. Janeway and Chakotay are with Paris at the Conn, looking at a starchart.

> CHAKOTAY
>
> We're heading into an area of open space . . . no indications of life or any kind of technology. We can carry out the procedure with no risk to anyone else.

> PARIS
>
> Except those two ships behind us.

> JANEWAY
>
> Can we stay ahead of them?

> PARIS
>
> Not for long.

> CHAKOTAY
>
> How soon can we clear the subspace ruptures and go to warp?

> PARIS
>
> Ten, maybe fifteen minutes . . . But those ships will catch up to us before then.

Janeway acknowledges, considering the situation.

> JANEWAY
>
> We have one advantage. We've got Omega. They won't risk firing at us . . . at least not until they run out of options. That should give us a chance to neutralize the molecules.

275

                    CHAKOTAY
Captain . . . we might have another problem.

She gives him a look.

                    JANEWAY

Seven of Nine?

                    CHAKOTAY
                     (nods)
She's convinced she can stabilize Omega.

                    JANEWAY
I thought we'd settled that question.

                    CHAKOTAY
While you were on the surface, she showed me a
pretty convincing simulation of how it could be done.

                    JANEWAY
I should have known she wouldn't just let this go.
                     (beat)
I'll be in Cargo Bay Two.

She EXITS to the Turbolift.

37   INT. CARGO BAY (OPTICAL)   37

Seven of Nine is working at the harmonic chamber. OMEGA is GLOWING
within the chamber, deep blue, crackling, with an otherworldly HUM.
Janeway ENTERS, her voice urgent.

                    JANEWAY
Seven . . . the procedure?

                  SEVEN OF NINE
It's working. Eleven percent of the molecules have
already been neutralized.

Janeway looks relieved.

                    JANEWAY
Let's see if we can speed up the process a little.

                  SEVEN OF NINE
Did Chakotay tell you about my idea?

> JANEWAY

Yes.

> SEVEN OF NINE

Then you will allow me to stabilize the remaining
molecules.

> JANEWAY

You know I can't do that . . .

Janeway steps toward the chamber, but Seven stands in front of the
controls. This is a subtle gesture, not threatening, but <u>protective</u>. She
doesn't want to let Omega go.

> SEVEN OF NINE

Your Starfleet Directive is no longer relevant. I've
found a way to control Omega.

> JANEWAY

I don't care if you can make it sing and dance . . .
we're getting rid of it.

> SEVEN OF NINE

A foolish decision.

> JANEWAY

But it's mine to make. Now, step aside.

Seven hesitates—the tension rises.

> SEVEN OF NINE

I could have done this without your permission . . .
but I chose to follow your command structure. I
should've made the attempt . . . I still can.

> JANEWAY

But you won't . . . you know I'm not trying to stop
you from finding "perfection."

This strikes a chord with Seven.

> JANEWAY
> (pressing)

I can't risk the safety of this Quadrant. Omega must
end here . . . we both know that.

Seven considers, torn . . . and finally, <u>she steps aside</u>. Janeway moves to the chamber controls. As they start to work . . .

> JANEWAY

Status?

> SEVEN OF NINE

Eighteen percent.

> JANEWAY

This could take hours.
> (beat)

Can you increase the harmonic resonance?

> SEVEN OF NINE

Yes . . . but it would rupture the chamber.

> JANEWAY
> (thinks)

How many molecules would we neutralize?

> SEVEN OF NINE

Forty . . . fifty percent at best.

> JANEWAY

That's good enough. Our torpedo can take care of the rest.
> (taps combadge)

Janeway to Bridge.

> CHAKOTAY'S COM VOICE

Chakotay here.

> JANEWAY
> (to com)

I want you to clear Deck Four, and put emergency forcefields around this section. Prepare to decompress Cargo Bay Two on my command.

> CHAKOTAY'S COM VOICE

Understood.

> JANEWAY
> (to com)

Tuvok, load the gravimetric torpedo. Once we've jettisoned the chamber . . . fire.

TUVOK'S COM VOICE

Aye, Captain.

Janeway turns to Seven.

JANEWAY

Harmonic resonance to maximum.

They work. The chamber emits a high-pitched whine . . . blue LIGHT plays on their faces . . .

37A   EXT. SPACE—VOYAGER (OPTICAL)   37A

As before. Voyager at high impulse, the two ALIEN SHIPS hot on our tail.

38   INT. BRIDGE (OPTICAL)   38

As before.

PARIS
(off console)
Commander . . . they're closing on us . . .

TUVOK
(off console)
They're attempting to stop us with a tractor beam.

CHAKOTAY

Adjust shields to compensate.

Tuvok works.

KIM

They're hailing us.

CHAKOTAY

On screen.

On the Viewscreen, we see an ALIEN CAPTAIN of the same race as the scientists in the research facility.

ALIEN CAPTAIN

Disengage your engines and prepare to be boarded.

CHAKOTAY

I can't do that.

                         ALIEN CAPTAIN
You've stolen our technology . . . abducted our
people.

                           CHAKOTAY
Your people are safe. They're receiving medical care.
I'll be glad to get them back to you when this is over.
But we're keeping the molecules.

                         ALIEN CAPTAIN
I won't allow this substance to fall into enemy hands.
I'll destroy it first.

                            TUVOK
                        (off console)
They're charging weapons.

                           CHAKOTAY
                      (to Captain, urgent)
You'll destabilize the molecules—we'll both be
destroyed!

                         ALIEN CAPTAIN
Return our technology. Now.

                           CHAKOTAY
I'm sorry. That's not possible.

A beat, then the Viewscreen goes back to a starfield.

39   EXT. SPACE—VOYAGER AND ALIEN VESSELS (OPTICAL)   39

The alien vessels are a short distance behind Voyager. One of them FIRES
an energy beam. It HITS Voyager.

40   INT. BRIDGE   40

The ship SHAKES slightly.

                            TUVOK
Direct hit. Shields down ten percent.

                           CHAKOTAY
Evasive maneuvers—try to shake them off!

Another HIT! Off the tension . . .

41   INT. CARGO BAY (OPTICAL)   41

Janeway and Seven of Nine working at the harmonic chamber . . . which is now sending out a loud whine of energy, unnerving. The BLUE LIGHT beyond the chamber window is GLOWING BRIGHTER, HOTTER.

> SEVEN OF NINE
> (over the noise)
> Harmonic resonance is at maximum, Captain!

> JANEWAY
> The molecules?

> SEVEN OF NINE
> Eighty percent remaining.

> JANEWAY
> We need to get that down to sixty.

The ship SHAKES hard from alien phaser fire. They both hang on.

> SEVEN OF NINE
> Any damage to our power grid could overload the chamber! Omega would chain react!

> JANEWAY
> The same thought crossed my mind!

Another SHAKE!

> JANEWAY
> Where are we now?

> SEVEN OF NINE
> Seventy-two percent.

> JANEWAY
> Close enough!
> (taps combadge)
> Bridge—start the decompression sequence!

> CHAKOTAY'S COM VOICE
> Acknowledged.

There's a sudden metallic wrenching SOUND from within the chamber. A BRIGHT BURST of BLUE LIGHT RADIATES from behind the portals. Seven checks a reading . . . reacts.

> JANEWAY
> What's wrong? What's happening?

> SEVEN OF NINE
> The molecules are stabilizing . . .

> JANEWAY
> What?

> SEVEN OF NINE
> I've done nothing. It's occurring spontaneously . . .

> JANEWAY
> That's impossible.

Seven moves to the portal, looks inside . . . light crackling on her face . . .

> COMPUTER VOICE
> Decompression in fifteen seconds.

41A   ON SEVEN OF NINE   41A

CAMERA PUSHING IN on her face . . . she's staring into the chamber . . .

41B   THE PORTAL (OPTICAL)   41B

CAMERA PUSHING IN on the window. Inside the chamber, we can see the deep blue ENERGY and MATTER of OMEGA swirling chaotically . . . but it's starting to COALESCE . . .

> COMPUTER VOICE
> Decompression in ten seconds.

41C   ON SEVEN OF NINE   41C

watching with a look of wonder . . .

41D   THE PORTAL (OPTICAL)   41D

CAMERA PUSHES BEYOND THE WINDOW, AND INTO OMEGA IT- SELF. We are now IMMERSED in the deep blue . . . which suddenly CRYSTALIZES into a beautifully complex MATRIX. Multi-colored, sparkling, kaleidoscopic—a cross between a fractal pattern and a stained-glass window. Electrifying . . . and somehow perfect.

41E   SEVEN OF NINE   41E

is transfixed.

> JANEWAY
>
> Seven—let's move!

Seven hesitates—she can barely tear herself away from the sight. But Janeway grabs her by the arm and they RUSH toward the doors.

> COMPUTER VOICE
> Decompression in five seconds.

42   INT. BRIDGE   42

As before.

> CHAKOTAY
> (to Paris)
> Tom, are we clear of the subspace ruptures?

> PARIS
> Almost.

> CHAKOTAY
> I need maximum warp in the next ten seconds or
> we'll be stuck at ground zero.

Paris turns quickly back to the helm, hands flying over the controls.

> PARIS
> Yes, sir.

> TUVOK
> (working)
> Decompression is complete . . . targeting the harmonic
> chamber . . .

> CHAKOTAY
> Fire.

43   43
thru   OMITTED   thru
44   44

45   EXT. SPACE—VOYAGER AND ALIEN VESSELS (OPTICAL)   45

The small harmonic chamber has been jettisoned from Voyager. A photon torpedo HITS, and the chamber EXPLODES in a spectacular display, sending energy tendrils in all directions, nearly lashing Voyager as it speeds away at warp.

46   INT. BRIDGE   46

Paris leans back in his chair, relieved.

                        PARIS
            We made it. We're at warp one.

Janeway and Seven ENTER from the Turbolift.

                        JANEWAY
            The alien ships?

                        PARIS
            Out of range.

                        JANEWAY
            Tuvok?

                        TUVOK
                    (as he works)
            Sensors show no traces of Omega molecules.

Janeway acknowledges, relieved and weary from the efforts of the past few days.

                        JANEWAY
                    (quiet)
            Mission accomplished.

She moves to take her place in the Captain's chair. Seven remains standing near the back of the Bridge, pensive, not sharing the same feeling of accomplishment.

47   EXT. SPACE—VOYAGER (OPTICAL)   47

as the ship flies along at impulse.

> JANEWAY (V.O.)
> Captain's Log, Stardate 51793.4. We've arranged for
> our guests in Sickbay to be taken back to their
> homeworld, and we can finally put this mission
> behind us. This will be my last encrypted log
> concerning the Omega Directive. The classified
> datafiles will now be destroyed.

48   OMITTED   48

49   ANGLE—A PLAIN, WOODEN CROSS   49

hanging on a wall. Lit by candlelight. REVEAL we are in—

50   INT. HOLODECK—DA VINCI'S WORKSHOP—NIGHT   50

Seven of Nine is staring at the cross, lost in thought, contemplating all that's
happened. After a beat:

> JANEWAY'S VOICE
> I wondered who was running my program.

Seven turns to see Janeway, who's just entered.

> JANEWAY
> (lightly)
> Master da Vinci doesn't like visitors after midnight.

> SEVEN OF NINE
> He protested . . . I deactivated him.

Janeway smiles a little . . .

> JANEWAY
> What are you doing here, Seven?

> SEVEN OF NINE
> This simulation contains many religious components. I
> am studying them . . . to help me understand what I
> saw in Cargo Bay Two.

> JANEWAY
> The data isn't clear why Omega stabilized in those last
> few seconds . . . but chances are it was simply a
> chaotic anomaly . . . nothing more.

Seven tries to put her adventure into words . . .

                         SEVEN OF NINE
              For three point two seconds, I saw perfection.
                                  (beat)
              When Omega stabilized, I felt a curious sensation. As
              I watched it . . . it seemed to be watching <u>me</u>.

Seven glances up at the cross.

                         SEVEN OF NINE
                               (continuing)
              The Borg have assimilated many cultures with
              mythologies that would explain such moments of
              clarity. I've always dismissed them as trivial.
                                  (beat)
              Perhaps I was wrong.

Janeway takes this in, intrigued.

                            JANEWAY
              If I didn't know you better . . . I'd say you just had
              your first spiritual experience.

51   EXT. SPACE—VOYAGER (STOCK—OPTICAL)   51

at impulse.

                                                          FADE OUT.

                           <u>END OF ACT FIVE</u>
                              <u>THE END</u>

STAR TREK: VOYAGER

''One''

#40840-193

Written
by
Jeri Taylor

Directed
by
Kenneth Biller

STAR TREK: VOYAGER

"One"

<u>CAST</u>

JANEWAY   TRAJIS

CHAKOTAY   BORG DRONE

KIM

PARIS

DOCTOR

TUVOK

NEELIX

TORRES

SEVEN OF NINE

COMPUTER VOICE

<u>Non-Speaking</u>

N.D. SUPERNUMERARIES

STAR TREK: VOYAGER

''One''

SETS

INTERIORS	EXTERIORS
VOYAGER	VOYAGER
BRIDGE	
ASTROMETRICS LAB	
CARGO BAY	
CORRIDOR	
ENGINEERING	
JEFFERIES TUBE	
MED LAB	
MESS HALL	
SICKBAY	
STASIS ROOM	
TURBOLIFT	

STAR TREK: VOYAGER

''One''

PRONUNCIATION GUIDE

MUTARA   myoo-TAR-uh

PARISSES   puh-REE-seez

NEURODES   NOOR-odes

TRAJIS LO-TARIK   TRAY-jiss low TARE-ik

STAR TREK: VOYAGER

"One"

TEASER

FADE IN:

1   INT. MESS HALL (OPTICAL)   1

Dinner in the Mess Hall. A number of the crew are there, including HARRY KIM and B'ELANNA TORRES, sitting together at one of the tables, eating. SEVEN OF NINE approaches them.

> SEVEN OF NINE
> Lieutenant, Ensign.

> KIM
> Hey, Seven.

> TORRES
> Would you like some dinner? The potato salad isn't half bad.

> SEVEN OF NINE
> I don't require nourishment at this time. I would like to talk with you.

They exchange a curious glance.

> KIM
> Okay . . .

> SEVEN OF NINE
> Ensign Kim, what is your place of origin?

An unusual request, but Harry is game.

> KIM
> You mean . . . where am I from? Well, I was born in New Mexico, but I grew up in—

She cuts him off and turns to Torres.

> SEVEN OF NINE
> Lieutenant Torres, explain why you became a member
> of the Maquis.

Equally odd. B'Elanna hesitates, but answers.

> TORRES
> It was through Chakotay. I met him . . . actually, he
> saved my life, and—

> SEVEN OF NINE
> (to Harry)
> List the sports you play.

Harry is definitely puzzled by this rapid-fire questioning. In the background, we see the DOCTOR approaching, listening.

> KIM
> Well, I've dabbled in quite a few . . . tennis, Parrises
> Squares . . . but volleyball is probably my favorite—

> SEVEN OF NINE
> (to B'Elanna)
> Specify the foods you find enjoyable.

B'Elanna wants to know what's going on.

> TORRES
> Seven, what is this?

But Seven of Nine ignores her.

> SEVEN OF NINE
> Describe the nature of your sexual relationship with
> Lieutenant Paris.

The last straw.

> TORRES
> Now wait just a minute—

> DOCTOR
> Computer, freeze program.

All but Seven of Nine and the Doctor freeze in a HOLOGRAPHIC EFFECT.
The Doctor pulls Seven of Nine away from the group.

> DOCTOR

Would you care to explain what you're doing?

Seven of Nine is genuinely puzzled.

> SEVEN OF NINE

I'm doing exactly what you instructed me to do.

> DOCTOR

I hardly think so.
> > (beat)

I created this program to help you become more comfortable in social situations—not to practice alienating people.

> SEVEN OF NINE

You made recommendations about how to carry on a conversation.

> DOCTOR

That's true.

> SEVEN OF NINE

You said it's helpful if people feel you're interested in them.

> DOCTOR

Correct.

> SEVEN OF NINE

And that "drawing them out" by asking them about themselves is one way to demonstrate that interest.

Now the Doctor understands.

> DOCTOR

But that doesn't mean subjecting them to an interrogation. You have to let them answer . . . listen to what they say . . . ask another question on the same subject . . . take your time.

Seven of Nine stares at him, not fully understanding.

> DOCTOR

Shall we try again?

Seven of Nine eyes him briefly, then—

> SEVEN OF NINE
> I am overdue for my weekly medical maintenance.
> We should go.

He gives her a knowing look.

> DOCTOR
> Seven, you've <u>never</u> volunteered for a check-up.

> SEVEN OF NINE
> It is preferable to remaining here.

And she EXITS, the Doctor following.

2   EXT. SPACE—VOYAGER (OPTICAL)   2

as it approaches a filmy nebula-like phenomenon.

3   INT. BRIDGE   3

JANEWAY, CHAKOTAY, PARIS, TUVOK, Kim, and N.D.s.

> JANEWAY
> What have we got here?

> KIM
> Looks like a Mutara class nebula . . . with a few trace
> constituents that aren't in our database. But they're
> showing up in minute quantities.

> TUVOK
> The nebula is vast, Captain. It extends beyond the
> reach of our sensors.

> JANEWAY
> Then I guess we won't try to go around it. Tom, take
> us in at one-half impulse.

> PARIS
> Yes, Ma'am.

He works controls.

> KIM
I'm detecting a slight radioactive field . . . it's . . .

Harry breaks off and winces slightly.

> JANEWAY
Harry?

> KIM
Nothing . . . just a headache coming on . . .

But then he takes a breath in pain, puts his hands to his temples. Janeway moves toward him.

> CHAKOTAY
Maybe you should go to Sickbay . . .

> KIM
Maybe so—

But now he clutches at his console, head down, trying to deal with the pain.

> PARIS
Captain . . .

She whirls to see that all the Bridge crew is reacting in pain, some clutching their stomachs, some their chests . . . then she, too, begins to feel it. A strangled cry from Harry makes her turn back. He's looking at the back of his hand, pressed up against the console.

4   INSERT (OPTICAL)   4

A horrible smoking BURN is eating through Harry's hand.

5   RESUME   5

One by one the crew crumples to the deck, in agony. Off the mystery—

FADE OUT.

END OF TEASER

FADE IN:

(NOTE: Episode credits fall over opening scenes.)

6   INT. BRIDGE   6

As before. Janeway is gripping the side of her chair, desperately hanging on.

                                    JANEWAY
                  Tom . . . turn us around . . . get us out of here . . .

Tom is on the deck, doubled over, groaning. But he struggles to get to his
feet, can't make it, sinks back down. At the rear stations, an N.D. covers his
face, writhing. Tuvok, with difficulty, steps from behind his console and
starts toward the conn.

                                    JANEWAY
                  Janeway . . . to Sickbay . . .

                                                              INTERCUT:

7   INT. SICKBAY   7

where the Doctor is treating one N.D. with a hypospray as a group of N.D.s
stumbles in through the door. They have burns on their faces. Seven of Nine
is there as well.

                                    DOCTOR
                  Yes, Captain . . .

                                    JANEWAY
                  We need help . . .

                                    DOCTOR
                  What's happened? I'm being innundated with calls!

                                    JANEWAY
                                   (weakly)
                  Hurry . . .

The Doctor gives Seven of Nine an instrument.

> DOCTOR
> Go to the Bridge. Use the dermal regenerator to treat
> the burns.

She nods and EXITS with the dermal regenerator.

8   ANGLE ON TOM   8

as he forces himself to try to crawl toward the conn, but each inch causes
him agony. He takes a deep breath, tries to clear his eyes. His face is
drenched in perspiration.

9   ANGLE ON TUVOK   9

who is also in pain, jaw clenched, perspiring, moving forward step by
painful step. He finally reaches the conn and collapses in the seat, and
enters instructions.

> TUVOK
> (with difficulty)
> Course laid in . . .

Then he bends over the conn, suffering.

10   TOWARD THE REAR   10

The N.D. who covered his face is writhing on the deck. Finally, he shudders
and lies still.

11   ANGLE ON JANEWAY   11

grimly hanging on. Then, gradually, her face relaxes and her eyes clear. She
draws a deep breath, looks up. Every else seems to feel a little better, too.
She manages to get to her feet, heads toward the collapsed N.D..

Harry has raised himself up, now studies his console.

> KIM
> We're clear of the nebula . . .

People begin standing up, returning to their stations. At that point, the
Turbolift doors OPEN and Seven of Nine comes onto the Bridge, looks
around, sees Janeway approaching the N.D. Seven of Nine joins her and
they roll him over and react.

12   THE N.D.—THEIR POV   12

Hideous burns cover his face.

13   BACK TO SCENE   13

Seven of Nine feels for his arterial pulse, looks up.

> SEVEN OF NINE
> He's dead.

And off the solemn moment . . .

14   INT. ASTROMETRICS LAB (OPTICAL)   14

Janeway and Seven of Nine stare at the dome, which displays a graphic
showing a representation of a tiny, dwarfed Voyager beside a nebula so vast
its borders are past the edges of the screen.

> SEVEN OF NINE
> The nebula extends for at least one hundred and ten
> light years. Possibly more.

> JANEWAY
> At the least, it would take us well over a month to get
> through it and more than a year to go around.

> SEVEN OF NINE
> The crew was unable to tolerate the nebula for even a
> few minutes. They would certainly not survive a
> month.

Janeway takes this in. Then—

> JANEWAY
> We've come fifteen thousand light years. We haven't
> been stopped by temporal anomalies, warp core
> breaches, or hostile aliens. I'm damned if I'm going to
> be stopped by a nebula.

Seven of Nine acknowledges her determination. She heads for the door.

> JANEWAY
> I'll be in Sickbay.

And she EXITS.

15   INT. MED LAB   15

The Doctor and Janeway.

> DOCTOR
> I've analyzed a sample of the gases from the nebula.
> I think the damage came from subnucleonic
> radiation . . . even the briefest exposure is devastating
> to organic tissue.

> JANEWAY
> Can you give us any protection against the effects?

> DOCTOR
> Yes.

Janeway waits expectantly.

> DOCTOR
> Stasis chambers. Independent life support for each
> unit.

She gives him a questioning look.

> JANEWAY
> Are you suggesting . . . that the entire crew be put in
> suspended animation?

> DOCTOR
> Yes. I, of course, would stay on line in order to
> monitor everyone.

Janeway considers the monumental implications of his suggestion.

> JANEWAY
> It's a drastic step . . . are there any other options?
> Adjusting the shields? Inoculations?

> DOCTOR
> I assure you I've considered all possibilities. This is
> the only way.

> JANEWAY
> There's more to getting through the nebula than
> monitoring the crew . . . who would regulate ship's
> systems? Make course corrections?

> DOCTOR
> (a bit stung)
> I think I've demonstrated that I have a command of
> the rudimentary aspects of piloting . . .

> JANEWAY
> Of course you have. And I know you could do it . . .
> (beat)
> But you need back-up. We have no idea what effect
> the nebular radiation might have on your holomatrix.
> What if you went off-line?

The Doctor ponders the situation.

> DOCTOR
> There was only one crewmember besides myself who
> seemed unaffected by the nebula . . .

And Janeway realizes who that is. It isn't the best choice in the world.

16   INT. CARGO BAY   16

Janeway with Seven of Nine.

> JANEWAY
> I want you to understand the seriousness of this
> responsibility. The lives of the entire crew will be on
> your shoulders.

> SEVEN OF NINE
> You doubt my ability to fulfill this task.

> JANEWAY
> Ordinarily, not at all. But this is an unusual situation.

Seven of Nine looks at her quizzically.

> JANEWAY
> After being in the Collective, it wasn't easy for you to
> adjust to a ship with only a hundred and fifty people
> on it. How would you feel with only the Doctor for
> company?

> SEVEN OF NINE
> I will adapt.

But Janeway still seems concerned.

> JANEWAY
> Most humans don't react particularly well to long
> periods of isolation. Borg Drones have even more
> difficulty.

Seven of Nine regards Janeway with her customary cool.

> SEVEN OF NINE
> As you've pointed out, I am neither Borg nor human.
> I can do this, Captain.

Janeway detects the note of pride in her voice—Seven of Nine <u>wants</u> to do
this, and to do a good job.

> JANEWAY
> All right. I'll work with the senior staff to draw up a
> list of duties.

She pauses, thinks it's necessary to add one more point.

> JANEWAY
> Let me make it clear that the Doctor will be in
> command. You're to follow his instructions as you
> would mine.

Seven hesitates.

> SEVEN OF NINE
> Follow the orders . . . of a hologram?

> JANEWAY
> (firmly)
> He's our Chief Medical Officer and he's thoroughly
> grounded in Starfleet protocols. You will report to
> him.

It takes Seven a second, but finally she acquiesces.

> SEVEN OF NINE
> I understand.

And off her always imperturbable gaze . . .

16A   INT. BRIEFING ROOM   16A

Janeway, Chakotay, Paris, Kim and Torres discuss the upcoming situation.

> CHAKOTAY
> The Doctor is preparing the stasis units now. We
> should be ready by seventeen hundred hours.

Paris seems uneasy with the whole idea.

> PARIS
> And . . . how long will this be for?

> JANEWAY
> We don't know for certain. At least a month. Maybe
> longer, if the nebula is larger than we estimate.

> TORRES
> I've never been in stasis. Are there any—side effects?

> JANEWAY
> The Doctor assures me it'll be just like taking a nap.
> We'll go into the units . . . our cardiopulmonary
> systems will be slowed . . . neural activity
> suspended . . . and we'll wake up feeling as though
> we'd had a good night's sleep.

In spite of these assurances, it's clear that the crew feels uneasy about this
prospect.

> KIM
> There are things that can go wrong . . . at least, that's
> what I've read.

> JANEWAY
> We'll have the Doctor and Seven monitoring us.
> They'll be checking our vital signs four times a day,
> taking care of any problems.

> PARIS
> I assume we've explored all the alternatives . . .

Janeway decides to confront the collective discomfort head on.

> JANEWAY
> I know you're all feeling uneasy about this. I'd be
> lying if I said I don't have concerns myself.
>   (beat)

I think it has to do with the loss of control. We all feel better if we think we're in charge of our circumstances. In stasis, we give up that control.
(beat)
No Starfleet officer likes doing that.

She looks around the room.

                    JANEWAY
Crews have been in stasis for much longer than a month. I think we can handle this.

No response. As positively as possible:

                    JANEWAY
All right. You're free until seventeen hundred hours. I'll make a ship-wide announcement when the Doctor's ready.
                    (beat)
Dismissed.

The others rise to go, but Chakotay waits. When they're gone . . .

                    JANEWAY
Something else?

                    CHAKOTAY
I want you to tell me . . . that this isn't a mistake.

She regards him quizzically.

                    JANEWAY
Your turn to get reassurance?

                    CHAKOTAY
Maybe. But my concern isn't about going into stasis . . .

He hesitates, not sure how to say this.

                    CHAKOTAY
It's about . . . who you're leaving in charge.

                    JANEWAY
You're worried about Seven.

>   CHAKOTAY
> Maybe you need to step outside yourself for a
> minute . . . look at the fact that here's someone who's
> butted horns with you from the moment she came on
> board . . . who disregards authority . . . and actively
> disobeys orders when she doesn't agree with them . . .

She gives him a long look, finishes the thought.

>   JANEWAY
> And this is the person I'm giving responsibility for the
> lives of the entire crew.

An ironic smile.

>   JANEWAY
> I suppose you want me to tell you I'm not crazy.

>   CHAKOTAY
> In a nutshell.
>   (beat)
> I know your bond with Seven is unique . . . different
> from everyone else's. From the beginning, you've
> seen things in her that no one else could.
>   (beat)
> But maybe you could help me understand some of
> those things.

She absorbs this, considering what he's said.

>   JANEWAY
> I don't know if I can. It's just instinct. There's
> something inside me that says she can be redeemed.
> In spite of her insolent attitude, I honestly think she
> wants to do well by us.

He considers, then acknowledges.

>   CHAKOTAY
> That's good enough for me.

She smiles, grateful for his support.

>   JANEWAY
> See you at seventeen hundred hours.

He turns and EXITS, leaving her to ponder her decision.

17   INT. STASIS ROOM   17

(NOTE: This is the Cargo Bay redressed.) Seven of Nine and the Doctor with
Janeway, Paris and Kim. In the room are a number of stasis containers (as
seen in "Resolutions"). Some already contain crewmembers. The Doctor is
wearing his mobile emitter.

> PARIS
> If I have to take a nap for a month, I'd rather do it in
> my own quarters.

> DOCTOR
> Everyone's being relocated here to Deck Fourteen.
> That will make it easier for us to monitor you. Hop
> in.

Harry climbs into his container, but Tom stands there, looking dubious.

> KIM
> Come on, Tom. Sleepy time.

But Tom doesn't move. Clearly he's uneasy.

> PARIS
> What if we had to get out in a hurry?

> JANEWAY
> You can unlock the unit from inside.

But Tom isn't particularly comforted, still hesitates.

> DOCTOR
> Do I detect a note of claustrophobia, Lieutenant?

Tom reluctantly climbs in.

> PARIS
> Did they have to design these things like <u>coffins</u>?

> KIM
> Should we replicate you a pillow?

Tom shoots him a look, and the Doctor prepares to close the hatch.

DOCTOR

Sleep tight.

He and Seven of Nine close both containers. Then they move with Janeway to another stasis unit.

DOCTOR

Please have no worries, Captain. You'll close your eyes and the next thing you know I'll be standing over you, telling you we're through the nebula.

Janeway climbs into her unit.

JANEWAY

I'm leaving the ship in good hands. I have every confidence in both of you.

She settles back.

JANEWAY

See you in a month.

The Doctor and Seven of Nine close the unit; he makes a few adjustments at the console. Then, looking around the room—

DOCTOR

Well—it's just the two of us now.

18   ANOTHER ANGLE (OPTICAL)   18

The room, optically enhanced, is vast, and filled with containers. Seven of Nine and the Doctor are two small figures at one end of the room, dwarfed by the long lines of stasis containers.

FADE OUT.

END OF ACT ONE

ACT TWO

FADE IN:

19   EXT. SPACE—VOYAGER (OPTICAL)   19

moving through the nebula.

> SEVEN OF NINE (V.O.)
> Personal Log, Seven of Nine, Stardate 51929.3. This is
> the tenth day of our journey through the Mutara
> nebula. I have created an efficient daily routine.

20   INT. CORRIDOR   20

Seven of Nine walking the corridor. The only SOUND heard is the ambient
HUM of Voyager's systems. She reaches the doors to the Mess Hall, which
open.

21   INT. MESS HALL (OPTICAL)   21

avoiding the windows. The room is deserted and at a low light level. Seven
of Nine moves to a replicator.

> SEVEN OF NINE
> Nutritional supplement fourteen-beta-seven.

The replicator provides a glass of beverage. Seven of Nine takes it and
crosses to one of the tables.

She sits in the empty room and sips at her nourishment.

                                              TIME CUT TO:

22   INT. ENGINEERING   22

Completely empty, a strange contrast to its usually bustling nature. Seven of
Nine ENTERS and walks to the console at the railing around the core, works
controls. She checks several other monitors. Then she turns and EXITS
briskly.

23   INT. BRIDGE   23

Seven of Nine ENTERS from the Turbolift and goes to the conn, sees
something she doesn't like.

SEVEN OF NINE
Computer, adjust heading by point three-four-seven
degrees starboard.

COMPUTER VOICE
Course adjusted.

24   INT. CORRIDOR   24

as Seven of Nine walks. Then she stops, seeing something just ahead.

25   OPEN DOOR—HER POV   25

Doors are open just ahead of her, and on the deck she sees an arm jutting
out from the room.

26   RESUME SCENE   26

She hurries forward, tapping her combadge as she does. Reveal Tom Paris
sprawled on the deck, unconscious.

SEVEN OF NINE
Seven of Nine to the Doctor.

INTERCUT:

27   INT. SICKBAY   27

DOCTOR
Go ahead.

SEVEN OF NINE
Lieutenant Paris has left his stasis unit. He's
unconscious.

DOCTOR
I'll be right there.

TIME CUT TO:

28   INT. STASIS ROOM   28

Seven of Nine and the Doctor have just finished loading Tom back into his
container and are closing the lid. The Doctor is wearing his mobile emitter.

> DOCTOR
> Apparently he's more claustrophobic than I thought.
> But he doesn't seem to have suffered any ill effects.

He makes an adjustment to the controls.

> SEVEN OF NINE
> Is this likely to happen again?

> DOCTOR
> It's not unheard of for people to come out of stasis
> and start wandering.
>   (beat)
> Leave it to Mister Paris to be just as much trouble
> now as when he's awake.

> SEVEN OF NINE
> You knew this might happen. Why complain about it?

And now we sense that these two are beginning to get on one another's
nerves. As they make adjustments to the controls . . .

> DOCTOR
> If you had even the slightest sense of humor, you'd
> realize I was making a small joke.

> SEVEN OF NINE
> Very small.

He shoots her a glance, annoyed.

> DOCTOR
> Give me his vital signs, please.

> SEVEN OF NINE
> Pulse, forty-two. Body temperature, ninety-seven-
> point-six. Blood pressure one hundred over fifty.

> DOCTOR
> Good.

> SEVEN OF NINE
> I'll continue on my rounds.

> DOCTOR
> I think not. We're paying a visit to the Holodeck.

SEVEN OF NINE
I have no time for frivolous pursuits.

DOCTOR
It's not frivolous—it's essential.

She looks at him, questioning.

DOCTOR
You've been getting more irritable and short-tempered
with each passing day.

SEVEN OF NINE
So have you.

DOCTOR
Only because I'm having to put up with you. You
need a little brush-up course in getting along with
people.

SEVEN OF NINE
(puzzled)
There's no one here to get along with.

DOCTOR
I'm here.
(beat)
This isn't a suggestion and it's not a request. It's an
order.

She gives him an icy look, but acquiesces. She turns on her heel and EXITS;
he follows.

29   INT. MESS HALL (OPTICAL)   29

As before, crowded with people in a festive mood. The Doctor is momentarily chatting with Janeway and Chakotay. Seven of Nine stands to one side,
sullenly alone, working at a PADD, ignoring the others. NEELIX approaches her.

NEELIX
Join the party, Seven. It's no fun to stand here by
yourself.

SEVEN OF NINE
I have no desire to "have fun."

> NEELIX
> (puzzled)

No?

> SEVEN OF NINE
> I am attempting to recalibrate the warp field in order
> to resist the nebula's radiation.

She eyes Neelix briefly, then gets an idea which will turn the Doctor's order to her own ends.

> SEVEN OF NINE
> I believe you have some knowledge of warp field
> theory.
> (beat)
> Perhaps you can help me.

She has purposely tapped into Neelix' desire to be useful. He takes her PADD, peers at it.

> NEELIX
> I'd be happy to give it a try.
> (reads)
> Let's see . . . the subspace field matrix looks right . . .
> Hmmm . . .

Janeway approaches.

> SEVEN OF NINE
> Captain . . . perhaps you could help as well. We are
> attempting to find a stronger warp field calibration.

Janeway is immediately intrigued. The Doctor is watching in the background.

> JANEWAY
> Interesting. Maybe if you vary the EM stress
> parameters, the warp field dynamic would increase.

> NEELIX
> Excellent idea, Captain. And if the warp coils were re-
> phased, it would increase power to the nacelles.

> SEVEN OF NINE
> There is an additional problem. We must compensate
> for a subspace induction drag on the engines . . .

> DOCTOR
>
> Computer, freeze program.

The figures FREEZE and the Doctor grabs Seven of Nine's arm, pulls her away.

> DOCTOR
>
> You're completely missing the point of this exercise. You're supposed to be mixing and mingling—not working on Engineering problems.

> SEVEN OF NINE
>
> You ordered me to participate in this program. You did not specify the topic of conversation.

The Doctor is definitely getting irritated. The nature of their conflict escalates during the next.

> DOCTOR
>
> You're splitting hairs. You know very well what purpose this program is supposed to serve.

> SEVEN OF NINE
>
> I find that it serves no purpose whatsoever.

> DOCTOR
>
> You're being intentionally perverse.

> SEVEN OF NINE
>
> Holodecks are a pointless endeavor, fulfilling some human need to fantasize. I have no such need.

> DOCTOR
>
> What you <u>need</u> is a means of curbing that tongue of yours. I don't want to put up with your crankiness for the next month.

> SEVEN OF NINE
>
> We can arrange to avoid each other.

> DOCTOR
>
> I wish it were that simple. Unfortunately, you have to report to me four times a day to keep me informed about the crew.

SEVEN OF NINE
We can minimize those reports—

But before she can finish, the ship TREMBLES. They react.

COMPUTER VOICE
Warning. Emergency procedures in effect.

DOCTOR
(alarmed)
Computer, what is the nature of the emergency?

COMPUTER VOICE
The antimatter storage tanks are failing.

This is a crisis. Seven of Nine and the Doctor rush out.

30   INT. CORRIDOR   30

Seven of Nine accesses a wall panel.

SEVEN OF NINE
A cascade effect is in progress. The warp field coils
are compromised . . . primary deuterium tank is
rupturing . . . plasma conduits are ready to breach.

DOCTOR
This is awful!

SEVEN OF NINE
We have to eject the antimatter tanks.

DOCTOR
We've got to coordinate the effort. You go to
Engineering, I'll go to the Bridge.

She nods and they hurry off in opposite directions.

31   INT. BRIDGE   31

as the Doctor runs in and goes to an aft Engineering station. He quickly
pushes controls, looks stricken.

DOCTOR
Doctor to Seven . . .

32   INT. CORRIDOR   32

as Seven of Nine hurries toward Engineering.

> SEVEN OF NINE
> Yes, Doctor?

> DOCTOR
> It's worse than we thought. Engineering is flooded
> with plasma. You'll never get in.

> SEVEN OF NINE
> I believe I can survive long enough to eject the
> assembly.

> DOCTOR
> It's too late. Sensors show plasma conduits rupturing
> on Decks Seven and Thirteen . . .

Seven of Nine is near the doors to Engineering.

> SEVEN OF NINE
> I can do it.

> DOCTOR
> (reacting to something on sensors)
> Seven—there's been another plasma discharge in
> Engineering! The hull is breaching! Get out of there!

But Seven of Nine is at the doors, which slide open. She reacts in surprise.

33   INT. ENGINEERING—HER POV   33

It is pristine. No gas, no explosions. The warp core churns comfortingly.

> DOCTOR
> Seven? Do you hear me?

> SEVEN OF NINE
> It's all right, Doctor.
> (beat)
> False alarm.

And off the mystery . . .

FADE OUT.

<u>END OF ACT TWO</u>

ACT THREE

FADE IN:

34   INT. ENGINEERING (VPB)   34

The Doctor is now there, wearing his emitter, and has called up an Okudagram of the neural gel-pack schematic. They are both studying it.

> DOCTOR
> I think I've found the problem.
> (beat)
> There are malfunctions in a number of neural gel-packs. As a result, false readings were fed to the sensors which detected an emergency where there was none.

> SEVEN OF NINE
> We must repair them.

> DOCTOR
> They seem to be in sequence six-theta-nine. We'll need replacement packs and a repair kit.

Seven of Nine collects an Engineering kit and another which contains the gel-packs. They move to the Jefferies Tube and ENTER.

35   INT. JEFFERIES TUBE—HORIZONTAL   35

Seven of Nine and the Doctor crawling. The Doctor doesn't enjoy this.

> DOCTOR
> These tubes certainly weren't designed with creature comfort in mind. It seems to me the shipbuilders should've created a space in which one can walk upright.

> SEVEN OF NINE
> But they didn't. And it doesn't help to complain about it now.

> DOCTOR
> I'll complain if I want to. It's comforting.

SEVEN OF NINE
(ignoring him)
We can access sequence six-theta-nine from there.

They stop at a panel and open it.

36   ANGLE ON GEL-PACK (OPTICAL)   36

They see one of the packs, clearly damaged. The Doctor takes a tricorder
from the Engineering kit and scans.

DOCTOR
Odd . . . I've never seen this kind of neural activity in
the gel-packs . . .

SEVEN OF NINE
In what sense?

DOCTOR
The neurodes are discharging in random bursts . . .
(beat)
I would imagine the nebular radiation is causing it. I
want to take this pack to Sickbay for further study.

SEVEN OF NINE
I'll reroute the command processor to bypass this
series.

Seven of Nine begins working controls.

DOCTOR
This journey certainly hasn't lacked for excitement. I
can't complain about being bored.

SEVEN OF NINE
But since you find it comforting, you'll undoubtedly
find something else to complain about.

The Doctor isn't offended by this, and smiles slightly.

DOCTOR
Undoubtedly. You really should try it—

But suddenly the Doctor FRITZES. Seven of Nine looks quickly back at him.

                          SEVEN OF NINE
What's happening?

He FRITZES again.

                             DOCTOR
My program is degrading . . .

                          SEVEN OF NINE
The mobile emitter?

                             DOCTOR
I don't know. I have to get back to Sickbay!

Seven of Nine has finished the replacement. She puts the damaged pack into
the kit and they begin crawling headlong out of the tube.

                             DOCTOR
    Hurry!

                          SEVEN OF NINE
I am hurrying.

                             DOCTOR
If the mobile emitter goes off-line while I'm out of
Sickbay, my program may be irretrievable!

                          SEVEN OF NINE
Don't panic. It's counterproductive.

                             DOCTOR
That's easy for you to say—you're not in danger of
being decompiled!

They reach the end of the Jefferies Tube and EXIT.

37   INT. JEFFERIES TUBE—VERTICAL (OPTICAL)   37

as they emerge into the vertical tube and the Doctor stands, he FRITZES
again—this time very badly.

                          SEVEN OF NINE
    Doctor . . .

Finally he stabilizes.

                              DOCTOR
                   If that happens again, I'll be gone!

They race out the door.

38   INT. CORRIDOR   38

The two of them running toward the Sickbay doors, which OPEN; they dash in.

39   INT. SICKBAY   39

The Doctor, gasping with anxiety, draws deep breaths. Then he straightens
up, realizing he's safe.

                              DOCTOR
                   Home sweet Sickbay . . . I never thought I'd be so
                   glad to see these walls . . .

                          SEVEN OF NINE
                   Give me the emitter.

He takes it off and she picks up a tool and begins tinkering with it.

                          SEVEN OF NINE
                   The electo-optic modulator is damaged.

He takes it from her and inspects it.

                              DOCTOR
                   You're right. It's as good as useless . . .

He looks at her, realization sinking in.

                              DOCTOR
                   There's no way I can risk using it now.
                              (beat)
                   I'm stuck here.

                          SEVEN OF NINE
                   The nebula is having a deleterious effect on all the
                   ship's technology.

                              DOCTOR
                   And we still have weeks to go . . .

He looks at her, assessing their situation.

> DOCTOR
> It's up to you to keep the ship running. We can't
> afford to break down in the middle of this nebula.

Seven of Nine hesitates. For the first time, we see a glimmer of doubt, of uncertainly, pass over her. But she finally lifts her chin with determination.

> SEVEN OF NINE
> I won't disappoint you.

And off their worsening plight . . .

                                                            FADE TO BLACK.

FADE IN:

40   CLOSE ON SEVEN OF NINE (OPTICAL)   40

She is turning slowly, against a white background. Gradually the camera pulls back and up . . . revealing a barren, icy environment . . . the snow-swept tundra . . . the top of a glacier . . . desolate. Seven of Nine is the only living thing visible. Camera pulls back until she is a tiny speck in the frozen wasteland.

> COMPUTER VOICE
> Oh-six-hundred hours. Regeneration sequence
> complete.

41   INT. CARGO BAY—CLOSE ON SEVEN   41

eyes opening in response to the computer voice.

She moves out of the alcove and proceeds to the console where she activates the recording device.

> SEVEN OF NINE
> Personal Log, Seven of Nine, Stardate 51932.4. The
> twenty-ninth day in the Mutara-class nebula.
>   (beat)
> I believe I'm beginning to feel the effects of this
> prolonged isolation. My dreams have been disturbing.
> But I'm determined to fulfill my responsibilities.
>   (beat)
> With the Doctor confined to Sickbay, I have taken on
> increasing responsibilities. Ship's systems are

beginning to require constant maintenance in order to
avert disaster. This morning I must purge the
auxiliary plasma vents.

                    (beat)
End log.

42   INT. BRIDGE   42

as Seven of Nine goes to the conn, inspects the readouts.

                    SEVEN OF NINE
Computer, trim heading by point-three-one degrees
port.

No response.

                    SEVEN OF NINE
Computer, respond.

Nothing.

                    SEVEN OF NINE
Computer, trim heading by point-three-one degrees
port.

Now, finally, the computer voice responds, but cuts out intermittently as
though there's a power problem.

                    COMPUTER VOICE
Attempting to make correction . . . stand by . . .
attempting to make correction . . .

A moment of static CRACKLE, then—

                    COMPUTER VOICE
Unable to comply.

                    SEVEN OF NINE
Manual override.

She enters the course correction in the conn, then moves toward the
Turbolift. As she goes . . .

                    SEVEN OF NINE
Computer, initiate a level-four diagnostic of your
command processors.

There's a beat, then—

                    COMPUTER VOICE
Diagnostic in progress.

43   INT. TURBOLIFT   43

                    SEVEN OF NINE
Astrometrics.

                    COMPUTER VOICE
Diagnostic complete.

                    SEVEN OF NINE
Analyze.

The computer voice is still cutting out.

                    COMPUTER VOICE
Quantum failures are present in thirty-three percent of
gel-pack relays.

                    SEVEN OF NINE
Reroute all functional relays through subprocessor chi-
one-four.

Now the voice is normal again.

                    COMPUTER VOICE
Rerouting complete. Relay failures bypassed.

44   INT. ASTROMETRICS LAB (OPTICAL)   44

Seven of Nine ENTERS, goes to her console.

                    SEVEN OF NINE
Display Voyager's current position within the nebula.

She views the display, which now shows Voyager about two-thirds of the
way through.

                    SEVEN OF NINE
How long to complete passage through the nebula?

                    COMPUTER VOICE
Six days, five hours.

There is a long beat as Seven of Nine stares up at the image of tiny Voyager, so near and yet so far.

                         SEVEN OF NINE
          Six days.

Finally, she EXITS.

45   INT. CORRIDOR   45

as she walks along. The corridor seems a little darker . . . shadows play on the bulkheads. Seven of Nine seems anxious, preoccupied. Then she hears—

                         PARIS' VOICE
          Seven . . . help . . .

She looks down the darkened corridor and sees—

46   TOM PARIS   46

disappearing around a corner. She follows.

She rounds the corner and doesn't see Tom. She moves to the doors of the Stasis Room, and they open.

47   INT. STASIS ROOM   47

as she ENTERS. She looks around . . . doesn't see Tom.

                         SEVEN OF NINE
          Lieutenant . . .?

Then she moves to his container and looks in.

48   PARIS—HER POV   48

still in stasis, sleeping deeply.

She looks around the room, and feels chilled suddenly. Then—

                         COMPUTER VOICE
          Proximity Alert. Vessel approaching.

This is surprising.

> COMPUTER VOICE
The vessel is hailing.

> SEVEN OF NINE
Open a channel.

As she talks, Seven of Nine moves to the door and EXITS.

49   INT. CORRIDOR   49

She continues the conversation as she walks the corridor.

> COMPUTER VOICE
Channel open.

> SEVEN OF NINE
This is the Federation Starship Voyager. State your
identity.

> TRAJIS' VOICE
I'm Trajis Lo-Tarik. I'm trying to get through this
nebula and I'm in need of a microfusion chamber.
Would you consider a trade?

> SEVEN OF NINE
Why are you in this nebula?

> TRAJIS' VOICE
Trying to get through it, as I imagine you are.

She considers, then—

> SEVEN OF NINE
Do you have liquid helium?

> TRAJIS' VOICE
You're fortunate. I have an ample supply.

> SEVEN OF NINE
I'll beam you directly to our Cargo Bay.

> TRAJIS' VOICE
I look forward to it.

Seven of Nine rounds a corner.

Seven of Nine with TRAJIS, a creepy-looking alien with a ferret-like face.
She is going through cargo containers, looking for the microfusion chamber.

> TRAJIS
>
> Seven of Nine . . . that's an unusual name. How did
> you get it?

> SEVEN OF NINE
>
> It was my Borg designation.

> TRAJIS
>
> Borg? Never heard of them.

She doesn't reply. He tries another tack.

> TRAJIS
>
> Are you alone on this ship?

> SEVEN OF NINE
>
> No. The entire crew is here, in stasis. And our Doctor
> is in Sickbay.

> TRAJIS
>
> I'm both pilot and crew on my ship. Fortunately, I'm
> resistant to the effects of the nebula.

> SEVEN OF NINE
>
> What about your technology? The radiation is causing
> damage to ours.

> TRAJIS
>
> I've had to rebuild my engines twice already. If
> you've been in the nebula for three weeks—you're
> doing well.

> SEVEN OF NINE
>
> I am hopeful that our propulsion system will remain
> operative for the next six days.

> TRAJIS
>
> I'll admit I was surprised to find another ship heading
> toward me. No one has ever managed to cross the
> nebula.

SEVEN OF NINE
If it weren't necessary, we wouldn't be attempting it.

TRAJIS
I'm here by choice. I'm determined to be the first to get through. I've failed five times before . . . but this time I'm sure I'll make it. I want to see what's on the other side.

SEVEN OF NINE
There is nothing remarkable.

TRAJIS
But I'll be the first of my kind to see it.
(beat)
Tell me . . . how are you handling the loneliness?

She gives him a glance.

SEVEN OF NINE
What do you mean?

TRAJIS
You know what I mean. No matter what you say— you're alone here.

Seven of Nine doesn't answer. She withdraws a device from the container.

SEVEN OF NINE
The microfusion chamber you requested.

Trajis takes it and inspects it, then looks back at Seven of Nine.

TRAJIS
I've heard that Drones can't stand to be alone. They're too used to the Collective.

She gives him a curious look.

SEVEN OF NINE
How could you know that?

TRAJIS
It's true, isn't it?

SEVEN OF NINE
You said you'd never heard of the Borg.

TRAJIS
Don't take offense. I've got no grudge with them.

Seven of Nine eyes him, suspicious.

SEVEN OF NINE
You have what you asked for. Now leave.

Trajis seems dismayed.

TRAJIS
I thought we could keep each other company for a
while . . . maybe have something to eat . . .

SEVEN OF NINE
No.

TRAJIS
And if I want to stay longer?

Seven of Nine pulls a phaser from the container.

SEVEN OF NINE
You will not be accommodated.

He lifts his arms slightly, in acquiescence. She gestures him out of the Cargo
Bay.

51   INT. CORRIDOR   51

Seven of Nine keeps the phaser trained on Trajis as they walk along. He is
carrying the microfusion chamber.

TRAJIS
There's no need for this, you know. I don't mean you
any harm.

She doesn't answer.

TRAJIS
I think maybe you're a little paranoid . . . that's what
loneliness can do to you.

No reply.

> TRAJIS
> You'd be a lot better off if you spent some time with
> me . . . we could get to know each other . . .

> SEVEN OF NINE
> Quiet.

Seven of Nine is stoic, keeps walking. Then—

> PARIS' VOICE
> Seven . . . help me . . . help . . . Seven . . .

Her head snaps around in the direction of the call; she's thoroughly
distracted. Then she turns around—and Trajis isn't there. She starts after
him, rounds a corner.

52   DOWN THE CORRIDOR—HER POV   52

She sees Trajis scuttling around the corner at the far end of the corridor.
He's gone.

53   BACK TO SEVEN OF NINE   53

She hits her combadge. Grimly—

> SEVEN OF NINE
> Seven of Nine to the Doctor. We have an intruder on
> board.

                                                          FADE OUT.

<u>END OF ACT THREE</u>

ACT FOUR

FADE IN:

INT. SICKBAY

as Seven of Nine and the Doctor confer over this newest calamity. They are
working at the free-standing console.

> **DOCTOR**
> He must have a cloaking device. Sensors show no
> alien lifesigns . . . and no evidence of a ship.

They ponder the situation.

> **DOCTOR**
> I've been working on my mobile emitter. I think I'm
> making progress, but I still can't leave Sickbay.
> (beat)
> You'll have to try to track him down. Arm yourself
> and use extreme caution.

The computer voice interrupts, and it is distorted, electronically SLOWED.

> **COMPUTER VOICE**
> Warning. Deuterium tank levels are fluctuating
> beyond acceptable tolerances.

> **DOCTOR**
> The computer sounds like it needs a stimulant.

> **SEVEN OF NINE**
> It's been experiencing relay failures. I haven't been
> performing my maintenance duties.

> **DOCTOR**
> Do what you have to, but keep your eye out for the
> alien. We have to assume he's up to no good.

Seven of Nine acknowledges, but is clearly troubled. The Doctor sees this.

> **DOCTOR**
> (gently)
> Seven . . . are you frightened?

There is a brief moment where Seven of Nine might admit this: she's unnerved by the voices and apparitions she's experienced.

But once again, she summons her strength.

> SEVEN OF NINE
> I am Borg.

He gives her an encouraging smile.

55   INT. CORRIDOR   55

Seven of Nine on the prowl, armed with a phaser rifle. The corridors seem more sinister now: shadows flicker on the walls . . . faint thumps and bumps are heard—each of them producing a reaction in Seven of Nine, who stops, turns, raises the rifle, expecting to see the alien.

56   ANOTHER ANGLE   56

Ahead, there is only darkness.

> SEVEN OF NINE
> Who's there?

No answer. Seven of Nine lowers the rifle. Then she hears a voice . . . faint, whispery, unreal . . . but it's unmistakably Trajis'.

> TRAJIS
> Seven . . . help me . . . Seven . . .

She turns in the corridor as though to locate the voice, but there's nothing. Steeling herself, she continues to walk.

57   ANOTHER CORRIDOR   57

as she approaches the stasis room. As she gets nearer, she hears a voice . . . then another is added . . . then another, until it's a chorus, a cacophony.

> PARIS
> Seven . . . help me . . .

> KIM
> Help, Seven . . . I need help . . .

> CHAKOTAY
> We need you, Seven . . .

> TUVOK

Assist us . . .

> NEELIX

I'm dying, Seven . . . don't let me die . . .

> JANEWAY

The lives of the crew are on your shoulders . . .

This chorus of ghostly voices is a thundering roar in her ears by the time she reaches the stasis room. The doors slide open and she looks in.

58   INT. STASIS ROOM—HER POV   58

Suddenly, there is silence. The comatose crew sleeps peacefully in their strange sarcophagi. There are no voices calling for help. Seven of Nine finds herself breathing deeply. Is that fear?

Seven of Nine moves into the room, checks readings. She constantly looks behind her, around her, as though expecting someone to jump out at her.

Then, having done what she had to, she EXITS.

59   INT. CORRIDOR   59

as she resumes her rounds. Then, cutting through the silence like a fierce Klaxon, the voice of Trajis on the com.

> TRAJIS' COM VOICE

Trajis to Seven of Nine . . . that's an unusual name.
How did you get it?

Seven of Nine doesn't answer.

> TRAJIS' COM VOICE

Don't want to answer me? That's all right, I don't
mind. I know you're not yourself today.

Seven of Nine marches stoically ahead.

> TRAJIS' COM VOICE

But you might be interested in what I'm doing
now . . .

Apparently not.

> TRAJIS' COM VOICE
> I know your sensors can't detect me . . . so if you
> want to know where I am, you'll have to ask.

She doesn't.

> TRAJIS' COM VOICE
> Playing stubborn? That's a mistake, it could lead to an
> unfortunate accident . . .

No answer.

> TRAJIS' COM VOICE
> Just to prove I'm willing to give you a fair chance . . .
> I'll ask you—what would happen if the structural
> integrity around the warp coils collapsed?

Seven of Nine stops dead in her tracks.

> TRAJIS' COM VOICE
> You wouldn't have much time to keep them from
> rupturing . . .

Seven of Nine takes off running.

60   INT. ENGINEERING   60

Seven of Nine dashes in and looks.

61   WARP CORE—HER POV   61

No one there.

62   RESUME   62

She moves to a console, checks controls, looks puzzled.

> TRAJIS' COM VOICE
> I couldn't bring myself to destroy your ship . . .

And with that, the lights go out in Engineering. Only the ghostly blue of the
warp core illuminates the room.

> TRAJIS' COM VOICE
> I hope you're not afraid of the dark . . .

Seven of Nine takes a breath, speaks as calmly as she can.

> SEVEN OF NINE
>
> Where are you?

> TRAJIS' COM VOICE
>
> Finally! I'm glad you're responding. It's going to be
> much more interesting if we play this game together.

> SEVEN OF NINE
> (firm)
>
> Your location.

> TRAJIS' COM VOICE
>
> A long way from you—on the Bridge. Command
> center of your ship, I believe. I can do just about
> anything from here.

Seven of Nine is about to enter a command when a voice from above makes
her stop.

> PARIS' VOICE
>
> Seven . . . help me . . .

Seven of Nine looks up to see—

63   TOM AND HARRY—HER POV   63

collapsed over the railing on the second level, extending their hands to her,
nothing but shadowy forms in the darkness.

64   RESUME SCENE   64

Seven of Nine runs for the ladder and starts climbing.

65   INT. ENGINEERING—UPPER LEVEL (OPTICAL)   65

as she emerges from the ladder, she sees Tom and Harry, sprawled on the
floor, moaning. Suddenly, they burst into FLAME.

She gets an idea, turns to a console. Then she hits her combadge.

> SEVEN OF NINE
>
> Seven to Trajis. Are you still there?

TRAJIS' COM VOICE
Of course. Do you think I'd leave now?

Seven of Nine begins entering commands.

SEVEN OF NINE
I'm enjoying this game. What's next?

TRAJIS' COM VOICE
That's better! Well . . . let's just imagine . . . that one
of the photon torpedoes was activated . . . but not
ejected . . .

SEVEN OF NINE
I'd have to get to the Torpedo Bay quickly.

TRAJIS' COM VOICE
And even then you might be too late. But of course
you have to try . . .

She is still working controls.

SEVEN OF NINE
Let's play another game. Let's imagine . . . that the
oxygen on the Bridge has been depleted.

A hesitation.

TRAJIS' COM VOICE
What?

SEVEN OF NINE
What do you suppose the results might be?

From the com, there's a rasping sound, a wheezing . . . someone trying
desperately to breathe.

SEVEN OF NINE
Computer, seal the Bridge with a level three
forcefield.

COMPUTER VOICE
Bridge sealed.

She waits a moment, hears nothing more. She taps her combadge.

SEVEN OF NINE
Seven of Nine to the Doctor.

INTERCUT:

66   INT. CORRIDOR   66

The Doctor, wearing his mobile emitter, on the move.

DOCTOR
I'm here.

SEVEN OF NINE
I have incapacitated the alien. He will not trouble us
again.

DOCTOR
Good work. I have my mobile emitter back on line.
Where are you now?

SEVEN OF NINE
In Engineering.

DOCTOR
I'll be right there. I have interesting news about the
neural gel-packs.

SEVEN OF NINE
Acknowledged.

She goes back to the ladder and descends.

67   INT. ENGINEERING   67

as Seven of Nine emerges from the top level. She turns to move toward the
doors, and sees—

68   TRAJIS—HER POV   68

standing in Engineering, near the doors, looking smug.

69   ANGLE ON BOTH (OPTICAL)   69

as Seven of Nine stares at him in amazement.

TRAJIS
In your heart, you knew you'd see me again.

Seven of Nine lifts the phaser rifle and fires. It hits him squarely—to no effect. He begins walking slowly toward her.

TRAJIS
You can't defeat me. You're too weak.

SEVEN OF NINE
Don't come closer.

TRAJIS
You couldn't stand being alone, could you? You felt vulnerable . . . afraid.

SEVEN OF NINE
Stop . . .

TRAJIS
Because you know what you are.
(beat)
At first you thought you could become human . . . but now you know that's impossible, don't you?

Seven of Nine stares at him, like a bird watching an advancing serpent, mesmerized.

TRAJIS
You're Borg . . . that's what you were meant to be. One of many.

Now there's a change in the lighting in Engineering . . . instead of the cold blue light of the warp core, a Borg-like green pervades everything. Seven of Nine glances at the warp core.

70   WARP CORE—HER POV (OPTICAL)   70

Now pulsing to a Borg green.

71   BACK TO SCENE   71

Trajis continues to advance.

TRAJIS

But your days of power are gone . . . you're alone
now. Weak. Pathetic.

72   INT. CORRIDOR   72

as the Doctor, wearing his mobile emitter, hurries along. He reaches the
doors to Engineering, which slide open. We hear Seven of Nine's voice.

SEVEN OF NINE'S VOICE

Don't come any closer.

73   INT. ENGINEERING   73

toward the Doctor, standing in the door, looking puzzled.

SEVEN OF NINE'S VOICE

I can kill you with my bare hands.

DOCTOR

Seven . . .?

74   ANGLE TOWARD SEVEN OF NINE   74

She is pointing the phaser rifle toward thin air, talking.

SEVEN OF NINE

And I will if you don't leave . . .

Then she turns around, sees the Doctor.

SEVEN OF NINE

Doctor—be careful. He's dangerous.

The Doctor looks from her to the blank space . . . back again.

DOCTOR

Seven—who are you talking to?

And now we see real fear on Seven of Nine's face. She lowers the rifle,
stares at the Doctor. Then she looks back where Trajis was.

75   HER POV   75

He's gone.

Seven is disoriented, not sure what's happening.

                    SEVEN OF NINE
          Where did he go?

                    DOCTOR
          There's no one here.

                    SEVEN OF NINE
          But he was . . . he was right here . . .

                    DOCTOR
          Seven, you're hallucinating.

                    SEVEN OF NINE
          No . . . I saw him . . .

                    DOCTOR
                    (firm)
          There was no one else in this room.

She stares at him, trying to accommodate this notion . . .

                    SEVEN OF NINE
          You mean . . . I imagined him?

                    DOCTOR
          Yes.

She takes a breath, trying to absorb this.

                    SEVEN OF NINE
          I heard Mister Paris . . . calling for help . . . I saw
          him, and the others . . . was I imagining them as well?

                    DOCTOR
          I believe so.
                    (beat)
          When I studied the gel-pack, I discovered the
          radiation was producing a degradation in the synaptic
          relays.
                    (beat)
          I'm guessing there's been a similar effect on your
          Borg implants.

He glances at her, but she doesn't answer. She isn't even looking at him, but seems thoroughly preoccupied with her own thoughts.

> DOCTOR
> The radiation could be destroying the neurotransmitters in your sensory nodes. That would explain why you're hearing voices . . . seeing hallucinations.

> SEVEN OF NINE
> They seemed real . . .

> DOCTOR
> Hallucinations usually do. That's what makes them so frightening.

She looks up at him for the first time. Makes an admission.

> SEVEN OF NINE
> Once, when I was a Drone . . . I was separated from the Collective for two hours.
> (beat)
> I experienced panic and apprehension.
> (beat)
> I am feeling that way now.

He realizes what an admission this is. He's affected.

> DOCTOR
> I'll do everything I can to help you.

She nods, but doesn't speak.

> DOCTOR
> We'll get you to Sickbay. An antipsychotic might help . . . at least until I determine just what neural functions are being affected . . .

He starts toward the door and she follows—when suddenly there's a huge FLASH in Engineering, and the sound of systems SIZZLING. The Doctor stops.

> SEVEN OF NINE
> What was that?

COMPUTER VOICE
Warning. Primary EPS system is overloading.

Now the Doctor FRITZES badly.

DOCTOR
I tied my mobile emitter into the EPS system!

Seven of Nine rushes to a console.

SEVEN OF NINE
Computer, reroute all available power to the EPS system.

The computer voice is still distorted.

COMPUTER VOICE
Unable to comply . . .

DOCTOR
My program's going off-line . . .

SEVEN OF NINE
No—

COMPUTER VOICE
Warning. Primary EPS system is overloading. Secondary systems are failing.

DOCTOR
Seven—you've got to hang on. Repair the EPS system . . . everything depends on you.

SEVEN OF NINE
I'm unable to function alone—

The Doctor FRITZES again.

DOCTOR
You have to! You're the only one who can save us now!

And he DISAPPEARS.

SEVEN OF NINE
No . . .

In a shot which reminds us of her ''dream'' on the tundra, camera LIFTS up, until Seven of Nine is a small figure in Engineering. Utterly alone.

FADE OUT.

<u>END OF ACT FOUR</u>

ACT FIVE

FADE IN:

78   EXT. SPACE—VOYAGER (OPTICAL)   78

still in the nebula.

79   INT. ASTROMETRICS LAB (OPTICAL)   79

Seven of Nine is working controls.

> SEVEN OF NINE
> Display Voyager's current position within the nebula.

> KIM'S VOICE
> It doesn't matter—you won't make it.

She ignores this voice and views the display, which now shows Voyager near the far edge of the nebula.

> SEVEN OF NINE
> Computer, how long until Voyager is out of the nebula?

The computer voice is still slowed down, elongated.

> COMPUTER VOICE
> Seventeen hours, eleven minutes.

80   WIDEN TO INCLUDE KIM   80

He is standing next to her, gazing up at the dome. His hands and face have horrible burns on them.

> KIM
> That's an eternity.

> SEVEN OF NINE
> Go away . . .

> KIM
> You can try to shut me out, but it won't work.

COMPUTER VOICE
Warning. Propulsion system failure in progress.

Seven of Nine turns and walks out.

81   INT. CORRIDOR   81

The corridor, like Engineering, has a faintly green hue. It's dark and smoky, and shadows play on the walls. Gradually, a chorus of voices is heard, moaning, crying . . . souls in torment.

Then a BORG DRONE steps out in front of her.

BORG DRONE
Seven of Nine, Tertiary Adjunct of Unimatrix Zero
One.

She stares at him.

BORG DRONE
You have left the Collective.

She turns and walks away from him, but he follows, inexorable.

BORG DRONE
It was a foolish decision. Now you are alone.

She walks a bit faster. He keeps pace.

BORG DRONE
You have lost the many. You are only one.

She tries to shut out the sound of his voice.

BORG DRONE
You have become human. Weak. Pathetic.

He lets this sink in.

BORG DRONE
Humans do not have our strength. They are imperfect.
Now you are imperfect as well.

SEVEN OF NINE
No . . .

BORG DRONE
You will not survive. You cannot survive without the
Collective.

SEVEN OF NINE
I will adapt . . .

BORG DRONE
By becoming weaker. Less perfect.

Seven now begins mouthing a "mantra" to herself, trying to keep a grip on
reality.

SEVEN OF NINE
I will adapt as an individual.

BORG DRONE
One. One alone. A Borg cannot be one.

SEVEN OF NINE
I will become stronger . . .

BORG DRONE
A Borg cannot be one. She will die.

Seven is heading for a Turbolift. The Borg is right behind her.

BORG DRONE
Weak . . . detached . . . isolated . . . one Borg cannot
survive. A Borg needs the strength of the Collective.

SEVEN OF NINE
(overlapping)
I am an individual . . . I will survive alone . . .

The Turbolift door opens and she gets on.

BORG DRONE
No. You are weak.

82   INT. TURBOLIFT   82

as she turns around and faces outward, he is standing just outside.

BORG DRONE
You will die alone.

The doors shut in front of him and Seven of Nine draws a breath.

> TRAJIS' VOICE
> He's right.

She whirls to see him with her in the Turbolift.

> TRAJIS
> You're in pain, Seven. I can help you.

She turns away from him.

> SEVEN OF NINE
> Bridge.

The Turbolift starts up.

> TRAJIS
> You don't have to beg me . . . you don't even have to
> ask. All you have to do is make a choice.

> SEVEN OF NINE
> I can survive . . . alone . . .

The Turbolift stops and the doors open.

83   ANGLE ON DOORS (OPTICAL)   83

Through the doors we see the interior of a vast Borg Cube (as seen in "First
Contact").

> TRAJIS
> That's home. That's where you belong.

> SEVEN OF NINE
> No . . .

> TRAJIS
> End your pain. Just walk through that door. You'll
> never be alone again.

> SEVEN OF NINE
> This . . . <u>isn't real</u>.

From the interior of the Cube, the Borg voice begins to speak.

BORG VOICE
Resistance is futile . . . you live to serve us.

Seven of Nine takes a breath.

SEVEN OF NINE
(insistent)
Bridge.

She looks again. The doors are open to the Bridge, and she walks out.

84   INT. BRIDGE (OPTICAL)   84

There, the entire Bridge Crew awaits her. All have burns on their faces.
Their casual, almost carefree mood is in sharp contrast to their appearance
and the import of their words.

JANEWAY
Seven of Nine—you look a little worse for wear.

KIM
I didn't know she was still on board . . .

CHAKOTAY
I never wanted her here in the first place.

TUVOK
She won't be here long. She can't survive alone.

PARIS
I'm taking bets on how long she'll last . . .

CHAKOTAY
She'll fall apart before we leave the nebula.

KIM
And then everybody will die.

JANEWAY
Well, blame me. I put my trust in her. I should've
known better.

COMPUTER VOICE
Warning. Propulsion system failure in progress.

(The computer voice is still slowed.) Seven of Nine goes to an aft station and begins keying controls. The others begin moving closer to her. Throughout this sequence, Seven of Nine's mouth is moving faintly . . . she's whispering her "mantra" mostly to herself.

                         TUVOK
What is she doing now?

                       CHAKOTAY
She's trying to keep the engines on line.

                         PARIS
Place your bets. Anyone think she can do it?

                          KIM
I'll lay odds she can't.

                     SEVEN OF NINE
Computer, how long until the ship is out of the nebula?

                    COMPUTER VOICE
Forty-one minutes.

                        JANEWAY
That's too long. She won't make it.

                          KIM
That's an eternity.

                     SEVEN OF NINE
Computer, reroute available power from weapons, sensors and environmental controls to the engines.

                    COMPUTER VOICE
Warning. Propulsion system failure in progress.

                     SEVEN OF NINE
Reroute all available power to the engines.

                    COMPUTER VOICE
Propulsion systems have failed. All engines are off line.

                          KIM
She's got herself a real problem now.

CHAKOTAY
I'll say. She's taken power from every available
system and it's still not enough.

TUVOK
But if she fails to get this ship moving, everyone on
board will die.

PARIS
What do you think she'll do?

JANEWAY
I know what she's thinking. She's thinking if she
could take power from the stasis units on Deck
Fourteen . . . she might be able to get those engines
back on line.

KIM
But that would mean sacrificing some of the crew.

CHAKOTAY
I don't think that would bother her too much . . .

TUVOK
What matters to Seven is efficiency. Sacrificing a few,
to save many, would be an efficient plan.

JANEWAY
She's already killed millions—what would a few more
matter?

Seven of Nine has been staring at the controls, whispering her lullaby to
herself. Finally . . .

SEVEN OF NINE
Computer . . . divert power from stasis units one
through ten . . . reroute to propulsion systems . . .

A brief beat, then—

COMPUTER VOICE
Engines are back on line.

SEVEN OF NINE
Resume course.

> KIM
> Look at that. She did it.

> JANEWAY
> But those people she disconnected are going to die.

> PARIS
> I win! I knew she didn't care about them.

But Seven of Nine is on the move, off the Bridge and into the Turbolift.

85   INT. CORRIDOR   85

Seven of Nine hurrying through the green-lit corridor. She is nearing the Stasis Room. Burned Janeway is standing at the door.

> JANEWAY
> Come to watch them die?

The doors open and Seven of Nine hurries in.

86   INT. STASIS ROOM   86

Alarms are flashing on the containers. Nitrogen is venting from several of them.

> COMPUTER VOICE
> Warning. Power to stasis units has failed.

She runs to look into the one that has Tom Paris in it. Burned Janeway is standing next to it, peering in. Tom is unconscious but gasping, twitching.

> SEVEN OF NINE
> Computer . . . how long to complete passage through
> the nebula?

> COMPUTER VOICE
> Eleven minutes . . .

> JANEWAY
> They won't last that long.
> (beat)
> What do you do now, Seven? It's all up to you.

Seven of Nine stares at her.

> SEVEN OF NINE

Computer . . . cut life support from all decks and reroute available power to the stasis units.

> JANEWAY

That will keep <u>them</u> alive . . . but what about you? No
oxygen . . . no heat . . .

Janeway looks at her matter-of-factly.

> JANEWAY

Good-bye, Seven.

Seven of Nine backs up to the wall and, sliding her back down it, sits down.

> SEVEN OF NINE

I am Seven of Nine . . .

Breathing is getting harder now.

> SEVEN OF NINE

I am alone . . .

She struggles for oxygen.

> SEVEN OF NINE

But I will adapt . . .

She begins to fail. With her last gasps . . .

> SEVEN OF NINE

I will . . .

And off that—

FADE TO BLACK.

FADE IN:

87   INT. SICKBAY—SEVEN OF NINE'S POV   87

Looking up: Janeway, Chakotay and the Doctor are peering down in
concern. They are their normal selves.

> DOCTOR

She's coming around . . .

who looks momentarily confused, struggles to sit upright.

>   DOCTOR
>   Not so fast . . . get your bearings first.

Seven of Nine relaxes a bit, takes some deep breaths.

>   SEVEN OF NINE
>   The crew . . .

>   JANEWAY
>   We came through the nebula in fine shape—thanks to
>   you.

>   CHAKOTAY
>   You were the one we almost lost. When the ship
>   cleared the nebula, the Doctor came back on-line and
>   found you unconscious. He reinitiated life support and
>   woke the crew.

>   JANEWAY
>   He tells us you had quite an adventure . . .

Seven of Nine assesses this statement. There's a lot for her to think about.

>   SEVEN OF NINE
>   It was . . . interesting.

Janeway puts a hand on her shoulder.

>   JANEWAY
>   When you're rested, I'd like to hear about it.

She and Chakotay turn and EXIT. The Doctor turns to Seven of Nine.

>   DOCTOR
>   I'm proud of you, Seven. You performed admirably.

>   SEVEN OF NINE
>   I am glad . . . I was able to help.

But we sense she is still troubled by the ordeal.

89   INT. MESS HALL   89

Some of the crew, including Harry, Tom and B'Elanna, are having dinner.
The doors OPEN, and Seven ENTERS. She stands at the door for a moment,
looking around. She seems more hesitant than normal.

                            KIM
          Neelix . . . this soup is great. What is it?

                            NEELIX
          That's my secret recipe. I've never told anyone what's
          in it.

                            PARIS
          Why does that make me nervous?

                            TORRES
          Come on, Tom—where's your spirit of adventure?

                            PARIS
          Not in my stomach.

Finally, Seven of Nine spots the table with Harry and Tom, and heads
toward it, stops and stands there a bit awkwardly.

                       SEVEN OF NINE
          Lieutenants Paris and Torres. Ensign Kim.

                            KIM
          Seven—I'm surprised to see you here.

                       SEVEN OF NINE
          May I join you?

There's a brief moment of surprise—this isn't like Seven.

                            PARIS
          Sure . . . have a seat.

Seven sits.

                            TORRES
          Do you want some soup? It's actually edible.

>   SEVEN OF NINE
>   I don't require nourishment at this time.
>   (beat)
>   I . . . felt the need for . . . companionship.

Everyone stares at her. This is the most vulnerable admission she's ever made. There's a moment of sympathy, and then, to break the tension—

>   PARIS
>   After a month with only the Doctor for company . . . I
>   can understand it.

>   KIM
>   Yeah . . . what was that like, anyway? Just the two of
>   you . . .

After a beat . . .

>   SEVEN OF NINE
>   The Doctor was quite helpful. I cannot fault him.

>   TORRES
>   Well, we all owe you.

>   PARIS
>   Yeah, just think—we would've died in those
>   coffins . . .

>   SEVEN OF NINE
>   I suspect you would've found a way out before that,
>   Lieutenant.

>   KIM
>   What do you mean?

>   SEVEN OF NINE
>   Mister Paris would not stay confined. On four
>   separate occasions, the Doctor and I had to put him
>   back into his stasis unit.

Harry is tickled by this image. To Tom—

>   KIM
>   Were you locked in dark closets as a child or
>   something?

PARIS
I just don't like closed spaces. Never have. I don't
know why.

SEVEN OF NINE
Perhaps . . . you dislike being alone.

And on that note—

FADE OUT.

<u>END OF ACT FIVE</u>
<u>THE END</u>

STAR TREK: VOYAGER

"Hope and Fear"

#40840-194

Teleplay
by
Brannon Braga & Joe Menosky

Story
by
Rick Berman & Brannon Braga & Joe Menosky

Directed
by
Winrich Kolbe

STAR TREK: VOYAGER

''Hope and Fear''

JANEWAY

CHAKOTAY

KIM

PARIS

DOCTOR

TUVOK

NEELIX

TORRES

SEVEN OF NINE

COMPUTER VOICE

ARTURIS

BORG

STARFLEET ADMIRAL

Non-Speaking

N.D. SUPERNUMERARIES

STAR TREK: VOYAGER

"Hope and Fear"

SETS

<u>INTERIORS</u>

VOYAGER
    BRIDGE
    ASTROMETRICS LAB
    CARGO BAY
    CORRIDOR
    ENGINEERING
    HOLOGRID
    MESS HALL
    READY ROOM
    BRIEFING ROOM

DAUNTLESS
    BRIDGE
    BRIG
    ENGINEERING

<u>EXTERIORS</u>

VOYAGER
SPACE
QUANTUM SLIPSTREAM
DUANTLESS

STAR TREK: VOYAGER

"Hope and Fear"

<u>PRONUNCIATION GUIDE</u>

ARTURIS   are-TOOR-iss

ICONOMETRIC   eye-kahn-oh-MEH-trik

RECURSION   ree-CUR-zion

TRIAXILATING   try-AX-ill-ate-ing

KU CHA MEE-ROCH   koo-CHAH-mee-ROCHHH

STAR TREK: VOYAGER

''Hope and Fear''

<u>TEASER</u>

FADE IN:

1   A VELOCITY DISK (OPTICAL)   1

is SPEEDING toward camera! An aerodynamic, metallic object, eight inches across, glowing from within—angry red.

2   JANEWAY (OPTICAL)   2

FIRES a hand-phaser at the disk! She's dressed in a sleek, sleeveless ''workout'' uniform.

3   THE DISK (OPTICAL)   3

is STRUCK by her phaser shot! It instantly CHANGES to a cold blue color, and radically ALTERS its course, heading toward—

4   SEVEN OF NINE (OPTICAL)   4

also wearing a workout outfit, a few subtle BORG IMPLANTS along her upper arm. She whirls out of the way . . . the DISK ZOOMS past her, then abruptly REVERSES COURSE and comes at her again! She FIRES a quick shot—HITS the disk. It turns red again, heads toward Janeway.

REVEAL we are in—

5   INT. HOLOGRID (OPTICAL)   5

Janeway and Seven of Nine are engaged in a furious game of ''Velocity''—a one-on-one competitive sport that's a cross between handball and a firing range. (Each player must avoid being hit by the disk by shooting it and sending it back toward their opponent. It's fast-paced, physical, both players in constant motion, ducking, spinning.) The game continues from Scene #4.

Janeway LEAPS out of the way, narrowly avoiding the disk, stops herself before she slams into the wall, but her phaser drops from her hands!

The disk comes FLYING back at her . . . but Janeway stays pressed against the wall, not able to see the disk, as though "sensing" just the right moment to move. In the blink of an eye:

Janeway jerks her body out of the way just as the disk SLAMS into the wall and RICOCHETS OFF IT and heads back for the Captain. Janeway carries her motion in a ROLL toward her phaser, grabs the weapon, whirls and FIRES at the disk, HITTING it!

6   OMITTED   6

7   SEVEN OF NINE (OPTICAL)   7

is caught offguard by the swift move. The now angry-red disk ZIPS into frame and STRIKES her in the shoulder! The disk VANISHES.

> COMPUTER VOICE
> Full impact. Final round to Janeway. Winner: Janeway.

The two of them are cooling down from the game. Janeway is breathing harder than Seven of Nine—the Borg have superior stamina. As Janeway grabs a small towel off the corner of the floor, dabbing her face and neck.

> JANEWAY
> Good game.

> SEVEN OF NINE
> For you.

> JANEWAY
> Come on, Seven . . . you won four out of ten rounds . . . nothing to be ashamed of.

> SEVEN OF NINE
> On the contrary. I have superior visual acuity and stamina. I should have won every round.

> JANEWAY
> (lightly)
> "Velocity" is more than a test of stamina—it's a game of wits.

> SEVEN OF NINE
> You are a . . . frustrating opponent.
> (beat)

During the final round, after you dropped your
phaser, you weren't even looking at the disk. And yet,
you managed to evade it.

Janeway walks up to her . . . naturally falling into her role as Seven of
Nine's "mentor."

                    JANEWAY
Intuition.

                    SEVEN OF NINE
Intuition is a human fallacy. The belief that you can
predict random events.

                    JANEWAY
Belief had nothing to do with it. At some level . . .
conscious or otherwise . . . I was aware of several
factors. The trajectory of the disk after I hit the
wall . . . the sound it made on its return . . . the
shadow it cast on the hologrid . . .

                    SEVEN OF NINE
Intriguing . . . but implausible.

                    JANEWAY
                    (lightly)
I won, didn't I?
                              (beat)
Thanks for the match.

Janeway turns for the door. But Seven of Nine wants to keep going.

                    SEVEN OF NINE
I wish to play again.

                    JANEWAY
Not today.

                    SEVEN OF NINE
You are fatigued . . . and concerned that I will defeat
you.

Janeway pauses, turns.

                    JANEWAY
Tired? Yes. Concerned? No.

                    SEVEN OF NINE
                       (to com)
        Computer—begin first round.

                      JANEWAY
                  (quickly, to com)
        Belay that command.

They lock eyes for a tense beat—and it's clear that there's more at stake
here than a simple game.

Seven of Nine is challenging her mentor, wants to beat her, prove her
superiority. But Janeway is calm, won't take the bait.

                      JANEWAY
        Try to be a good sport, Seven. The game's over.

Janeway turns and EXITS. As Seven of Nine watches her go, the look of
challenge still on her face . . .

                                                        FADE OUT.

                    END OF TEASER

ACT ONE

FADE IN:

(NOTE: Episode credits fall over opening scenes.)

8   EXT. SPACE—VOYAGER (OPTICAL)   8

at impulse.

> JANEWAY (V.O.)
> Captain's Log, Stardate 51978.2. It's been five months
> since we received the encoded message from the
> Alpha Quadrant.

9   ON A DESKTOP MONITOR (OPTICAL)   9

It shows a DAMAGED DATA STREAM—a chaotic jumble of symbols and
alphanumerics racing across the screen.

> JANEWAY (V.O.)
> (continuing)
> We know that the transmission was from Starfleet
> Command . . . but we still can't decrypt it.

10   INT. MESS HALL   10

After hours, dimly lit. Janeway sits alone at a table, working on the desktop
monitor. Coffee and PADDS spread all around.

> JANEWAY (V.O.)
> (continuing)
> B'Elanna thinks it's a lost cause . . . but I haven't
> given up. I keep hoping inspiration will strike . . .
> somehow.

Over this log, CHAKOTAY ENTERS and walks up to her.

> CHAKOTAY
> Good morning.

> JANEWAY
> (surprised)
> What time is it?

                              CHAKOTAY
Oh-six-hundred.

                              JANEWAY
Well, then . . . good morning.

                              CHAKOTAY
I just heard from Tom and Neelix . . . they're about to
leave the trading colony.

                              JANEWAY
Any luck?

                              CHAKOTAY
According to Tom, the shuttle's so loaded with
supplies, he won't make half-impulse.

Janeway smiles.

                              CHAKOTAY
                             (continuing)
Neelix is asking permission to bring one of the locals
on board. He's been very helpful . . . and Neelix
wants to repay him by giving him passage to the next
system.

Janeway stifles a yawn.

                              JANEWAY
Permission granted.

                              CHAKOTAY
You might want to grab some sleep . . . we've got a
big day ahead.

                              JANEWAY
In a while.

                              CHAKOTAY
                             (re: monitor)
Still hunting for buried treasure?

                              JANEWAY
We found the treasure . . . I just can't pick the lock.
                             (frustrated)

I've tried over fifty decryption algorithms. Every time
I piece together a datablock . . . ten more come
unraveled.

Janeway eyes the monitor, thoughtful.

> JANEWAY
> (continuing)
> What did Starfleet send us? A map, the location of a
> wormhole? If I decode this today, we could be home
> tomorrow.
> (beat)
> Then again, it could be Admiral Chapman's recipe for
> the perfect pound cake. I've been pinning our hopes
> on this message, but I'm starting to wonder . . .

> CHAKOTAY
> One way or another, we've got to find out.
> (upbeat)
> I'll talk to B'Elanna . . . you could enlist Seven of
> Nine.

> JANEWAY
> (nods)
> She should have a few Borg algorithms up her sleeve.
> If she's in the mood . . .

> CHAKOTAY
> Problems?

> JANEWAY
> I don't know if she's getting restless . . . or if it's just
> me . . . but we're butting heads more than usual
> lately. She seems to challenge everything I say.

> CHAKOTAY
> She's learned a lot from you over the last year. Maybe
> the pupil thinks she's outgrowing the mentor.

> JANEWAY
> Maybe . . .

A quiet beat.

                              JANEWAY
                            (with humor)
        Well, this is one mentor who could use another cup of
        coffee. Join me?

                              CHAKOTAY
        Love to.

                                                          CUT TO:

11   EXT. SPACE—VOYAGER (OPTICAL)   11

      at impulse. A Voyager SHUTTLECRAFT is approaching the ship.

12   INT. CARGO BAY   12

      (NOTE: The Borg alcoves remain off-camera.) FOUR STARFLEET N.D.s are
      busily sorting through CARGO—containers of various sizes and shapes.
      Chakotay and PARIS are directing the job.

                                PARIS
                        (to N.D., re: container)
        That goes to Engineering.
                          (to another N.D.)
        Sickbay.

      A third N.D. walks over, carrying a bizarre-looking ALIEN OBJECT—it's
      covered with gnarled tendrils and spiny projections.

                              CHAKOTAY
                              (lightly)
        I hope that's not going to the Mess Hall.

                                PARIS
        I don't remember <u>what</u> this is . . .
                            (calls out)
        Neelix!

13   NEW ANGLE—JANEWAY, NEELIX AND AN ALIEN   13

      are standing nearby. The alien—ARTURIS—is an exotic-looking humanoid
      with an enlarged cranium. He's from a highly intelligent species, soft-
      spoken, charismatic. Neelix is playing Ambassador.

NEELIX
(to Janeway, re: Arturis)
Captain, he's a genius! I was trying to negotiate with a
xenon-based lifeform . . . when the Universal
Translator went off-line. Arturis here stepped in and
acted as a perfect go-between. And he'd never heard
either of our languages!

ARTURIS
They're simple.
(to Neelix)
No insult intended.

PARIS' VOICE
<u>Neelix!</u>

NEELIX
On my way.
(to Janeway, Arturis)
If you two will excuse me . . .

Neelix rushes off.

JANEWAY
(to Arturis, lightly)
Welcome to Voyager. We may be a linguistically
simple folk . . . but we're happy to give you a ride.
Let's see if we can find you some quarters.

They start walking toward the doors. Arturis looks touched.

ARTURIS
Neelix was right . . . Voyager is a welcoming place.

JANEWAY
We do our best.

14   INT. CORRIDOR   14

Moments later. Janeway and Arturis are walking along.

JANEWAY
I can't say I've ever met a living Universal Translator.

ARTURIS

My people have a way with languages. I myself know
over four thousand.

JANEWAY

And to think I still struggle with basic Klingon.
(intrigued)
You couldn't have heard Neelix say more than a few
phrases . . .

ARTURIS

That's all I needed. It's enough to grasp the grammar
and syntax.

JANEWAY

Impressive.

ARTURIS
(modest)
Not really. It's a natural ability. Some species are born
with great physical prowess . . . others, like yours,
with a generosity of spirit.
(off her smile)
My people can see patterns where others see only
confusion.

A beat, and then Janeway looks at him, her mind working.

ARTURIS

Is something wrong?

JANEWAY

No . . .

(pointed)
Tell me . . . how are you at computational languages?
Algorithms . . . trinary syntax . . .

ARTURIS

It's all the same to me.

JANEWAY

I was wondering . . . if you might do us another favor.

Off Arturis, puzzled . . .

                                                    CUT TO:

15   THE DAMAGED DATA STREAM (VPB)   15

as seen before—chaotic alphanumerics racing across a MONITOR.

                        ARTURIS' VOICE
            You weren't exaggerating, Captain. This data stream is
            badly damaged.

REVEAL we are in—

16   INT. ASTROMETRICS LAB (VPB)   16

It's a short time later. Arturis is working the console monitor. Janeway and
Seven of Nine look on.

                           ARTURIS
                       (continuing, beat)
            I'd like to see the entire transmission again.

Janeway nods to Seven of Nine, who works the console. Arturis glances at
Seven of Nine, curious.

                           ARTURIS
            Are you Borg?

                        SEVEN OF NINE
                          (working)
            Yes.

                           ARTURIS
                           (lightly)
            You're more attractive than the average Drone.

                        SEVEN OF NINE
            I'm no longer part of the Collective.

Arturis studies the monitor, absorbed.

                           ARTURIS
            Yes . . . yes . . . I see the problem . . .
                          (re: console)
            May I?

                           JANEWAY
            Please.

Arturis starts tapping controls, focussed, never taking his eyes off the monitor.

                    JANEWAY
                (to Seven of Nine)
Have you encountered his people before?

                 SEVEN OF NINE
Species One-One-Six.

Arturis is still absorbed in the work, but seems perfectly capable of carrying on a conversation at the same time.

                    ARTURIS
Is that what you call us?

                 SEVEN OF NINE
Yes.
                  (to Janeway)
The Borg have never been able to assimilate them.
Not yet.

                    JANEWAY
Seven . . .

                    ARTURIS
             (working, good-natured)
It's all right, Captain. The Borg Collective is like a
force of nature. You don't feel anger toward a storm
on the horizon . . . you just avoid it.

The console BEEPS and Arturis looks pleased.

                    ARTURIS
Ah! Here it is.
                  (to Janeway)
It's a simple matter of extracting the iconometric
elements, and triaxilating a recursion matrix.

                    JANEWAY
                    (wry)
Now, why didn't I think of that?

                    ARTURIS
                   (works)
There's a great deal of information here, Captain . . .
it might be helpful to utilize the other monitors.

Janeway moves to the console and works alongside him. A beat, and then:

17   THE DOME (OPTICAL)   17

COMES ALIVE WITH INFORMATION—a MULTISCREEN DISPLAY, each section filled with different kinds of DATA—schematics, coordinates, and one section shows a STARFLEET ADMIRAL talking to camera, another an image of EARTH. All of it is heavily FRITZED. SOUND fills the room— beeps, clicks, the Admiral's distorted voice, etc.

> JANEWAY
> You've done it . . .

> ARTURIS
> Almost. I've reconstructed over sixty-eight kiloquads of information . . . but a lot of it's still garbled.

> JANEWAY
> (nods, off console)
> What about this datablock—fourteen alpha?

> ARTURIS
> That part of the message is too degraded to recover.

Janeway takes this in. Then:

> SEVEN OF NINE
> Captain—I've found a spatial grid.

Janeway rushes over.

> JANEWAY
> It looks like a map of a nearby sector . . .
> (studies it)
> They've marked a set of coordinates . . . it's less than ten light years from here . . .

> SEVEN OF NINE
> Maybe Starfleet wants us to proceed to that location.

> JANEWAY
> Maybe.
> (energized)
> There's only one way to find out.

CUT TO:

18   EXT. SPACE—VOYAGER (OPTICAL)   18

RACES past camera at high warp!

19   INT. BRIDGE   19

Janeway, Chakotay, Paris, TUVOK, KIM, N.D.s at their stations. Seven of
Nine is at an aft station. Arturis is there, as well, standing by Janeway. This
is an exciting moment for everyone.

> PARIS
> We're approaching the coordinates . . .

> JANEWAY
> Take us out of warp. Scan the vicinity.

A suspenseful beat. Tuvok's console BEEPS.

> TUVOK
> I'm picking up a vessel.

Reactions.

> JANEWAY
> On screen.

20   INCLUDE THE VIEWSCREEN (OPTICAL)   20

It shows a STARSHIP, glowing with power, hanging in space. It's sleek,
bullet-shaped, as though built for speed. And it's roughly half the size of
Voyager. (We'll come to know this vessel as the "Dauntless.")

> CHAKOTAY
> Identify.

> TUVOK
> Captain . . . unless I'm mistaken . . . the warp
> signature is Starfleet.

Off the moment . . .

                                                        FADE OUT.

                        END OF ACT ONE

ACT TWO

FADE IN:

21   OMITTED   21

22   INT. BRIDGE (OPTICAL)   22

As before. Everyone watching the Viewscreen, which shows the Starfleet
vessel. The crew is transfixed by the sight. But Janeway stays calm,
cautious, taking this one step at a time.

                          PARIS
                          (quiet)
          I'll be damned . . . they came through.

                          JANEWAY
          Tuvok.

                          TUVOK
          Hailing them . . .
                          (works)
          No response.

                          CHAKOTAY
          Lifesigns?

                          SEVEN OF NINE
                          (works)
          There's no organic matter of any kind.

Reactions.

                          KIM
                          (off console)
          No sign of damage to the outer hull . . . primary
          systems are on-line . . . including life support.
                          (anxious)
          Something must've happened to the crew . . .

                          JANEWAY
          The answer is somewhere in that Starfleet
          transmission . . . we need to finish decoding it.

She turns to Arturis.

                        JANEWAY
May I call on your talents again?

                        ARTURIS
Of course.

                        JANEWAY
                      (to Chakotay)
Take an Away Team. Secure the vessel.

                        CHAKOTAY
                      (on the move)
Tuvok, Tom.

Chakotay, Tuvok and Paris head for the Turbolift. Janeway stares at the
image of the Dauntless, thoughtful. Arturis considers her.

                        ARTURIS
Captain . . . I won't pretend to know you well . . . but
I'm surprised you're not more encouraged by this
discovery.

                        JANEWAY
I've learned to walk the line between hope and
caution . . . we've had other opportunities that didn't
work out.
                      (smiles)
But I will admit . . . I'm leaning toward hope this
time.

He returns the smile warmly. As Janeway and Arturis head for the door,
Seven of Nine following . . .

                                                        CUT TO:

23   INT. DAUNTLESS—BRIDGE (OPTICAL)   23

Gleaming, sexy, cutting-edge Starfleet technology. The room is deep,
cylindrical, curvilinear. There are no crewmembers, but the room is
pristine. Chakotay, Tuvok and Paris MATERIALIZE. They glance around,
impressed.

                        PARIS
Wow.

TUVOK

Wow indeed.

Chakotay stops at a console, works it. The console LIGHTS UP with a SCHEMATIC of the ship.

CHAKOTAY

I've never seen this kind of hull geometry . . . looks like they've taken a whole new approach to starship design . . .

TUVOK
(off console)
USS Dauntless. Registry NX Zero One-A. Launch Date . . . 51472.

CHAKOTAY

Sixty thousand light years in three months?

A mysterious beat. Tuvok works the controls . . .

TUVOK

I'm trying to access the crew logs . . .
(reacts)
But there are none.

PARIS' VOICE

I don't think there was a crew.

They turn to him. Paris is studying another station.

PARIS
(continuing)
The helm was set for autonavigation to these coordinates.

They consider.

TUVOK

Logic would suggest that Starfleet has provided us with a new ship.

CHAKOTAY

Let's not pack our bags just yet. I'd like to know how they—

The ship TREMBLES slightly, and we hear a LOW RUMBLE.

> PARIS
> (off helm)
> I'm reading power fluctuations in the warp core . . . if
> you can call it a warp core. I don't recognize this
> engine configuration . . .

Another tremor.

> CHAKOTAY
> Let's go take a look.

He spots a Turbolift, heads for it . . . stops.

> CHAKOTAY
> It might help to know where we're going.

> TUVOK
> (off console)
> Engineering. Deck Six, Section Twenty-Four.

As they head for the door . . .

                                                          CUT TO:

24   24
thru   OMITTED   thru
26   26

27   INT. DAUNTLESS—ENGINEERING   27

A dimly lit chamber, with an ENGINE DOME in the center of the floor. The
dome is roughly four feet high, GLOWING with deep, shifting COLORS. A
circular console surrounds it. At the moment, we cannot see the actual
engine core—it's down below. A RUMBLING sound fills the room.

28   ANGLE—CHAKOTAY, TUVOK AND PARIS   28

ENTER the room . . .

> PARIS
> (re: dome)
> I think we've found our engine core.

Paris moves to the dome and peers down through the clear surface. Tuvok and Chakotay join him . . .

29   OVERHEAD VIEW—ENGINE CORE   29

The CORE itself is a glowing mass of ENERGY. Huge, exotic, powerful.

30   THE AWAY TEAM   30

eyes it, the light playing on their faces.

> CHAKOTAY
> Some kind of new warp drive?

> PARIS
> That's not antimatter . . . it's . . . I don't know what it
> is . . .

Paris moves to a nearby console, looking for answers. The ship TREMBLES . . . and the room RUMBLES loudly. The LIGHT from the engine dome FLARES briefly.

> PARIS
> (off console)
> They call this thing a . . . quantum slipstream drive.

> TUVOK
> "Quantum slipstream"?

> CHAKOTAY
> I've never seen that in the engineering manuals.

The RUMBLE grows in intensity . . . the room VIBRATES. ALARMS start to sound. Paris checks a readout.

> PARIS
> The ship is powering up! Autonavigation's kicking in!

31   EXT. SPACE—THE DAUNTLESS (OPTICAL)   31

starts to MOVE forward!

32   INT. VOYAGER—BRIDGE   32

N.D.s at their stations. Kim in command, checking the armchair console.

> KIM
> (to com)
> Voyager to Away Team. What's happening over there?
> (beat)
> Chakotay?

Nothing.

> KIM
> (to com, urgent)
> Bridge to Janeway—the vessel's moving away at high
> impulse!

INTERCUT:

33   INT. ASTROMETRICS LAB   33

Janeway, Seven of Nine and Arturis are working. Various monitors and
displays show the STARFLEET DATA, as seen in Act One.

> KIM'S COM VOICE
> (continuing)
> I can't raise the Away Team.

> JANEWAY
> Pursuit course, Ensign!

34   INT. DAUNTLESS—ENGINEERING   34

As before. The ship is RUMBLING violently now, the engine core GLOW-
ING wildly.

> PARIS
> (working)
> I can't shut down the drive!

> CHAKOTAY
> (to com)
> Computer, disable propulsion!

> COMPUTER VOICE
> Unable to comply.

> PARIS
> Hang on!

They brace themselves . . .

35   EXT. SPACE—THE DAUNTLESS (OPTICAL)   35

ROARING at HIGH IMPULSE. The NOSE of the Dauntless starts to GLOW
and DISTORT in a strange effect, and the entire ship VANISHES from view!

36   OMITTED   36

37   INT. VOYAGER—BRIDGE   37

As before.

> KIM
> (to com)
> Bridge to Janeway—they're <u>gone</u>.

Off his surprise . . .

38   EXT. SPACE—QUANTUM SLIPSTREAM (OPTICAL)   38

A TORRENT of ENERGY whipping past us at blinding velocities! The
Dauntless is RACING through the raging river of energy at breakneck
speeds!

39   INT. DAUNTLESS—ENGINEERING   39

LIGHT from the engines STROBING, a harrowing experience. Over the
noise:

> PARIS
> (off console)
> Look at this! Energy from the quantum drive is being
> routed through the main deflector!

> CHAKOTAY
> Is that what's creating the slipstream?

> PARIS
> It looks that way!

> TUVOK
> Fascinating! Can you make it stop?

> PARIS
> I'll try accessing the helm controls!

Paris works . . .

40   EXT. SPACE (OPTICAL)   40

A starfield. And then, with a BLAST of ENERGY, the DAUNTLESS comes
ROARING out of the quantum slipstream and into normal space!

41   INT. DAUNTLESS—ENGINEERING   41

Alarms stop. LIGHT from the engine core dies down.

                        PARIS
            We're back in normal space . . .

                        CHAKOTAY
            Scan for Voyager.

                        TUVOK
                        (works)
            No sign of them.

                        (reacts)
            Commander . . . we've traveled over <u>fifteen light</u>
            <u>years</u>.

Off their surprise . . .

                                                        TIME CUT TO:

42   EXT. SPACE—VOYAGER (OPTICAL)   42

at impulse.

                        JANEWAY (V.O.)
            Captain's Log, Supplemental. After two days at high
            warp, we've rendezvoused with the Dauntless.

Voyager FLIES INTO VIEW of the DAUNTLESS, which is hanging in space.

                        JANEWAY (V.O.)
                        (continuing)
            Arturis has helped us reconstruct most of the Starfleet
            message. The pieces of this puzzle are finally coming
            together . . .

43   ON A STARFLEET ADMIRAL (OPTICAL)   43

on a WALL MONITOR, fritzing slightly. Mid-message:

> STARFLEET ADMIRAL
> Slipstream technology is experimental and high-risk.
> But it's come a long way in the past year.

As the Admiral speaks, REVEAL we are in—

44   INT. BRIEFING ROOM (OPTICAL)   44

Janeway, Chakotay, Tuvok, Paris, Kim, TORRES, Neelix, the DOCTOR (wearing his mobile emitter) and Seven of Nine are gathered around the table, watching the monitor.

> STARFLEET ADMIRAL
> (continuing)
> We've conducted forty-seven trial runs . . . all of them
> successful. But each flight lasted only five days . . .

As we listen, CAMERA MOVES across the crew's faces, expectant.

> STARFLEET ADMIRAL
> (continuing)
> In order to reach Earth, you'd have to remain at
> slipstream velocities for a full three months. Can your
> crew survive that long? We believe they can . . . and
> we encourage you to try. Everything you'll need is on
> the Dauntless. Power cells, supplies, living quarters.

The Admiral's voice softens.

> STARFLEET ADMIRAL
> (continuing)
> Safe journey. We hope to see you soon.

The transmission FRITZES OUT, replaced by a Federation symbol. There's a somber pause as everyone takes in the situation. No one says anything, no one even breathes. Finally, Janeway turns to her crew.

> JANEWAY
> (lightly)
> Admiral Hayes. Good man. Fine officer. But
> something of a windbag.

This breaks the ice—everyone laughs. The tension is released.

JANEWAY
(to business)
Let's talk about the risk. Doctor?

DOCTOR
I've examined the Away Team for signs of cell
damage or physiological stress. Nothing. Their little
joyride didn't harm them in the slightest.

JANEWAY

Long-term effects?

DOCTOR

I'm running medical projections right now . . . so far,
the results are encouraging.

JANEWAY
(to Chakotay)
And the Dauntless itself?

CHAKOTAY
I'd say it's in pretty good shape, considering . . .

TORRES
(chiming in)
I've been looking over the primary systems. Helm,
Ops, Tactical—they're comparable to Voyager's. But
it's a lean ship, Captain. No Shuttlecraft, only one
Transporter . . . no Holodecks, no replicators.

JANEWAY
Well, Mister Neelix . . . you may have your work cut
out for you.

NEELIX
Ready and willing, Captain.

KIM
So what are we waiting for?

SEVEN OF NINE
Your enthusiasm is premature. Voyager is a proven
vessel. We'd be reckless to abandon it so quickly.

KIM

Come on, Seven . . . where's that Borg spirit? We'll adapt!

SEVEN OF NINE

My "Borg spirit" gives me an objectivity you lack.

TUVOK

She has a point. This would mean leaving Voyager behind . . .

CHAKOTAY
(to Torres)

Is there any way we could modify Voyager to create a slipstream?

PARIS

In theory. But I don't think the ship would hold up very long under the quantum stresses.

JANEWAY
(to Paris)

Try to make the modifications. If there's a way we can bring Voyager along for the ride, I'm all for it.
(orders)
B'Elanna, Harry—take an Engineering team to the Dauntless. Start working on a way to shut down that slipstream drive at a moment's notice.

TORRES

Aye, Captain.

JANEWAY
(to Paris)

Once we've got that safeguard in place, we'll start making test flights.
(to Chakotay)
The entire crew should familiarize themselves with that ship. See to it.

He nods. Janeway takes a moment . . . glances around the room itself . . . she's facing her biggest decision yet.

JANEWAY
(to all)

Dismissed.

Everyone swings into action, heading for the door. Janeway stares out the window.

                    JANEWAY
          Tuvok.

Tuvok stays behind. Janeway waits until they're alone, then . . .

                    JANEWAY
          Big day.

                    TUVOK
          Indeed.

                    JANEWAY
          A way home. We've been waiting for this moment for
          years . . .
                        (beat)
          Why don't I feel more enthusiastic?

                    TUVOK
          Perhaps my mental discipline is finally rubbing off on
          you.

                    JANEWAY
                        (smiles)
          Hmm . . . perhaps.
                        (beat)
          What do you think about this little "miracle" of ours?

                    TUVOK
          I share your concern about the crew's safety. We
          must take every precaution.

                    JANEWAY
          Somehow, I don't think the standard diagnostics and
          security protocols are going to make me feel any
          better.

                    TUVOK
          Captain?

Janeway looks at him.

                    JANEWAY
          All of this is too . . . perfect. The alien genius with the

answers to all our problems . . . a message from
Starfleet telling us everything we want to hear . . . a
starship delivered right to our doorstep. What more
could we ask for? They even turned down the
beds . . . the only thing missing is chocolate on the
pillows.

Tuvok considers.

> TUVOK
> It does seem . . . convenient.

> JANEWAY
> I can't put my finger on it . . . but from the moment
> this all started, I've felt something was wrong . . .

> TUVOK
> It started when Arturis boarded Voyager.

> JANEWAY
> Exactly.

She thinks, makes a decision.

> JANEWAY
> We'll proceed as planned. But I want you to
> investigate that ship from stem to stern . . . and keep
> an eye on our guest . . . see if you can find out more
> about him.

> TUVOK
> Understood.

> JANEWAY
> Let's hope we're suffering from nothing more than
> good, old-fashioned paranoia.
> > (beat)
> Keep me posted.

Tuvok nods, turns and EXITS. Off Janeway . . .

FADE OUT.

END OF ACT TWO

ACT THREE

FADE IN:

45   EXT. SPACE—THE DAUNTLESS (OPTICAL)   45

drifting next to Voyager.

> JANEWAY (V.O.)
> Captain's Log, Supplemental. So far, the crew hasn't
> found any evidence to support my doubts about
> Arturis . . .

46   INT. DAUNTLESS—BRIDGE   46

As seen before. Janeway, Chakotay and FIVE STARFLEET N.D.s are busily
checking consoles, making adjustments, etc. Paris and Kim are there, too—
exchanging smiles and laughter while they work.

> JANEWAY (V.O.)
> . . . nevertheless, I've told them to keep looking and
> to keep their optimism in check. But that's one order I
> don't expect them to follow to the letter . . .

Over the last few words of Janeway's log, we OVERLAP a LOG by Seven of
Nine and DISSOLVE TO:

47   INT. ASTROMETRICS LAB (VPB)   47

Seven of Nine is studying a GRAPHIC of a quantum slipstream. Arturis can
be seen working in the b.g.

> SEVEN OF NINE (V.O.)
> (overlapping)
> Daily log, Seven of Nine, Stardate XXXXX.X. I've
> analyzed the quantum slipstream technology of the
> Dauntless. It's similar to the transwarp drive used by
> the Borg. As a result, my expertise will be crucial to
> the mission's success.

48   INT. VOYAGER—CORRIDOR   48

Seven of Nine walking along. Starfleet N.D.s are hustling past. She studies
them as they pass by.

>   SEVEN OF NINE (V.O.)
>   (continuing)
> Voyager's crew is counting on that success . . . but I
> find myself ambivalent. So I'm carrying out my
> assignment, nothing more . . .

Over the last couple of words, we OVERLAP back to Janeway's Log and
DISSOLVE TO:

49   INT. READY ROOM   49

Janeway at her desk, working at a desktop computer.

>   JANEWAY (V.O.)
>   (overlapping)
> Despite my apprehension, I can't help but wonder
> what I'll be doing in three months' time.

Janeway pauses for a moment, stares out the window.

>   JANEWAY (V.O.)
>   (continuing)
> Still guiding Voyager through the Delta Quadrant . . .
> or looking up old friends in Indiana?

OVERLAP and DISSOLVE TO:

50   INT. CARGO BAY   50

Seven of Nine is working at a Borg alcove.

>   SEVEN OF NINE (V.O.)
> . . . If we do return to Sector Zero-zero-one, will I
> adapt to human civilization? A single Borg, among
> billions of individuals?

Off Seven of Nine's face . . .

                                                              CUT TO:

51   51
thru   OMITTED   thru
52   52

53   OVERHEAD VIEW—THE DAUNTLESS ENGINE CORE   53

The glowing ENERGY, as seen before. Torres, Kim and Seven of Nine are
standing at the console overlooking it.

                              TORRES
              Initiate emergency shutdown on my mark . . .

54   INT. DAUNTLESS—ENGINEERING—CONTINUOUS   54

Torres, Kim and Seven of Nine at the console.

                              TORRES
         Now.

The three of them work . . . and we HEAR the RUMBLE of the engine core
start to SUBSIDE . . .

                              KIM
              Quantum field strength down to ninety percent . . .
              eighty percent . . .
                         (reacts)
              It's leveling off at seventy-five.

                         SEVEN OF NINE
              We need to dampen the field by at least fifty percent.

                              TORRES
              Try reversing the quantum field polarities.

Seven of Nine works . . . the rumbling sound starts to dissipate . . .

                              KIM
              Seventy percent . . . fifty-five . . . forty-nine percent!

55   OVERHEAD VIEW—THE ENGINE CORE   55

The glowing sphere of energy SLOWS and the rumbling noise fades to a low
hum.

                              TORRES
              We did it!

56   RESUME SCENE   56

Torres is excited—more upbeat than we've seen her in a while.

                    TORRES
We've got our safety net.

                     KIM
One step closer to home.

Torres and Kim exchange a satisfied look.

                SEVEN OF NINE
                 (to business)
Tuvok wants us to run a metallurgical analysis of the
bulkheads . . . to look for anything unusual.

Torres glances at her, slightly annoyed that she spoiled the moment.

                    TORRES
Thanks.
                   (to Kim)
You two run the analysis. I'll be on the Bridge with
Arturis. Our "resident genius" said he'd help me
figure out those control sequencers.

Kim nods. Torres starts preparing an Engineering kit. Seven and Kim pull
out tricorders and start scanning the bulkheads. Seven of Nine glances at
Torres, pensive.

                SEVEN OF NINE
Lieutenant . . . you seem eager to return to Earth.

                    TORRES
Eager? I wouldn't go that far.

                SEVEN OF NINE
                  (probing)
You were a member of the Maquis. Starfleet
Command will no doubt hold you responsible for a
multitude of crimes. You will find nothing on Earth
but adversity.

                    TORRES
                  (sarcastic)
That's looking on the bright side.

But the inquiry does catch Torres offguard . . . and she considers.

                              TORRES
                            (continuing)
                Let's put it this way . . . I'd rather face the music
                back home than spend the rest of my life in the Delta
                Quadrant.

Seven takes this in.

                              TORRES
                            (continuing)
                What about <u>you</u>? Looking forward to seeing Earth?

                          SEVEN OF NINE
                No.

                              TORRES
                I'm not surprised. You think people are going to
                resent an ex-Maquis . . . what about an ex-Drone?

Seven looks troubled.

                              TORRES
                I'm kidding, Seven. A joke.
                            (softer)
                Look . . . I know how you're feeling. Part of me is
                dreading going back. But if I can do it, you can do it.
                            (lightly)
                We'll be outcasts together!

But Seven doesn't smile.

                              TORRES
                Work on that sense of humor—it'll help you make
                friends on Earth.

With that, Torres EXITS.

                               KIM
                           (off tricorder)
                I'm reading an anomalous energy surge behind this
                panel.

Seven scans it.

                    SEVEN OF NINE
    There are no power conduits running through this
    section.

As they work, Kim glances at Seven of Nine. He can tell she has a lot on her
mind.

                         KIM
    Believe me, Seven . . . one look at that big blue
    marble, and you'll fall in love. It's got just about every
    ecosystem you can think of. And hundreds of different
    humanoid species live there. Bolians, Vulcans,
    Ktarians . . .

He glances at her. She's staring at him, unimpressed.

                         KIM
                    (trailing off)
    If you . . . like Ktarians.
                       (beat)
    There are plenty of other planets to choose from.

                    SEVEN OF NINE
    If you will excuse me, Ensign. I must speak to the
    Captain.

He nods. Seven of Nine heads for the door.

                         KIM
    Seven?
                    (she stops)
    For what's it worth . . . it won't be the same without
    you.

Seven of Nine gives him an almost imperceptible smile. In their own offbeat
way, they've bonded over the months.

Kim watches her go . . . then snaps his tricorder shut, belts it . . . moves to
a nearby control panel . . . removes the covering and starts adjusting the
circuitry within . . .

57   NEW ANGLE (OPTICAL)   57

The ENTIRE BULKHEAD SHIMMERS IN AN ALIEN HOLOGRAPHIC
EFFECT, REVEALING EXOTIC ALIEN TECHNOLOGY BEYOND.

Kim reacts in surprise.

                                KIM
                           (taps combadge)
            Kim to Tuvok.

                        TUVOK'S COM VOICE
            Tuvok here.

                                KIM
            I'm on the Dauntless . . . in the engine room . . . and
            I've found something that qualifies as "unusual."

                               TUVOK
            I'll be right there.

As Kim keeps working the wall circuits . . .

                                                                    CUT TO:

58   EARTH (OPTICAL)   58

The big blue marble against starry space. After a beat, technical DATA
appears all around it—this is one of the images we saw from the Starfleet
message in Act One.

59   INT. ASTROMETRICS LAB (OPTICAL)   59

Janeway is working a console, the image of Earth on the Dome in front of her.

                             JANEWAY
                             (to com)
            Computer—display datablock fourteen-beta.

We hear the computer work. Janeway studies a console, intent. Seven of
Nine ENTERS.

                             JANEWAY
            Seven—I could use your help.

Seven of Nine moves to her.

                             JANEWAY
                           (re: console)
            I'm trying to reconstruct that last fragment of the
            Starfleet message.

> **SEVEN OF NINE**
> Arturis said it was irreparably damaged.

> **JANEWAY**
> I know . . . but I have a feeling he gave up too easily.

> **SEVEN OF NINE**
> ''Intuition.''

> **JANEWAY**
> (with humor)
> It's intuition if I'm right . . .
> (re: console)
> I've designed a new decryption algorithm. Let's give it
> a try.

Seven of Nine and Janeway work a moment, the image of Earth looming
large between them. Then:

> **SEVEN OF NINE**
> Captain . . . I will not be going with you to the Alpha
> Quadrant.

Janeway glances at her, calm.

> **JANEWAY**
> (gently)
> I can understand your reluctance. It's been hard
> enough dealing with a crew of a hundred and fifty
> humans. The prospect of an entire planet must be
> overwhelming . . .

> **SEVEN OF NINE**
> I am not overwhelmed. I simply don't wish to live
> among humans.

> **JANEWAY**
> Whether you like it or not, you're one of us.
> (beat)
> You've come a long way from that Drone who
> stepped out of a Borg alcove nine months ago. Don't
> turn your back on humanity, now . . . not when
> you're about to take your biggest step. <u>Earth</u>. Your
> home.

Seven of Nine considers.

> ### SEVEN OF NINE
> I may have "come a long way" . . . but not in the
> direction you think.
> > (beat)
> You've attempted to influence my development . . .
> you've exposed me to your culture and ideals. You
> hoped to shape me in your own image. But you failed.
> > (beat)
> You may have noticed our tendency to disagree.

> ### JANEWAY
> > (wry)
>
> Oh, I've noticed.

> ### SEVEN OF NINE
> Then you should also recognize that I don't share your
> values. Your desire to explore space is inefficient . . .
> your need for familial connections is a weakness.

She indicates the Dome.

> ### SEVEN OF NINE
> > (re: Earth)
> Your infatuation with this planet is irrational.

> ### JANEWAY
> I won't argue that you've turned out . . . differently
> than I expected . . . and that we often have conflicting
> points of view.
> > (beat)
> But right now, there's more at stake. This crew needs
> your expertise. Abandon them and you diminish their
> chances of getting home.

> ### SEVEN OF NINE
> Irrelevant.

> ### JANEWAY
> No, it's not. We've given you a lot, Seven . . . it's time
> you gave something in return.

> ### SEVEN OF NINE
> I have . . . on many occasions. Now, I refuse.

A tense beat. Janeway takes a different tack . . .

> JANEWAY
> What would you do—go back to the Collective?

> SEVEN OF NINE
> I don't know.

> JANEWAY
> Then what, exactly, do you have in mind?

> SEVEN OF NINE
> (an edge)
> I don't know.

Seven doesn't have an answer.

> JANEWAY
> That's my point. You're asking me to cast you adrift
> in the Delta Quadrant . . . alone, without support. I
> wouldn't grant that request to any member of the
> crew. It's too dangerous.

> SEVEN OF NINE
> I'll survive.

> JANEWAY
> On what—Borg perfection?

> SEVEN OF NINE
> Precisely.

They're at an impasse.

> JANEWAY
> I don't buy it. This isn't about your independence or
> your superiority . . . it's about your fear.
> (off her look)
> You're not making this choice because you've
> outgrown humanity. I think you're afraid to go back
> to Earth.

This challenge hangs in the air . . . then the console starts BEEPING.
Janeway checks it.

> JANEWAY
>
> The algorithm's working . . . it's reconstructing the
> datablock . . .

Janeway works . . .

60   NEW ANGLE—A WALL MONITOR (OPTICAL)   60

It shows the STARFLEET ADMIRAL, as before. The image is fritzing slightly, and we can't understand what the Admiral is saying. Janeway and Seven move to the monitor.

> JANEWAY
>
> Strange. I thought we already recovered this part of
> the message.

> SEVEN OF NINE
>
> Perhaps it's an addendum from the Admiral. You did
> designate him a "windbag."

But Janeway is dead serious.

> JANEWAY
> (off console)
> I don't think so. The data index doesn't match. This is
> a completely different message . . .

She works a moment. In response, the Admiral's image CLEARS UP a little, and we can hear his voice. Mid-message:

> STARFLEET ADMIRAL
> (fritzing slightly)
> . . . apologies from everyone at Starfleet Command.
> We've had our best people working around the clock,
> trying to find a wormhole, a new means of
> propulsion—anything to get you home. But despite
> our best efforts . . .

The Admiral looks somber. Janeway and Seven of Nine exchange a look.

> STARFLEET ADMIRAL
> (continuing)
> I know it's not what you were hoping. But we've sent
> you all the data we've collected on the Delta
> Quadrant. With any luck, you'll find at least some
> part of it useful . . . maybe enough to shave a few

years off your journey.
                    (somber)
Safe journey. We hope to see you soon.

The message ENDS, replaced by a Federation symbol. A stunned beat.

                    SEVEN OF NINE
Your intuition was correct.

                    JANEWAY
Unfortunately.

                    SEVEN OF NINE
Arturis must have created a false message.

                    JANEWAY
                    (tight)
It sure as hell looks that way.

A grim beat.

                    JANEWAY
                    (to com)
Janeway to Tuvok.

                    TUVOK
Yes, Captain.

                    JANEWAY
My suspicions have been confirmed.

                                        INTERCUT:

60A   INT. DAUNTLESS—ENGINEERING   60A

Tuvok and Kim are working at the bulkhead seen earlier (it has a normal
appearance right now).

                    JANEWAY
                    (continuing)
Arturis tampered with Starfleet's message. The
Dauntless isn't what it appears to be.

Tuvok and Kim exchange a look.

TUVOK

I agree. We've discovered alien technology behind a bulkhead in Engineering. I can't identify it.

JANEWAY

Where's Arturis now?

TUVOK

On the Dauntless Bridge—working with Lieutenant Torres.

JANEWAY

Go there, but don't tip our hand. I'll meet you with a full security team in a few minutes.

TUVOK

Understood.

JANEWAY
(to Seven)

Grab a phaser.

As Janeway and Seven of Nine head for the door . . .

FADE OUT.

<u>END OF ACT THREE</u>

ACT FOUR

FADE IN:

61   INT. DAUNTLESS—BRIDGE   61

As seen before. Arturis is studying a console. Torres and two Engineering N.D.s working nearby. As they talk, Tuvok ENTERS in the b.g., wearing a phaser on his belt. He silently observes . . .

> TORRES
> (to Arturis)
> Don't touch that!

She moves to him.

> TORRES
> (re: console)
> You almost kicked us into slipstream drive.

> ARTURIS
> Oh . . . I wouldn't want to do that.
> (in Klingon)
> Ku cha mee-Roch. (My mistake).

> TORRES
> No problem.
> (surprised)
> You speak Klingon.

> ARTURIS
> I do now. Your Captain was kind enough to let me review your linguistic database.

> TORRES
> I only know a few phrases myself.

> ARTURIS
> Shame. It's a robust language.

> TORRES
> A little too robust for me.

He smiles warmly . . .

Janeway, Seven of Nine and TWO SECURITY GUARDS MATERIALIZE
suddenly, armed with hand-phasers and phaser rifles—all of them aiming
directly at Arturis! Tuvok takes up position alongside them, phaser drawn.
Startled reactions around the Bridge.

                    ARTURIS
                    (innocent)
        Is there a problem?

Janeway glances at Torres, as the Guards take up positions around Arturis.

                    JANEWAY
                    (quickly, to Torres)
        Evacuate the repair teams.

                    TORRES
        Captain?

                    JANEWAY
        Do it.

Puzzled, Torres and the Engineering N.D.s EXIT to the Turbolift. Janeway
faces Arturis.

                    JANEWAY
        Explain yourself.

                    ARTURIS
        I don't know what you're talking about.

                    JANEWAY
        You fabricated the message from Starfleet.
                    (off his look)
        I recovered the real transmission . . . the one you said
        was irreparably damaged.

                    ARTURIS
        That's absurd.

                    JANEWAY
                    (pressing)
        Starfleet didn't send us this vessel . . . and you aren't
        here to help. Is this your ship?

                          ARTURIS
                        (diplomatic)
Please . . . stay calm . . . I'm sure there's an
explanation.

                          JANEWAY
I tried to ignore my gut feelings, because I got carried
away by the excitement of getting home. But you
preyed on that, didn't you? You took advantage of our
hopes . . . and I want to know why.

A long, tense beat. Arturis looks disturbed.

                          ARTURIS
I believe there is a threat here, Captain . . . but not
from me.

He looks at Seven of Nine.

                          ARTURIS
                      (re: Seven of Nine)
I didn't feel it was my place to make accusations . . .
but I saw her reconfiguring several key algorithms.
Two days ago . . . in your Astrometrics Lab.

Seven of Nine reacts.

                          ARTURIS
                        (continuing)
It seems obvious . . . she must've been tampering
with the Starfleet message.

                       SEVEN OF NINE
You are lying.

                          ARTURIS
                        (to Janeway)
She's been sabotaging your efforts to reach Earth. You
don't have to believe me. You'll find all the evidence
you need in her personal database.

For a brief instant, Janeway glances in Seven of Nine's direction. Then:

JANEWAY
(to Arturis, hard)
Evidence you undoubtedly put there. Just in case you
got caught.
(to Tuvok)
Take him to Voyager . . . throw him the Brig.

Tuvok steps toward Arturis, whose expression tightens. All hell breaks
loose:

63		63
thru	OMITTED	thru
66		66

67   ARTURIS   67

BOLTS for a nearby console, KNOCKING a Security Guard off his feet with
a SMASHING BLOW!

68   TUVOK (OPTICAL)   68

FIRES his phaser!

69   ARTURIS (OPTICAL)   69

takes a direct HIT! He stumbles, but keeps going in a display of remarkable
strength. He grabs hold of a console panel, RIPS it away, revealing a set of
ALIEN CONTROLS beneath.

The second Guard LUNGES from behind, grabbing hold of him, but Arturis
THROWS him off and the Guard goes FLYING!

Arturis rapidly TURNS a circular control, then hits two more controls in
quick succession!

69A   ANGLE—A CONSOLE (OPTICAL)   69A

SHIMMERS in an ALIEN EFFECT—and TRANSFORMS into an ALIEN
CONSOLE, surrounded by ALIEN TECHNOLOGY.

70   WIDE—THE BRIDGE   70

The ENTIRE ROOM has transformed into an ALIEN BRIDGE. Consoles,
lighting, bulkheads—they now have strange and unfamiliar configurations.

71   TUVOK (OPTICAL)   71

reacts. A narrow ALIEN FORCEFIELD FLASHES around his body, trapping him in place.

72   JANEWAY AND SEVEN OF NINE (OPTICAL)   72

As two similar FORCEFIELDS APPEAR around them. We HEAR two other forcefields flash on offcamera. Trapped!

JANEWAY
(taps combadge)
Janeway to Voyager—beam us out of here!

Arturis reacts to this, starts working a console in response.

72A   INT. VOYAGER—BRIDGE   72A

Red Alert. Chakotay in command, Paris, Kim, N.D.s at their stations.

KIM
(working fast)
He's trying to deflect our transporters . . . stand
by . . .

72B   INT. DAUNTLESS—BRIDGE (OPTICAL)   72B

Tuvok and the two Security Guards DEMATERIALIZE in a Starfleet effect. Arturis keeps working furiously . . .

72C   ON JANEWAY AND SEVEN OF NINE (OPTICAL)   72C

Also DEMATERIALZING, but the effect stops midway through!

72D   INT. VOYAGER—BRIDGE   72D

As before, Red Alert.

KIM
I've got everyone but the Captain and Seven of Nine!
He's found a way to block their transport.

PARIS
The ship's going into slipstream mode!

CHAKOTAY
Pursuit course!

72E   INT. DAUNTLESS—BRIDGE   72E

As before. Arturis is at the helm, working the alien controls. The ship is
TREMBLING and we HEAR the familiar RUMBLE of the engines . . .

73   73
thru   OMITTED   thru
77   77

78   EXT. SPACE—THE DAUNTLESS (OPTICAL)   78

roaring at high impulse, the nose of the ship GLOWING and DISTORTING
as seen before. The ship VANISHES from view!

79   INT. VOYAGER—BRIDGE   79

As before.

                              PARIS
                We've lost them, Commander.

Chakotay considers.

                            CHAKOTAY
                Tom—bring the warp core modifications on-line.
                We're going after them.

                              PARIS
                Sir—we haven't even had a trial run!

                            CHAKOTAY
                No time like the present.

Off Chakotay, determined . . .

                                                         CUT TO:

80   EXT. SPACE—QUANTUM SLIPSTREAM (OPTICAL)   80

The Dauntless RACING through the torrent of energy at breakneck speeds.

81   INT. DAUNTLESS—ALIEN BRIDGE   81

As before. Janeway and Seven of Nine standing in place, trapped by the
unseen forcefields. Arturis is at the helm, navigating the ship. The deep
RUMBLE of the engines can be heard.

SEVEN OF NINE
Where are you taking us?

ARTURIS
(simply)
Home.

Janeway and Seven exchange a look.

JANEWAY
How'd you create the Starfleet Bridge—holograms?

ARTURIS
Particle synthesis. Beyond your understanding.

JANEWAY
Is this what your people do—prey on innocent ships?

Arturis turns to her, a flash of anger in his eyes.

ARTURIS
(an edge)
"Innocent." Typical of Captain Janeway. Self-
righteous.

JANEWAY
If I've done something to offend you or your people,
please tell me.

ARTURIS
Diplomacy, Captain? Your "diplomacy" destroyed my
world.

She reacts. Arturis take a beat, he's been waiting a long time for this
moment. He begins circling his captives . . .

ARTURIS
(continuing)
You negotiated an agreement with the Borg Collective.
Safe passage through their space . . . and in return,
you helped them defeat one of their enemies.

SEVEN OF NINE
Species Eight Four Seven Two.

> ARTURIS
>
> In your "colorful" language, yes. Species Eight Four
> Seven Two.
>> (to Janeway)
>
> Did it ever occur to you that some of us in the Delta
> Quadrant had a vested interest in that war? Victory
> would have meant the annihilation of the Borg.
>> (beat)
>
> But you couldn't see beyond the bow of your own
> ship.

> JANEWAY
>
> In my estimation, Species Eight Four Seven Two
> posed a greater threat than the Borg.

> ARTURIS
>
> Who were you to make that decision? A stranger to
> this Quadrant!

> JANEWAY
>
> There wasn't exactly time to take a poll. I had to act
> quickly.

Arturis eyes her darkly.

> ARTURIS
>
> My people managed to elude the Borg for
> centuries . . . outwitting them . . . always one step
> ahead. But in recent years, the Borg began to weaken
> our defenses . . . they were closing in. Species Eight
> Four Seven Two was our last hope to defeat them . . .
>> (to Janeway, emotion rising)
>
> You took that away from us!

Arturis is visibly shaken now—his fury at Janeway coming to the fore.

> ARTURIS
>
> The outer colonies were the first to fall . . . twenty-
> three in a matter of hours. Our sentry vessels were
> tossed aside . . . no defense against the storm . . .
>> (beat)
>
> By the time they surrounded our star system . . .
> hundreds of Cubes . . . we'd already surrendered to
> our own terror.
>> (haunted)
>
> A few of us managed to survive . . . ten, twenty

thousand. I was fortunate. I escaped with a vessel.
Alone . . . but alive.

He trails off . . . reliving the horrible memory.

> ARTURIS
> (re: Seven of Nine)
> I don't blame <u>them</u> . . . they were just Drones acting
> on Collective instinct.
> (to Janeway)
> <u>You</u>. You had a choice!

Janeway is moved, upset.

> JANEWAY
> I'm sorry for what happened to your people. But try
> to understand . . . I couldn't have known.

But he doesn't hear her . . . gives her a long, cold stare . . .

> ARTURIS
> It took me months to find you. I watched, waiting for
> an opportunity to make you pay for what you'd done.
> (pointed)
> Then . . . the Starfleet message. And I knew your
> selfish desire to get home would surface again . . .
> that I could lure you to this vessel . . . and see to it
> that you would all be assimilated, and spend the rest
> of eternity as Borg.
> (darkly)
> I was hoping for your entire crew . . . but I'll settle
> for the two of you.

He moves back to the helm and checks the coordinates.

> ARTURIS
> (continuing)
> In a matter of hours, this ship will return to my
> homeworld . . . inside <u>Borg space</u>.

> SEVEN OF NINE
> When that happens, <u>you</u> will be assimilated, as well.

> ARTURIS
> That's . . . irrelevant.

He considers Seven for a moment.

                    ARTURIS
          This is what you've wanted all along, isn't it? To go
          back to your Collective?
                              (cold)
          You should thank me.

He returns to work. Janeway glances at Seven, whose face is neutral. Off
the moment . . .

                                             FADE OUT.

          <u>END OF ACT FOUR</u>

ACT FIVE

FADE IN:

82   EXT. SPACE—VOYAGER (OPTICAL)   82

ROARING at high impulse, the nose of the ship GLOWING and DISTORTING—about to enter a "slipstream!"

83   INT. VOYAGER—BRIDGE   83

Red Alert. TREMBLING. A deep RUMBLE can be heard. Chakotay, Tuvok, Paris, Kim, N.D.s at their stations. Tense:

> CHAKOTAY
>
> Report!

> PARIS
>
> We're at full impulse—but we're not breaking
> through the quantum barrier!

> TUVOK
>
> I'm having trouble controlling the field parameters! I
> need more power to the deflector!

> CHAKOTAY
> (to com)
>
> Bridge to Torres—

84   INT. ENGINEERING   84

Red Alert. Trembling. The warp core is PULSING rapidly—and there a few MODIFICATIONS to the core itself, Starfleet plant-ons, etc. Torres and several Engineering N.D.s are rushing around the room, working.

> TORRES
> (overlapping, to com)
> —Already on it, Commander! Stand by!
> (to N.D.)
> Reroute auxiliary power to Deflector Control!
> (to another N.D.)
> Make sure that quantum warp field is stable!

85   INT. BRIDGE   85

As before. There's a heavy SHAKE!

                        TUVOK
                       (working)
     Deflector at maximum . . . I'm focusing the quantum
     field . . .

                         KIM
     Make it quick! Hull temperature's at critical!

Suspense as the ship trembles . . . then:

86   INCLUDE VIEWSCREEN (OPTICAL)   86

The starfield EXPLODES in a BURST of LIGHT and COLOR as we enter a
QUANTUM SLIPSTREAM. Tunnels of energy ROAR past.

87   THE CREW   87

hangs on.

                        PARIS
     We're at slipstream velocity!

                         KIM
     Structural integrity's down by nine percent. We've got
     less than an hour before the hull starts to buckle.

                        PARIS
     We're right behind them . . . in the same slipstream.

                       CHAKOTAY
     How far behind?

                        PARIS
     A few minutes . . .

                        TUVOK
     Is there any way to increase our speed?

                        PARIS
     None. We're at maximum.

                       CHAKOTAY
     Maintain course.

(beat)
If I know the Captain . . . she's already got a plan.

88   JANEWAY (OPTICAL)   88

as her hand touches an ALIEN FORCEFIELD, which flashes on briefly.

                        JANEWAY
Any ideas?

REVEAL we are in—

89   INT. DAUNTLESS—BRIG   89

Janeway and Seven of Nine are standing in the small chamber. They've
been stripped of their weapons.

                     SEVEN OF NINE
Not presently.

                        JANEWAY
We'd better think of something. We come face-to-face
with your former family in less than an hour . . . and
that's one reunion I'd like to miss.

Seven is silent. Janeway studies her.

                        JANEWAY
Unless you're looking forward to rejoining the
Collective.

                     SEVEN OF NINE
                        (thinking)
I don't believe I am.

                        JANEWAY
Not the ringing opposition I was hoping for, but I'll
take it.

Janeway glances around the room.

                        JANEWAY
                      (continuing)
A Drone could walk through this forcefield like it was
thin air . . .

(beat)
Is there enough Borg technology left in your body to
let you adapt?

SEVEN OF NINE
If I activate the appropriate nanoprobes, I could alter
my bio-electric field.
(beat)
However, I would need to adjust my cranial implant.

JANEWAY
(thinks)
Would a microfilament do the trick?

SEVEN OF NINE
It might.

Janeway takes off her combadge, starts to OPEN it.

JANEWAY
(re: combadge)
Then let's get you one.

There is no bench in this spare setting . . . so Janeway takes a seat on the
floor. Seven of Nine hesitates, then joins her.

JANEWAY
(points)
Once you're outside, access that control panel and
disable the forcefield. Then we'll try to reach the
engine room . . .

SEVEN OF NINE
(catching on)
And deploy the emergency shutdown procedure.

Janeway nods . . . works the delicate circuitry within the combadge . . .
pulls out a thin, tiny WIRE. Seven of Nine eyes it.

SEVEN OF NINE
Sufficient.
(instructing)
You will need to cross-link the third and sixth
nodules.

Seven of Nine turns to face her . . . Janeway reaches out with the filament.

Seven of Nine pulls back slightly, and Janeway hesitates . . . it's a little
awkward . . . being this close . . .

Janeway carefully begins to make minor adjustments to the Borg implant
above Seven of Nine's eye.

> JANEWAY

Déjà vu.

> SEVEN OF NINE

Captain?

> JANEWAY
> (working)

As I recall, this is where our . . . relationship began.
In a Brig. Nine months ago. I severed you from the
Collective . . . and you weren't exactly happy about it.

> SEVEN OF NINE

No . . . I was not.

A quiet beat. A lot has happened between these two characters in the past
year . . . both of them with mixed feelings.

> JANEWAY
> (working)

In case that happens . . . and I never get a chance to
say this . . .
> (beat)

I realize I've been hard on you at times. But it was
never out of anger . . . or regret that I brought you on
board. I'm your Captain. That means I can't always be
a friend.
> (beat)

Understand?

Seven of Nine eyes her.

> SEVEN OF NINE

No.
> (beat)

However, if we are assimilated, our thoughts will
become one . . . and I'm sure I'll understand
perfectly.

Janeway pauses, gives her a look.

> SEVEN OF NINE
> A ''joke,'' Captain. You, yourself have encouraged me
> to use my sense of humor.

Janeway smiles, charmed . . . keeps working on the eyepiece.

> JANEWAY
> (lightly)
> It's nice to know you're taking <u>some</u> of my advice to
> heart.

Seven looks thoughtful.

> SEVEN OF NINE
> You were correct. My desire to remain in the Delta
> Quadrant was based on fear. I am no longer Borg . . .
> but the prospect of becoming human is . . . unsettling.
> (difficult)
> I don't know where I belong.

> JANEWAY
> (gently)
> You belong with us.

Seven looks at her, uncertain. Then we hear a Borg fritzing SOUND.

> SEVEN OF NINE
> The adaptations are complete.

Janeway pulls back, and they both get to their feet . . .

90   NEW ANGLE (OPTICAL)   90

as Seven of Nine moves toward the archway . . . pauses . . . then effortlessly STEPS THROUGH the CRACKLING FORCEFIELD.

91   INT. DAUNTLESS—ALIEN BRIDGE   91

As before. Arturis at the helm. An ALARM is sounding from a nearby
console. He rushes to it . . . reacts with concern . . . then moves to another
station . . .

91A   INT. DAUNTLESS—BRIG   91A

Seven of Nine is working the wall panel. We HEAR the alien forcefield flash
off. Janeway joins Seven of Nine.

                    JANEWAY
    We're in business.

As they quickly move off . . .

CUT TO:

91B   EXT. SPACE—QUANTUM SLIPSTREAM (OPTICAL)   91B

    The Dauntless ROARING along.

92   INT. DAUNTLESS—ENGINEERING   92

    LIGHT from the offcamera engines flashing, rumbling. (NOTE: This is the
    same set as before, no alien modifications.) Janeway and Seven of Nine
    ENTER and move to the console around the engine core.

                    SEVEN OF NINE
    I can't initiate the shutdown procedure . . .

They work.

                    JANEWAY
    Our commands are being blocked from the Bridge.
    He's detected us . . .

The engines RUMBLE louder and there's a TREMBLE. Seven of Nine
checks a console.

                    SEVEN OF NINE
    The ship's velocity has increased . . .
                    (reacts)
    At our present speed, we will enter Borg space in less
    than twelve minutes.

A tense beat as they think . . . engines REVVING behind them . . .

                    JANEWAY
    Do we still have access to the power distribution grid?

                    SEVEN OF NINE
    Yes.

                    JANEWAY
    If we can't throw on the brakes, let's swerve the
    wheel.

(off her look)
Send a power surge into the starboard thrusters.

SEVEN OF NINE
The torsional stress at these speeds could tear the ship
apart.

JANEWAY
It's either that . . . or join the Hive.
(on the move)
Do it. If we're still in one piece, try to gain control of
navigation. I'll be on the Bridge.

Janeway reaches the door . . . turns:

JANEWAY
We have a game of "Velocity" scheduled for
tomorrow on Holodeck One. I expect you to keep the
appointment.

SEVEN OF NINE
Aye, Captain.

A final beat between them, then Janeway EXITS . . .

CUT TO:

93   EXT. SPACE—QUANTUM SLIPSTREAM (OPTICAL)   93

The Dauntless speeding through the torrent. Suddenly, we see a THRUST-
ER on the starboard hull FLARE OUT—causing the ship to CAREEN out of
control!

94   INT. DAUNTLESS—ALIEN BRIDGE   94

SHAKING HARD! Arturis hanging on for dear life! He struggles to the
helm, works it . . .

95   EXT. SPACE—QUANTUM SLIPSTREAM (OPTICAL)   95

The Dauntless out of control! The ship SPINNING and SLAMMING against
the sides of the slipstream, causing powerful DISCHARGES of ENERGY!
After a harrowing beat, the ship begins to SLOW and its course evens out.

96   INT. DAUNTLESS—ALIEN BRIDGE   96

The shaking subsides. Arturis looks relieved. He begins to work again, when suddenly:

> **JANEWAY'S VOICE**
> Sorry about the bumpy ride.

He whirls to see Janeway, who's just stepped into the room.

> **ARTURIS**
> You can slow this ship down, but you can't stop it.
> (beat)
> In four minutes, Captain Janeway will be gone . . .
> and a new Drone will be born.

> **JANEWAY**
> Don't count on it.

The ship ROCKS again! Arturis works the helm desperately . . . then the shaking subsides.

> **JANEWAY**
> Seven of Nine has accessed your navigational systems.
> You taught us how to use this ship a little too well.

Arturis moves to another console, works it with intent. Janeway tries to reach him on an emotional level.

> **JANEWAY**
> (compassionate)
> I can't begin to imagine your loss . . . but if you can
> try to see beyond your desire for revenge . . .

> **ARTURIS**
> Revenge is all I have left!

> **JANEWAY**
> No . . . as long you're alive . . . there's hope. Your
> people's knowledge, accomplishments, dignity . . . can
> survive . . . in <u>you</u>.
> (quiet)
> End this.

He glances at her, and it looks like he might be persuaded by her words . . . then he taps a final control.

97   INT. DAUNTLESS—ENGINEERING (OPTICAL)   97

Seven of Nine working a console . . . when an ENERGY DISCHARGE
CRACKLES around the entire console! A section of the panel BLOWS OUT
in a SHOWER OF SPARKS! Seven of Nine recoils.

98   INT. DAUNTLESS—ALIEN BRIDGE   98

As before. Arturis turns to Janeway.

                              ARTURIS
                I've just destroyed the navigational controls. No one
                can stop this ship, now . . . not even me.

Janeway rushes to a panel. Arturis takes satisfaction in her anxiety.

                              ARTURIS
                Two minutes to Borg space.

A long, terrible beat . . .

WHAM! The ship JOLTS. They both stumble! Arturis looks shocked—what
now?

99   EXT. SPACE—QUANTUM SLIPSTREAM (OPTICAL)   99

The STARSHIP VOYAGER is CAREENING toward the Dauntless, FIRING
TORPEDOES, which SLAM into the enemy ship!

100   INT. VOYAGER—BRIDGE   100

Red Alert. Chakotay, Tuvok, Paris, Kim, N.D.s. Fast action:

                              TUVOK
                Direct hit!
                              (reacts)
                The vessel's shields are down. Transporters standing
                by.

                              CHAKOTAY
                Get a lock on our people!

Kim works . . .

101   INT. DAUNTLESS—ALIEN BRIDGE (OPTICAL)   101

As before, SHAKING HARD. A couple of consoles EXPLODE, SPARKING! Arturis is on his feet, rushing from station to station, panicked, his world coming unraveled.

> ARTURIS
> (off console)

Voyager.

Janeway reacts.

> JANEWAY
> Come with me—it's not too late!

Arturis grabs an alien HAND-WEAPON from out of a station. He whirls on Janeway.

> ARTURIS
> It is for you.

Janeway DEMATERIALIZES. Arturis FIRES but the discharge goes right through her without effect!

Another JOLT! Arturis is thrown to the floor!

102   INT. VOYAGER—BRIDGE   102

As before.

> KIM
> I've got them, Commander—Transporter Room Two!

> CHAKOTAY
> Alter our slipstream—hard starboard—take us back
> the way we came!

103   EXT. SPACE—QUANTUM SLIPSTREAM (OPTICAL)   103

Voyager BANKS hard! The SLIPSTREAM BANKS with the ship, BRANCH-ING OFF the original slipstream as Voyager flies offscreen!

104   THE DAUNTLESS (OPTICAL)   104

keeps going in its own slipstream at top speed! As it ZOOMS off into the distance . . .

105   EXT. SPACE (OPTICAL)   105

A field of stars. In a blast of energy, the DAUNTLESS comes ROARING out of the slipstream and into normal space. It decelerates to a slow drift . . . and the CAMERA PANS to reveal—

106   FIVE BORG CUBES (OPTICAL)   106

heading right toward us!

107   INT. DAUNTLESS—ALIEN BRIDGE   107

Peaceful now, no shaking. Arturis is on the floor. He sits up . . . dazed . . . but recovers in time to HEAR the voice of the COLLECTIVE:

> BORG
> We are the Borg. You will be assimilated. Resistance is futile.

Off Arturis . . . bracing for the inevitable . . .

                                                        FADE TO BLACK.

FADE IN:

108   EXT. SPACE—VOYAGER (STOCK—OPTICAL)   108

at impulse.

> JANEWAY (V.O.)
> Captain's Log, supplemental. We remained in the quantum slipstream for an hour before it finally collapsed. Our diagnostics have concluded that we can't risk using this technology again . . . but we did manage to get three hundred light years closer to home.

109   INT. HOLOGRID (OPTICAL)   109

Janeway and Seven of Nine in their workout clothes, engaged in a game of ''Velocity,'' as seen in the Teaser. Seven of Nine is FIRING her phaser at the glowing blue DISK, but misses, and the disk GLANCES off her arm and VANISHES.

> COMPUTER VOICE
> Full impact. Final round to Janeway. Winner: Janeway.

Seven looks frustrated. As the two of them cool down . . .

                    JANEWAY
          Nice play. You almost had me.

                    SEVEN OF NINE
          Almost.

                    JANEWAY
          Go again?

                    SEVEN OF NINE
          I must report to the Astrometrics Lab. There is work
          to be done.

                    JANEWAY
          Work? I gave the crew strict orders to take some R &
          R over the next few days . . . that includes you.

                    SEVEN OF NINE
          There are more pressing needs. I'm attempting to
          design another method of traveling at slipstream
          velocities . . . without damaging Voyager.

                    JANEWAY
          I thought that was impossible.

                    SEVEN OF NINE
          "Impossible" is a word that humans use far too often.
          I wish to continue my efforts.

Janeway looks at her, surprised.

                    JANEWAY
          A few days ago, you were ready to abandon ship . . .
          and here you are, practically laying in a course to
          Earth.

                    SEVEN OF NINE
                    (thoughtful)
          As we approached Borg space, I began to reevaluate
          my future. I found the prospect of becoming a
          Drone . . . unappealing.

>   JANEWAY
> Sometimes you've got to look back, in order to move
> forward.
>   (gently)
> Sounds to me like you're starting to embrace your
> humanity . . .

>   SEVEN OF NINE
> No.
>   (beat)
> But as I said . . . nothing is impossible.

Janeway smiles. A moment between them. Then:

>   JANEWAY
>   (to com)
> Computer—one more game.

They take their stances. We HEAR a SERIES of escalating BEEPS . . .

110   A VELOCITY DISK (OPTICAL)   110

APPEARS in mid-flight, red-colored, racing directly TOWARD CAMERA!
As it FILLS THE SCREEN—

                                                          CUT TO BLACK.

                        <u>END OF ACT FIVE</u>

                        <u>END OF SEASON FOUR</u>

                           <u>THE END</u>